Welcome to Cemetery

By C. J. Daley

C. J. DALEY

WELCOME TO CEMETERY

Copyright © 2025 C. J. Daley/BestGhost Books
All rights reserved

No part of this book may be reproduced, or stored in a retrieval system, or transmitted in any form or by any means, electronic, mechanical, photocopying, recording, or otherwise, without express written permission of the publisher, except for the inclusion of brief quotations embodied in critical articles and reviews.

The right of C. J. Daley to be identified as the author of this work has been asserted by him in accordance with the Copyright, Designs, and Patents Act 1988.

The characters and events portrayed in this novel are fictitious. Any similarity to real persons, living or dead, is coincidental and not intended by the author.

Cover by Miblart
BestGhost Books Logo created by Miblart
No AI has been used in the making of this novel

For my Gwendolyn,
You deserved more
I miss you

Contents

1. Part I: 1
2. Intro   2
3. Ch 1   4
4. Ch 2   18
5. Ch 3   28
6. Ch 4   36
7. Ch 5   44
8. Ch 6   57
9. Ch 7   69
10. Ch 8   81
11. Ch 9   93
12. Ch 10   104
13. Ch 11   117
14. Part II: 128
15. Ch 12   129

16. Ch 13 — 140
17. Ch 14 — 149
18. Ch 15 — 162
19. Ch 16 — 174
20. Ch 17 — 184
21. Ch 18 — 196
22. Ch 19 — 206
23. Part III: — 211
24. Ch 20 — 212
25. Ch 21 — 222
26. Ch 22 — 230
27. Ch 23 — 236
28. Ch 24 — 241
29. Ch 25 — 248
30. Ch 26 — 257
31. Ch 27 — 264
32. Ch 28 — 273
33. Ch 29 — 283
34. Ch 30 — 291
35. Ch 31 — 298
36. Ch 32 — 305
37. Epilogue — 322

Part I:

Seasonal Highs

Intro

Welcome to Cemetery

The town of Cemetery, New York sat damn-near invisibly among the other villages of the Hudson River Valley. It's not that it was hard to find, or out of the way. Nor was it that hidden—practically only an hour outside New York City. Rather, it was just typically forgotten. Most of the townsfolk thought that the name was funny or silly originally, but with the passing of time, they started to think that it was part of the reason it was overlooked—as if people couldn't get past the fact that the name was of an entire town and not a place. "What was the name of that town again?" visitors might ask each other while passing through. "I don't remember, I think I only saw a sign for the cemetery."

The town itself had a single long road that ran the entire length of it called Route 17. This was from the time long forgotten when a route or highway could be labeled for a single two-lane road. The townsfolk just referred to it as Main Street. However, any single turn off the main street was practically, and immediately, back road. A neighbor might be several turns away, but only a short drive or walk away.

Not overpopulated, streets were filled with trees. American beech, sugar maples, yellow birch, and great swaths of pine trees stretched way high into the sky. Cemetery wasn't known for any single trade, but more often than not, truck advertisements and tee shirts in supermarket lines boasting employment with *Cemetery Town & Lumber* could be seen. Some might say the town and the surrounding area were beautiful; it just didn't stand out above the rest.

Demographically, Cemetery was of an average size, in an average area, with average workers, townsfolk, and children; an average climate; and even an average unemployment rate. The only thing about Cemetery that wasn't average, was the number of crimes that went unsolved and unpunished.

Now it wasn't that the police force was too small, too negligent, too unproven. It was simply that they were inundated with a mysterious, arguably devilish level of disappearances and deaths, and insufficient evidence to solve them. Even with the most experienced wracking their brains for a solution, a lead, or a single shred of evidence, nothing was found, and nothing was solved. Over the years, many of the retirees from the police department became true crime enthusiasts, taking to continued researching and speculation over crimes long unsolved in their newly found free time. One group that had gotten a semi-substantial following, started calling themselves Closed Case Resurgence. The team worked hard to keep alive the hope on cases long put aside.

Regardless of the way the townsfolk felt about the town, their way of life was often marred with shock and loss, as if a long shadow was cast over the town a long time ago.

Enough time spent somewhere begins to feel like home…

Ch 1

CEMETERY TOWNSHIP

I

SHORT ON DETECTIVE WORK for the day, and having already made a pitstop for in-home questioning for a case she was buttoning up, Detective Abigail Williams cruised around aimlessly in a squad car. Since she was a child, it was never more than Abby, and since entering the force, it was Williams only. She was convinced her coworkers had no idea what her first name was. That had become her preference, not because she didn't want to feel seen by them, but simply because she always felt embarrassed correcting people about her first name.

As one of the two detectives in the department, she did have something less conspicuous she could drive around, but today she wanted to drive the Dodge Challenger for the hell of it. It had been a gift from the mayor to the department after it had come to light how many outdated Crown Vics were still in circulation.

Coming around a bend, she passed a sign that said "The Nowack-Prendergast Parade." It was a yearly parade funded by what she always assumed were two big league town members. The parade was a good time though, and since making detective, she was finally off detail and able to go. Small victories.

Getting back toward the center of town, she approached the red light and idled next to a recently refurbished McDonald's. It always amazed her how some of the town's elderly frequented the fast food restaurant daily, as if it were some local small business deli. Mr. Cody, an elderly man with crows feet eyes and a mop of shaggy white hair and who Williams wouldn't have been able to pick out of a crowd if he didn't happen to be her neighbor, ambled out of his parked car, headed for the door. As he looked both ways and went to cross the parking lot, cane in hand, he saw her staring and waved.

Fuck, she thought, *just what I need, to look like I'm checking out the old people. He's probably going to wave at me every time I leave or enter my house now, too.*

The light turned green, giving her a reprieve from her internal chastisement. She drove off, turning right. She passed a gas station, an old pizza place, an empty building, and another pizza place—or a card place—or was it the florist now? She couldn't keep track anymore. She remembered as a young kid it was one of the coolest places to get Pokémon cards. It had this larger-than-life sign that read "WHAT'S HOT," the outside giving away nothing of the treasures locked inside.

Three miles down the road she passed what was easily her least favorite location in Cemetery, a ramshackle collection of two two-story buildings called the James Motel. Motel was the word they used, but it's not what any normal, decent person would picture when thinking of a motel. However, somehow the owner had legally gotten the rights to the property, collecting the rent in what can only be called a ghostly fashion, as nobody had ever seen them.

With only negative thoughts attached to the place now, Detective Williams saw the stages of her life through the property. As a child, she was continuously cautioned that "if anyone from that place ever approaches you, for anything at all, you tell mommy and daddy immediately." As a teen, it was the easiest place in the entire town (and neighboring ones) to score weed. It was also the cheapest place to knock on a door and play "Hey Mister" for some underage beer. Then, as a young adult and rookie on the CPD, it was the place she'd frequented the most for petty theft, domestic disputes, and assaults.

The reminder of her childhood smarted more than she expected. As a child, her father had, unbeknownst to her mother, allowed her to be used during a police sting operation. She had been young, far too young to understand what had happened, but the trauma had gotten to her in other ways. The morbid fascination of which more than likely was the driving force that led her to police work. When she had arrived on the force, she had been beside herself to read through the report and find that the perp had specifically been after *her*. Before his death, her father had sworn that was the precipice that plummeted her parents toward divorce. And if the perp was after her, did that mean that she had caused her parents to split? Although she had been much older when he told her, it didn't make it feel any less hard to hear.

Another five minutes down the road and she arrived at her intended destination. This gas station was out of the way, further from the station than the one she already passed, but she always liked this one the most. Eight years on the force and it still bothered her that the station didn't have its own supply of gas, at least for convenience's sake, and emergency situations, not that she'd speak up about it.

"Enough time to get gas, get back to the station, swap cars, and start my off days a little early," she said, smiling as she pulled up to the gas pump.

She filled the car and headed toward the station, eager to start her time off.

II

Two hours later, Williams was drenched in sweat, out of breath, and finishing up one final set at the gym. The idea of relaxing had felt strange to her, like it had been engrained in her that not having work to complete was her fault. She still had three full days after this, right? Might as well get a good workout in. Work herself into exhaustion now, then finally settle in for her days off. At least that was the plan.

Williams set her feet, leaning forward to begin her final set of deadlifts. She was just about spent, which was entirely the point. She would head home, grab a shower, order in something to eat, and probably crash on the couch.

She worked hard, harder still to gain respect in the precinct, but three days off in a row still felt like an undeserved luxury. It grated on her to have the time off.

Too bad the relaxation wouldn't last.

III

Once outside the town itself, the roads of Cemetery are winding and long, practically circling in on themselves. Unlike its neighboring town of Warwick, there's no farmland, just trees. The town itself doesn't have a particular forest, but no one told the town that.

Detective Williams received the call thirty minutes ago, getting dressed immediately. Although she had finally settled in, the erasure of her personal time had somehow still felt right. As she pulled up, the oscillating blue and red of the police lights cut through the dead of night, filling her windshield.

Williams got out and walked over to her partner, Senior Detective Reyes. Subconsciously, as if trained, she had begun waiting for him to speak first. A trait that was two parts embarrassment and anxiety, and one part respect.

"What are we looking at here? It's two o'clock in the morning for Christ's sake." Reyes, an expert at his craft, spoke while taking a drag of his cigarette.

"Uh, a car crash?" Williams asked, uncertain. She strained her neck to look over at the scene. "Jesus, I know the Cemetery force isn't huge, but they called both detectives in for an accident?"

"Ain't no body in the car, kid." Senior Detective Reyes, as his title suggested, had been with the force for over twenty years. Regardless of his seniority, he'd only recently taken to calling her kid. A fact that Williams continually pointed out to no avail.

"Cut that out, I'm almost thirty, Reyes. I-I think I've earned it—" Williams cut herself off, Reyes' previous statement finally settling in. "There isn't a body? Like, the person was ejected through the windshield or something...and they called us in for that? Did they check further down the road for it?"

"I just got here, kid, same as you. My guess would be that they already did, the Chief doesn't like us called in for nothing." Reyes took a final drag and rubbed the cherry out of his cigarette with his index finger and thumb. His voice still had the distinct trill on several words with the letter "r," gathered from being first or second generation Mexican, but otherwise had taken on an almost distinct New York accent. His shirt, stretched across his chest and stomach, had seen better days. Or at the very least, better days when Reyes was of a smaller size. As his years with the force passed, his cynicism, and belt size, grew.

Williams noticed his need for a cigarette had grown recently. He'd even taken to long bouts without shaving, as if he couldn't be bothered. The caramel skin tone of his cheeks was being overtaken by a black beard speckled in grey and white. Williams had thus far let it lie, unsure of how to broach the subject. She knew he was jaded—hell, the entire department could tell—she just wasn't sure they'd passed a point where she could ask.

Williams on the other hand was still young enough—and new enough to the force—that she aimed to keep in shape, working out whenever possible. After years of her parents forcing her to play soccer as a child, she ended up loving the sport, continuing all throughout high school and even some of college. As height had never been gifted to her, she used her more squat, muscular build to her advantage, often using her back to block out the competitor as they both went for the soccer ball, ponytail swinging. Now she kept her hair more shortly cut, a bob. However, she still clung to her desire to keep the competition away from the ball, turning it to ambition instead, as the world is less forgiving than a soccer pitch. Her ambition, and honed skills, always fought for the surface, her uncertainty entering the force the only thing holding her back.

"So the options are what, accidental self-ejection, or foul play? Therefore, they need to call in the entire force?" Williams quipped, still searching for her footing.

"Astute detecting, kid, really tip-top," Reyes retorted.

Embarrassed, Williams stared at the ground, pushing a sheet of hair behind her ear to hide the reddening of her cheeks.

"What do you think then? You have to give me something to go on. You might have just arrived, but I know you're thinking something," Williams said, her lips downturned in frustration.

Williams' comfort, or lack thereof, was not lost on Reyes as he held his hand up to stop an approaching officer. He placed a calming hand on her shoulder.

"I think Chief gets a call in the middle of the night and is told there's a flipped-over car right outside of Cemetery and it's missing a body. My take on the situation is I don't know, he don't either, and therefore, it's a big deal until we do, kid." Reyes shrugged, releasing her and pulled out his pack of cigarettes, gesticulating with them as he talked. "You know what you're doing. The officers see it too, or at least they will if you let them. Now why don't you go over to the car and look instead of badgering me for the answers, okay?"

The police walkie attached to Williams' hip chirped, pulling away her attention. The call wasn't for her, but she listened to the back and forth anyway, wondering if it pertained to the accident. It didn't. Dispatch was calling for a response to a disappearance at the Old Mayor's Mansion. A local haunt for kids that wanted to test their mettle in what was coined the town's biggest paranormal hotspot. To Williams, even when she was a teen who could have been susceptible to the pressures of others, she still thought the place was all bullshit. She turned the walkie down, giving her attention back to the task at hand.

Williams walked toward the accident, calling, "Hey, Brennan and Shotz, what have you got so far?" She wanted to listen to Reyes, knew he was right, and figured asking the officers' their opinions were the fastest option. Now, if only she could stay out of her own way.

Brennan and Shotz, two of the department's uniform officers, had been on and off their walkies and phones since she stepped out of the car. Finally free, she aimed to question them too. Brennan was tall, while Shotz was not, with a head of salt-and-pepper hair that didn't quite match his eyebrows yet; and Shotz had a hooked nose that could make a '90's witch jealous. Even at the unholy hour both were in full Cemetery Police Department uniforms.

"Answers have been hard to come by given the hour, but we just got back confirmation that the car is registered to a Cynthia Wickam. We tried to contact her or her husband but haven't heard anything back just yet. We requested to have someone go over to their residence, but it looks like it might have to be us whenever we get finished here," the taller of the two said.

"Do we have any reason to believe that she wasn't the driver?" Williams asked.

"That's still unknown, but we're looking for anything at this point," Brennan replied.

"And what do we have coming in the way of clean-up?" Williams continued, kicking chunks of glass off the road with the heel of her boot.

"Officers Dans and Riggs have some flares and a couple of squad cars blocking the way into Cemetery, as well as a couple of road flares, and Officers Prescott and Owens posted a little up the road toward Cemetery. Figured we better wait until everyone arrived before blocking that side. Gonna keep them closed at least until the scene is cleared." The shorter officer removed his police cap and ran his hands through his hair. "Whole thing is pretty freaking weird if you ask me...I mean, where's the body?"

"I'm simply looking for something to go on here," Williams replied, her tone more clipped than intended. Practice made perfect.

"I'm just saying, Detective, this is unusual even for us," Shotz replied, replacing his police cap. "We don't have much else for you yet though; everything was left exactly how it was when we arrived. We figured we better wait for it to be photographed. Then we heard you and Reyes got the call, too."

"I'll hold my judgments for some actual facts for starters...thanks though, to you both. You better get back to it," Williams said, stepping away from them with a nod. She had wanted to play it cool; to show them she had things handled, but maybe Shotz was right. Was it a little too weird?

No. She was being ridiculous.

Brennan was an officer who came on the force around the same time as Reyes. When he wasn't doing something involving his hands, he was known for spinning an old class ring on his pointer finger. Whether it was because he was proud to be educated, or just some kind of tick, Williams was unsure. Shotz, on the other hand, was new blood. She remembered the day he joined. *There's nothing weird about an accident*, she thought. Perhaps the two of them were partnered to balance each other.

Regardless, they were both waiting on her.

The car appeared to have come around the bend in the road at substantial speed. It had clearly rolled and spun on its hood until finally stopping in a ditch. Williams found herself playing it out in her head; the driver losing control, possibly drunk, an overcorrection, a curse and shout, then the inevitable crunch. *Or* a dirty look at a local bar, words exchanged, someone followed the driver into the parking lot, and it leads to this? Or, a case of road rage—the driver's, or someone else's—leading to an untimely end.

Or some kind of kidnapping.

The windshield of the Chrysler 200 was cracked and missing chunks of glass, all of which had kindly placed themselves at dangerous angles all over the road and hill of the ditch, like so much vehicular flotsam. Williams carefully stepped her way through and squatted down, taking a closer look. The upside-down view gave her a weird feeling, as if she were the one that was topsy-turvy, suspended, but she pushed through. The driver side airbag had deployed, now deflated. There were obvious rips and tears through it from the glass. *But where is the body?*

There were a few things that stuck out as odd to her, though.

"Reyes, come look at this!" she called up to her partner.

Lighting up again, Reyes panned his flashlight over to her and the car. "I can see great from up here out of the glass. What is it?"

"Well, it's weird. The glass missing from the windshield couldn't have fit a body through it, not even a small one, not even at high velocity. But the driver-side window is entirely gone. There're various blood spray patterns inside the car, as well as some blood wiped on the door, but nothing substantial. It's all just passive drops, nothing's splattered in it. And whoever heard of a car accident where the person involved is rocketed through the driver-side window? I don't know that I believe that's even possible, honestly."

Detective Williams stood again, shaking her head and running her hands up and down her thighs. She shone her flashlight back and forth over the driver-side of the car, thinking hard. "This is interesting too; if the driver had survived the crash and was conscious enough to pull themselves out, the glass from the window would have been blown outward, most of it outside the car. And if it had blown out during the flip there wouldn't be so much of it here. I mean, I can't be positive with the windshield glass here too, but it looks like this window was broken inward. *Toward* the driver. Are we sure there's been no arrivals to the local hospitals? Maybe a witness saw it happen and tried to rescue them on their own?"

"Without calling it in?" Reyes said. "I mean people are stupid, but everyone knows you're not supposed to move someone when they're hurt. They still teach kids that, right? They got to."

"I don't know, but that hardly matters. The passenger side airbag didn't deploy, so most likely they were alone. Unless it malfunctioned. We need to get on this. If someone saw and tried to help, or if there was a passenger, the victim could already be at a local hospital. Let's try Middletown or Newburgh even—no idea how bad the person was banged up, but Saint Luke's is good."

"Alright, this is good stuff. Let's give it a shot, but I doubt we wouldn't have heard if they had," Reyes replied.

Detective Williams climbed precariously back up the ditch. "Yeah, I feel the same way. We would have heard by now. Still worth a shot though. I know it might sound stupid, but I typically have some inkling, some feeling toward the cause or a path to take, but this?" Williams gestured back and forth between the glass, the flipped car, and the flood of activity around them. "But this is stumping me. What in the hell would even make someone flee? Or if it was a witness or passenger helping, who doesn't call to notify the appropriate authorities?"

"Panic," was the only word Senior Detective Reyes offered in reply, exhaling cigarette smoke.

"Excuse me?"

"Panic. The dude probably panicked. How often do you flip a car? Dude probably got out of it mildly hurt and panicked. Panic makes people do strange shit." Reyes' shoulders raised, not looking nearly as concerned as he should have been.

"And why are you so certain it's a man all of a sudden?" Williams shot back.

"Listen, I've been doing this a long time. Nine times out of every ten, if something real stupid's been done, it's a man's done it. Better yet, most likely a young one too." He shrugged again, smiling around his cigarette butt. "I don't make the rules, kid."

Williams' attention shifted as an ambulance pulled up. Two paramedics got out and pulled a stretcher out of the back. One of the paramedics, pulling latex gloves over his hands, looked left and right, a rather confused look on his face.

"You guys took your sweet time." Williams smiled, shaking her head. "Ehh, doesn't matter anyway, no one's found a body…"

IV

Detective Williams stared down at the coffee Reyes had handed her. Cloudy, greyish brown with bits of white floating in it. *Creamer. I fucking hate creamer.* The oily excuse for a milk alternative always turned her stomach in circles. By now, she thought Reyes would have remembered that, but after the night out they had, she'd drink it black, or shovel the grounds directly into her mouth. Anything to stay awake at this point.

A crowd of people from town had amassed, answering the call for volunteers. All they had been notified of was that there was a missing person. The car and glass had been removed hours ago.

The crowd slowly headed toward a tarp-covered portable pavilion, the kind from Target or Dick's Sporting Goods. It was a purchase that Williams had been sent to make when she was a uniform cop, some four or five years ago, and Chief still said it was the best purchase they ever made. To him, the thing exuded control. Or power. Or at the very least it commanded attention, which was all the Chief of Police wanted when he made appearances. Usually known for his pomp and circumstance, he had dressed down for the day: hiking boots and slacks, and a tucked-in flannel with a police windbreaker overtop. His hair, a usual staple for being perfectly placed, was no different today, the wind unable to defeat it. He raised his hands and smiled, gimlet eyes turning to the crowd.

"Ladies and gentlemen, some of you may already know me, but I am the Chief of Police for the Cemetery Police Department, Raymond Carter. I want to thank you all for showing up on such short notice. This is quite a turnout, and I'm yet again humbled by the great town of Cemetery."

The crowd gave a subdued round of applause, while many in the crowd continued to shake their heads and stare at the Chief of Police. The Chief had been appointed by the mayor, but he was an unusual pick. The pool of applicants had featured several older, more qualified individuals, so the choice had surprised many of those invested in the selection. The rumor mill had spit out that there was possibly an outside source making the final call, but nothing was ever confirmed. The Chief, though, had proven himself to be calm and steady, offering something Cemetery often needed in spades.

Chief Carter gave them all a small smile and nodded his head in recognition. "You can clap, you certainly all deserve it. And look, I know many of you have questions. Questions I am not prepared to answer. Not yet at least. Please, let me put your minds at ease. At this point this is a missing person. We are looking for them. We aren't currently looking into any suspected foul play, so please put all of that to rest. We just need your help to find them; to bring them home safely." A few hands were still raised straight into the sky, like beacons, readying to undo the tentative calm the Chief had elicited. He did his best to cut them off, "That's why it's so important for us to stop wasting time here! Let's be orderly, let's be safe, and let's do this together."

Some of the older generation, those especially keen on law enforcement, applauded again. They were joined by those that found the Chief to be impressive as well. The Chief smiled but directed his attention back to the table he had been standing over. The surrounding woods had been broken into manageable quadrants, then even smaller sections so that groups could be assigned targeted search areas. Officers Dans and Owens started handing out high-vis vests to the volunteers. Each of them would also be provided with a flashlight. It was early morning, but there was rain in the forecast, and the police department didn't want anyone to feel the need to bend down to get a look into any tight or dark places. They had enough on their hands without added injuries to worry about.

Williams and Reyes approached the Chief from behind the pavilion, still slurping their coffees. Both looked haggard, but the changes showed the most on Williams. She had dark circles under her eyes, the right side of her shirt was untucked, and she sported a coffee stain on her shirt that she was still self-conscious about.

Reyes replaced the cigarette in the corner of his mouth with a fresh one, barely putting one out before starting another. "Lovely morning we're all having, wouldn't you say, Chief?"

Chief Carter pinched the bridge of his nose and took a deep, calming breath. Looking down at a list he said, "I want you two separated for this. I need two good sets of eyes out there, and I don't want them both in the same search area. Williams, you'll be with a volunteer named Katherine. Reyes, with Declan and April."

Every person in the crowd had donned their high-vis vests, flashlights in hand. They collectively looked left and right, as if in search of a final directive. More than a fair share of the volunteers seemed overly concerned, as if they were spooked before ever stepping foot in the woods. Carter felt it was necessary to wrangle them back in one final time before sending them on their way:

"Everyone! Everyone please, listen up for just a minute more. You've all been provided with your vests and flashlights by now. This is not something to take lightly; please ensure you are wearing the vests and using the flashlights everywhere you go. We're all here to find a missing person, we don't want to go getting lost ourselves now do we?" At this he smiled at the crowd, though few smiled back. "As you all must be aware, we do not have enough officers to assign to every group but know that we have separated them so that they are as spread out as possible. Stay together with your partner or group, stay hydrated, and if you feel yourself getting uncomfortable, don't be afraid to say so—we're all volunteering here. The grid we've created is much smaller than you may think; call out if you need any help and someone should be able to hear. Thank you."

During his second speech, Williams had approached the woman Carter had pointed out. Katherine was a short woman with glasses, mid-twenties, with dark brown skin and beautifully curly hair. She wore a pink sweater over a button-up with no jacket, even though it was supposed to rain. After exchanging names—all that Williams found to be strictly necessary—she led the woman to the edge of the woods.

I've been up for an ungodly number of hours, Williams thought, *and now they stick me with a fucking librarian.*

It wasn't that she had anything against reading, or libraries, or librarians even—she actually enjoyed them. It was the fact that she was ten hours late to bed, which also meant that she was ten hours late to her day off. Neither of which really got to the issue at heart—the fact that she was shy one body. The missing person had continued to niggle at her the entirety of the night. There was the accident itself, the smashed in window, the glass being blown *inward* rather than out, and the fact that there was next to no blood. Williams, so often entirely sure of herself, felt like she was floating in the unknown. Weightless and aimless, on a precipice.

She was probably just overtired, but her anxiety bled out as sarcastic snark.

"So, what exactly do we do?" Katherine said, pulling Detective Williams back in. "Or I guess I mean, what exactly do we look for? Am I stumbling on a body or looking for clues? Do we get deputized then?"

"Pardon me?" Williams said, yawning and pulling her hair up as best as she could into a ponytail.

"Sorry, sorry, I'm most definitely rambling. I guess I'm just a little anxious and once I started talking it just keeps coming and coming. I never realized until just a second ago that we could possibly stumble across a body out there...oh god what if I even *trip* on it?"

"Katherine, look at me," Detective Williams said. "You're not going to trip on anything. You have your flashlight, yeah? Use it. Pay attention. Keep your eyes peeled, and we'll find whatever we're meant to find. I'm personally hoping for the missing person to be recovered alive, thank you." She paused to breathe deeply after each statement.

Use it. Breathe. *Pay attention.* Breathe. *Keep. Your. Eyes. Peeled.*

All things considered, they might have stuck Katherine with someone less sleep deprived, less venomous. Or they might have thought to stick Williams with someone who didn't need babysitting.

"Sorry," Katherine mumbled, crestfallen. *Don't be stupid*, she mouthed repeatedly to herself, but not discreetly enough that Williams couldn't see.

"Don't worry about it, I'm not exactly comfortable with all this myself, you know," Detective Williams said, trying to reel herself in. Katherine not so different from how she actually felt. "They have us covering a pretty small area, not that that will mean it's easy to do. We'll walk this direction for two miles, keeping an eye out. If we see anything of note, I'll radio in. If not, we'll more than likely be instructed to keep going deeper, as long as we're up for it."

They walked in silence for several minutes, flicking their flashlights left and right. They didn't walk at any predetermined pace, nor did they take it unnecessarily slow. Detective Williams wasn't sure what she expected at this point. Or, more importantly, she wasn't exactly sure what she wanted—should she be the one to find a clue, a body? It could just as easily be someone else, somewhere else. Of course, there was no way of knowing; she just felt conflicted with the possibilities. On the one hand, if she found something, she could show them that she could handle herself well. On the other, she really wasn't positive she wanted to be the one.

If anything, it would likely be the group that had Eric Mathers in it. He and his son were diehard hunters, and they had a dog with them. Williams was a skeptic on the whole "hunters can be great trackers" thing, because isn't hunting just an extreme sport of patience, sitting in wait until something passes? The dog could be a great help though.

"Oh shit, *oh god*, what is that?" Katherine said, pulling Detective Williams from pondering.

Shit.

Ch 2

SEARCHING

I

DETECTIVE WILLIAMS WHIPPED HER flashlight around frantically, trying to spot what had made Katherine freak out. To their right, she saw nothing. To their left, about fifty feet from where they stood, was a clump of leaves and detritus. To her, someone with a bit more experience looking for people and looking at bodies, it appeared to be a ground-up pile of leaves, nothing more. She had to admit, though, it was of a body shape.

The two women edged forward. Katherine practically choked off blood supply to Williams' arm, gripping tighter than a blood pressure cuff. Williams pulled them forward, closing in on the leaf pile. She was almost positive it was nothing more than what it looked, but something still felt off about it. Williams removed Katherine's hands from her arm and lightly pushed her toward the right. Williams skirted around to the left; she had a sickening feeling in the pit of her stomach, her hand creeping its way toward her holster.

By the time Katherine got up the courage to stumble out front and center, Williams was already squatting down to appraise the situation. The area in front was devoid of leaves and twigs, almost as if someone was attempting to make a snow angel without snow. The closer Williams looked, the more bits she seemed to pick up on. Under her right foot was a pull straight through the leaves. She directed her flashlight and saw gouges made in the dirt, almost as if they were nail marks. She removed her phone and started taking pictures of the surrounding area.

Katherine let out a breath that she had most definitely been holding in. "Not a body," was all she could get out.

"True, but look at this, someone *was* here. It looks like someone was on the ground, pushing up the leaves. Then there's these gouges in the dirt, like they were putting up a fight. I'm not great with this stuff, but there doesn't seem to be any obvious footprints. But if they put up a fight, that…that means that whoever pulled them from the car wasn't trying to help. It wouldn't make sense to bring them a mile into the woods to get them help either," Williams said, pieces falling into place.

"So, we *are* looking for a body?" Katherine said, whimpering.

"Hold on, let me call this in," Williams said, grabbing her walkie.

II

Chief Carter asked for Detective Williams to get clear photos before heading in. The forecasted rain had started in earnest, spoiling the chances of a real police photographer getting into the woods. The chief waited for them under the pavilion. A few other people, including Senior Detective Reyes, waited with the Chief.

"Ah, Detective Williams, Katherine, I'm glad you've made it back in one piece," Carter grimaced. "Sorry, a figure of speech. Apologies. Please, let me see the pictures."

Carter swiped through them slowly, looking at each and zooming in randomly. As he got toward the end of the pictures, the ones Williams assumed were of the fingernail grooves in the dirt, he zoomed in and took an even longer look at each. He passed the phone to Reyes and turned back to the group of people. "This definitely looks like a struggle of some kind. However, nothing shows anything that indicates a second person. Could the driver have run off into the woods confused or disoriented? The struggle on the ground could have been them trying to get back up? Especially if they were drunk or concussed. Reyes, what do you make of it?"

Reyes finished with the pictures, tossing Williams back her phone. With a fresh cigarette between his two fingers, he nodded. "I'm with you on that, Chief. Nothing shows a second person by any means. Concussed or drunk fits a few of the theories that Williams put out there, too."

This was their way, Williams and Reyes. He centered her, reminding her of what needed to be done and that she was good at it, and then he let her do her thing. Reyes ensuring the Chief was aware that Williams had good ideas was just another layer to it. It wasn't lost on Williams that she was the one out there, the one taking the pictures, yet Reyes was the opinion the Chief cared about.

"So maybe you should double down on all the local bars in the area that were open last night. If someone had their keys taken from them, that could lead us right to them."

"I- I'm not sure about that anymore." Williams' face burned bright at having interrupted. "When we were out there, the way the leaves looked from the back, it almost seemed heavy. Like the body had impacted the ground, maybe sliding a little—and that's why the leaves were pushed up. I guess an injured or inebriated person could drop that hard to the ground, but the whole thing just feels off."

"It seemed intentional, violent even," Katherine offered.

"Thank you so much for the help, Katherine, as well as the rest of you kind folks, but if you'd step out to the tent over there, there's water and some light food. We'll be back with you in just a couple of minutes," Chief Carter said, dismissing them as diplomatically as possible.

As they filtered out from under the pavilion, Carter made a face. "I'd forgotten they were here to be honest with you both. I don't like this. Our timeframe for a lead is disappearing right before our eyes and we don't even have a person or a body recovered. There might not have been significant blood on or in the car, but broken bones? Internal bleeding? Our time window to find a living person seems to be running out."

Reyes pointed toward the trees. "So send us back out there. The rain sucks, but it's not an actual impeding factor. We need to search, so send us searching. Far as I'm concerned, we're bound to find *something*."

The way Reyes emphasized something made it clear he didn't believe it could be a *someone*. At least not anymore. Reyes lit a new cigarette with the butt of his last. He put the first cherry out with his first two fingers and flicked the butt. Something about this investigation seemed to be unraveling him, as if he knew he was up against something unbeatable.

III

Thanks to Mathers and his son, Detective Williams and Katherine were now the proud borrowers of a four-wheeler. As they needed to head deeper into the forest, the hunters had briefly left to get their ATVs for the growingly difficult terrain. Truth be told, Williams thought ten quads for a single family was a bit over the top, but for the moment she'd swallow the commentary and give their legs a break.

Williams was particularly thankful since the engine and tight quarters meant focusing intently—no time for Katherine to ramble. They had just hit a dense area of woods where the branches and brambles seemed to lean down and grow up in menacing angles. Katherine's breath caught in her throat. Williams simply lowered her head and drove right through them. She wasn't going to let it get to her. Wasn't going to let Katherine's sighs, gasps, and circulation-ending grip pull her into her hysterics.

She wasn't leaving these woods till she found something. That was not entirely what the Chief wanted, but he needed a break in the case, so she was going to find it.

Williams figured they were around three, three and a half miles in, having driven for a decent amount of time. It was afternoon, and aside from a few walkie call-ins that were eventually debunked, or insignificant, no one had found anything of particular interest. The rain, on the other hand, had taken its sweet time starting, but was now coming down in sheets, the wind making it a horizontal onslaught that they were unfortunately driving straight toward.

Drenched to the skin and awake for over thirty hours, Williams pulled the four-wheeler around a final tree before stopping and keying it off. Grinding her teeth had been the norm for the entirety of the drive. She was passed exhaustion, now on her third, fourth, or even fifth wind. The teeth grinding had given her a mind-melting pressure headache, which did nothing for her mood. She needed to be on the ball more than ever. The rain, the current cloud cover, as well as the waning light, were bound to make it difficult enough as it was.

Get it together, Williams thought, *do your job already*.

The rain whipped at the perfect angle to sting her eyes, and even the light from their flashlights was making her head hurt. She felt like she might vomit, but she swallowed it down rather than appear weak in front of Katherine. A twig snapped to her left and she whipped her head around.

"Over here, Detective, I think I see something," Katherine called from what appeared to be a clearing a bit up the path.

Williams headed toward Katherine, keeping her flashlight pointed at the ground to ensure she wouldn't miss anything. Entering the clearing to the side of Katherine, she saw another area of mushed leaves, practically identical to before.

"This one's larger than the first one, right?" Katherine asked.

"At least double the size. Easy," Williams replied.

At that moment, the detective's walkie gave off a loud bout of static. Within the clearing, it echoed twice as loud. Katherine let off a clipped scream.

Williams shushed Katherine, trying to be soothing. "It's just the walkie. Let's try to listen."

More static rang out in two decisive bouts, nothing intelligible. Williams started walking around, in and out of the clearing, with the walkie held slightly in the air.

"You really think that'll work? Are police walkies anything like cellphones, even?" Katherine asked.

"Shit, I don't know," Williams retorted, incredulous. "My mother's house used to sit right outside a pretty large area of woods. Service was great, then over the years it got worse and worse. Who's to say whether or not it had anything to do with the woods. But no, this walkie should work much better. With the storm and the woods though, all bets are off."

The walkie static chirped again. Katherine let out another scream. This one longer and increasingly shrill. The kind of scream that brings "bloodcurdling" to mind.

What the fuck is she doing?

Williams turned around and stepped back into the clearing. Katherine, having found some kind of bravery within herself—or idiocy—had stepped up to the leaf pile. Her cheeks had blanched, and tears ran down her face. The look on her face was one of pure dread. As Williams approached, she felt as if each step forward elongated the distance between them by two. A trick of the mind of course, her brain giving her time to decide "fight" or "flight." Williams just couldn't figure out if it was in favor of, or against, her psyche. Her breathing hitched as she edged closer.

Circling around the backside of her, Williams came into full view of the cause of Katherine's distress. The air was redolent of earth and the sickly-sweet aroma of decay. Intermixed with the leaves was a body. Or, more accurately, what remained of one. Filthy and torn clothes covered a rigid and prone form. Williams steadied herself with a deep breath and panned her flashlight from the shoes upward: one shoe was missing, the foot itself tinged blue and filthy, various cuts and abrasions evident. What remained of their lower half shared a similar fate, but with the added filth of released bowels post mortem. Their shirt was completely torn in two, the flat chest emaciated and bruised, the sleeve of the tee shirt still present on the left shoulder, the arm stuck out at an unnatural angle. With the remainder of the left side gone, the chest could be seen; practically skin and bones, tight and malnourished. Blue and cold from the look of it, the wet sheen from the rain gave it an odd quality, one that Williams would try for the remainder of her days not to think about.

The right side of the shirt, still loosely readable as having once been white, was brown and spotted with bits of rust—what vaguely registered to Williams as dried blood. The victim's neck was another story. Torn and popped viscera and muscle, as well as a thin layer of fat, showed at the peak of what once would have been connected to their head. The victim's head, still possibly within the area, was not attached to the body.

Oh shit!

Katherine vomited off to Williams' right, pulling her attention back to the living person that she still shared the clearing with. Katherine was shaking and sobbing uncontrollably. "If it wasn't...wasn't for the leaves, I...I really could have tripped over it!" she stuttered.

"I'm so sorry you had to be the one to find it."

Katherine's shaking continued and it became clear to Williams that she was on the cusp of shock. The hours of being in the cold downpour weren't doing them any favors either.

Why the hell didn't she wear a coat?

"We went to high school together," Katherine mumbled weakly before slumping toward the ground, passed out. Williams was just able to grab her before she hit her head on the ground.

It's always the strangest moments that bring memories back to someone. In Williams' eighth-grade health class they were shown a video on reproduction. For the most part the class thought it was a little gross, but mostly funny. One kid, though, was especially squeamish and passed out, hitting his head off the desk next to his. One of the high schoolers that was running the class jumped right into action. Afterward, he ran the class through what he had done, stating that the lightheadedness that happens before passing out is due to a lack of blood flowing to the brain, and that elevating the legs helps to circulate it back faster.

With the memory ripe in her mind, the need to help someone else grounded her. She ripped off her coat and put it under Katherine's head on the ground. Next, she elevated her legs, leaning Katherine's shoes against her hip to keep them in the air. When Katherine started to come to, she passed her a water bottle and instructed her to take slow, deliberate sips.

When Katherine was finally steady enough to get up and sit on the four-wheeler, Williams instructed her to stay put—that she'd be right back. The shock still showed on Katherine's face. Williams imagined that if she were more herself, she would have squealed, "*Don't leave me here with...it!*"

Outside the clearing, Williams was finally able to get a clear chirp out of the walkie. She walked for a couple more minutes before pressing the button, "This is Detective Williams, over."

"Kid, it's Reyes, over. Been trying to reach you on your cell for probably an hour now."

"Sorry, the storm and woods are really messing with the service. The walkie too, over," Williams responded. "We found them, Reyes. They..." She released the button and took a deep breath. "They didn't make it. Look, Katherine's definitely in shock. We'll need an ambulance for when we get back. Were you able to get a hold of the owners of the vehicle? Someone will have to let the wife know. The victim is male, over."

"Shit. Look, Brennan and Shotz finally contacted the owner of the vehicle from last night...the Chrysler 200 was stolen. The entire family is on vacation, so they didn't even know." Reyes answered. "Whoever you found, we'll still need to investigate to get an ID, over."

"Stolen?" *Back to square one, again?*

"You okay, kid?" Reyes called over the walkie.

Williams' cheeks burned red at the fact that he would even ask, over the department radio no less. He should know better. She wasn't any less angry that he was just looking out for her. "I'm fine. Look, I tried to drop a pin on my phone, but it died from trying to search for service for so long. I'll have to come back out here to try to find the spot again with the recovery team. I'm fine, over." She let go of the button, cursing herself for saying it twice. No one would believe her; they could probably tell just from her voice. She didn't even believe it herself. She was anything but fine, but no one else needed to know that. She needed to be strong, to appear strong. She was no one's problem but her own.

If she had just been faster, better, this could have been avoided, couldn't it? It wasn't her fault, she knew that, but she couldn't shake the feeling all the same. Just like the stake out that broke up her parents. If she had done better, gotten whatever they needed from her right, everything would have worked out.

IV

The ride back in the rain had been a difficult one. When they had finally made it out of the woods, an ambulance was waiting for them both. Two paramedics helped Katherine off the back of the four-wheeler and into the ambulance. Senior Detective Reyes had pulled his car up right in front of Williams, getting out and opening the back door for her, ushering her in and brokering no arguments. He drove off right in front of Chief Carter, who didn't look happy.

The back of Reyes' car was where Williams had woken up, hours later, with a thick wool blanket covering her. Reyes sat in the driver's seat, the window cracked open, smoking the butt of a cigarette. "This rain is foul—didn't want to leave you alone with the car running."

"You didn't have to do that. What time is it?" Williams asked.

"A little after eight. You needed it, kid," Reyes replied, smiling.

He wasn't wrong there; she most definitely had needed it. Still did; another twelve hours probably wouldn't do her justice. "You need sleep too though, you've been up just as long as me. We both worked Friday."

Reyes laughed heartily, belly shaking. "I'll tell you two things you missed. After our final questioning on Friday, you decided to go driving around like a jackass, and I napped in the office. I'm also a single, middle-aged man. I went home and had a beer or five and passed out on the couch at eight. Knowing you, you were probably still awake when we received the call early Saturday."

Right again. "Alright, fine, whatever, old man. Thanks for this. The blanket too," Williams smiled. "I soaked your backseat though."

Detective Williams tried to look out the car window, but the rain and her sleeping had fogged up the inside. "Where are we, the precinct?"

"Yeah, kid, Chief Carter is waiting for us. They recovered the body," Reyes answered.

The *body*. The misfortune of the entire day came back to her in a rush. That's the beauty and sin of a real "is that person alive?" sleep; the utter bliss of waking up with no idea what's happened or where you are. She remembered now, and briefly wished she didn't.

She pushed down her guilt at having a moment of joking with her partner. "Oh god," Williams groaned, "Is Katherine alright?"

"Yeah, they gave her something to calm her, and made sure she was drinking enough fluids. She's probably home now."

Williams sat up and Reyes offered her a water bottle and a hot coffee; she chose the latter. Taking a slow sip to test the temperature, Williams took a deeper pull, finding it serviceable. She took a deep breath, releasing it loudly. "What the fuck are we going to do about this case, Reyes, 'cause we've clearly got something going on here," she said reluctantly, not wanting to put it out there, even though she needed to. "The body we found looked like it was flesh and bones, practically no substance. The first spot we found looked like there was a struggle…the body we found, well shit, it didn't look like it could have struggled against a thing. Then they go another two or three miles or so—then they get their fucking head cut off? It makes zero sense. I need more than that. I'm trying to make connections; I just don't know what we're dealing with."

Already Williams was worried that what Shotz had said was sticking with her. She had been working far too hard to appear rattled already, she couldn't slip up just because things weren't making any sense.

"I'm sorry, kid, but it gets stranger," Reyes said, frowning around his cigarette. "A lot stranger."

Ch 3

Autopsy

I

Inside Chief Carter's office, Williams and Reyes were given two of the more comfortable chairs, but they had been pushed to the left side of the room.

The office had a row of filing cabinets off to the right side of the room, the kind that came with lock and key. Carter's desk was a nice, solid wood, possibly oak. It was otherwise rather spartan, the need for personal effects or flairs something the Chief had long done away with. The only thing that had remained since his first day was a framed photograph of the Chief with several young men in military uniforms. A West Point Academy alum, the Chief took pride in showing off the members of the Hudson Valley he had graduated with.

Taking in the photo, Williams couldn't for the life of her remember who the other people were. Business owners and even fellow officers; she just couldn't place exactly who was who. Their importance was obvious, but Williams spent most of the time in this office giving the Chief her undivided attention or studying her shoes as he consulted with her partner. She did wonder why he was being so laid back since this started. Typically, Reyes taking off with Williams for a much-needed nap would never fly, but it was almost as if he were trying to be nice. Too nice.

Williams smiled slightly to herself, just a small twitch at the corners of her mouth as she thought about how stereotypical the room was. *If you've seen literally any cop TV show, this is the chief's office.*

Dr. Devin Kenmore, the police pathologist, was setting up shop. Carter had allowed him to roll a cart into his office, which was positioned at the center of his desk like an added appendage. He sat himself to the right so that he could face them. After gingerly placing a manilla folder on the rolling cart, he pushed his glasses back up the bridge of his nose and opened the folder, exposing a series of photographs and hastily written notes.

"I apologize for the wait and crappy handwritten notes. I originally intended to send my autopsy tech Sam Kristi, but he is a bit unreliable. He is good at shorthand though, so I should be able to dissect these notes for you."

"No worries, Devin," Carter started. "You remember Reyes and Williams, right? They're heading the investigation and need any pertinent information you may be able to offer."

"Of course I do," Dr. Kenmore said. He nodded at both of them in greeting. "You been hitting any of the local pubs lately, Reyes?"

"Uhh, no," Reyes replied. "Not exactly a lot of time on my hands."

"Well, you just let me know. I'm always looking for a new wingman and women love to hear all the nitty gritty—"

"Devin, please. They've been working straight through since Friday morning. They're tired, I'm sure they're hungry—well, maybe not after what they're about to see, but you get my point. Giving them something to go on will make you their best friend at this point." Carter pinched the bridge of his nose and motioned for Devin to take the floor. "Maybe they'll want to hit the pubs with you after you help them catch whoever's responsible."

Dr. Kenmore was a man of perhaps forty years. He had a head of orange hair that had seen better days, now sparse. He wore beige khakis and a light blue button-down tucked in. He was the kind of person that wore his lab coat twenty-four seven, often taking it home. Williams often wondered if it was to wash it or continue wearing it around the house, perhaps fulfilling some sick fantasy. Known for being good at his job, perhaps even too good, his morbid curiosity creeped out everyone else around him. He took it in stride though, wearing it as confidence.

Settling himself, Dr. Kenmore began spreading out the photographs and notes from the folder on the cart in front of him. He attached a note to each photo so that he could share insight with each piece the autopsy had gleaned. "I'm ready, but if you wouldn't mind, I could certainly do with a cup of joe. Hanging with the dead is tiring work."

Chief Carter's face, typically neutral and controlled, looked like he was prepared to say, *"Does this look like a fucking Starbucks?"* Instead, he smiled, using the intercom for coffees. Williams noticed that he hadn't removed his fingers from the bridge of his nose. Clearly, this was getting to him as well. Probably not the way it was affecting her, but the man at the top was the first stop for answers, and she knew that meant something.

After sipping his piping hot coffee, Dr. Kenmore took a deep breath and, rubbing his hands up and down the thighs of his heavily pressed khakis, began:

"The first photo here is from the examination of the skin itself. We didn't find any remarkable identifiers; however, the victim does have a single moth tattoo on the back of their left arm...I've brought a picture of that to leave with you as well. The contusions seen, covering vast swaths of body, are pretty typical for a heavy, if not fatal, car accident. Or, it's important to note, seen frequently in cases where the victim put up a significant fight. At this point I cannot definitively say one way or the other which instance this is from, although, I was of the initial opinion that some of the rather darker bruises came from addition injuries—i.e., both the crash and a struggle." Dr. Kenmore took a breath and sipped his coffee again. Williams thought for a second there was a gleam in his eye. "An additional note of import would be the overall state of the body. It has telltale signs of youth; however, it's rather malnourished, the skin tight over the bones...a rather *desiccated* look to what was a living person. Just an idea so far, as I couldn't find any typical track marks, but perhaps they were an addict of some kind?"

Chief Carter leaned forward, his desk chair creaking, "Sorry to interrupt, Devin, but you said that this was your initial opinion? Are you saying that opinion changed?"

"Possibly. This second set of photos are additional images of the outside of the body. More specifically the cuts, tears, and breaks of the skin. What we're seeing here is several cuts to the cutaneous, and sometimes subcutaneous, layers. There are, perhaps, seven prominent cuts overall. Four of which I would state are definitively not from a car accident. They are not deep, mostly scrapes, and that is why the area was lacking any blood in substantiality. Two more are both located on the victim's foot, which was shoeless, and are caused from movement within the woods. One appears to be from some type of root or branch as it's more of a tearing than a cut, and I removed what appears to be bark or some similar wood fiber from the area. The second foot injury is from glass; however, it appears to be from some kind of bottle rather than a car accident. The glass still present in the foot was brown, like that seen in beer bottles. Both of which were heavily plastered in mud, leaves, and other gunk, and that is why the area was not covered in a layering of blood from the injuries." Dr. Kenmore took a break to again sip his steaming drink.

Williams felt the slightest tremor in her hand. She hoped nobody had noticed that she looked pale, perhaps a little sweaty; maybe even on the verge of green and sickly.

"The next photo provided is of the neck itself. The lack of blood plays heavily into my decision making as to whether or not this took place post-mortem. It's quite easy to lean one way, as an injury this grievous would have covered a significant area around the body in the victim's blood.

"A few options do come to mind. The first is that this is not the cause of death—I am almost certain of that at this point—meaning that this heinous act was committed posthumously. The lack of a beating heart could certainly have contained a portion of the blood, which would somewhat explain our current situation, but not to the extent that we're seeing." At this, Dr. Kenmore did appear rather taken with himself, or the subject matter. Williams' stomach did a final flip as she imagined the tightening of this creep's pants around his crotch.

"You hanging in there, Williams?" Carter asked, leaning forward again to take in the detective's face.

"Yeah, you're lookin' a little green at the gills, girl," Dr. Kenmore added. As a detective, Williams was forced to work rather closely with the man. Most often, she found his fascination with dead bodies to border on outright creepiness, so to see him looking downright gleeful, knowing the state in which she had found that poor soul, was too much to take.

Williams swallowed it down, her anger bubbling out before she could rein it in. "Are you finished gawking, Victor Frankenstein?"

Dr. Kenmore laughed before continuing. "No, unfortunately not finished yet. The most likely option, from what I can see, is that this was caused by some wild animal or beast. A wolf or bear in this area is not farfetched. It sounds mildly ridiculous to even speculate, but as the injury caused to the neck appears to be more of a tear, rather than a series of cuts, I'd think a bite from an animal would be rather more likely than another human doing this. There is one portion on the lower right side of the neck that still has some unaffected skin on it. This spot in particular bears a marking that could easily be from some type of tooth, or fang. This—"

"Teeth or fangs, sure," Williams interrupted. "What about a clumsily done needle injection? Could the first hole be from the victim struggling?"

"I can't answer that for sure, as that would require a blood test, but yes, I suppose that is within the realm of possibility. Now please, let me finish." Dr. Kenmore rubbed his hands on his thighs, an act that seemed like he was steeling himself, although he looked right at home. "This still supports the theory that this took place after death, as animals are rather more confident when their human meals are not moving, but I can't say for certain yet. The injury itself does not appear to have visible bite marks that I can make out; however, it does appear to be similar to the tearing off of chunks of meat."

Williams stood abruptly, mouthing an excuse and rushing from the office.

"Come on, Devin, you were practically goading her with that ending." Reyes laughed, removing his cigarettes from his shirt pocket. He used them to gesticulate as he spoke. "Anyone else think the body looked like a kid's crumpled up juicebox?"

Carter released a loud *tisk* as the words left Reyes' mouth.

"What do you think about this animal theory?" Chief Carter said, course correcting the conversation and appraising his lead detective.

"I particularly enjoyed his use of the word 'beast,' as if an animal, just being its animal self, was somehow a level above that. Kind of funny honestly," Reyes replied. "Ridiculous, even."

II

When it became apparent that Williams wasn't coming right back, they took a break for an hour. Chief Carter remained at the station to do damage control.

She had definitely puked, that Reyes was a hundred percent right on, he just wasn't sure how many times. It seemed to have helped settle her though.

Reyes took them to their usual haunt, the Cemetery Diner. All through their quick meal—a greasy burger for Reyes, and eggs with fries for Williams—she couldn't shake the pit in her stomach. It wasn't nausea anymore, more anxiety, or fear. It was this niggling uncertainty. She wanted to know what was happening. How to solve this case. How to bring the victim justice for what they suffered. Again, it all weighed upon her shoulders, even if they didn't have an ID. *Especially* because they still didn't have an ID. Williams knew that the typical TV show drama *The First 48* was a bit of a sham; most of their investigative work continued on for much longer than that. However, spending almost the entire first day searching for the missing person? Now that was an issue. A rushed autopsy still didn't leave them with much to go on, other than a small moth tattoo on the back of the victim's left arm. She didn't have much faith in the system bringing anything back on someone processed with that kind of tattoo, although with the car being stolen, there was a bit of hope.

She needed a direction soon, something solid. She knew herself too well to keep floating in the unknown.

Devin Kenmore strode back into Carter's office. Williams was still slightly sweaty, but some of the color had come back to her cheeks, and now mostly she felt embarrassed. "I apologize. I appreciate the patience. I'm surprised that I got that rattled."

She shook her head, feeling heat in her cheeks.

"Hey, it's okay, kid," Reyes offered. "Is it really that bad?"

Dr. Kenmore smoothed the lapels of his lab coat, some of his former gusto gone. He gave a side-eyed glance at Reyes before he continued:

"I'll get back into it then, if you will. Finished with the cutaneous examination, I made the typical Y-shape incisions from shoulders to pelvis. One of the first things I noticed was just how...tainted everything looked. Even before removing the ribs, the victim's internals had quite an odd coloring to them. Then I cut and placed the ribcage to the side. They were perhaps more brittle than they should have been, but with the body in such a malnourished state, it shouldn't come as a surprise, having seen it yourselves." He held up the three photos taken of the incision, the cavity, and the removed ribs, before passing them around. Once they were out of his hands, he yet again smoothed the lapels of his lab coat.

"Now, bear with me for this final part of the report here, for it's bound to get awfully...strange."

Reyes and Williams gave each other a confused look.

The pit in Williams' stomach doubled in size. She wished she hadn't eaten. *It was going to get stranger?*

"Yes of course, Devin," Chief Carter said. He smiled, either out of politeness or confusion at the serious look on the pathologist's face. "Please, finish."

"At first glance, with the organs all in situ, it looked almost as if the body had been shrunken, shriveled even. The strange coloring continued to the rest of the organs as well, and even though everything was in the correct place, it just looked...off."

There it was, that word again. Since Williams had arrived at the scene of the accident it was all she'd been hearing. Even using it herself. The whole thing simply felt...*off*. Inexplicably so.

Dr. Kenmore looked to Williams, though his earlier smirk was missing. "As I removed several of the organs, one thing became increasing clear to me: the body wasn't strangely experiencing a lack of bleeding—from the accident, the struggle in the woods, the heinous decapitation—there was a mysterious lack thereof of blood. None. I mean zero." He laughed, almost maniacally. For once his humor seemed a little uncertain.

"What the fuck are you saying, Devin?" Senior Detective Reyes demanded.

"This is why my opinion has changed. This body, the victim, is entirely exsanguinated. Not enough time passed for the victim to be transported elsewhere and returned. They couldn't have been trussed up somewhere and drained. And I tell you this, this is the most thorough de-blooding of any body I've ever seen. I mean it's simply *gone*...not even a drop." He laughed, and this time there was a definite crack in his overall facade. "I am of the official opinion that this was not the body you were searching for, just the body you found."

Ch 4

Reprieve

I

After Chief Carter escorted Devin Kenmore from his office, he set about planning what to do next with Williams and Reyes. Once he felt comfortable enough with their course of action, he sent them both home and told them he better not see them until noon the following day.

Williams had slept, rather soundly at first, but then she had tossed and turned, dreaming in violent and strange nightmares. Gloved hands in a children's playground, brandishing a knife. A police officer, who had been pretending to be her father just moments before, brutally stabbed to death. His hot blood splashed across her cheek. The look, that hungry look in the criminal's eyes.

She woke with a start each time. Her past was never far from her mind, but at night, while she slept, was where it lived. Nightmares, while inexplicable, are where trauma breeds.

Her memories were foggy at best, childhood trauma doing its best to block out the entire situation. Her dreams were all she had to go on, unsure if that's even how it happened.

After that she paced. She lived alone, so bothering another sleeping person wasn't an issue. She cleaned, she vacuumed, she mopped the entire house. Then she took a mug of tea outside to her porch swing, intent on calming her nerves. A shiver ran down her spine; she told herself it was from the chill of the night.

II

Detective Williams had cleaned until ten thirty, then showered, grabbed her keys, and left. As previously feared, old man Mr. Cody was right at his front window, waving to his newest friend. Williams didn't have time to give it another thought.

At the precinct, she overheard two officers talking about the disappearance at the Old Mayor's Mansion. It was the same call she had heard come over the walkie the morning of the accident. She usually focused on her own stuff and kept her head down, but this morning she let her ears prick up. They were still searching for the kids; apparently some self-proclaimed ghost hunting group. The officers assumed the disappearance was a stunt for YouTube, so she tuned it out and headed to the precinct's kitchen.

With two cups of piping hot coffee, she hooked a right into the one labeled "Detective Reyes, Williams." As "senior detective" was a non-existent position given to Reyes when it became apparent that the department most grievously needed an additional detective on hand, they had never bothered to change the sign. The position did little more than make the "detective" role appear vacant for filling, as well as probably explain the wage gap between the two. That's what twenty years of experience did though, so Williams didn't mind. It also meant that they had smushed another desk into the office, the two now constantly looking at each other across what little space was left. Williams didn't mind that either, as the type of work they did most often left them partnering rather than working alone.

"Let me just say this first thing, right off the bat," Williams said, sitting the coffee down on Reyes' desk. "This whole thing is off. Everyone is saying it, and honestly, I can't shake it. You know I'm no superstitious fool, but there's just something odd about this whole thi—" Williams cut herself off, finally facing Reyes full on. "Wait, you smoke in here?"

"My name on the door, hell of a case, Chief's out of the building…call it seniority or some shit," Reyes said, cigarette held aloft.

"Where is the Chief?"

"I'd guess he's most likely organizing something again after last night's revelation. You remember, the discovery that there were two bodies instead of one…not my favorite last-minute reveal, personally," Reyes responded, violently stubbing out his cigarette on the edge of his desk.

Williams took her coffee and walked around the side of her own desk. Sitting down, she looked at Reyes, now sipping his coffee, looking as if nothing in the world was bothering him, a strawberry frosted donut on a plate to his right. For a stereotypical cop, his desk was actually rather spartan—no excess of reports piled high or trash littered around; his garbage can was empty and clean. He was a neat person, just lacking on the person-side of cleanup. It was a surprise whenever they met back up in the office.

"I know you think all of this is off, odd, strange. It's our job to keep all of that shit on the sidelines, remember that—*facts*, Williams," Reyes coached. "I'm waiting on a call back from the medical examiner. After yesterday's revelation, and the fact that the body was removed quickly due to the number of witnesses, I've asked for an additional check-in on the time of death. Especially to help us narrow down if this really isn't the body we're looking for. They should be calling soon, hopefully."

"So say that it isn't the body of the driver, then what? We're left with zero clues, and the need for another body—to make two separate IDs. The odds keep stacking up, don't they? We're not so much back to square one as ten paces behind it. And what about all the cuts from the glass and struggling if the victim from yesterday wasn't in the car?"

"I'm not pretending to know the answers. I don't know shit," Reyes began, taking a second to dunk his donut in his coffee. "But the police pathologist said it wasn't the body we were looking for, right? He didn't technically say the body wasn't in the car, or at the very least, *a* car. I know you know this by now, but I'll say it again: I'm of a mind to not guess, but to *know*. Right now we don't, so let's find out, not guess. Guess work ain't police work, kid. You want to tell me you have a gut feeling, a hunch or something, I'll follow you nine times out of ten, but I don't see where this is getting us."

At that moment the phone rang, cutting off whatever response Williams was cooking up. Reyes let it ring a second time before picking it up. After a brief back and forth Reyes returned the phone to the receiver and looked back up at Williams. Placing a cigarette in the corner of his lips, he lit it and took a long drag.

"Medical examiner is pretty positive the victim from yesterday has been dead for a couple of days," Reyes began.

"Pretty positive?" Williams responded, wanting to say more, but Reyes raised his hand to cut her off before she could.

"She said that with the blood being removed, as well as the body being outdoors, it opens the door for a few possibilities we wouldn't be looking at otherwise. I didn't get into the science with her, you know I don't get it, but the discoloration is something they have seen with older bodies. She thinks the pathologist was thrown off because the body wasn't in rigor mortis. It's something she's not sure on but thinks it could be due to however the body was drained. The shrunken organs were a mystery to her entirely, but they're still working through the body."

Williams took her time digesting this information. So, they surely had the wrong body. That sadly opened the door for additional headaches—including the one she was suffering from now—as they needed to search again. They were potentially looking at two separate crimes, two separate scenes, and two separate investigations. She wanted to be sure of herself, but she was better off working directly with Reyes in this situation.

Reyes' computer dinged, signaling the arrival of a new email. The pit in Williams' stomach persisted, despite her attempts to be positive.

Reyes tapped away on his keyboard briefly, then scrolled with this mouse until he got to the window he wanted. "Ah, here it is. All these years later and I still hate these things. We didn't get a hit on the moth tattoo, so when I got here, I figured I'd email it over to my buddy from Goshen PD and have him take a look. He said he vaguely remembered something he had worked on a few years ago and would make some calls. He sent me over a news article. Guy has a great memory for stuff."

"So, we have an ID?" Williams asked, holding out for an ounce of hope.

"Yeah, we do, but read the article. I'm forwarding it to you now, you know I'll just mess it up if I read it out loud," Reyes said, clicking away on his computer again.

Williams logged in while she waited for the article to come through. It could have been the case, or the heinous images and report she sat through last night, but the wait felt eternal. The dread cut like a knife through her gut...like whatever had happened to the victim, happening to her.

A minute or so later, her computer dinged. She brought the email up; it was a scanned document of a newspaper from last month. She leaned forward and read:

UPSTATE YOUTH MISSING

By TOM DUMBRELL

Goshen police elicit help from additional towns in the search for missing teen, seventeen-year-old, Robert Elton.

With no indication that he planned to run away, the teen left home earlier this week and has not been seen or heard from since. As of now it is known that he did not attend high school either, but reports are coming in that he may have been seen with friends that evening in Cemetery. However, when questioned, his friends claimed he hadn't been.

HAVE YOU SEEN THIS MISSING PERSON?

When last seen he was wearing a pair of blue jeans, black Nikes, a white tee shirt, and a zip up hoodie that said Goshen High School. His parents admit to him being a troubled child, often dealing with addiction, but state that nothing in his behavior ever alluded to something like this. That he was a loving boy. Robert is about 5-feet-7 and weighs about 130 pounds. He has short black hair and green eyes. On the back of one arm, he has a moth tattoo, pictured beside a photo of Robert. If you or anyone you know has information concerning the whereabouts of Robert Elton, contact the Goshen Police Department (914)938-4586.

Williams stared at the screen for a long time after finishing. It could have been several minutes, an hour, a day—she couldn't say. The only thing typed in the email body read "still a missing person."

"A month? An entire month ago? What the hell, Reyes?"

"I know, I know, I read it just the same as you, kid. A whole month. Could explain the malnourishment, right? I mean how much money could a teen have on them? Long time to not eat. Or drugs could have done him in and then the animal theory looks better and better," Reyes offered.

"Jesus, Reyes, show a little respect, he was just a kid," Williams said.

Reyes took an exaggerated drag of his cigarette, rolling his eyes. "Pardon me if I don't go crying my eyes out for another druggie in Cemetery. I've been doing this a long time, kid, let me break it to you nice and quick: when it comes to shit like this, the hits keep coming."

Williams opened her mouth but decided to close it. She didn't need his approval, so why did she feel her cheeks turning red? Not in front of him, no way. Maybe she was still more idealistic than the others, but protecting came first, and justice was above all. It didn't matter where you came from, what you'd done, or who you were. Not in the least.

"No way, Reyes. I mean, come on...no one deserves what happened. No one deserves that," she spat out, making sure she didn't blink, not allowing the moisture in her eyes to turn to tears. "Everyone across the board deserves justice. He was just a high schooler."

Reyes waved her away and stubbed his cigarette out. "Don't let my shitty cynicism get you down, kid, okay? I'm sorry. We'll work hard to get them justice, alright? It's just this whole thing, it's getting to us all differently, okay?" Reyes was placating her, but she was sure he didn't mean it.

"We just need to get something going here. *I* need it. Before whatever forced calm Chief has going on begins to dissipate."

"Well, if you're up for it...I do have possibly uplifting and semi-related news," Reyes teased.

"Yeah, and what is that?" Williams bristled rather than opening up, worrying once more that there was something she'd missed.

"You have to promise to keep an open mind here. And no assault!" Reyes said, laughing.

"Not unless you tell me what it's about," Williams said, not trusting him, but mostly kidding now.

"Well, the hint I'll give you is that I said semi-unrelated, not entirely. Now promise," Reyes said, a twinkle in his eye.

"Fine, fine. I promise," Williams said, not quite ready to give in to it fully.

"Well, the precinct received a call today from a Ms. Jackson. A Katherine Jackson. She was enquiring after you, Williams. You weren't here yet, so I took the call. It's the Katherine from the volunteer group. She called looking to speak to you, hoping to apologize for what happened in the woods. I told her she could take you to dinner," Reyes said, smirking around his cigarette butt.

"No. *Abso-fucking-lutely* not. No way, Reyes, I mean it. It's not happening," Williams shot back. A panic of a different kind hit her hard. She worked hard to seem agreeable—more herself with her partner than others, but she still tried not to curse or act outright combatively. Williams could already tell what he had in mind.

"Yes, way. Absolutely, kid. You need this," Reyes said back, suddenly serious.

"No. Thank you, but no," Williams shot back, not willing to agree to being set up.

"You need this, *Abby*. You do," Reyes said, smiling.

The use of her first name—especially the use of it in her preferred shortening, something heard so seldomly in the police circles—made her genuinely smile for the first time since all of this started.

"Alright, alright, Ed. Maybe." Abby Williams let herself smile; hope.

Ch 5

INTELLIGENCE

I

DETECTIVE WILLIAMS HAD ALLOWED herself to genuinely smile for five minutes before putting her head back in the game. Reyes' buddy from Goshen PD had already notified the parents of their son's death, so they had one less awful task on their to-do list. They did, however, still have to go to the parents' house for questioning.

Williams felt good, like a ship captain with a heading, finally aiming towards something. A lighthouse spotted offshore, guiding her in. She hadn't been being ridiculous when she said she needed this. A clue. Without it, the aimless floating might have subdued her entirely.

Reyes drove so she didn't have to worry about letting her mind wander. What came next was something she allowed herself to feel certain of. This was the police work she hit out of the park: the questioning, the connecting of dots. When it was just her and Reyes in the field. One of the few times she felt comfortable within her own skin.

There was still that nagging feeling of something being misaligned though. *I'm glad to have a next step finally but fuck if I know if this is even for the same case anymore. All bets are off until the second person is found.*

Second body.

The longer it took to find the missing person, the lower the chances were of finding them alive.

Reyes pulled into a driveway off the main road. The quick glimpses Williams had picked up on subconsciously were few and far between. She had, however, noticed when they passed "Village Pizza," an on-the-nose name for an above average pizza place. Maybe Reyes would agree to stop there before heading back to Cemetery.

Reyes knocked on the door with a heavy thud, much harder than Williams thought was necessary. When no answer came, he took the cigarette from his mouth, flicked it out into the street and called, "Mr. and Mrs. Elton, this is the police. I'm Senior Detective Reyes, and this is my partner, Detective Williams. We have a few questions that need asking. Open up."

Reyes really couldn't play the part of the concerned police office.

"Pardon me if I don't go crying my eyes out for another druggie in Cemetery," rang hollow in Williams' head.

Reyes heavy-handed the front door again, "Police, open up!" Apparently, his "good graces" could be exhausted in half a minute.

The door cracked open, still chained, and a woman with red and swollen eyes stared out. She had clearly been crying, and there were heavy black bags under her eyes. Her stare was unforgiving; void. She eventually slammed the door shut and they could hear the chain being undone. The door reopened and the woman they assumed was Mrs. Elton walked into the living room without looking back. She was still in a nightgown and slippers; apparently Goshen PD had shown up to notify the family as soon as they heard. Clearly, she hadn't given much thought to her appearance since, which was understandable.

Williams wasn't too worried yet, not about this. Over the years she'd been working for the police department she had been met with a gamut of responses from civilians. From joy to violence. Some people loved cops, some simply did not. Her experience had taught her that it didn't matter who you were, nor what lifestyle you chose to live. A serial killer could open their door with an unerring smile; a grieving mother could give you dirty looks and slam a door in your face when you're trying your hardest to bring justice to their child.

She remembered one in particular, a grocery bagger from the local store, had actually spat at her. So, so far so good.

Mrs. Elton sat in a rickety recliner and motioned for them to sit in the available seats across from her. She leaned back, her brunette hair, all split ends, hidden against the headrest. She could have easily passed for fifty, her frown lines pronounced, but one could argue for younger. Williams figured a missing child could do that to you.

Williams took a seat on the loveseat opposite, hoping to put the woman a little more at ease. The room itself wasn't overly cluttered, having a tv in the corner and family photos on the wall. Every seat had an accompanying blanket, and although they weren't neat, it was…cozy, lovely. She tried to motion for Reyes to do the same, but he hadn't looked her way.

"We're so sorry for your loss, ma'am," Williams spat out, hoping to get a word in before Reyes. This broke his staring, and she got him to take a seat. Her words felt hollow: they hadn't saved her son, and they all knew it. It wasn't even her department or her town, but Williams wondered if she could have done more.

"Yes, I'm sure you're all just pouring out with sorrow for my dear boy," Mrs. Elton said with obvious venom. "Where was that fire while he was missing? I'll tell you plain, same as I just did to the other officer that took my baby away from me: none of you cared a wink. You saw a troubled kid and wrote him off. This. Could. Have. Been. Avoided."

Each word hit like a punch, tears rolling down Mrs. Elton's cheeks as she spoke.

"We're from Cemetery PD, ma'am," Reyes offered. "Not Goshen. We aren't the department that headed the investigation, so I won't pretend to know what went on during it. But we didn't mishandle anything."

"The other officer told me that your town was where my son was found. My darling boy. So don't sit there and pretend you couldn't have done more, he was right under your fucking noses!" Mrs. Elton sobbed in earnest now.

At this outburst, a man, presumably Mr. Elton, came out from behind a door. Williams caught a glimpse of a small kitchen behind him as the door swung shut. He was wearing grey chinos and a maroon sweater over a white button up. Williams assumed he was getting ready for work when the police arrived. He took Mrs. Elton by the hand and tried leading her away.

"I want to stay, Jon," Mrs. Elton said, pulling her hand away from his.

"Then you have to calm down and answer the questions they have, honey. This isn't productive. They aren't the cause, and they won't bring our Robbie back, but they could bring us peace," her husband replied, soothing.

Mrs. Elton sniffled and turned her nose up. It was clear she wasn't ready to relent, but she did quiet down. Williams thought she understood, or at the very least, was comfortable admitting to herself that she didn't know how she would react to something terrible like this.

A son gone, forever.

"Mr. Elton, not to be a broken record, but we're sorry for your loss. If there was something more we could have done, we would have—we're just sorry we didn't know," Williams offered. Suing for peace.

Mr. Elton smiled, though his eyelids were puffy and red. "It's settled then. How can we help you two? We want justice. You came prepared with questions—ask away."

Williams removed the notebook from her jacket pocket. Where to start? Sometimes if you asked the wrong question first it led to a tangent you never intended to be on.

"Well, I'd hate to make you relive more than necessary," began Reyes. "But I think it best if you took us through the disappearance. Like I said, we aren't the department that handled your son's disappearance. Perhaps something will stick out to us that didn't for them."

Well, that derailed Williams' desire for tact, but having the questionees take you through something you already knew was a pretty foolproof way to get them to open up. It tended to get the storytelling juices flowing. She could work with this. She sat back for the retelling, giving her full attention to Mr. Elton.

"Okay. It was a month ago now. On the morning of September third, Robbie woke up and got ready for school. He acted normal, dressed normal; still managed to eat an entire box of waffles. Nothing told my wife and I that something was up. I feel like people often say that there was a cloud overhanging them or something ominous the day that something happened, but for us it was nothing like that. We sadly thought that everything was fine. Robbie told us that he needed to re-up his tab at the school cafeteria, so I gave him a little extra money. I guess I could have taken that as odd, as we had just done so a few days prior for the start of a new month, but I figured…you know kids, they buy twice as much as they need, and twice as often, and more for their friends besides." Mr. Elton ran a hand down his face, stopping to cup his chin and jaw in a vicelike grip. He tilted his head to the left and right, cracking his neck. He shifted in his seat next to his wife.

"We didn't notice that he didn't take his backpack!" Mrs. Elton shouted, sobbing anew. "Us, his own parents, sent him off to school, not even noticing the signs right in front of our faces that he clearly didn't have any intentions of going there."

"It was an oversight, yeah. Our son got into some trouble in the past, but he'd ensured us he was on the straight-and-narrow. He met all our deadlines, his schoolwork was finished, he checked in when he was out with friends. He was clean, I know he was clean," Mr. Elton said, getting a little loud.

"Oftentimes like this," Williams said, "it's hard not to look back and question the decisions you made, the things you may have missed. That isn't your fault. The small things that change from day-to-day slip through the cracks. I know that doesn't make it any easier, but it's the truth."

Reyes stared from beside her.

"Thank you. Forgive us if we aren't ready to let it go just yet. Robbie is—was—our only child. He was everything to us," Mr. Elton said. At the changing from present to past tense, Mrs. Elton let out a choked sob, clutching her hands to her heart. "After Robbie left for the day," continued Mr. Elton, "we went about our business as you typically would. I left for work and headed to the city; my wife stayed home. She works...she just works retail. Because of that, she happened to be home when the school gave us a call, stating that Robbie hadn't shown up for school and that it was an unexcused absence. My wife called me, but we weren't quite frantic yet...you never assume the worst, or maybe you just tell yourself not to, I don't know. I told her to drive the route to school, check his usual hangouts, and give me a call back. I figured he was just blowing off class. Who hasn't? My wife though, was immediately worried that he might have fallen back into his old habits. Even then, that was something we were playing close to the chest. Few others knew about it. By the end of the day, we were panicked. I rushed home and we called the police. It was four thirty-two in the afternoon when we called. I'll never forget that time until the day I die."

Williams scribbled down a few last notes that she thought could end up being helpful. Nothing seemed pertinent, but she'd refer back later, not make assumptions. Just like Reyes had taught her.

"I'll apologize, as I'm sure you've been asked this before to some degree, but is there anything you can think of out of the ordinary when you put your mind to it that could have been abnormal for your son? Something like the leaving of a backpack? Anything like that could help," Williams inquired.

"No, nothing." Mr. Elton said, gripping his hands together and shaking his head. "I'm sorry. I've wracked my brain every day since his disappearance, hoping something would come to mind, but it hasn't. He was totally normal."

"Is there anyone that could have wanted to cause your son harm?" Reyes asked.

"Why would anyone want to hurt our precious Robbie?" Mrs. Elton snapped.

"You said your son had had some troubles. Drugs, alcohol, those things tend to make harsh situations harder. Was your son dealing? He could have been working for someone. Could your son have made enemies?" Reyes leaned forward.

"I don't—" Mr. Elton rung his hands and shook his head again. "No I don't believe so. He would have told us. We would never have let something happen to our son...never. He knew that, and he would have asked for help if he needed it. Even if the situation was bad."

"No run-ins with bullies in school, or fallouts with friends?" Williams asked, trying to steer back toward the land of their son being the victim. She didn't like it, but she knew deep down she'd have to say something. Reyes' approach was entirely off, bordering on unacceptable.

"He was beloved at school, kind of popular. I guess that could have made some of the less popular kids dislike him, but we never heard anything specific. His friends were great, some of them still stop by," Mr. Elton said.

"Would you be willing to provide us with information about that? A list of his friends?" Williams cut in. Better to cut this short than to let Reyes get them kicked out.

"I mean, I really don't see how that could help, but sure. A list of friends should be easy. The Goshen police should already have one," Mr. Elton said, standing.

"Great, I can get that sent over to me," Williams said. "Here's my card. If anything changes, if anything comes to mind, call me immediately."

II

Climbing back into the passenger seat, Williams snapped the door shut harder than was necessary. She wasn't sure why, but she thought if Reyes assumed she was upset with him, that this next part would go easier. He had almost blown the interview no less than a couple of times. Not to mention his approach had started wrong right from the way he had knocked.

Williams stared at her feet, taking in the mat beneath them in vivid detail. Every piece of discolored leaf, crumb, cigarette ash, and pebble. This would have to be outright confrontational. As partners, they had bickered before—hell, bickering was practically their main form of communication—she just wasn't sure how to approach something more serious than that.

"What is it?" Reyes finally asked.

As always, he spoke first.

"I'm really not sure how to say it, so I just will," Williams began. "This whole chip on your shoulder thing, it really needs to level itself out. I get that I'm the new one here, and lord knows I'm trying to show you I know what I'm doing, but you went off the rails in there. You think I'm naïve, and maybe I am, but that was uncalled for. You were being a dick to a mother and father that just found out their *son* was gone for good."

Finishing, Williams put her hands over her face, applying pressure over her aching eyes. She hoped she looked more annoyed than nervous, but she wouldn't hedge any bets on it. Now that it was out in the open though, she felt oddly relieved. She waited for Reyes' tirade to come, to tell her all the things she was doing wrong. Or how she would be better off minding her own business. But as the silence dragged on, she started to wonder if she had somehow gone too far.

Reyes removed his cigarettes from his shirt pocket, slapping the pack until one popped out far enough for him to grab it between his lips. He lit up and released a heavy sigh with his first drag.

"They're not the only people that lost a child, kid."

What the hell *does that mean?* Reyes hadn't sounded angry; there wasn't the typically jagged edge that accompanied his jaded tone. Was he saying that they weren't important, or was he including himself in that statement?

If anything, he just sounded…sad.

Reyes drove them straight past Village Pizza, and they spent the rest of the journey in a dead silence.

III

Williams climbed out of the passenger side. Reyes had parked in front of the Cemetery Diner. There was a small gap between the diner and the lot behind it that Williams headed into. The connected lot served as additional parking for the diner but was also parking for a strip mall. The strip's Dunkin' Donuts was a frequent stop for the local kids. Williams had spent an ungodly amount of time outside of it herself in her late teens, so she should know.

One of the names listed for Robbie Elton's friends had stuck out like a sore thumb. James Rictor, a twenty-year-old with a hell of a reputation. He hadn't done anything necessarily illegal, but it was considered a matter of time for the kid. Minor infractions and the knack for always being where something went wrong had gotten him police notice.

Williams walked toward the Dunkin' in hopes of spotting him. It was a bit early for his crew, only two in the afternoon, but they were taking a chance. Williams ordered two coffees, hoping to settle the waters between them with a quick peace offering. But on her way out she practically collided with the kid. James wore a Monster Energy hoodie and a pair of skinny jeans. He had on a beanie and Nikes. He just looked...normal, with a small, pimply face. He took one look at her, registering the recognition on her face, and ran. Williams dropped the coffees and set off in pursuit as she saw him running for the split in the strip mall.

"Stop—we just have some questions about your friend, Robbie!" Williams called after him. He hit the corner of the building where it split and turned, picking up speed. "Damn it!" she shouted after him.

As she rounded the corner, she saw that Reyes had the kid by the collar of his shirt, his car completely blocking the back exit of the drive thru.

"Hey, did you plan that?" Williams asked, doubling over and taking a breath. It was a short run, but there was something about entering a pursuit that threw out all cardio training.

"Hangs by the Dunkin' and this is the closest way to disappear. I took a chance," Reyes replied, shrugging. He pushed the kid up against the hood of the car, motioning for him to stay. He placed a cigarette in his mouth and gesticulated at the kid with the box. "Keep your ass planted and I won't ask any questions about why you were running. We just want to ask some questions about your friend Robbie Elton. I'm Senior Detective Reyes, and this is Detective Williams."

"Couple cops already bothered me at home about it. Dad beat my ass after too, thinking I was up to something," James Rictor spit out, still catching his breath. "I don't know a thing about what happened to Rob. He wasn't here the night his parents said he left either—that was bullshit."

"Did he have any enemies? People who would want to cause him harm?" Reyes asked.

"Enemies? What is this *CSI: Cemetery*? He was just a kid, younger than me. Who would want to hurt a kid?" James asked, his tone mocking.

Reyes stepped toward him, motioning like he was going to grab him again. James flinched and reddened.

"Stop treating this like a joke, you little rat," Reyes said with a bit of venom. "Someone must have wanted to cause him harm. There must be something that comes to mind, now *out with it*." He emphasized the final words like there was a threat there. With how they'd all been feeling, Williams wasn't sure there wasn't.

James gulped and looked between the two detectives. "I told you—I don't know anything. I really didn't see him that day, nor since. Honest. I don't want anything to do with this, just let me leave."

"Not until you give us something," Williams said. "Until then, you stay."

"You can't just hold me here, what the fuck!"

"Like I said, kid, you ran from the police. You want a ride to the precinct instead?" Reyes threatened, not empty this time. "That could take what, Williams—ten, maybe twelve hours? It'd be a huge affair at that point. We'd have to book you, do some paperwork too. And I am *terrible* at paperwork. Terribly slow that is." He exhaled his cigarette smoke in the kid's direction, as if it could carry the threat for him.

"Alright, alright, Jesus. Just don't take me in. And don't smoke that shit near me, my dad will lose it if he smells it on me, okay?" James said, the redness still in his cheeks.

"Twenty and still living with mommy and daddy?"

As soon as we get him to cooperate...Reyes has to go and be himself, Williams swore.

"Dude...officer...whatever you even are...it's 2022, everyone wants to move out and no one can afford it. Does it look like I'm being sent to college? No. I fold jeans for shit pay," James replied, a bit of his earlier personality coming back.

Reyes just shrugged, nonplussed. "Fair enough."

"Let's not forget why we're here," Williams said. "Robbie Elton disappeared on September third. You swear you didn't see him that day? Haven't heard from him since? Seen him at all?" She hadn't wanted to speak over Reyes and risk sparking something else, but this was going nowhere fast. James immediately opened his mouth to answer, but Williams cut him off, swiping her hand through the air. "*Think*!"

James screwed his face up in thought. The look made Williams realize it wasn't farfetched that he wasn't being shipped off to college if remembering a single month took that much mental power. On the other hand, she remembered being younger too; she was only nine years his senior. At twenty, people don't often bank memories with friends based off the idea of mortality. This would be new for him.

As she watched him, she realized he really did look like a kid. Perhaps just another reason to be annoyed that Reyes still took to referring to her as such, but that was thought for later. It was a good reminder for her that not everything was black and white, nor was anyone inherently bad. Now if only she could get Reyes on board.

Finally, James opened his mouth to answer. When no one objected, he said, "Alright, so I might have seen him the day of, but it was early, not at night, which is how the news made it seem. And, and it was in passing! Like he was heading somewhere…we only talked for a minute, and he didn't tell me where he was headed or why he wasn't in school. It was odd, now that I'm saying it, but I didn't think of it like that that day, I just assumed he was busy!"

"You withheld this from the police originally, because…" Reyes said, flicking his cigarette right past the kid's ear.

"Because I didn't want to be involved! Because I figured that if I admitted to seeing him, they would have taken me to the station," James said shrilly. "Everyone assumes the worst of me already, my dad included. My dad the most. Think I still got some bruises to prove it."

"Alright, James. I accept your reasoning, but we need your help," Williams said, placing a hand over her heart in sincerity. "Do you remember anything else? Like you said, the day itself you just thought he might have been busy, so it wouldn't have tracked as weird then. I mean *now*. Does anything at all stick out as weird now?"

James took a minute and thought the questions through again.

"Well, the paper had said that nothing at home had indicated he would run away." James finally said. "When I saw him, he didn't have anything on him at all."

"How do you mean," Reyes asked.

"Well, no bag or nothing. No additional clothes or shoes. Who runs away without clean underwear? Seems like shit planning to me. Not saying I've thought about it..."

"That's true, James, good catch. And did he maybe say anything that didn't stand out then, but sticks out now?"

"Well, maybe, but I don't know if it's true," James said. He shrugged and pulled his hood over his head.

"Go ahead, kid. No stopping now," Reyes said. Rather gentle for him.

"Well, he said some weird shit about thinking that someone was watching him. Said he maybe saw someone staring into his window a few times." James said, adjusting himself on the car. "He'd been saying that for a while though—but hadn't mentioned it the day he disappeared. We thought he was crazy; he was always an anxious kid. We made fun of him for it. Said mommy and daddy would let him share the bed and shit like that. I don't know though, Rob was from fucking Goshen, man, nothing happens there."

"Crime happens everywhere, kid. You should have told the police that," Reyes barked.

"Rob said he told his parents every time he thought he saw someone. At first it slipped my mind, but after I figured his parents would just bring it up. Not like I'm going out of my way to approach you people."

Williams gave James her card, telling him if he remembered or needed anything, to give her a call. As he walked away, the anxious pit in Williams' stomach returned twofold. *Facts*, Reyes had said, *facts*. Well, the facts weren't adding up.

Why had Robbie Elton's parents withheld that information from police?

Ch 6

A Body

I

THEY ARRIVED BACK AT the precinct after four, Reyes wanting to eat at the diner first. Their lunch was filled with speculation rather than hashing out what had happened in the car back from Goshen. Reyes had reached out to his friend at Goshen PD to update him on what James had said. They hadn't heard about someone lurking from any of the interviews conducted. Reyes thought the kid was spewing nonsense so that they'd let him go. Williams thought otherwise, taking the concern for Robbie to be sincere.

Williams realized she hadn't gone back to apologize for dropping the coffees. *Guess I can't show my face there ever again.*

As they headed to the Chief's office to appraise him on what little they had found, Carter shouted from the door for them to hurry up.

"We've got a second body," was all Carter said in lieu of welcome.

"When?"

"Where?"

"Same woods as the other—this one better hidden though. Looks like maybe the perp has gotten wise," Carter replied.

"You think these are related? You sure this is the body from the car accident this time?" Reyes inquired.

"This body was ruled fresher, at any rate," Carter replied, the bridge of his nose pinched tight between his finger and thumb. "Still exhibiting a lot of the same strange features as the other: desiccated look, shrunken and shriveled innards, a strange tinge to the body. Oh, and "absolutely bloodless," like Cemetery is now the set of a horror film."

"Do we have an ID this time?" Williams asked.

"Yes," Carter replied, shaking his head. "This one has a head. Facial recognition came back with one, Brendan..." he stopped and consulted the sheet in front of him, "Err, Brandon Doty. Dental confirmed it. Kid is apparently a friend to your Robert Elton. Though he's older, and car theft is a rung up from anything Robert was into as far as we know. Maybe this Brandon was a ringleader of some kind for troubled kids."

"Well shit, Chief. We just spoke to one of the Cemetery kids on the list of Robbie Elton's friends. He claims that Robbie was complaining about feeling like he was being watched. Apparently even told his folks that he had seen someone looking in his window a few times." Williams put her right hand to her mouth, thinking hard. "I know Reyes thinks the kid was lying, but that's two in a row...what if he actually did see something and these kids are being targeted?"

"Nah, that's ridiculous, kid. Think. In that scenario, how could the perp know the kid was driving just outside Cemetery in a car that wasn't even his?" Reyes asked, throwing what he felt was logic into the wheel spokes of her momentum.

"Ease up, Reyes. Think for a second. If the perp was watching Robbie, why couldn't they be watching this Brandon kid too? Say they watched him stealing the car...that right there explains it well enough. Don't forget that one of my original theories was that the accident could have been caused by someone else."

Reyes shrugged, reaching for his cigarettes until he remembered where he was. "Alright, yeah, that could possibly track, but I still think the James kid was loading us with crap so that we'd let him go. Why wouldn't a single other interview have turned that info out...why would the parents withhold that if it was true?"

"Damned if I know, Reyes," Williams replied, "but people withhold stuff from us all the time. You plan on continuing to act like that isn't the norm or something? Maybe Robbie swore them to secrecy, maybe it collectively slipped their minds, or maybe they thought it sounded ridiculous, like you, and therefore they decided to say nothing instead. Certainly not the most far-out idea nowadays."

Reyes opened his mouth to retort, clearly raring up to dish it out, their previously unfinished business spilling over. "Look—"

"Alright, that's certainly enough," Chief Carter said, cutting them both off. "I pay you both to work together to solve crimes, not to be of a like mind. If you disagree, investigate both possibilities, there's nothing wrong with that. We're clearing two days in with next to nothing to show for it but double the trouble. We really can't afford to rule anything out. Although I'm rather inclined to agree with Reyes at this point, I'm always up for being proven wrong. Kids spew nonsense all the time, but let's do our due diligence to ensure that's the case, that's all. Now look at this before I send you back out. I told them no more rushed work, so the autopsy isn't here yet, but Dr. Kenmore sent over this beauty."

Chief Carter placed a single photo on top of his desk. Reyes and Williams had to get out of their chairs to see what was in front of them. It was the picture of an arm, or lack thereof, as the tissue around the elbow was mangled and torn. They were presented with viscera, torn and pitted muscle, fat and skin, and split veins.

The ever-growing pit in Williams' stomach reared its ugly head. This looked exactly like the neck of Robbie Elton. Williams felt nauseous, like the world was spinning, but she swallowed it down.

Fuck.

Directly above the torn appendage were two obvious puncture wounds in the skin, which could easily have been hastily done needle marks or a bite from a wild animal. But if they were from a needle, why would there need to be two? A lack of experience? A struggle?

"Look at the bruising under these two punctures, here and here. See?" She pointed to the two spots on the photo and waited for them to acknowledge her. "Don't those look like wheal marks?"

II

They spent the majority of the following day in their office making various calls and notes. Mrs. Elton feigned ignorance when called and questioned about her son seeing things, rude as ever. Williams had a little more luck, securing two more interviews for the following day with a friend of Robbie's, and an ex-employer.

Home now, Williams stood in front of her bedroom mirror and stressed over a "date" she never asked for—with Katherine from the search party. Or was it not a date? She had never been the type to stress over her looks, her body, or makeup—not being superficial herself. It was more an inner battle of 'what do you wear to a possible date that you didn't ask for or want?' Jeans or leggings? A dress, or skirt? She didn't intend to be standoffish; she was just busy and hadn't sought to connect with anyone in a couple of years. All the other attempts ended rather poorly. She wasn't against the idea of it, but with the current case especially, she just didn't have it in her to argue over the small things like who left the dishes in the sink. With the crime rate in Cemetery, and people dying, everything else just seemed meaningless. Her feelings of that showed, and more often than not, she'd been left, not the other way around. She was fine with it either way, as getting close usually meant disclosing her troubled past.

Her house wasn't very large, and the bedroom's layout left a lot to be desired. Regardless she had outright refused to have anything smaller than a king bed. Having suffered through a dorm room twin for four years, she was never going to settle for anything less. Her bed was positioned exactly opposite from the door. She had two nightstands on either side of the bed, although she only used the one to her right, never the left. Her closet was next to the nightstand, and she wished there were more room. There was no TV in the room, she went there for sleep.

Williams showered quickly, washing her hair and brushing her teeth. She found herself right back in front of the mirror. After slacks and a blouse made her feel more like she was going to work than out to dinner, she gave up the attempt and put on jeans. She kept the white blouse though.

Get it together, she thought, *what, are you nervous now? What if it's not even a date?*

Thirty minutes later she pulled in front of *Benucci's*, Cemetery's only Italian restaurant. She had always found it to be overly pricey but felt it worth it in the moment every time. Katherine had picked it. A momentary thought of Reyes brought anger back to the surface, but she stuffed it down. She took a deep breath and stepped out of her car.

Williams spotted Katherine and took another deep breath. She felt almost immediately calmer having seen her. It's not every day that at your first meeting you see the other person cry, vomit, and pass out all at once. Unless you met them at a college frat party. There was the little added caveat of the victim, though. Not many frat parties included finding a body, right?

Katherine wore a black dress that had red roses patterned throughout with a short leather jacket on top. Williams was pleased to see that she was wearing Vans though, so she wasn't completely underdressed. She thought Katherine looked beautiful. Now that she was less overtired and venomous, she found that she liked the librarian glasses.

Katherine spotted Williams and smiled, extending a hand. Her face was thin, with a nose that broadened at the bottom, and full lips. Her eyes were brown but reflected the light like layers of honey. Her eye shadow was a brown a few shades lighter than her skin, accentuating her eyes and beauty. "Hi, I'm Katherine Jackson. I figure now that the circumstances are so different, we should probably get an actual introduction?"

Williams found herself smiling too. "Yeah, sure, that makes sense. I'm Abigail Williams, Abby...just Abby, please." She stammered. She tried to recover, however awkwardly. "How are you?"

"I'm doing well, thanks." Katherine motioned toward the front doors, "You want to maybe head in now? It's chilly." She rubbed her hands up and down the arms of her jacket.

They walked together into the restaurant, queuing behind a family waiting for the hostess. The restaurant was in an odd location, squished within a strip mall, spread out by necessity over two floors to accommodate guests. The bar was directly to the left of the front door. Williams found herself wondering how many more tables they could fit if the bar wasn't practically the length of the building itself. Any time she'd ever been to eat at the place, the bar was empty, say for the occasional person or two. Clearly the guests came for food. It didn't give off much of a hangout vibe. It was fancy.

After the family had been walked upstairs and seated, the hostess came back down to see to them. "Waiting on the boys, ladies?" she said, smiling. She meant well, but Williams had always found that hostesses and wait staff felt the need to assume things as a way to appear kind; it led to rather awkward conversation.

Instead of being awkward, Katherine just smiled brightly and said, "nope, just us girls tonight, thank you."

She doesn't miss a beat, Williams thought, smiling to herself. *Who the hell is that kind?*

They were seated at a small table toward the back of the first floor, which was fine with Williams. She found the second-floor stairs to be awkward. Not only was the bar downstairs, so was the washroom.

"Did we really go to high school together?" Williams asked.

"What?"

Williams was afraid of being awkward already. She nervously pinched her thigh. "Sorry, but right before you passed out you had said we went to high school together. At first, I just thought it was a confused comment made as you were about to pass out, but I have been wondering…"

"We did, actually," Katherine said, color creeping into her cheeks. The first time she'd looked anything but at peace. "I thought I dreamed that. Damn.

More than a little embarrassing, especially seeing that you don't seem to remember me."

Williams smiled, attempting to belay Katherine's embarrassment. "Don't be, I've been thinking about it, so that's reason enough for me to be embarrassed too. I don't remember though, I'm sorry. It's true though?"

"Yes, it is. You were a grade above me though, so it makes sense you don't remember me. Older kids don't pay much attention to younger kids. It's the younger kids that notice the older ones," Katherine answered.

"Yeah, I guess that's true," Williams said, allowing herself to open up a bit more. "I should have noticed you, though."

Katherine blushed slightly again, smiling. "I didn't know you liked girls then."

Williams almost sighed audibly. This wasn't really a topic she ever liked to discuss, but she had just chosen to open herself up more. "I do like women...men too. I'm bisexual if anything, honestly. I know some people have their stories about knowing for as long as they can remember, but that just wasn't it for me. I don't think I would have even explored the idea if I had noticed back then. My mom's something of an asshole in that region—"

At that exact moment the waiter approached the table. Williams turned crimson. There was something about sharing personal information and having it overheard by a waiter that made it so much worse. There was also the added pressure of being overheard cursing by a member of staff that still made you feel like you were underage and being caught by an adult, saying something naughty. And criticizing her mother no less.

Her father had been agreeable, supportive of it even, but that was his MO, right? Always on her side, as if that could tip the moral scales over for him.

"Hi, I'm Aaron. I'll be taking care of you this evening. Can I start you off with something to drink?" he asked. Williams felt like the corners of his mouth were turned up just a little too much. *This motherfucker heard me!*

Before Williams could say anything about it, or order, Katherine ordered them a bottle of wine and two waters. The waiter went off to fulfill the request, and with him went her anger toward him. "Wine, huh?"

"Sorry, should I not have? I told Senior Detective Reyes I wanted to apologize for what happened in the woods and he suggested that you might be interested in a nice dinner. Nothing says "nice" to me like wine and Italian food!" Katherine smiled warmly.

"It does, and it is nice. You don't have too though. I'm not worth,"—she gestured to the restaurant and the incoming bottle of wine—"all this, though."

Katherine looked sternly at her. "That's not true. You are, and it's my treat. It's just dinner between two possible friends if you like. I'm not looking for anything, you have nothing to worry about."

Williams took a deep breath again to steady herself. "Thanks, Katherine, really. This is really nice of you. All of it. Future reference though, never listen to a word Reyes says, he's an ass."

Katherine laughed at that, loudly and unashamed. It was cute. "What should we eat?"

The waiter poured wine for them while they perused the menu and chatted away. Williams was pretty set on something chicken, with cheese of course, while Katherine was more of a pasta person. Katherine ordered them fried risotto to start with bread and butter. They picked their entrees, and the waiter left again.

Williams contentedly sipped at her wine. She was enjoying herself, the pit in her stomach finally quieting enough to let her enjoy where she was at, as well as the company. Her phone buzzed in her pocket, but she chose to ignore it. She was happy that Reyes had insisted on the Cemetery Diner earlier, having lunch the only reason the wine wasn't overwhelming her before the food arrived.

Katherine sighed into her wine glass, seemingly content as well. She smiled across at Williams, replacing her glass on the table, and refilling both. "Where were we?"

"Well, I'm afraid to ask the most stereotypical question ever for a date, but you obviously know what I do for a living, so what about you?"

"Oh, I'm a librarian, actually. I work at our local library as well as the high school," Katherine answered.

Williams found herself laughing a little more heartily than was technically necessary. When the color rose in Katherine's cheeks she immediately stopped.

She did notice that Katherine hadn't balked at her officially calling it a date. "Sorry. It's just that that was my immediate impression of you when we first met outside the woods that day. I'm good, but I didn't realize I was that good." She smiled to convey sincerity. "That's really cool. I'm surprised you'd step foot in Cemetery High again, though. By choice no less!"

"My experience there was a pretty good one, honestly. With a high school that big it was easy to fit in and find your people. And everyone is so used to seeing different kinds of people that no one was giving me any grief for being me. That always stuck with me. As a librarian, it's all about helping people for me, even if it's just with finding books. Well, honestly, it's more than that, especially at the high school." She was in her element now. "If I can help a student with a project, a paper, a class, that feels good for me, I like to do it. Now if I can help a random kid find their love for reading within those walls, now that's what's especially powerful for me. It makes it worth it."

Williams smiled warmly at Katherine; she liked that explanation. "We have that in common then. I know it's idealistic of me—particularly in Cemetery—but I always felt like becoming a cop meant helping the people here. Even if I didn't love high school as much as you did. It's not just about justice and putting away the bad guys for me, it was always about working hard to protect the good ones, those in trouble. I don't know…I just like the idea of being a force for good. If that makes sense…"

"It definitely makes sense," Katherine said, smiling around her wine glass. Two full-blown idealists then. "Here comes some of our food now."

Their waiter carried a tray of food in one hand and a metal foldout holder in the other. He set the tray on the stand and passed the food to each of them. They sat in a contented silence for a time, nothing but the sounds of silverware—eating together and enjoying the meal. Williams' phone buzzed another two times in her pocket, and she felt a slight unease creeping in. She slugged wine to dull her anxious stomach. The chicken parmesan was far too good to be distracted. Katherine poured the remains of the wine bottle into Williams' glass.

Katherine took another bite of food, smiling while she chewed, enjoying herself. "So, how is work going? I know that the search and everything must have been a lot. Have you made good headway at least?"

Williams shrugged. She had been hoping to avoid talking about work and the case in general, the pit in her stomach yawning to life like a savage beast. She supposed she should have seen the topic coming though, as involved as Katherine was. It didn't help her feelings about it in the least though. The sobering effect of a question that throws a person off, as it so often does, made her realize how quickly she had been approaching drunkenness. It wasn't usual for her, but the wine was good, the food better, and the company great. Her fear of messing it up had already started to build, so she had leaned into the wine in hopes of loosening up. Perhaps too much. "It's not going well."

"I'm sorry to have brought it up then."

"No, it's totally fine. We've been searching, overturning stones, and trying to make connections, and you know what, we aren't finding a thing. We met with the parents of the deceased, the kid's best friend, and we've still not gotten a lead. The entire case is one big shit-show. Reyes and I can't seem to agree on a single thing, Chief Carter is applying pressure as he always does, and we're two bodies in without a thing to show for it," Williams rambled. Was she slurring?

"Wait, they found a second body?"

Williams finished her wine to keep her mouth shut, no longer connecting that the wine was the issue. She shook her head, trying to will herself sober. She couldn't tell if the nauseous feeling in her stomach was from drinking too much too fast, or her anxiety finally winning out. That was not information that should be making its way into the public. She was conscious of the waiter's presence more than ever. She looked over her shoulder for him, and of course, he was right around the corner.

Williams leaned across the table and stared desperately at Katherine. "Shoot, I should not have said that. Please keep it between us."

Katherine laughed, but then realized how serious Williams was and nodded, "Of course."

Williams' shoulders slumped in relief. "Thank you. With the stress of work, my nerves, and the fact that I don't do this often, the wine is kind of running right through me. I'm so sorry."

"It's totally okay, everything's fine," Katherine smiled. "Just means we have to do this more often, that's all."

They made eye contact, and Williams let it linger longer than intended. She realized she would like that.

Katherine motioned for the waiter and asked for the check. Williams still felt awkward and offered to pay, which Katherine smoothly declined. After paying she stood up from the table and put her jacket back on. "Come on, Abby, I'm driving you home."

"Like hell you are," Williams practically shouted. Lowering her voice and looking around her, she said, "I'll be fine. Really, I'm good."

"Badge or not, you're you are seriously not driving right now!"

Williams relented and allowed herself to be pulled to Katherine's car. She was embarrassed and more than a little ashamed, feeling the heat of it all in her cheeks. It wasn't just the alcohol. She had to admit to herself she didn't mind the feeling of leaning into Katherine...she certainly smelled nice.

III

When Katherine pulled into the driveway, she parked and got out to help Williams to the door. She had no intentions of anything going further than that, certainly not with the state that the night had deteriorated into. However, when they reached the door Williams kissed her. It was nice and warm, and she allowed it to happen for a bit longer than what technically qualified as "just a kiss." Breaking the contact, Katherine said, "that was nice, but maybe we should do this another time?"

Williams sighed, leaning her head back against her door. She looked to her left and saw Mr. Cody standing in his yard smiling. He had his little dog on a lease next to him. *Plausible deniability*, Williams thought. He waved and called out, "You two ladies have a nice evening?"

"That's my neighbor, he's always freaking looking at me." Williams reddened and banged her head against the door. "I'm sorry, but you should probably go. I had a really nice time though."

"We had such a super nice night, thanks for asking," Katherine called out to Mr. Cody, her voice high and artificial. Smiling, she pecked Williams on the lips again and headed toward her car. "Goodnight, Abby."

All in all, what should have been a perfect night left her feeling a bit dejected. She should have been smiling, but all she could think was, *I need another drink.*

Ch 7

Home Alone

I

Williams poured herself what she considered to be a healthy portion of white wine. Others might have called it indulgent, excessive even, but she was far past caring. She had swapped out the jeans and blouse for grey sweats and a ratty old tee shirt that she'd had since high school, the Cemetery High across her chest barely visible anymore. She added a purple hoodie over the top.

She *had* looked at her phone, but she gave it little of her attention. When she saw that it was Reyes texting, she figured it was him trying to mess with her while she was on a date. It was the exact kind of thing he would do—set her up, convince her to go, and then text to annoy her the entire time. That or he had finally decided to apologize. Perhaps the less likely option, but she wasn't ready for it either way.

She glanced at the time on her phone screen, but never opened the texts. It was nine o'clock now. She tossed her phone on the bed and took her wine downstairs with her, pausing long enough for a refill, and then heading outside for the porch swing. It was late enough that she didn't think she had to worry about Mr. Cody.

On the porch swing, Williams sipped away at her wine, spilling a little here and there, but thinking nothing of it. Well and truly drunk now, she swung the swing back and forth, allowing her feet to drag. The swing had been her father's idea, a present from him when he randomly decided he was a handy man. She remembered it being a real pain in the ass for her father to do. Primarily because he had no idea what he was doing. From what she could remember from life with him, he was always more of a "pay for what you want" than "work hard and do it yourself" kind of guy. *If only he could see me now*, she thought.

After finishing the glass of wine—or rather, what she had managed to get into her mouth, leaning sideways as she was—she lightly dosed on the porch swing, slightly swaying before coming to a halt.

She woke to a slight chill down her spine. She shivered, sitting up. For some reason, she felt spooked, something giving her the creeps. However, it was October, so a chill while drunkenly dosing off was a pretty normal thing.

She looked around her porch, which had an overhang, giving it the appearance of being enclosed. Everything looked normal. She breathed. Why did the air feel so...*threatening*?

Williams stood and looked across the lawn. The street, a simple two lane, was flanked on the opposite side by Cemetery's lovely trees. She usually loved only having to see neighbors on one side of the street, but tonight it felt eerie instead. As if someone was lurking. It was a dense area, but not without moonlight flickering through. For some reason, it made Williams feel even worse. The swaying of the trees in the wind and the flashing in and out of the moonlight had her on edge. She scanned the trees, not sure what she was looking for. She felt fear building in her stomach. That or she was about to vomit.

Williams edged down the bottom of the porch steps, squinting into the trees. She found herself wishing she had taken her phone outside for the flashlight at the very least, weak as it was.

She stopped and scanned to the right. There, right in front of her very eyes, was a silhouette. She could just make out the slight outline of a person standing behind one of the oak trees. Her blood turned as cold as ice as she stopped to wonder who would stand in the woods in the middle of the night staring at people.

The silhouette stepped forward and Williams screamed, falling flat on her ass.

She lay there, the blood pounding in her ears. She sat up too quickly, feeling faint, and planted her elbow in the grass. She scanned left and right and found nothing...no one. Just the trees and the wind, swaying and creating spooky little movements in the night. She sighed, slapping her hand to her forehead. Laughing she rolled over and got to her feet, albeit rather shakily.

Heading back up the stairs, Williams chided herself repeatedly. That stupid stunt probably woke up the neighbors. Williams would be known as Detective Kook, nobody taking her seriously. What if she had woken up Mr. Cody?

"You're piss drunk, you idiot." She continued the self-deprecation. "You couldn't see well enough to unlock a freaking door, let alone spot a ghoul in the dead of night. Maybe if you're lucky that's your perp watching you. The only way your stupid ass is going to catch them is if they catch you instead!" Williams turned back toward the street, shouting so anyone hiding could hear her, "Come right on in if you want, make yourself at home, you murderous shit!"

II

Inside, Williams threw the bolt into the lock. It stuck a bit, but then again it always had. The bottom floor of the house was an open concept. When she had first bought the house, she and her father had decided that to maximize space, the walls had to go. She still found herself designing the furniture in a way that left a clear demarcation. From the front door, the kitchen was off to the right. The cabinets fit snuggly into the corners and there was a beautiful marble counter island. To the left was the living room, with her favorite piece of furniture she had ever bought, a feather cushioned sectional. Part of the sectional's back stuck out from the wall, breaking the room up. Her TV was one of the curved kinds and she had it mounted in the room's corner above a propane glass fireplace. Identical tile kept the entire floor cohesive, giving it a well finished feeling. At the back of the floor, in the dead center, was the entrance to the second-floor stairs, and off to the left, the basement door.

She was experiencing a second wind. She poured another helping of wine, sloshing merrily, microwaved popcorn, and threw pizza bites in the toaster oven. She had never been one for calorie counting. There was something cathartic about getting drunk and needing to eat every little thing in sight. It wasn't something she experienced often anymore.

When the popcorn and pizza bites were ready, she stacked the plate on top of the popcorn bowl and moseyed her way to the couch. She sat down with a satisfying plop, feeling the feather cushions welcome her home.

She spent some time stuffing her face, not ungracefully she thought, before grabbing the remote and turning the TV on. She found the first horror movie she could find, *SCREAM*. Slumping further into the corner, she shoveled popcorn. She loved this movie, but if she was honest with herself, her vision was a little fuzzy. *How much have I drunk?*

The movie was already in the climax, Neve Campbell's Sidney already at the party. That much she could tell. She had always been a little uncomfortable with the need for high schooler sex, regardless if they were supposed to be seniors. Regardless if they were played by actual adults. It made fantasizing easier for the disgusting type of people she dealt with in her daily work life.

A half an hour later all her snacks were gone, her glass was dry, and the movie was over. She contemplated getting more, but the longer she stayed awake the more she kept circling back to work. Back to the silhouette in the woods. As much as she felt confident in the fact that she was a drunken idiot, it had seemed so incredibly real, hadn't it? How about incredibly convenient too. James' comments behind the Dunkin' earlier crept their way back into her disorganized mind.

"Well, he said some weird shit about thinking that someone was watching him, said he maybe saw someone staring into his window a few times."

Williams was not superstitious, not even a little bit. However, she hadn't been able to stop herself from being rattled since being called to the scene of the crime. So many unanswered questions, so many atypical connections. She stood and headed for the stairs, certain that staying awake any longer was a bad idea.

"Said he maybe saw someone staring into his window," trailed her all the way up the stairs.

III

Williams slept fitfully at first, having dropped corpse-like on top of the comforter. She had still felt that overall strangeness she had been experiencing so much lately, but she was too drunk to stop the ever-present ticking of the night.

Hours later, she ripped the covers off the bed, sending her phone flying off the duvet, where it smashed against the wall. She covered herself without giving it a second thought and fell back to sleep. With the warmth and comfort of the comforter on her side, she slept like the dead.

Therefore, she didn't hear the slight creak that her front door hinges always made. The way the handle jostled slightly as someone held it tightly, shouldering it closed and letting go. The muffled movements below that could only be made by someone, by something, as they rifled through the contents of the kitchen: cabinets and drawers, open mail on the kitchen island, taking in the spare photos and fridge magnets. She couldn't hear the squeak of the eighth step, where there's a mini-landing in her turn-staircase. Couldn't hear someone ever-so-slowly creep up the stairs. Down the hall, they quietly trailed their fingers along the white walls, nails scaping slightly, the light sound following them toward the bedroom.

The door was ajar, and all they needed to do was slip inside. They hesitated, ever so slightly; this was their favorite part after all. The hunt. They took their time, relishing it. How often did they get this bliss?

Inside the bedroom, Detective Williams lay prone in bed, covered by the comforter. The figure edged forward, silently, breathing it all in. They could literally smell her, the type of smell that can only truly be found while a person sleeps soundly. They leaned forward, tasting it. Soap, shampoo, perfume, even sweat and drool. The scent of sleep. The slight burn in the nostrils from the heavy scent of alcohol. Perhaps even the remnants of the garlic seasoning from dinner, now permeating her skin. They had a keen nose for scents after all.

The figure waited, and when the detective didn't wake, they took in the room in the faint moonlight. Nightstands with nothing on them but lamps. A closet to the side, door closed. There really wasn't much. But there: a hamper in the corner. Rifling through, the figure took their time imagining her outfits from days past. Button ups and slacks in various shades, ever the diligent worker through and through. And of course there were more: bras, panties—the figure inhaled deeply, this sickly intimate and one-sided intrusion into what lay beneath when the detective worked. And of course, those closest to the top, the outfit from the date. Hours earlier, as the figure watched her house from outside, their bated breath pulsing through the leaves that camouflaged them, there was a moment where they feared that the night would be ruined by the other woman joining the detective inside. But it was meant to be.

Back to the bed, a pale, long-fingered hand reached out of a loose sleeve, caressing Williams' cheek. Pushing her hair away from her face, almost like a lover. They leaned forward, breathing in deeply. The breath was unusually rattled. As if a handful of BBs were stuck in their lungs, and each breath brought them smacking up.

They kept their hand there, applying the slightest pressure, leisurely breathing in the moment. As much as they relished occasions like these, Detective Williams wasn't a usual target, having not started out as anything close to such. As they leant in, ever closer, they didn't account for one thing: as a child, Williams had been terrified of spiders and other creepy crawlies getting on her in the dead of night, her body practically training itself out of sleep. It hadn't diminished in strength after all these years.

Abby Williams woke up screaming.

IV

Williams screamed on and on. She flailed against her attacker, pushing back. What she hoped would be a punch ended up being more of a closed fist shove. They immediately retreated and she reached for her phone. Her phone, which had been sent sailing into the wall earlier in the night, was somewhere underneath the nightstand. Instead, she reached for her standard issue Glock 17, just inside the top draw. A slight creak came from across the room, where shadows clung black against the bedroom door. The darkness moved like liquid; stilling, then shuffling again. She fired four rounds toward her bedroom door in fast succession. She put one hand to her ear, the sound inside her small bedroom almost deafening, but refused to give up her grip on the pistol with the other.

The darkness continued its undulation, making it impossible to tell if she hit anything. Or if they were still there.

Reaching for the lamp on her nightstand, she flicked it on. Nothing. There was no one there.

But I felt them.

She was certain it hadn't been a dream. She had felt breath on her; someone's touch, an overwhelming presence. You don't dream in that kind of realness—you just don't. She knew the level of intoxication when she fell asleep was well within the realm of not dreaming at all...she was *certain*.

Sliding off the edge of the bed, she stood and raised her pistol. The door was still slightly ajar. She took a step, her heart in her throat, the blood pounding a sickening beat in her ears. This was the most shaken she had been in her entire career.

Stepping up behind the bedroom door she shouted, "Freeze! You better not move, or I will shoot you. What are you doing in my house?"

Kicking the door wide, she turned, and again...nothing. There was no one there. *But I felt them.*

Edging her way down the hall, she took fast, painful breaths. As she neared the top of the staircase she flipped the light switch on her right, then regripped her pistol. The light was a bit much all at once, but she refused to blink, afraid the assailant was still in the house.

She turned at the top of the stairs and lowered the sight of the pistol. Still nothing.

Slowly working down the stairs, she took deliberate care with each step. She skipped over the eighth step, knowing that it would make a squeak, giving her away. At the turn in the stairs, she tried for a steadying breath, knowing her breathing was ragged at this point. The turn awarded her nothing, no assailant, no bleeding intruder—no jump-scaring home invader with an axe either. *I felt them.*

Before descending the final step, she kicked her sock-covered foot out to hit the light switch opposite her. A quick scan of the bottom floor of the house showed her that there was no one inside. The kitchen had various cabinets and drawers opened, but nothing else looked amiss.

The front door stood wide open.

Approaching it, she looked left and right out into the street. She was certain she saw nothing this time. She slammed the door shut, locking both the bolt and the chain.

Williams climbed back up the stairs to find her cellphone. She dialed for Reyes before searching the entire house top to bottom again.

V

Williams sat on the edge of her bed, hands shaking at her sides; her pistol beside her, still within reach. She couldn't remember ever having felt worse in her entire life. The chiaroscuro of oscillating police red and blues flashed across her face as her coworkers rushed to the rescue.

A little late, right, and for what?

Reyes reached her bedroom, his old snubnosed .38 in his outstretched left hand, his face flushed in worry. He registered her sitting on the edge of the bed, unharmed, and then he bent over at the waist, panting. He took heaving breaths in and out, like a track star if they had taken to smoking several packs of cigarettes a day.

"Thank God you're alright," he panted, looking her over. Her hair was also a mess, her eyes twitchy and hands shaking. She looked pale and sickly. If he hadn't been told what had happened on the phone, he might have assumed she had seen a ghost. She looked anything but alright. "You okay, kid?"

Williams didn't answer—couldn't. She shook her head slightly, the only indication that she wasn't he was going to get. Truth be told, she was so unbelievably happy to see him. He was the first person she had thought of for help when she'd woken up. She no longer cared that they had been at odds. Unbidden, tears tracked their way down her face. She sniffled, fighting them back, always doing her damnedest to fortify herself, but the dam had too many cracks.

Reyes knelt before her and pulled her into an embrace. He smelled of sweat, beer, coffee, and cigarettes. It was his usual smell. It was a comfort, a constant to latch on to. She let herself cry for a minute more and he held her all the tighter.

"I thought I was going to die, Reyes. Holy shit. I mean—I'm unharmed, but I just thought...I thought that was it."

"You didn't. You're okay, Abby. I've got you. You can let it out if you need to, but we'll have company in a minute," Reyes said.

Wiping her eyes, Williams shook herself hard. The last thing she wanted was for anyone to see her and think her hysterical; meek. Weak even. This kind of thing could shake anyone, but she wouldn't make it a habit. There was nothing standing between her and succumbing to absolute darkness, save for herself.

At that moment Chief Carter walked into her bedroom. His hair was a mess, he was sweaty, and he wore a bulletproof vest. He looked rather annoyed as opposed to glad at the fact she was okay. Just what she needed. Was the tirade incoming too?

Good god, even the Chief? What did you do, Reyes?

Carter took in the room, then looked to Reyes and Williams. "Well detectives, where is this intruder?" Again, with the air of annoyance about him. Just like the last time they had all been together, that layer of stock-still calm was diminishing.

"Look at the door behind you, Chief, I-I shot at them. They wouldn't exactly wait around, would they?" Williams said, wanting to sound annoyed, but coming across as defeated.

"We have the entire team here now," Carter said, still looking around as if the scene would change before his eyes. "They're powdering for fingerprints and looking for forced entry. The front door wasn't damaged, so that couldn't have been it. Do you have a back door or basement windows? We have officers in the woods and some speaking to neighbors, asking if they saw anything. If there's someone out there, we're going to find them."

"The front door was open when I ran down the stairs," Williams said, cheeks burning. "But I can't be sure if that's how the intruder entered. The basement windows are far too small for entry, and the door down there is literally chained up. It was secured when I checked. I'm really not sure, Chief. It's confusing...I know I locked the door before I went to sleep,"

"And you're positive you saw someone? Literally with your own eyes, lights on?"

"Well, no, not exactly. But I woke up screaming; I could feel them touching me. Before I switched the light on it looked like someone wearing black was moving around the bedroom door," Williams said, head spinning.

"I have two dead bodies, both freakishly bloodless no less. We've just received a call for another missing kid, too. Concerned parents and citizens calling me nonstop, coming to the precinct, demanding answers. They stop me in the grocery store; they don't let me finish my morning coffee order without bothering me, without interrupting and interrogating me. You mean to tell me you called us here because you're seeing ghosts?" Carter gritted out, practically spitting.

This was the closest to cursing Williams had ever seen him.

Taken aback, and too dangerously close to losing it again, Williams became submissive. "I didn't know what the hell was going on. What was I supposed to do, go back to sleep?"

"We protect our own, Chief," Reyes yelled, his face purple. He edged his way in between the chief of police and his partner, protecting her.

"Alright, alright. Don't give me that crap. This wasn't an invitation to gang up. My patience with the two of you is razor thin at the moment, I tell you. We're days in, and the two of you have absolutely nothing. Nothing!" Carter exploded. "What am I to do when my only two detectives haven't been able to find a single thing? Kids are dying and you're what, out partying? It smells like a bar in here!"

It was clear that his anger and frustration was coming out on them, rather than being caused by them. Everyone at some point is force-fed the crap in their work life. That kind of thing rolls downhill. Someone above Carter was blowing him up. This morning it was his turn. The fact that it was coming out on the cusp of Williams being touched in her sleep, mere minutes after there had been an intruder in her house, and the fact that he was yelling at them like children in her own bedroom, was far too much for her to take.

For the briefest moment, she wished her anger could spark through her eyes and burn him like lasers.

How dare he, she thought, *what an asshole*!

Reyes stayed right in between them. He was fuming, and as part of the alcohol sweat was pouring off him and not just Williams, he was probably equally insulted. "And what if she hadn't been alright, Chief? What then? I bet you'd be singing a different tune. She's one of us!"

Carter stayed still a second longer. Then he turned on his heels and headed out the bedroom door. Stopping in between the threshold, he knocked on the door right below the group of bullet holes. "If we had found anything, Detective Williams, literally anything..." He shook his head and left.

Reyes followed him out like a guard dog. Williams waited until she heard him descending the stairs, each clunk on his way down bringing Williams an ounce more of peace. But instead of releasing the pressure, she stewed, waiting for Reyes to return before boiling over.

"What was all that about?" Williams asked the second he turned into the doorframe.

"This case is not looking good, but that was nuts," Reyes placated. "He'll shake it off and be fine later at the precinct."

"What the hell was all that about not finding anything anyway?" Williams spat. "There was someone inside my house!"

"Well...about that, Abby," Reyes began. He looked uncomfortable, and he was reaching for his cigarettes. "We haven't found a thing—no fingerprints, forced entry, or footprints—no torn clothes from a snag during a hasty retreat. Ain't no blood if you shot someone. But of course, I'm sure we will, kid. Only a matter of time."

"God, not you too, Reyes?" Williams whined. "I said I shot *at* someone; I did not say I shot them. You know there's a difference, right?" She put her head in her hands and shook it back and forth. "This whole thing is off, Reyes, I'm telling you. You must feel it too. There's something wrong here."

Reyes shook his head, face creased with sorrow. "I know you feel that way, kid. I hear you, but I think this one's just got you shaken is all. It's in you, it's got your blood all worked up. The alcohol didn't do you any favors either, I'm sure." He took a step forward and placed his hand on her shoulder in a move that was meant to be reassuring.

Instead, Williams pulled away and stared at him, looking patronized.

"You can't possibly expect me to believe that I'm the only one feeling it," she said. "And you can't just play off the Chief like any of that was normal! He's eerily calm, like nothing out the ordinary is happening. Then he's randomly explosive like he can't contain it anymore. That's not strange to you?"

Reyes looked grim. "We're looking at multiple bodies at this point. So far, all kids under your age. No one would blame you for being a bit shaken up is all I'm saying. But this talk of things being off…it's turning some heads. This is Cemetery for crying out loud. Just don't cry wolf, Abby. *Facts*. Remember what I said, we deal in facts. And as of right now, the facts point to some sick bastard, not a ghoul in the night. And not the goddamn chief of police…"

"There was someone in my fucking bedroom with me, Reyes!"

Ch 8

Ambiguous

I

Williams had kicked Reyes, as well as the other officers, out shortly after. She didn't have the time to fight with everyone over whether or not she was losing it. She knew what she saw; that was good enough for her. She knew it had happened. However, her anxiety had become a tight knot. She was having trouble keeping anything down, water included. That could have been the raging hangover, though.

Her other issue was the stack of paperwork that would accompany her night of frivolous inebriation. Intruder or no—which was a whole different set of paperwork anyway—she had to account for discharging a firearm. Just what she needed.

The impenetrable stack of work that needed doing for her actual case had lengthened tenfold as well. Williams reached for a bottle of Advil and noticed her hands were still shaking. Snapping the cabinet shut, she shoved a handful of pills into her mouth and took a small sip of water. She'd fight like hell to keep that down at least, otherwise an hour from now, she'd still be wishing for a dark corner in a quiet room.

After everyone had left, she locked herself in the bathroom and moved the semi-filled hamper in front of the door. With her Glock 17 well within reach, she took all of her clothes off. She looked down at the Cemetery High shirt, so faint it was hard to make out what it said. How incredibly different she had felt last night when putting it on. She looked at herself in the mirror, feeling empty. More than that, she looked gaunt; hollow.

Maybe she really was shaken. She took the coldest, and then hottest, shower she could stand, washing away what felt like weeks' worth of grime. She wanted more than anything to just stay there under the running showerhead; however, the longer she did, with eyes closed, the more her nightmares forced their way into the light.

Why did her brain try so hard to jumble up her trauma? Like someone drawing a bag over her head, making her a prisoner to her own memories. Yet no matter how hard or how jumbled they became, they still plagued her. Holding her down. Or holding her back.

It wasn't just being exposed to a near-fatal incident; it was the introduction to evil. To horror. Her brain's trauma response did far more than just messing with the stake-out her father put her into to catch a killer; huge patches of memories featuring her father were a blur. While not the evil himself, he was at fault, he was the exposer, and she never fully separated him from it.

Turning to the side, the hot water running down her face flashed, and for a second she was there again. The water, now the hot sticky blood, splashed across her little face. Williams slammed the water off and reached for a towel.

She returned to the edge of her bed, still wrapped in the towel. Entire weeks of life could be lost while sitting on your bed in nothing but a towel. It was its own kind of black hole. Williams reached for her phone. Twelve missed messages. She unlocked it, the first three from her mother, asking about doing dinner soon. She ignored these. The next conversation was the texts she had missed from Reyes last night. She read them now:

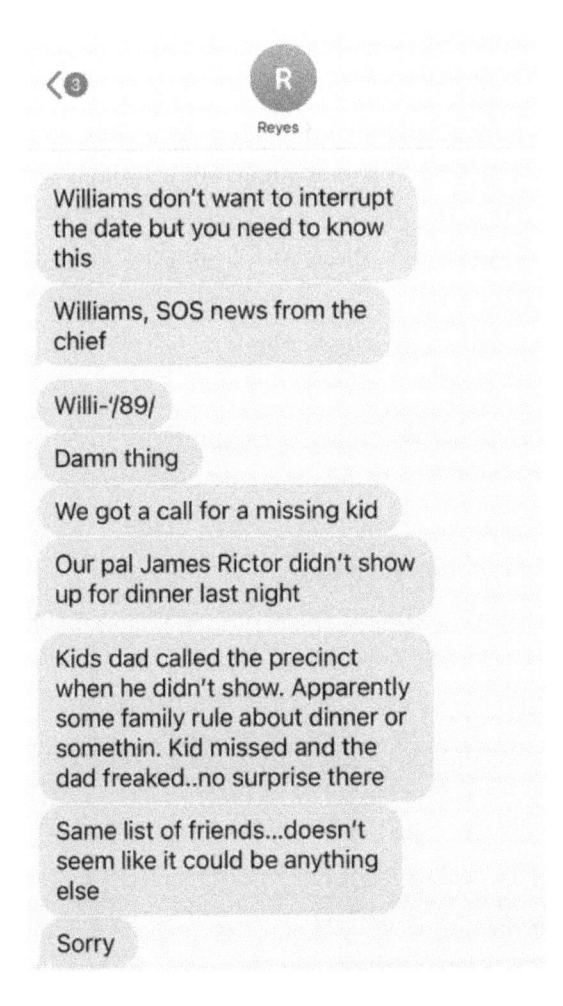

> Reyes
>
> Williams don't want to interrupt the date but you need to know this
>
> Williams, SOS news from the chief
>
> Willi-/89/
>
> Damn thing
>
> We got a call for a missing kid
>
> Our pal James Rictor didn't show up for dinner last night
>
> Kids dad called the precinct when he didn't show. Apparently some family rule about dinner or somethin. Kid missed and the dad freaked..no surprise there
>
> Same list of friends...doesn't seem like it could be anything else
>
> Sorry

Williams sat and stared at the phone. They had just questioned James Rictor yesterday afternoon. She had given him her card, told him to reach out for help if he ever needed it. Something about his pimply face made Williams think he was years younger than he actually was. She wondered what had transpired between handing him her card and these texts. Wondered what she could have done. Where he was.

She couldn't help but feel like this was yet another failure.

II

Back at the precinct, she figured she would be beating Reyes by a handful of hours. Instead, she walked into the office, only one coffee in hand, to see Reyes behind his desk. He looked more put together than he had in months, but a cigarette was still affixed to his lips.

"Damn, a little fight and you no longer bring me a coffee?" Reyes said, attempting to break the ice.

"Shit, I thought you wouldn't be here for at least a couple of hours," Williams replied.

He looked uncomfortable, color coming to his cheeks, "Thought I wouldn't be, or hoped?"

"We don't have to do this now, Reyes. I'm fine. It's whatever," Williams replied, sounding anything but fine.

Senior Detective Reyes looked like a reprimanded child, but he didn't push the subject. Instead, he changed it. "So...see anything different?"

"Yes, you look like a regular member of society again. Shaved, parted your hair, probably showered...at least this week?" Williams said, allowing a bit of their typical banter to return, but without its usual warmth.

"Yes, to all three, thank you very much, but I shower every damn day," Reyes said, the color leaving his cheeks. A smirk replaced it.

"And thank god for that," Williams said. She was glad the fighting wasn't continuing, but she knew it wasn't over. She wasn't ready to let it go, either. She had needed him, confided in him, and he had brushed it off. Not returning his crooked smile, she continued. "Unfortunately, we've got to get down to business. What the hell happened to James?"

"I'm not too sure anymore, kid," Reyes replied. "Could he have just ran away? His home life wasn't anything to brag about."

"With him being on that list of friends, are you really hedging any bets on this being unrelated?"

"Betting, no. Hoping? For his sake." Reyes took another drag and pondered. "The mangled flesh? A different body part every time, too, which could fit the animal theory. Or are they trying to tell us something?"

"If they are, they could have just called. I have no idea what we're looking at here. The teeth marks that could just as easily be needle marks. I don't get it; it's not adding up."

Williams sat behind her desk and powered up her computer. She was determined to finish at least one of the reports from last night. She slurped her coffee while she waited, anxiously tapping away on her thigh. This whole case, from start to finish, was something she'd never expected. Who drained bodies of blood in such a way that it was ruled *bloodless*? Where was the why of it? Was some madman simply bottling up human blood for safe keeping—or was it for something more sinister?

A more ridiculous possibility started to brew in her head. She wanted to turn it away, to give it no credence, to not even let it come to the surface. She was losing the fight.

What if the perp was…drinking it? An irrational moment took hold as Williams imagined what, or *who*, could turn a body into a malnourished husk.

Detective Williams' computer finished powering up. She entered her credentials, the knot in her stomach growing as she shook off the crazy thought. Her coffee now had a sour taste to it.

She rushed her way through a report about the home invasion. Her mind raced the entire time, never finding its way to settling on the actual task in front of her. She grew more unsettled the longer Reyes puffed away at his cigarettes, seemingly content. Now that she was angry at him, his ever-present steadfastness peeved her, rather than giving her balance.

For a moment she felt annoyed that it annoyed her, but she didn't have the time to unpack it. She needed action.

She grabbed her keys and fled the office.

III

Williams pulled her car into the Rictors' driveway and keyed it off. Although she had cleaned herself up before coming to work, she still couldn't be certain she didn't look like a madwoman. The unexpected loss of James had derailed her schedule, the planned interviews all getting postponed.

She approached the door of a small white, ranch-style house with a porch that had lived long past its youth. This was known as a sketchier part of Cemetery, which may or may not be true, but it was definitely a cheaper area. Dilapidation and neglect were evident with many of the Rictor's neighbors. Lawns, ancient pools, and roofs were all a wreck, long forgotten. Compared to the poor standard around them, it appeared the Rictors did put forth a modicum of care.

Williams precariously climbed the porch and carefully knocked on the front door. It was freshly painted, as if they were in the process of getting their act together and sprucing the place up. She could only imagine this latest setback to the family would heavily dampen that cheer.

The door cracked to a small woman with blonde hair staring out. She, much like Robbie Elton's mother, was puffy and red eyed, the kind of crying that can only accompany a mother's worry. "Hello, can I help you?" she asked, with what could have possibly been the warmest voice Williams had ever been met with while out investigating.

"Hi, I'm Detective Williams from the Cemetery Police Department, I was wondering if I could come inside and ask you a few questions? It'll only take a moment," she said, trying to match the woman's warmth.

"We already talked to an officer this morning..." the woman said, looking suddenly crestfallen. "Let me check, my husband prefers I ask him these things first—let him make the decision, you know."

She shut the door and Williams heard muffled talking. The man inside was talking in much more than a whisper.

"My husband prefers I ask him these things first, let him make the decision"? Yep, definitely an abuser. Williams breathed in to calm herself, hoping it would lessen the chances of her smacking the man inside. She still really wanted to; she just figured the breathing would help her appear like she didn't.

A part of her had latched on to James when they were questioning him, that's why she had given him her card. Call it blind optimism, more of her so-called naivety, or maybe she saw some of herself in his youthfulness, but she had wanted to keep him safe. From his dad—from someone that made decisions like *her* father. She hated the abuse of power. It wasn't the entire reason, but it was the driving force that led her to police work in the first place.

The door swung wide open, and a man stood before her. He was short, unexpectedly so. He was clearly muscular, wearing only a tank top and basketball shorts. Like even in October, he wanted to be seen. He was also clearly balding but refusing to let it go. He wore an angry expression, and Williams would bet a year's salary this guy was compensating for several things. Most abusers were.

At his side was a truly massive dog. Williams couldn't pin down a breed, but several descriptors came to mind when looking at it, the least of which was *beast*. It was literally slavering, saliva pouring down ripples of jowls. It snarled, lunging forward. It would have attacked if it wasn't being held on a very short chain. Williams, not knowing very much about dogs, reckoned this was the kind of thing that had to be made, not born.

She pressed on anyway. "Uh, Mr. Rictor? I'm Detective Williams. I was hoping to ask you a few questions pertaining to the case."

"Case? You mean questions pertaining to my *missing* son?" Mr. Rictor asked, his voice squeakier than she had imagined it would be. He cleared his throat and attempted a growl. "What more do you people want?"

One exchange in, and Williams was certain she would have to smack him.

"To find him, sir? To ask questions pertaining to the case to hopefully catch the bastard that's done this? To bring James home safe? To bring you the satisfaction that there will be an end to whomever did this to your son?" Williams pushed, leaning into it a little more than was strictly necessary. "Should I go on?"

"What good will any of that do if he's already dead?" Mr. Rictor shot back, getting loud. His wife, standing behind him, began to cry.

"Perhaps we could take this inside, sir? It is rather chilly out here, and your neighbors are noticing?" Williams pressed again, hoping his ice-cold attitude wouldn't outlast his desire to keep his neighbors from witnessing.

He shrugged, walking off and heading for a dog kennel that looked more like an ad for Made-Well-Fence down the street than any actual dog crate Williams had ever seen. As he turned, the dog snapped at Mrs. Rictor, nearly catching her hand. Mr. Rictor did nothing in the way of reprimanding the dog, just continued dragging it. He used a legitimate padlock on the dog's door, then he headed for his kitchen. Mrs. Rictor held the door open for Williams, attempting to smile, but it was clear she was a ball of nerves.

The dog continued to snarl as Williams entered.

Okay, so not a family animal?

The inside of the house was a mess, like an episode of *Hoarders*; the Rictors had too many things and not enough space. Not to mention an apparent lack of will to part with any of it. The living room had several mismatched sofas in it. A small TV was stuck in the corner, stacked on a collection of cardboard boxes and newspapers.

Following Mr. Rictor into the kitchen, she saw more of the same. The walls were tiled in what could only be referred to as an off-yellow. The countertop was pitted and stained. The room was filled with appliances that might not have even worked in a modern outlet. The whole thing looked like it had needed to be updated since the 1960s.

Mr. Rictor sat at a rickety dining table off to the left of the room, covered in more newspaper and other household flotsam. Williams saw that he had taken the time to grab himself a beer. He didn't offer her a seat, or a drink. "Ask away. Let's get this over with, I've got work."

"Drinking beer before operating a motor vehicle?" Williams queried.

"Are you here to give me the third degree for having a refreshing pre-work drink, or are you here to ask questions about my *missing* son?" he retorted, taking an elongated pull of his beer.

Every time he said "missing son" he emphasized the word missing as if it meant "dead." Each time he did, Williams saw a little more of the light in Mrs. Rictor's eyes diminish. Tears streamed down her face, and she rung her hands in a constant loop.

"James is a good boy. He...he's a little lost, but he has the potential to be anything he wants. If he had applied himself at school, or even a trade, he could have gone places," Mrs. Rictor offered, sniffling all the while. "He was just a little timid, and he let the wrong people lead him astray. He sees the best in everyone, even when they ask the worst of him."

"James is a little shit," Mr. Rictor yelled. "Won't take any advice from his old man, never wanting to do as I say. He works for some shit company folding jeans for crying out loud, what kind of *man* is that? He's not turning any heads either with a pimply face like that. He needs to assert himself and be a man, but he won't."

His dog snarled and barked at its owner's raised voice, rattling against its crate. With each shake, Williams felt her blood pressure rise.

Mrs. Rictor lost all composure, sobbing openly. She staggered toward the kitchen counter, barely catching herself. She cried for her missing son, for what he could still be if Williams could find him. "Don't you dare talk about *my* James like that!" she shrieked.

Suddenly, Mr. Rictor stood and stalked toward his wife. He looked angry, but as if this was their normal—nothing new. So, no, Williams had not been reading the situation wrong. Mr. Rictor raised his right hand in what would have landed as a backhanded slab to his wife's face.

This wasn't exactly what she had meant by needing action, but there was nothing she could do about it now. She had seen enough. Knew enough men like this in her line of work. And this was something she could finally stop, could handle on her own.

Williams was a coiled snake, and she allowed herself to strike. In a fluid motion she stepped forward and grabbed Mr. Rictor's left arm, twisting it behind his back, and pulling it up toward his shoulder blades at the wrist. She twisted him around and smashed him face first into one of the piles of newspapers on the table. She was far past being gentle with the man. She pulled on his wrist ever harder.

"Listen to me you disgusting piece of shit," Williams snarled between gritted teeth. "We are dealing with two dead kids in as many days. Now your son is missing, too. All kids who could have had a future, one who was under the age of twenty still. Cemetery is bad enough without pieces of shit like yourself inhabiting it. Now please, I'm genuinely begging you, give me even the tiniest reason and I'll break your arm."

She wasn't actually sure if she could break it. Nor was she able to tell where this lake of strength was coming from, but her anger was feeding it, and for the first time in who knows how long she felt in control.

Mr. Rictor's entire personality shifted, darkened. He winced and whined into the newspapers. "Get your hands off of me, you bitch!" At this, part of Williams feared the padlock wouldn't be enough. The dog bucked in the other room, the shake of the crate a constant.

"That's Detective to you. Now tell me, is there anyone that could have wanted to harm your son? His friends?" Williams gave his arm a final tug upward before releasing him. Her eyes were on the mother, not the abuser.

"My James," Mrs. Rictor said, "had told me that one of his friends…Rob, that is, had complained about seeing someone. Like he was being watched or something. He said it like his friend was going crazy, like it was all a big joke, but I could tell that he thought it was creepy. A mother always knows. He wouldn't have brought it up otherwise, would he?"

"That's right. He told us that Robbie said that, too. He said that Robbie told his parents but was being brushed off. Had he mentioned anything like that to you?"

At that, Mr. Rictor let out a wet laugh, having been in the middle of sipping his beer. "Yeah. I've met up with Jon a few times at the bar. He seems to think his son was having nightmares like a little kid. Kept it from the police because he thought his son was being a pussy." He laughed again, clearly agreeing. "If my son had brought some bullshit like that to me, I'd have done more than ignore him."

Mr. Rictor got back up out of his seat and headed to the sink as if he was going to rinse his empty beer. He shoulder-checked his wife, clearly trying to make it look like an accident, and mumbled something to her that Williams couldn't make out. His wife paled, looking as if she was going to be sick with fright. She looked at Williams with an almost pleading look in her eye.

Williams had so much to do, too much. She needed to make moves and make them faster than she was. But she couldn't let this lie. Call it that overly idealistic view of what it means to be on the force again, but she just couldn't, she simply refused.

"And in your gracious opinion, Mr. Rictor, do you believe that what they may have seen is now possible, seeing that your son was kidnapped, and Robbie Elton was murdered by a stranger in the night?" Williams said, purposefully hoping to egg him on.

"My son's a deadbeat. No matter what I did, he wouldn't man up. He probably asked for it. Couldn't handle his own business. Good riddance, I say. Is that what you want to hear? Good Riddance! I'm not proud of the son I have, so might as well not have one period," Mr. Rictor said, practically frothing.

With each word Mrs. Rictor's heart shattered into smaller pieces. Williams wasn't done yet, she couldn't be.

"Like father, like son, though right, Rictor? James must have learned from the best, I'd guess. You're what, five-foot-four? Not much to live up to, I'd say. I just spoke to James yesterday; he was already a bigger man."

Mr. Rictor let out a scream and lunged. He held his arms straight out, his eyes ablaze with rage and hatred, like he intended to strangle Detective Williams to death on the spot. That or snap her neck. He never got the chance. Williams was on him: she side stepped, dodging, and he sent himself crashing into the kitchen wall. Dazed, she grabbed him.

The dog, now more of an afterthought to Williams, continued its snarling, spitting, and barking in the living room. It was apparent the crate would hold. She briefly wondered if he'd ever sicked the dog on his own family. Maybe even on a friend of the family?

She batted his hands away, now practically limp in his daze, and threw him to the floor, flipping him over. She wrestled his hands behind his back, cuffing him. As she read him his rights, she pulled him to his feet entirely by the handcuffs. There were ways that you could arrest someone easily, and there were ways that you could do so otherwise. Williams was excited to do everything the hard way for this piece of work.

As she pushed him out the front door, she was pleased to see that the neighbors had come outside to see what the screaming had been.

"You're under arrest for obstruction of justice and attempted assault on your wife, as well as a police officer. Intent to operate a motor vehicle under the influence of alcohol, too. And you're under arrest for the suspected murder of three people, your son, James, included." Williams did nothing to keep her voice down, if anything she let it ring out. She was positive that last one wouldn't stick, but she felt good about it in the moment.

Ch 9

Disambiguation

I

WILLIAMS PULLED INTO A spot in front of the precinct. On the way through Cemetery, they had shared some words. She told Rictor all about how much she hated men like him and how his wife now had her card and personal cellphone number. How she'd come pick him up each and every time he disrupted his wife's life, any time he touched her. She asked after the dog, how someone could raise an innocent puppy to be such an aggressive and angry spirit. She pointedly asked if he had used the dog to intimidate and harass his wife and son. And others.

Then Williams pointed out just how disruptive she could be within the confines of the law. Popping up at his local haunts, tailing him while he went out with friends, even making appearances at his work. When she had asked him how long he thought it would take for them to become fed up, to get rid of him entirely, he had quietened down, not saying a word since.

As they entered the precinct, Chief Carter faced her from behind the desk. He must have been looking for some kind of paperwork or something as she couldn't think of a single other reason for him to be standing where he was. He raised an eyebrow at her and her arrestee.

"Mr. Rictor...the missing kid's father," Detective Williams said by way of greeting. She pulled him along, Mr. Rictor wincing.

"And you've arrested him?" Carter said, looking more than a little shocked.

"He assaulted his wife. Then he tried to strangle me," Williams replied. "Probably would have sicked his dog on me too, if he'd gotten loose from me." It wasn't stretching the truth, much.

"Book 'em then," Carter replied, smile stretching ominously wide. Last night's fight like water under the bridge. "Got something more for you. One hell of a day's brewing. You need to follow me."

Thankfully, Williams was able to pass Mr. Rictor off to a uniform officer. The officer didn't even bat an eye, just took him by the arm and led him away. Good, she thought, let the officer pat that asshole down for weapons, possessions, and anything else that could be hidden. She felt that if she had to touch him any longer, she'd knock his teeth in. The further away the better. Who beats their wife and kid? Who couldn't care less that their son was missing?

II

Snapping the cruiser door shut, Williams stood, her back cracking as she straightened. She could see the deluge of police activity: spools of caution tape, forensic photographers, brazen flashing red and blues. The chilly October air snapped any unzipped coats in the oppressive breeze. The front of Cemetery Elementary was flooded with angry parents and suspicious onlookers.

Though outside, Williams felt claustrophobic. Chief Carter motioned her to the side.

He broke the ice. "Look, I'll start by saying I'm sorry that things got out of hand. All of the stress is getting to everyone. It's no excuse, but then again, it is what it is. I won't pretend it didn't happen." He ran a hand down his weary face, placing pressure on his eyes. "However, it does look like while the department was combing your block, our perpetrator took advantage of the empty Cemetery streets."

Senior Detective Reyes, who had been hovering, interrupted the Chief, hoping that from him, the blow might be softened. "Late this morning, a third body was found. The perp left the body on display this time, and it isn't James. They were found by a group of kids going to recess. Whole things a freaking mess. The parents and school are in an uproar about it and the kids are obviously shaken up to hell. I tried calling, but your phone was off." It was obvious that Reyes was still trying to right the wrong and even the score with Williams. He added, "this ain't on you..."

The Chief couldn't be bothered with softening the blow. They didn't have the time. He motioned for them to follow him onto the school's playground, ducking as an officer raised the caution tape for them.

Boots crunching in the playground mulch, and gravid with unease, Williams' focus shifted to Dr. Kenmore, who was orchestrating the forensic research. She knew the situation was dire for the pathologist to be dragged out of his morgue to a crime scene. The entire area had a woody smell, mixed with vinegar and ammonia, indicating to the detective that the mulch was fresh.

They stopped at the center of the playground, Carter miming for the pathologist to speak.

Dr. Kenmore cleared his throat and began. "Real preliminary findings here, but the ID is obviously confirmed." Brennan and Shotz stepped closer to hear as the doctor motioned toward the victim's exposed face. "Our perpetrator chose to truss up their victim on our elementary school's Geodome Climber. We're not sure how the parents and staff didn't see this before the school day started, but it seems unlikely that the crime could have taken place after that."

Williams readied herself to look at the devastation before them—immediately wishing she didn't have to. The victim had been hung up on the playground equipment, arms and legs splayed out and tied at the joints to support her weight. She was completely naked, dark skin drained pale with the loss of life, and her left breast and chest cavity were shredded open. She looked so...young.

"ID is one Lizzy Bowman, aged sixteen, about to be seventeen," Dr. Kenmore said, looking at Williams as she turned away from the trapeze corpse. "There is fatal damage to the cutaneous layers and the ribs themselves. As typical with this case—if we can call any of this "typical"—her body is entirely exsanguinated. Again, no blood on wounds that undoubtedly would have produced a great deal of it. Our killer is clearly escalating at an exponential rate." Dr. Kenmore seemed to be less jubilant today; sad even, if anything. His useful information had been few and far between, and he was feeling a measure of guilt realizing that.

"The damage on the skin and bones looks to be caused by scratching, or perhaps clawing into the ribcage—hastily done, though no less *brutally*—however, until I can do further analyses it could just as easily be enraged stab wounds, as I'm sure Williams was about to ask. So, are there still signs that point to an animal's possible involvement here? Yes." At this, he stood out of his crouch and signaled to the poor soul set on display. "But no animal could have done all this...oh, and we've yet to locate the victim's heart, if you can believe it."

Reyes lit a cigarette, releasing a lungful of smoke—breaking practically every crime scene procedure as he ashed into the playground mulch. The look on Carter's face was one of reproach, but Reyes cut off his retort. "This is the first victim that's not white. With everything else following the script, it could be nothing. But it could be important."

Carter nodded his head as he spoke. "We're not sure if this is a shift in the perpetrator's MO, or if this is another friend of the other victims. Her name didn't appear on the list, but we've all seen parents leave off girl friends, girlfriends, and ex-girlfriends in the past before, so that could mean nothing."

Williams sent a silent prayer up that the Advil was doing its job, the throbbing headache from her hangover more of a dull reminder than at the forefront. It was helping to keep her stomach steady as well. No way was she going to allow it to happen again, especially with all the extra eyes out today.

"What about the heart?" she asked.

Dr. Kenmore overheard her even though he had been fielding questions from his team. He stepped aside. "How do you mean?"

"Are there signs of the same brutality around where the heart should be? Does it match the damage done to the ribcage?" Reyes had caught her train of thought.

Dr. Kenmore's brows furrowed in surprise. "Well, it's funny you mention that. I was hoping to get to study it under the lights in the lab to be sure—but no, it looks as if it has been removed with some measure of *care*."

What level of care could be employed in the forceful removing of a teenager's heart? What did this mean for the investigation?

Williams took another long look at the corpse of Lizzy Bowman. The sight eternally burned into her retinas already, but she forced herself to be a witness. To see. "Unless the body was left out somewhere first, this throws a massive-sized wrench in the animal theory..." Williams' voice petered out as she tapped her chin. "It feels like every couple of hours we're uncovering something else withheld from us. Anyone feel like the Eltons might have left out just a bit too much?"

"Their son was missing. And after searching for him, they've found out that he's been murdered. We can't know what's going through their minds." Carter turned away from Reyes' smoking and came to a decision. "This one is out in the open, and three deaths and a possible kidnapping is too much to keep under wraps anyway. I'm going to have to address the public soon. Better from me than the media running with it. Reyes and Williams, I'll need you on it with me. We need to appear strongly united. Brennan and Shotz, I'm entrusting you with reinterviewing the Eltons. We need to know when and if their son actually thought he was seeing something. Dates, times, descriptions. Ask after a Lizzy Bowman in their son's life as well, even if it was old news or seemingly not a big deal. Dr. Kenmore, back to the lab and find me something solid, okay? We've all a part to play, and this is boiling down to the wire. Let's not fumble here."

They split up into separate conversations. Williams watched Dr. Kenmore switch back into forensic mode, pointing things out to the photographers and taking various samples from the area.

As everyone was about to leave, Carter motioned for Williams to hang back. Reyes made eye contact with her, raising an eyebrow, but she waved him off.

When Carter deemed that the others were far enough out of earshot, he took a moment and swallowed. "I figured it be best coming from me before you get home and find out anyway, but your neighbor, Mr. Cody, was found dead this morning on his living room couch. They believe he had a heart attack."

Just like that, another body for Williams to make the perp pay for. They had intruded on her while she was sleeping, slaughtered defenseless teens, and now caused an elderly man to have a heart attack from the excitement happening around *her* house.

Someone was going to pay, she just hoped it wasn't her.

III

Early morning, Williams and Katherine met for a quick breakfast. Williams realized only after sending the text that it had only been two days since their dinner date. She had enjoyed herself once she'd opened up, or rather the alcohol did, and if she were honest, she just needed the distraction. She didn't care.

Katherine had answered immediately.

They sat hip to hip in a booth at the diner, Katherine browsing a menu while Williams wondered what Reyes would have to say if he found out she was here without him. They ordered breakfast plates and coffees, rye toast for one, wheat for the other.

Katherine turned her head to face Williams. "I really wasn't sure I'd hear back at all. I've been wondering if Mr. Cody cut us off or saved you the trouble of asking me to leave."

Williams sipped her coffee to give herself a second to think, burning her mouth in the process. "I told you I had fun. We're so busy with the case that I don't have a lot of free time on my hands, but I figured a quick breakfast was better than no contact at all?"

She let the question hang between them like the gossamer strands of a spiderweb. If Katherine wanted, it could be a safe connection between them; a bridge, not a trap. Williams figured it was best to keep the home invasion, as well as Mr. Cody's death, to herself for the time being. That, and she came here to be distracted.

Katherine's face finally split into a wide smile. She was beautiful, and even if the smile was a little crooked, Williams found she liked that even more. "I get that you're busy. And I'm okay with that. I'm glad you called."

When their food came, they ate in silence for a while, simply enjoying the slight pressure of each other's legs touching.

Once outside, they briefly hugged. Katherine asked when she could see her again.

"I'm not entirely sure, but I'll let you know. This was fun. You can always text me too, I'll answer when I can."

After, Williams rushed off to the precinct for the chief's press conference, Katherine around the block to the library. Williams knew they had undoubtedly hit it off. Despite her nerves and the horror story that followed later that night, she hadn't felt this calm around someone in a long time. Maybe it was that everything else in her life seemed to be spiraling; the fact that Katherine was unrelated to work—or perhaps it was how cool and collected Katherine seemed, but she knew she wanted to continue seeing her.

IV

With the morning sun still high in the sky, Chief Carter, Reyes, and Williams regrouped outside for the press conference. It had been arranged for some interested news outlets to come to the precinct. A podium had been brought outside and someone had raked the leaves and discarded cigarette butts off the sidewalk out front.

The precinct's camera was set up dead center so they would have a copy of what was said, just in case any of the outlets tried to spin something. Carter wanted their undivided attention. He was good at smoothing over and controlling, but he had no intentions of being played.

Williams thought of at least a quarter million places she'd rather be as the news media people started filing in. She recognized the journalist from *Cemetery Times*, Meadows. She had worked in a minimal capacity with him in the past.

The others were a little smaller in size, coming from the surrounding towns of Middletown, Goshen, Chester, and Newburgh.

With towns so close together, Williams had expected more. Maybe news wasn't spreading to the smaller areas as fast. Maybe they just figured it was business as usual for Cemetery. Mostly, she figured it was because they hadn't been notified of the other bodies yet. Public murders drew attention, but serial killer territory typically drew fanatics and media in droves.

Carter approached the podium, clearing his throat and straightening his jacket. Williams stepped up to his left, crossing her arms in front of herself, Reyes copying her on the right.

Carter looked out over the crowd, giving a bit of attention to each person. He had that way about him. "Thank you for coming at such short notice. I certainly wish the news and circumstances were better. Before I get into the details, I want to assure you that we are doing everything we can to put a stop to these needless killings. To my left and right are Senior Detective Reyes and Detective Williams. They have worked tirelessly to bring us clues to bring down the evil perpetrator." He paused, looking into the police camera.

"The department received a call yesterday morning and responded to Cemetery Elementary, where a heinous scene was uncovered. We have identified the victim, notifying next of kin, and we will not stop until she has justice. Just yesterday, on my authority, Detective Williams arrested a man suspected of killing four young adults within the Hudson River Valley area. He was arrested just hours after the 911 call came in."

At that, Williams and Reyes looked at each other. Reyes' face was comical, Williams' mutinous. Williams hadn't truly believed Rictor had done it, not really.

But what came next shook her faith in herself.

"He was arrested right before he could drive through the streets of Cemetery on his way to work, armed with a handgun and possibly searching for his next victim. Investigators began watching the suspect after receiving tips and finally arrested him in Cemetery, where two of the victims were from." Chief Carter paused again, taking a sip of water from the bottle placed in the podium for him. "The perp's own son is missing, and no number of added patrols or door-to-doors has turned much out yet. But with the father in custody, we hope to have information that will bring him home safely soon."

Williams' head spun. Could Carter have sent officers to Rictor's house already and found something incriminating? And why hadn't Reyes or Williams been the ones involved if that was the case? She knew the dog wouldn't hold, so why was he acting so certain? She turned her head to the side, biting her lip. Two minutes ago, she was certain she had the wrong individual, now the chief of police was talking like the case was closed. She just hoped this didn't come back to bite her.

Carter answered a few questions, giving clipped, nondescript answers. After refusing to divulge the identity of the man they had arrested twice, he raised his hands, calling for quiet. He smiled, thanking the crowd for coming, and promised justice once more.

As the crowd dispersed, Carter was certain to keep the smile plastered to his face, nodding at each individual as they passed. The kind of smile that showed confidence, but a clear regret and respect for the situation. The kind one might give someone at a wake or funeral they don't know very well.

Carter waited for so long that Williams feared he'd keep them in the cold for the entire day. Until the final guest left for their car, Carter remained vigilant.

Finally, as he turned, Reyes came right out and confronted him. "Chief, what the hell was that? Did you find something we don't know?" Williams shuffled closer so she could hear.

"We found a few incriminating things in the search of Rictor's house. And his prints came back as a match for an old missing person's case."

"Why were neither one of us informed?" Williams asked.

"You're my detectives, but you're not the only cops in Cemetery, you know." Chief Carter still hadn't dropped his camera smile. "With everything going on, did you really think I'd send the two of you to fulfil a simple search warrant?"

"I'd think you would when it directly links to our investigation?" Reyes' tone was biting, no longer filled with the usual lack of care attitude. As he placed a cigarette in his mouth, he tried to catch Williams' eye.

Carter laughed in a way that sounded forced. "Listen, relax, guys. This is a good thing, okay?"

Well, shit, Williams thought. *Shit. Shit. Shit.*

V

Williams took the case file for the missing person from Chief Carter. She wondered why he would have it on his desk, but figured it was because of the developing case. He'd never taken files himself before, but everyone was up in arms. With her and Reyes not being informed about the search warrant, he'd probably just taken the file to hand it over anyway.

Williams had mostly arrested Mr. Rictor because he had assaulted his wife and tried to assault her. She never thought any of the other things would stick, although the dog was certainly weird. For it to come back and seem like it was him just didn't sit right.

At her desk, she opened the file. It had all the typical fanfare that it should: the initial police report, a transcription of the missing persons calls, photos of all of the evidence. Everything seemed to be there. Nothing within a case file was ever good, but it appeared to be in order—*normal.*

However, there was a sheet of paper that stuck out at an odd angle. She noticed it immediately. It looked as if someone had thrown it in the folder recently, but she figured it was just the connection made to Rictor's prints.

Now that it was in front of her though, she could no longer ignore the glaring differences. The handwriting was similar, but with some differences. It was in a different color, which she wouldn't typically find odd, but she noticed while studying the file that it was done by Officer Daniels—and she never used blue ink. She was honestly a little odd, but that was a thing that Williams had picked up on—she was one of the only people in the precinct that was particular about pens. So why the change?

The additional page was the piece about the missing persons car and the found fingerprints. Several of the statements on the sheet identified them as being from the original investigation. But as she flipped back now, she realized that

Daniels' original report didn't mention a fingerprint of any kind being found. This blue-inked sheet wasn't dated, nor was it signed, another difference between all of Daniels' work and this. So, where was this information coming from, and why the two different stories?

Ch 10

Developing

I

Williams returned to the precinct early from handling one of her postponed interviews. One of Robert Elton's teachers had agreed to meet with her. She was trying to feel out if his parents had been lying about how he was perceived at school, but the teacher, while forthcoming, had been next to useless. He was so far removed from Robert's day to day in school that Williams hadn't taken a single note. Exasperated, she left.

Now she faced Chief Carter as he sat behind his desk. She knew what she wanted to say, but still was anxious over the how. Carter finished explaining something to Officer Shotz before sending him on his way.

"What can I do for you, Detective Williams?"

This case, this single concatenation of events, had driven Williams to the very edge. She had to step out from Reyes' shadow if she ever wanted to get things done for herself. She felt cold uncertainty burning in her belly, but she had to fight it, fight through it. She looked Carter in the eyes, staring into their icy depths, and took the plunge.

"I want the interrogation room."

"Senior Detective Reyes is just finishing up with one of your rescheduled appointments. He won't be much longer. I want him to take a crack at him first," Carter replied.

Instead of asking the Chief why, or complaining outright she asked, "why did you choose me?"

His eyebrows shot up in question, but he didn't answer.

"For the job, Chief. Why did you pick me out of the pool of applicants?"

"To be honest, I thought you were naïve. That and you were young. Young enough to teach. And you seemed like you genuinely cared about the town. You didn't strike me as the 'my way or the highway' type of person, and I thought your idealism might rub off on Ed."

"Okay, well I'm new to the role of detective, but I've been around the block. I think I can handle interrogating my own arrest. I don't need Reyes holding my hand." Regardless of her prior uncertainty, Williams felt good being so direct. "How about a little trust?"

II

Williams felt her high begin to drop as she descended the stairs to the investigation room. Even after studying the case file for the missing person, she still felt off about it. It wouldn't stick, unless she could needle away at him until he bled, giving himself away. But even then, she didn't like Rictor for the murders.

After all that she found herself wishing Reyes was here with her. She was beginning to realize how much she relied on his presence, even if it was her doing all the work—even if he had been a prick more than usual recently.

Williams waited for the buzz and pulled the door open. It was a cement room, drab and damp. It was a converted basement that they hadn't even bothered to paint. The door snapped shut behind her and buzzed again. She approached the sparse metal table, which was bolted to the floor. Mr. Rictor was handcuffed to the opposite side of it, facing her. Distain read clearly across his angry face.

Let him sit and stew.

As she approached the table, she opened the folder with the missing person information. She began rifling through it as she sat. "Evan Rictor, age forty-five, height...approximately four and five as well."

Evan Rictor's face purpled.

So easy to ruffle his feathers. Perhaps this would be easy after all. "So, when did you decide to start turning your toxic masculinity into something far darker? When did you decide to kill?"

He turned in his seat, pulling at his reins. The veins in his neck popped and bulged. Spittle filled the corner of his mouth. "Shut your mouth you pathetic bitch!"

Williams kept her cool. Calm, even. "You really are a piece of work, Evan. Woman beater, child beater, an abuser through and through. Not even caring that your *son's* missing? Now that's cold. Even for you. The way you've trained your dog. Truly horrific. One could even say...evil. Did you know our victims have each been mutilated in different ways? Perhaps by just such a beast. I bet you do know something about it. Don't you, Evan."

"I'd never kill a person, I'm not a monster!" Evan Rictor said, "I won't let you vilify me for something I haven't done."

"You aren't a monster? Did you not just hear all the things I said? Who raises a hand to a defenseless woman and child, their own flesh and blood? If you're anything at all, it's a monster."

"I want a lawyer," Rictor spat.

There. Williams had it, her pivotal moment. Sometimes you pushed and it was just enough, and sometimes you pushed, and they went over the edge. She had him where she wanted him, but it was close.

"Sure, we're on that right now for you." She waved her hand above her head as if there was someone watching the camera. There wasn't. "Let me ask you though because this might be important. Long shot here, okay, but where were you on the night of February sixteenth, 2020?"

Rictor's face scrunched up. It blanched slightly, before going completely neutral. "Who remembers that kind of shit?"

"You don't remember possibly drinking a few too many with your buddies? Getting into a bar fight or two maybe? Following someone outside the bar on their way home? Maybe you thought it would just be an argument...maybe you felt slighted and knew exactly what you intended to do. That's not for me to decide, I leave that to the courts. Tell me, Evan, why did your fingerprints match those found in a missing persons vehicle if you had nothing to do with it?" She flipped to a different page in the file folder. "His friends filed the police report, stating, 'I had work early, so I finished my beer an hour or more before leaving at nine, but Derek didn't want to leave. He stayed. The last place we saw him was at O'Leary's Pub.' Isn't that your usual spot, Evan?"

Rictor opened his mouth to retort but closed it clearly having thought better of it.

It was amazing what people would give away if you simply watched them. He remembered something, and he wasn't going to give her anything about it at this rate.

"Let me get that lawyer ordered right up for you," Williams said, smiling. "Shouldn't be more than a couple of hours. While you wait though, give a long hard thought for where your son might be. We could still save him."

Evan Rictor protested, spouting the usual slew of mistreatment and rights. Williams ignored him.

III

Reyes pulled his car into the parking lot of Old Street Tavern in Goshen. He asked his buddy to meet him for lunch and a beer or two, saying it had been too long. Really, he had questions about the case. Robbie Elton had been from Goshen, but he didn't remember there being calls for help when he turned up missing.

The list from Goshen PD was turning out to be more of a hit-list than a friend-list. He knew that the list hadn't been publicly shared, he just wanted to know how it had gotten out.

On his way to Goshen, Reyes had placed a call to Jon Elton. The story he told was rather contrary to what had been shared with the detectives. By Elton's reckoning, Robbie and Lizzy were an established item, having been together for four months. Nothing eternal, but months to teenagers often seemed like they were. Elton also swore up and down that her name had, in fact, been placed on the list given to Goshen PD.

Reyes took a final drag of his cigarette and got out of the car. He scratched his face, feeling the five o'clock stubble already coming in under the razor burn. *Yep, disheveled it is from now on. Not worth this hassle.*

Approaching the bar, he ordered two Budweisers, already seeing Officer Dumbauld entering the door. He thanked the bartender, tipped, and found a booth in the corner.

"Hey, Dick, how's it hanging?" Reyes said.

"Ed, you're looking older and older, aren't you?"

They shook hands and Reyes passed him his beer. Dumbauld was far broader than Reyes: stoat, but not heavyset. They sat in a semi-awkward silence and drank.

"I hope you don't mind, but I got Brennan on his way here too. It's been too long since I've seen you boys."

Truthfully, Reyes did mind. He knew that Dumbauld had always been close to Officer Brennan, or at least closer than he had been, but he hadn't figured on him being invited. He'd have to watch how he went about questioning his old friend.

Officer Brennan walked to the table, full Cemetery blues on display except for his hat. He smiled at the two of them, placing another three beers on the table. "Damn, it's been too long, Dick. How are ya, Ed?"

Brennan's height far exceeded that of either Reyes or Dumbauld, a scar of his right cheek the most dominate feature on his face. The grey fighting its way up his temples was the only true indicator of his age.

"So I saw the news, and heard around the precinct that you boys in Cemetery were starting to feel the heat?" Dumbauld said so merrily, taking a sip of beer. He knew this meeting was off business hours, and as such, he hadn't a care in the world.

"Hey, you know me, Dick. Never was one for doing more than was asked," Brennan replied. Smirking, he said, "never did more and never moved up. I might not be taking the heat like Ed here, but the Chief's got my partner and I doing all the bullshit for sure."

"Yea, it hasn't been great," Reyes said. This was not going the way he wanted. If anything, he needed to reel these two back in. As they made further small talk, Reyes paid especial attention to his beer, hoping they'd run out of platitudes before long.

Finally, a waitress approached, passing them menus, and asking if they needed anything else, which they declined.

Reyes sipped his beer and rubbed the side of his face. "I shave once, and this is all the reminder I need why I stopped in the first place. The burn ain't worth it."

Officer Dick Dumbauld, clean shaven, shook his head and sipped away. "You clearly don't know how to do it. Old as ever, but still like a pubescent boy, just scratching away."

Officer Brennan had a stereotypical police mustache that grew sparse on the side where it met scar tissue. He chuckled at Dumbauld's joke but didn't give his two cents.

Reyes knocked his knuckle on the table twice. Better now than never. "Meaning to ask you about a Lizzy Bowman, sound familiar?"

"No. Why?"

"She was dating Robbie Elton at the time of his disappearance. She wasn't on the list of friends you sent me, but Robbie's father swears she was," Reyes said.

"Hey, must have been an honest mistake, I guess," Dick replied.

"Lighten up, Ed. I'm sure we didn't come here to fight?" Brennan interceded.

"Right, sure," Reyes replied. He sipped his beer, already close to needing a third. "Honest mistakes happen all the time while sending over scanned documents..."

He let the implication hang in the air.

Dick opened his mouth to reply but was interrupted by the waitress. She had three more beers and her pad in hand for their order. She smiled brightly. Presumptuous, but why else come to a pub at three in the afternoon? Even cops have a type.

Having been cornered into ordering and staying longer, Reyes took the beers and ordered a burger. Dick ordered a salad and Brennan got a buffalo wrap. They sipped their beers in silence, letting the air thicken. Reyes was trying to understand his angle here, why his friend would have missed information—seemingly purposefully—and then act as if it was meaningless. This wasn't the Dick Dumbauld he remembered.

"Jon Elton asked me not to share it. After you visited his house, he called me. I thought it was odd, but I respected his wishes, figuring his son had just been found dead and all," Dick said.

"You withheld information because what—the Elton's didn't want the public to know their son had a girlfriend?"

"He said he wanted to spare her more anguish. I thought he was being a nice person and the request was simple enough to honor for the guy," Dick said. He shrugged, grabbing his beer and drinking it down faster than was strictly necessary. "Come on, Reyes."

"Because of that lack of information, she's now dead!" Reyes yelled.

However, that wasn't strictly true and Reyes knew it. They had the list of friends, and originally, having nothing linking them to the murders, Cemetery PD had done nothing to protect the kids. Even now, he hadn't heard of any police detail stationed outside of any houses. He'd correct that after this.

"They're all a bunch of druggie kids. A bunch of troublemakers. What are we crying about here?" Dick Dumbauld asked, echoing the words of Reyes not too long ago: *"Pardon me if I don't go crying my eyes out for another druggie in Cemetery."*

Maybe Williams was rubbing off on him, or maybe the idea of a serial killer in Cemetery had changed his tune. Either way, he couldn't stand for it.

"Dick, come on, man, how long we known each other?"

"Friends twenty-four years now. A little less for Brennan here, but still a long time. Been patrolling the streets a good while," Dick replied.

"It's no excuse for shoddy police work, and you know it. That information should have been released. It wasn't even his kid's name. He had no right to withhold it. You should have told him to take a hike."

"Twenty-four years and not once have I told you how to do your police work, Reyes. Why are you starting to tell me how to do mine? You know what, you're starting to sound an awful lot like that partner of yours. Stick up your ass and everything," Dick said, getting angry. "You know I was one of the first people there for you. When—when everything happened. First Isabel. I was the first one there for you that night. And then again when Maria left. You don't get to just question me, Ed."

Brennan looked away from the table in disbelief. As if he couldn't believe that Dumbauld had taken things there so quickly. If they weren't seated in a booth, he probably would have pushed his chair away from the coming storm. He frantically spun the class ring around his finger.

It had been fifteen years since Reyes' daughter Isabel had died. They had tried everything, but her early onset heart disease got progressively worse. And when the medicine stopped working, they'd hoped more than anything that she could last long enough to get to the top of the donor list. Heartbreakingly, small enough hearts were hard to come by.

It broke Reyes in a way that could never truly be explained. He was a happy, proud father of one. He was in love and living the life he always wanted for himself. Sure, it had taken him a tad longer than others to find it, but he had, nonetheless. Then, as if overnight, he was someone else. When he couldn't find his way back, his work had suffered; he'd became brusque, he'd drank heavily, and more often than not he hadn't made it home. He and his wife had grown apart, as so many do after the loss of a child, and one night Reyes had stumbled through the door to find Maria gone. He hadn't even had it within himself to look for her. Just accepted it as his lot in life.

"Perhaps I've been thinking like you for far too long. Maybe I'm jaded, Dick, and maybe I've been spending years with my partner spewing hateful bullshit so that I could feel a little better myself. Maybe the fact that she's better than me has always been the problem, or maybe it's the fact that I see such a spark—" at this his voice broke and a tear carved a jagged path down his face. "—A spark inside her that's just a little too like my Isabel's, too much like what I've lost to tell her. But we have a crazy person running around killing *kids* in Cemetery. We need help, not roadblocks from our own."

Dumbauld frowned, knowing he'd gone too far. Brennan's face of disbelief could have been called comical, if he wasn't so afraid that Reyes was going to strike one of them.

Reyes sipped his beer and pulled his wallet out, putting two twenties on the table.

"Not sure what is going on, but there's something wrong here. Makes me lose my appetite."

IV

Williams had been getting another run in at Evan Rictor. She figured she might as well, and the second time he hadn't mentioned a lawyer. She had called a lawyer though, but they told her tomorrow would be the earliest.

Lawyers, the top paid job title in Cemetery, and the second busiest job.

What she hadn't realized was that someone was watching the camera this time. Someone was listening in.

Chief Carter had pulled up the camera system on his computer, his office door shut. Scowling, and listening to the information Williams was trying to peel out of Evan Rictor. Typically, he would be glad to have his best on something like this. The only cause for worry was that he knew she was *too* good. He would have preferred to have Reyes stumbling his way through the interrogation.

As chief of police, was there something more he should have been doing? Perhaps, perhaps not. Another murder and he might be fine; another string of them though, and it was his ass on the chopping block.

The mayor and town officials had added their voices to the constant calls he was receiving. It was inevitable, but he had found himself hoping for more time. He sat pinching the bridge of his nose between his first two fingers, applying as much pressure as he could stand. They pushed and pushed, never expecting him to burst. He knew eventually he would.

Carter reached for his cellphone as it vibrated wildly across the desk. His scowl deepened the furrows along his brow as he saw the name of the caller come across the screen.

"This is Carter," he answered, his clipped tone about as diplomatic as he could manage. The tinny voice on the other end of the line sounded like it was echoing off a large area, the voice almost doubled as it came through the phone. "Yes, I did it. No, she's in there with them right now." Carter paused again as the voice on the line grew agitated. "No, listen to me, I said I would and I did, but that's *it*."

Carter ended the call and slammed his phone back down on his desk.

Turning back to the camera, he had a feeling that they'd be the death of him.

V

Williams took to pacing the small interrogation room, patrolling back and forth in small circles. She still wished Reyes was around, but she had hit a stride on her own. His often brusqueness would have rubbed Evan entirely wrong. She did too, she could tell he obviously hated answering to a woman, but the challenge of it was propelling him as well.

"And you're still going to give me the same nonsense about not knowing what happened that night at the bar? We keep circling it. Just talk to me, Evan, what could it hurt now?"

He had thus far been adamant about his lack of knowledge from that night, stating he never saw the guy.

Derek Chan had gone out with a small group of friends to one of the popular local bars, O'Leary's, on February 16, 2020. They had gone out for a beer or two, but Derek, having a good time, had elected to stay. His friend who had first called it in had left around nine by his best estimate, with the three other friends staying. As the night progressed, the two other friends caught an Uber home, with Derek again electing to stay.

That much had been caught of the CCTV the bar had. What was also caught on camera, although the quality was far from favorable, was Evan Rictor present at the bar as the drunk and stumbling Derek Chan approached for another round.

Williams replayed the video for Rictor, wanting to do away with further arguing.

"I go to that bar a couple nights out of every week. You know how many drunk assholes bump into me or my barstool while ordering? This shows nothing." Rictor refused to relent.

Williams sighed, "You know, I'm trying to help you here."

"Help keep me here, more like it."

"Help me understand," Williams urged. "Walk me through what you remember of that night."

Rictor stretched, cracking his spine. He leaned forward, huffed out a breath, and smiled at Williams. "I went to the bar, got my usual seat, got my usual drink. As my bar ladies take care of me, my usual drink kept coming all night long. Couple of the other regulars showed up, friends of mine you could say. We got to talking, so I stayed later than usual. And yeah, that Asian kid bumped me. I said something of my usual style in response, and he wanted nothing to do with it, even offering me a drink to make up for it. I left the kid alone. *That's* what happened that night."

The door buzzed behind Williams, and she inwardly cursed. Chief Carter stuck his head into the room. He said her name and left, the door buzzing behind him.

"If you *didn't* do this, you're going to have to give me more than that, I'm trying for you here."

Williams had spent more time daydreaming about smacking Evan Rictor than helping him. Often, during his insults and screaming, she had thought back to smashing him into his own kitchen table. And part of her still felt as if she wanted to nail the guy, but this fingerprint thing was just one more piece of a mismatched puzzle.

VI

As Williams left the interrogation room, she almost walked straight into Senior Detective Reyes. She smiled at him despite herself—at least he was back. He didn't look the least bit happy though.

"Chief's office, now," Reyes said and was off.

"Hi to you too, Reyes," Williams shot back, jogging to catch up.

"No time for niceties, kid. Something's about to go down."

As they neared the chief's office, they could tell there was a buzz about the place.

Inside, the chief stood behind his desk. Several uniform officers filed out as the detectives turned to enter. Chief Carter shook his head and sighed before noticing he wasn't alone.

"Just got a call from the mayor. He wants to call in the FBI if—and I quote—'you can't get your goddamn shit together in Cemetery.'" Carter looked overwhelmingly stressed.

Without thinking, Williams laid into the chief. "I was going to get Rictor to talk, but you pulled me out! What the hell, Chief?"

"We just received a nine-one-one call. An emergency about a suspected kidnapping. Lizzy Bowman's younger sister, Ebony, was in class at the middle school when Lizzy was found. Her parents thought it best to let her finish out the day with some normalcy. But Ebony never made it home yesterday. One of her teachers, Ms. Andrea Nowack, is also missing."

The room was sucked into a vacuum of silence. No one breathed or moved an inch.

"We're unsure at this time if they are related crimes, if the teacher was an innocent bystander, or if she is the kidnapper herself," Carter finished.

Williams' world spun. She gripped the back of a chair for support and actually felt the world tilt. The anxious knot in her stomach was nothing short of a gaping hole, causing her real, physical, tyrannical pain.

She steadied herself enough to lean forward, saying, "When did the call come in?"

"An hour ago," was all that Carter offered.

An hour ago, Williams was already interrogating Evan Rictor, having locked him in that room hours prior.

It can't be him.

Williams needed a minute. She used the back of the chair to crutch her way around and plopped down into it. Breathing heavy, she looked to Reyes. Something wasn't right.

Reyes had a sheen of sweat on his brow. He looked pale. The hits kept coming at them nonstop, without giving an inch.

"And what about the search for James? His father still swears he has no idea where he is," Williams asked from her slumped position.

"We've obviously upped the number of police patrols and turned up nothing. Now we have to widen that search area even further," Carter replied. He too looked slicked in sweat, hunched, as if the situation was entirely on his shoulders.

Brennan and Shotz burst into the chief's office. They looked frantic.

"We called the Eltons all morning; no answer," Brennan said.

"So we went out to Goshen, and they aren't home," said Shotz.

"None of the neighbors saw them leave, but the house was empty," they said together.

Ch 11

Three Steps Forward

I

Williams and Reyes left Chief Carter's office. They looked at each other, making strained eye contact. Reyes had already placed a cigarette in his mouth, done with any attempt at pretending to care.

The second she was sure they were out of earshot, Williams said, "Listen, I know you think I'm overreacting, or jumping at ghosts, but just listen. While you were gone, I was interrogating James' father. I went through the missing person file that the Chief said his fingerprints were linked to, and I think something is seriously wrong. Not only was there a report in there that didn't match the others, but I have more than a sneaking suspicion that it was planted there. I don't know why he would, but I can't think of anyone else that could have done it, Ed. The report was in *his* office. Not only that, but he didn't want me to go in there at all—he said I had to wait for you. Then when I was finally getting somewhere, he pulled me out. And seriously, what the hell is with Carter not including us in a search warrant to begin with?" At this she stopped walking, stalling Reyes and making eye contact with him. "I know I've been cold lately, and we haven't hashed it out, but I need you with me on this."

Reyes started walking again. When he didn't respond immediately, Williams feared the silence would end her. Not only had she pulled the Chief into more of her delusion, but she had aired out their dirty laundry. Was Reyes going to go for her head again?

As they rounded the precinct's front desk, finally he spoke.

"Something *is* off, kid. Ain't sure what it is though," he said under his breath. "This whole thing is starting to stink to high heaven."

Part of Williams wanted to hug him, or high five him, or punch him in the face for taking so long. Instead, she simply nodded, increasing her pace. Through the entryway it felt as if everyone was staring at them. Like the feeling you get when you think everyone knows you have a secret.

As they headed toward the front door, Officer Caruso, a middle aged Italian NYPD transplant, looked up at them and asked them where they were headed. Were they being watched, or was it in their heads?

"Can't exactly smoke in here, can I?" Reyes said, taking the unlit cigarette from his mouth and waving it about like a candle.

"Williams doesn't smoke though, does she?" the officer asked.

"There's an active murder investigation going on, you want to fucking hold Williams' hand, too?" Reyes practically screamed it, startling the officer, who made a hasty retreat.

Reyes looked left to right, challenging the other officers to make a sound. He could be an imposing figure when he wanted to be, a shadow of the less bulky guy he used to be.

Reyes and Williams stepped outside, stopping short for him to light his cigarette. "What in the hell was that? It felt like being in a pool of piranhas and you're covered in cuts."

"I know the mayor is on the Chief, but he's acting weird. Weirder than usual." Williams replied. "And the FBI? Why wouldn't he welcome their help?"

"There ain't no way for us to know that," Reyes said.

Williams tilted her head back, leaning against the front of the precinct. She tapped the back of her head off the brick a few times, thinking. She let out the breath she had been holding in. It did nothing to calm her. "We need to go check out the Eltons. Something just doesn't feel right."

"Okay," Reyes replied, "to do what, kid?"

"I don't know, Reyes," Williams said. "Brennan and Shotz are weird, but that sounded almost rehearsed. Like the freaking twins from *The Shining*."

"Alright, alright...fine," Reyes offered, "but I'm driving, I need to smoke. I gotta think. Brennan was out to lunch with me and an old friend. I guess he could have checked on the Eltons, but Shotz sure as shit wasn't with us."

Stopping for a second, Reyes looked directly at Williams, "look, there's something I should probably tell you, too..."

The sky cracked with thunder and lightning. The wind blew leaves around the precinct. The kind of harsh gusts that smack the hair into your face and steal the breath from your lungs.

It was going to be a long day.

II

The fog had followed the rain like clouds of deception, cloaking the road in front of Williams and Reyes. He cursed; his window so nearly closed he was practically ashing his cigarette onto the car mat. The fog was nearly solid, making the usually stunning drive into Goshen a winding death trap.

Williams tapped her fingers on her thighs, feeling sick. She wasn't sure if it was the forced secondhand nicotine intake or the general feeling of despair. Reyes had tried more than once to start talking, but each time he'd stopped. The cat must have had his tongue. Fifteen minutes into their drive the Chief had tried to call them back into Cemetery for seemingly no good reason.

Reyes and Williams had ignored the radio after that, remaining silent.

As they approached the Elton's, the weather crashed ever harder. It was as if nature was trying to match the month they were having. The sheer magnitude of negativity within the air boiling over, seeping out in roiling waves of punishment.

They pulled into the Elton's driveway, the family car still in front of theirs in plain view. "Well, I see what Brennan and Shotz meant about the neighbors not seeing them leave, but they had to of checked at least, right?" Williams asked.

She was not all that excited to get out of the car with the storm coming down, who loves getting absolutely drenched? However, it was her idea, so she popped the car door and jogged for the front stoop.

Reyes was a bit slower. Williams figured he didn't want to be soaked any more than she did, or he just didn't want to jog. Amazingly, the rain wasn't able to put his cigarette out.

Williams knocked hard, hoping to be heard over the torrential rain. "Mr. and Mrs. Elton? It's Detective Williams and Senior Detective Reyes! We just wanted to check in," she shouted.

Their front door was unfortunately not the kind with windows. Williams felt her pulse strong in her ears. She knocked hard again. "Reyes, go around the back."

"Why can't you be the one to go out into the rain again?"

"Just do it, Reyes!" Williams yelled. "Now's not the time." She knocked again, harder. "Mr. and Mrs. Elton, are you home?"

Reyes relented, heading back into the torrent of rain. He kept his head slumped, smoke billowing from underneath his head until he disappeared around the house.

Williams continued pounding the door, getting steadily more aggressive. She couldn't understand why they wouldn't answer. She knocked so hard her knuckles hurt. Calling out more and more shrilly, almost pleading.

She couldn't have described it if she tried; she just knew something was wrong. Just as she had decided to start shouldering the door, a hand gripped her shoulder hard. She let out a scream. She twirled around, reaching for her gun.

But it was just Reyes returning from the back of the house.

"What the hell, Reyes, you almost gave me a heart attack! I could have shot you."

"You knew what I was doing, kid. Really weren't expecting me to return? Calm down and come with me."

Williams nodded at him and descended the stairs. He was right, and she had allowed herself to get spooked anyway. She followed close behind Reyes as he led the way. Each step felt like a mile to Williams as she wondered what Reyes had seen.

As they reached the back of the house, there were all the telltale signs of a breaking and entering. There were deep footprints from when Reyes had squelched around the back in the rain, but there were others too, from what looked like at least one other person. The back door was cracked and pitted, as if someone had taken a crowbar to it. One of the lower panel windows was crashed in with what looked like splashes of blood. Williams figured they had tried for a stealthier approach before cutting themselves.

Williams was going to be sick.

Reyes unclipped his holster and removed his snubnose .38. He edged around Williams, placing his hand on her shoulder. He gave it a solid squeeze.

"Come on, kid. I need you."

Williams nodded, punching herself lightly on the thigh. Amping herself up. She nodded her head again, swallowed, and unholstered her Glock 17. The lightning flashes overhead illuminated the basement beyond in fits and stops.

She put her hand on Reyes' back, signaling she was ready, and followed him into the black of the basement.

III

Katherine sat behind the counter of the library. It had been a slow morning, and she suspected the torrential downpour wasn't going to give the Cemetery Free Library any help. She had heard of libraries in other places being incredible. Doing community outreach and sponsored events was something Katherine would love to do, but in Cemetery it seemed like readers were a dying breed. Instead of events and outreach, the library used any help they could get just to stay afloat.

Today, she had rented out a single book. The book was required reading for the local college no less, not even a reader out renting for fun.

So Katherine sat behind the counter on her stool and continued on with her lunch. Today it was roast beef on rye bread, American cheese, and a paper-thin layer of mayo. Nothing fancy. She had already finished her bag of chips and was now sipping her water bottle and toying with tossing the rest of the sandwich.

Truth be told she hadn't been eating very much since that day in the woods. She wasn't sleeping very much either. What she had seen replayed itself in her mind every bite she took, every dream she dreamt. It had been the closest she had felt to giving something back to the community that she could think of, and it had been a disaster. Her living nightmare. Her dinner with Detective Williams, then their subsequent breakfast, had been the only reprieves since, and slight ones at that. She had let herself hope for a minute that she would be invited in. The drink was at the very least a dulling numbness to the memory; the possibility of sex would have been an acceptable distraction. A half bottle of wine and postcoital bliss were her best shots at a night's sleep.

Instead, she had gone home and tossed and turned all night. Which was an acceptable outcome, as she didn't want to be perceived negatively by Abby. That text for breakfast had solidified she was right about it.

Katherine grabbed her phone off the counter and looked at her text string with Abby. She had already done the unthinkable and double texted. Still no answer. Detective work was long and intense hours though, so a lack of texts back didn't amount to all that much, right?

She typed out a dozen text options before settling on, **Keep it together out there, I want to see you again!** and pressed send.

She smiled. That was friendly enough without being pushy. Triple texts were never cute, but what the hell.

IV

All throughout the basement Reyes and Williams were in near absolute darkness. The only reprieve, coming in flickers and flashes, was the lightning appearing through the high-set basement windows.

"You don't have a flashlight?"

Reyes leaned back to get closer to Williams' ear. "This wasn't exactly planned."

As they reached the stairs to the first floor, Reyes stopped, allowing himself to catch his breath. There's something about not being able to see, while a gun is drawn, that makes you exponentially out of breath with each step. Drawing a service weapon, in general, has the power to make all the hairs on the body stand on end—the body's response to the anticipation of action.

Williams felt rainwater, or sweat, running down the length of her back. She thought it was probably the latter. She drew in a deep breath, holding it for as long as she could before releasing. It did nothing to steady her, but she signaled for Reyes to resume.

Reyes took the first tentative step onto the old wood of the staircase. To his surprise, it made no noise, but he wouldn't bank on that kind of luck for the rest of the way up. With each step he made his was slowly upwards. For a man of his size, he tried to move with deliberate care, easing each shoe sideways onto the stairs, hoping to dull any thudding by using the arc of his foot, rather than the heel. Out of age-old habit, he reached for his pack of cigarettes, now soaked through, before he realized where he was and what he was doing. He shook himself as he neared the door at the top of the stairs.

Williams followed close behind him, doing her best to mimic his moves as they seemed to be working. Only once or twice did she hear anything above the typical sound a moving body makes. Even then, the sounds of thunder, lightning, and the pounding rain would likely silence anything—even in the basement it was deafening.

A surprisingly harsh strike of lightning was followed by a house-shaking thundering. Something audibly clicked off behind her. The furnace died in the middle of running the heat, so Williams figured it was the house's power cutting out. Even though they were already in darkness, something about knowing there were no lights above made it feel all the darker.

Reyes slowly turned the handle to the first floor, peeling the door open. He pushed his snubnose revolver through the opening and strained his eyes for any movement. This was normally the moment where police would re-announce themselves, but families don't often sit in complete darkness right after a storm blows the power out. There'd be shuffling and searching for flashlights, candles, matches, and each other. Reyes vaguely remembered Williams saying new phones had flashlights on them, but he wasn't sure if she was messing with him. He'd never gotten one, the kind that flips doing the trick just fine.

Easing his way out of the stairwell, Reyes entered the darkness of the first floor. The basement door had let out into a kitchen. The lightning flashes were more illuminating upstairs, but it felt more as if he were being plunged back into darkness rather than seeing the light. He slowed, trying to time the movements so that each step forward was a move within the light. He hoped that it would help him avoid bumping into anything, but it was an imperfect art.

Williams followed behind him. She tried to signal to him to go right, while she moved toward the left, but it was too dark, and his concentration was elsewhere. It was shocking to her, that even though this house was an entire town over, it was strikingly similar to the way hers was set up before they tore into it for the open concept. The kitchen opened both on the left and right. The left led directly into a living room, while the right led into the dining room.

Williams moved to the left anyway; they were used to scoping places out and meeting in the middle. She moved a little faster than him, keeping her feet closer to the floor to avoid making too much noise. She took a final look back at Reyes. He saw her now and was nodding, motioning that he was going forward with his gun. Busy glancing at him, Williams missed her second-long window to step in time with the lightning, however she stepped forward anyway.

She stepped on what felt like a pile of Legos, but with the distinct feeling of it being flesh and bone—the way you know you've stepped on your animal's tail before they react. She quickly shifted her weight to the other foot, stepping off whatever was on the floor as quickly as possible. As the lightning struck, she caught the scream in her throat as it threatened to tear its way out of her. She leapt back, banging into a hutch and clattering the neat standing China inside.

The thunder cloaked most of it, but it was enough for Reyes to stop and turn around. A moan escaped Williams and she motioned him over. He moved quickly.

Together, they stared down at the black-and-blue face of Jon Elton. His outstretched hand stuck out from behind the kitchen counter. It must have been what Williams had stepped on. His face was bloodied and beaten; puffy, with one eye swollen shut. The second eye stared, lifeless. A thickening pool of blood eked out from underneath him, still stretching outward.

"*This. Just. Happened.*" Williams mouthed to Reyes, barely a whisper, yet somehow a scream.

She pointed to the growing puddle of blood beneath him. Reyes nodded his understanding.

Lightning struck again, and Williams was hit with the full impact of what was before them. The kitchen cabinets were splattered with blood, which also ran down the window behind the sink. Mr. Elton's shirt had several bloodied holes in it. The castoff streaks from the work of a knife. Williams did the easy math...the killer was caught in the act, and Jon Elton fought. He lost, but at least he had fought.

It didn't relieve the horror on his dead face, frozen forever.

Williams stepped away from the hutch, not realizing that her back had wiped blood off of the old wood.

A pained gurgling noise drew their attention. The detectives raised their guns in front of them, gripping them like a lifeline. They made eye contact one final time. Reyes turned left, Williams right. This time they both headed out of the same side, heading straight for the noise and the living room beyond. The darkness around them ungulated and pulsed, as if every corner were home to unspeakable terrors.

Williams felt energy crackle through her that had nothing to do with the thunderstorm outside. As they stepped fully into the living room, the horror continued with each blink of the lightning. With each step, she continued to hold her breath, as if taking even the briefest intake of oxygen would release a massive scream. Williams had been doing this for years, but nothing dulled the terror that came with seeing what a demented human could do to another. Her disgust wanted a release more than anything.

Williams finally exhaled. With each step she was welcomed by more and more blood, until finally, she could make out Mrs. Elton, still seated in her rickety recliner, now flipped on its back. Her hand hung limply above her head, covered in blood, the gravity having pulled it away from her gaping throat after death. Her eyes had glassed over, but there were still faint pulses of arterial blood popping from the yawning wound in her neck.

Reyes approached from behind Williams. He closed Mrs. Elton's eyes before standing back up, groaning in effort. He had avoided getting blood on his clothes, but their shoes were a different story. There was nowhere left to step, nothing left unaffected.

Williams backed away, turning toward the darkness in the hallway beyond, the route they hadn't taken. As the lightning flashed outside the house, her phone pinged. It was so unexpected in the bleak and silent house that it drew her attention. Therefore, she didn't see the hulking figure standing before her in the shadowy hall.

As her eyes readjusted to the dark, the momentary blindness was only part of the reason for her slow reaction time. In the lightning flash that followed, she saw gloved hands holding onto a chef's knife. *Gloved hands* that were far too familiar to Williams—too close to a near fatal childhood trauma to distinguish real from fantasy.

The figure lunged forward; Williams' phone, now forgotten, bounced through the blood on the floor. She lowered a hand, but there was little hope of stopping the blow, slowed as she had been. The knife slid through her forearm and Williams felt it bite into bone through the searing pain. The tip of the kitchen knife slid into her gut. The air was knocked out of her in a guttural groan, and she felt the assailant turn the knife before being tackled by her partner.

Reyes was screaming. *"No. No. You bastard!"*

Williams fell backward and slumped against the bottom of Mrs. Elton's recliner. She held her uninjured arm against her bleeding stomach but could do nothing to staunch the bleeding from her right arm. Her Glock 17 was lost somewhere among the blood.

She chided herself, even now, but the thoughts were beginning to muddle together. *Should have been paying attention. Should have been faster. Should have been prepared for this. Reyes said he needed me, and I froze! The killer's still in the fucking house!*

Williams watched in horror as Reyes tried to fight off the larger man. She knew she should help, but she felt weightless, as if the strength that she tried so hard to maintain, so hard to exude, had fled from her. Her hand kept slipping from the wound in her gut. Was she falling asleep? What a terrible time to be so utterly tired. She could faintly tell that Reyes was calling out for something, but she couldn't make out what.

Williams shook herself hard, taking in the scene before her with blurry eyes.

"Radio it in, Williams!" Reyes was yelling. He had knocked the assailant's knife away, but he was overmatched in both wingspan and strength. He held on anyway. "Call it in, kid, come on!"

Williams sent dire messages from her brain, urging her arm to reach for the walkie attached to her hip. The problem was, she kept her police issue walkie on the right side, and her hand laid limp to her side, pulsing blood. She figured the assailant must have severed something. Try as she might, she couldn't reach the walkie with her left hand, and each time she tried, the lean to the right produced such an immense pain that her vision went black. Each lean saw crimson squirt down into her lap, but she continued to try. Even mid-blackout she worried Reyes would become just like the officer from her childhood.

Her world permanently faded as the house echoed with an incredible bang.

Thunder.

Part II:

Height of the Storm

Ch 12

Colossal Step Back

I

Reyes stood in the downpour, the wind whipping so hard the rain was practically sideways. He had retrieved a new pack of cigarettes from his car, the other having been soaked and crushed in the struggle. He had a lit cigarette between his lips, and he was taking deeper drags than breaths. This had led him to vomit twice since exiting the house, but he was sure he was fine. He'd just overexerted himself.

Tears mixed with the rain running down his face, but he didn't care. Williams—Abby—had been unresponsive, out cold. He'd feared she was gone. The paramedics had pulled her away before he could even say goodbye. What he really had wanted was to get in the ambulance with her, but he knew he couldn't. Goshen PD was called in, and a call was placed to the chief. Williams and Reyes technically weren't supposed to be there. A murder investigation allowed them to conduct interviews wherever they needed, but apparently the chief had no qualms with being loud and clear on the fact that he had tried to rein them in.

He couldn't exactly complain about it either, the chief wasn't wrong. If he had answered the walkie, if he hadn't nodded along and enlisted in Williams' crusade...maybe she'd still be by his side. This wasn't her fault though; he'd never blame her. The fault was his own, and he'd have to live with that.

Reyes keeled over, vomiting again, and reeling from everything that had just befallen them. He let his sobbing slowly bleed into his body-shaking retching. Williams had said that the murder had just happened. Reyes had agreed, and still he wasn't alert enough to catch the killer before he got to Williams.

He had the experience. *He* should have been ready.

II

Chief Carter had pulled up, police poncho on and eyes that looked ready to shoot fire. Instead, he had taken one look at the sorry state of Reyes and put him in a squad car to be taken home. He was mad, but he wasn't a monster, nor could he afford to lose officers—detectives especially—not in Cemetery.

He approached the officer in front of him, still needing to figure the situation out. "Hey, Chief Carter from Cemetery PD. What happened here?"

"Hey, Chief, I'm Officer Dumbauld. You may not remember me, but I actually came up at the same time as Reyes. Academy and everything together."

"Right, I remember," Carter said, though it was obvious he didn't. "And today?"

"Right, sorry. I responded to a call for two people snooping around a neighbor's house. When I got the address, I had a pretty good inkling to who it was. When I finally got here, the front door was locked, and nothing looked amiss. I honestly was close to responding that it was a prank call. The house was dark, but the entire street had lost power, so I hung around. I banged on the door a bit but didn't get an answer. When I heard a voice yelling from inside, I could tell it was Reyes. I kicked the door in, and when I got inside, I couldn't believe my eyes, man, I'm telling you." Dumbauld stammered the last part, clearly shaken.

"Yes, I can understand how that must have been, but please, cut out the personal commentary, we're in the pouring rain here."

"Sorry. So, anyway, when I stepped into the house, I entered a living room. Inside I saw the bloodied corpse of Mrs. Elton, Williams clutching her gut and looking not too far behind if I'm honest. In the hall, Reyes was fighting some muscle man. I called out to him, and he managed to kick the assailant off of him. When the guy got himself back off the floor, he had a kitchen knife in his hand. I called for him to stop, but he didn't, so I fired. He didn't drop until the fourth bullet hit him. Never seen anything like it."

"*Jesus*," Carter muttered under his breath, shaking his head and pinching the bridge of his nose. "It sounds like I owe you a thank you. I might have lost both of my detectives today if you hadn't arrived."

Dumbauld shook his head. "No thanks needed, sir. I only wish I'd been faster. Could have saved Williams from that brutal attack." He coughed, clearing his throat. "I'm thinking it would have been better if they had been faster too, no? Showed up while the damn murderer was still in the house! Another twenty minutes and they might have cut the bastard off."

"Imagine that."

Carter thanked him for his time and walked away. Although he didn't want to, he toured the murder scene himself. He took a few pictures and looked through some of the living room family photos. Pictures of the Eltons hung on the walls, now splattered with blood, but it was obvious the family had been close. Or at least portraying that fact on the walls of the home. He was having a little trouble connecting "a" to "b" when "a" was a loving family and seemingly normal middle-class home, and "b" was a troubled kid running with a crowd from Cemetery. Not that this was unheard of, though. His girlfriend Lizzy Bowman hadn't been a shining star by any means, but did young love have enough pull to redirect a good kid's life in such a big way?

If only they could see that route led to pain and death.

Chief Carter hung back for a bit longer, allowing the Goshen Police Department to do their work. He wanted answers but was unlikely to find them. This family was linked to the Cemetery murders, but the murderer here was mutilating victims with a chef's knife. None of his murders were like this. Not to mention the elephant in the room—blood. His victims were *absolutely bloodless*. Mutilated, true, but only on one specific part of the body—even if he wasn't sure what the specifics were at this point. This murderer was whipping blood about like some avant-garde psycho killer. This could lead to more problems than solutions, and Carter was out of time for either.

The problem was, no matter how much he wanted to wash his hands of it and walk away, this felt targeted, linked, intentional. He strained himself, mentally looking for the link, the key that would connect everything together. He didn't expect it to come wrapped in a pretty bow, but it would be nice. For once, something could be simple, right?

Pushing his phone into the crook of his shoulder, he listened to it ringing as he lowered himself into his car. He jumped down their throat the second the line connected. "This is *not* what we discussed."

III

Senior Detective Reyes poured over the police report Dick Dumbauld had forwarded him. He hadn't apologized for his comments and yelling, and he wouldn't, but he was glad the communication line was still open between them. He had to wonder if his comments weren't hitting home a little harder than expected right now. Was Dick blaming himself for this? First the son, now the parents. An entire family and family name wiped from the records of Goshen, from the face of the earth.

Morbidly, he reminded himself that none of them had been buried yet, so not *exactly* wiped from the face of the earth.

Reyes scoffed at himself. His feet were on his desk, he had a lit cigarette between his fingers, and he was drinking Evan Williams Bourbon straight from the bottle, knowing that drinking it down would lead to pain that he deserved all too well. Tears threatened to bat their way from his eyes, so he took another slug instead, blinking them away rapidly. He was trying to keep it together, but the self-blame was near crushing him now.

Why hadn't he forced his way onto the damn ambulance; why hadn't he insisted? Why did he take the easy way out and play distracted in the car instead of finally telling Williams the truth? *Fear. Pain. Desire to not see the inevitable, to not lose her too.*

Deep down Reyes knew that his job wasn't done, and even though he was hurting like hell, the department needed him to buckle down more than ever. You can't just bow out because of grief; you use it, pushing through the pain and fighting for a brighter outcome. Reyes wasn't sure that kind of thing was possible in Cemetery, but he'd do it for Abby Williams.

Poor Abby. He wished he could call her *kid* one more time, watch her face flush with anger, but something else, too. She liked it deep down, and he knew it. In a way, he had always viewed her as a kind of adopted child, or like he was a surrogate father. Not a replacement for Isabell, but a continuous reminder to the *good* that she was. Taking Williams under his wing was one of the few things to bring him joy in the bleakness that had become his life. He knew deep down he wouldn't have lasted these last few years without her. Not just having his back but bringing that deep belief in the role back to him.

He had never let her know it though, and he cursed himself for it now.

He smoked in silence, slugging randomly from the bottle of Bourbon. He stayed until he was ready to start swaying in his seat, wallowing in his misery.

A knock at the door was followed by the Chief sticking his head into the office.

"Come on, Reyes, I'm taking you home."

IV

Reyes awoke on his couch. Still fully clothed and with a ground-shattering quaking in his head. He smiled, stretching and welcoming the pain. It came in waves, like a floodgate opening, the stretch doing nothing but enhancing the yawning throb behind is temples.

He didn't recall getting home. He didn't recall getting on the couch. He didn't recall anything really. That was fine by him.

What wasn't fine by him was that he came home so drunk that he hadn't thought about the state he was in from the night before. The rain had tried its best, but he was still caked in blood from the crime scene. Some of it the Eltons', Williams', and even the killer's. His couch looked like its own murder scene now.

Perhaps he could auction it off to some horror nut somewhere, or else incinerate it.

He took every stitch of clothing on his body and put it into a garbage bag, shoes included. He couldn't believe the Chief had let him go around looking like that. The way he had been after the fact, though, it probably would have led to an explosive fight, perhaps even a physical one. Carter probably took the high road and let it be.

As he took the hottest shower he could stand, the previous day's nightmares came flooding back to him. He sobbed heavily, screaming out and welcoming the claws of grief.

How could he let this happen? He was better than this.

But was he? Hadn't Ed Reyes, the lead detective in Cemetery, New York, spent the last fifteen years being this exact kind of failure? Unable to save his dying daughter, unable to save his marriage as it held on by the very threads of grief? He may not have been a surgeon, a doctor, but he had—at least at one point—been a loving husband. Why hadn't that been enough to see the sorrow in his wife, to embrace the grief with her, rather than run away?

Hadn't he just continued to use the same techniques with Williams? A four-year degree and a top student of the academy—anyone would have been incredibly lucky to have her as a partner. Instead, he applied his brusque demeanor, his potty mouth, his know-it-all attitude to keep her at arm's length. Even though he saw the potential in her.

Coming up through the ranks when he did had been anything but easy. Doing so, and being Hispanic, was even harder. Especially when, coming on the force in the '90s, so many of the lead suspects looked like him. He had always kept his head down and looked for the facts, trying his best to create a better life for him and Maria. And in time, people learned, the racist comments *meant* as jokes lessened, but they were never truly gone, just bubbling under the surface. So when Williams was brought into his office, introduced as his new partner, the wide-eyed, bushy-tailed youth looking at him like he was the greatest thing in the world, he had trouble believing it.

Better to keep her at arm's length than to let her in. To fully care again.

And truly, what had that done for him? It hadn't even worked. With each day he saw more and more of his Isabell in her. Her undying light and good. Her unabashed idealism toward the force; towards a better future. He had fallen in love the same way he would have watching his own daughter grow up into an adult, and now, *again*, he had lost the chance to tell her.

As Reyes dried himself off and dressed, he called the Chief. Carter told him that there had been a call about suspicious activity last night and that he would text him an address. At the moment, the two departments were sharing information but investigating separately. Goshen PD felt that there wasn't any convincing evidence pointing to the crimes being linked, but that they'd continue searching. They were waiting on their own reports from the murders and investigating their own leads.

Carter was hopeful that this call of suspicious activity was linked to Ebony Bowman and the missing teacher. If they could somehow also find James, even better. He said the address he was sending over was for some house linked to a man who was seldom seen in Cemetery anymore. Colin Metlan, a businessman, was a property owner among other things, and spent most of his time in other countries, meaning the likelihood of the property being empty, and ripe for an undiscovered break in, was high. The Chief was hoping they had finally caught a break with the call in.

Reyes assured him he would head right over, and the Chief promised he would meet him there, as he was now down a partner—saying it was better if no one was alone right now. He opened a kitchen cabinet and grabbed a coffee cup and a pack of cigarettes from the box. As the coffee brewed, Reyes changed his mind, replacing the cigarette box and taking out the entire carton to bring to work with him. That was where he was at this month, so why the hell not?

He shoveled stale Cheerios into his mouth, spilling milk onto his brand-new shirt. At least this one fit. He shrugged, refusing to change, and headed for the door. As he locked the door, he lit a cigarette, inhaling deeply.

V

Senior Detective Reyes arrived at the given address. It was up a long private road off the main street through town. It opened up at the very end to a large house, far larger than most in Cemetery. It had four floors, beautifully tall windows and peaked roofs, reminding Reyes of this businessman's supposed wealth. When Reyes had thought to call the Chief back and ask what the caller had said was suspicious, he told him the neighbors had simply said someone coming and going a couple of times had been enough. The house was mostly vacant, save for a groundskeeper who came weekly, and the neighbors knew his vehicle.

The place loosely reminded Reyes of the Old Mayor's Mansion right outside of town, but smaller, though probably not by much. It instantly gave him the creeps. The brief feeling of kenopsia overtook him as he imagined the lives that were once lived here, now moved on.

There wasn't a car in the circular driveway, but the neighbors did say they had called after seeing the car leaving. Maybe he had made it just in time. They had reached out to the owner, who was apparently in Germany according to his assistant, but they hadn't gotten a hold of him. His assistant assured them the owner wouldn't mind them entering, especially because they were doing him a favor checking the place out.

Reyes popped the car door and stepped out. He wore a brown coat over his stained shirt, the October wind still blowing in an unforgiving torrent, regardless of the rain subsiding. His cigarette, perfectly placed at the corner of his lips, wasn't in danger of going anywhere, but the wind made it burn twice as fast. Thankfully he had taken the carton after all.

Reyes was still under the impression that James Rictor had just gotten out of Dodge. Whether it was to avoid more interrogation or to get away from his father, Reyes wasn't sure. Taking in the house before him though, he had to admit this would be a rather luxurious way to lay low.

Reyes stood in the wind a couple minutes longer, smoking and awaiting Chief Carter's arrival. When it got to around the ten-minute mark, and Reyes was on his third cigarette, he figured the Chief was caught up elsewhere.

Where the hell is he?

As Reyes approached the front door, he saw nothing out of the ordinary. There was nothing indicating forced entry—no broken windows, no caved-in door, no footprints indicating use around the porch. With yesterday's storm, Reyes remembered the squelching steps he had taken at the back of the Elton's house, how unavoidable the tracks would be. If the neighbors were correct, someone had been coming in and out of here, often, so no footprints were awfully strange.

Reyes clicked on the flashlight he had taken from the car. He headed back down the porch and around the side of the house. The house sat on a beautiful property, with the trees and bushes kept back by active landscaping. The house had more of the tall windows around the side, which should have given Reyes a clear view into the house, if it weren't for the fact it was pitch black. Reyes stopped in his tracks and imagined what a killer, or even a lowly window-shopping-creep, could witness through these windows. The amount that could be seen through them with some lighting would be astounding. He could barely imagine what size curtains would be needed to cover them, but he knew it'd be expensive.

Reyes passed his flashlight over the center window and stopped, frozen. For a split second he thought he had seen a leg stepping off the staircase, but that couldn't be right, could it? The cigarette dropped from his lips, and he took a shaky breath, blood pounding in his ears at the spike in his heartrate.

He had startled himself, that was all. He pointed the flashlight left and right—there was nothing there. He was seeing ghosts.

Get it together, man. Turn your back on Williams just to start doing the same? He took a deep breath in, held it, and then released. If he continued thinking like that, he wouldn't be able to reel it in.

As Reyes rounded the back of the house, he gave the backyard an admiring glance. It was wide open and spacious, with a firepit, inground pool, and a tennis court. The woods had been cut back in a perfect square that must have cost a pretty penny to manage. What exactly did this business guy do? Reyes had obviously spent the last twenty or so years in the wrong profession.

Twenty years and all it had gotten him was a sickening nicotine addiction, a newly ruined couch, and a butchered partner. He was allowed to be bitter. He was allowed to second guess. He was allowed to be in pain. And that was only touching on the professional issues. The rest he couldn't blame on work, but he was just as bitter.

The porch led up to a beautifully decked area. The back door was one of the double-sliding glass types. It stuck out in great contrast to the Elton's that he had passed through just yesterday. He found himself hoping this wouldn't be some kind of fancy repeat to what he had lived through last night. However, without Williams here, it meant that he was the one to go, and that struck as alright with him.

He flashed the light around the sliding glass door, approaching close enough to lean in, covering his eyes to see past the glare. The inside of the house was immaculate, but he figured that was a result of the weekly groundskeeper visits or something similar. A guy this wealthy could pay to keep an untouched house livable; could afford to travel to the house at any unannounced minute.

Reyes jumped back, dropping the flashlight and falling on his ass.

He thought he had seen...but it couldn't have been...a face in the dark?

You've got to be kidding me, Reyes thought. *It's an empty fucking house!*

Reyes picked himself up and brushed the back of his pants off. He lit another cigarette, smoke billowing around his head in great puffs before being swept away in the wind. He headed around the other side of the house, still cursing to himself.

This side of the house was practically identical to the other. Large windows cut straight through to the other side. With a bit of light, he was certain you could see everything inside. It felt almost purposefully dark inside, perhaps they were tinted? The only difference on this side was a small window and vent cut into the foundation, which probably led to the basement. The vent itself did look a bit jostled, out of place. He wrote it off as it wasn't the size of a full-grown person anyway. He took a few pictures of it, not that his old flip phone would do it any justice, but at least he could file it away that he had checked.

He texted the pictures to Carter and told him it was nothing, probably just some Cemetery kids playing a prank. He sent another to say he was headed back in, and for the Chief to not bother coming. He didn't wait for an answer.

As he continued around, he decided to reapproach the front door. He flicked his cigarette away before climbing the porch steps. He knocked hard, rang the doorbell, and called, "Cemetery PD—if you're in there open up!"

For the briefest moment he thought he heard someone approach the door from the inside. When no answer came, he knocked again, hard. "Police, open up! We got a call about some suspicious activity around the place. If you're the owner of this property simply open up and tell me to fuck off and I'll be on my merry way."

Reyes looked around the side of the house again. He really had thought he heard something. Just as he was about to turn and leave, the front door pulled open and a pale hand reached out from the depths of the dark, pulling him in.

Ch 13

Waking Nightmare

I

Williams lay on a bed that could have passed for concrete. Her eyes fluttered and tried to remain open. They felt heavy, the lids gunky and sticky. Her vision was blurry to the point of remaining out of focus, even though they were fully open now. The room was dark, no lights, save for the light bleeding in from the open door that led out to a white hallway. She couldn't think straight, but her mind settled on two facts—it was *night*, and this was a *hospital*.

She tried to ease herself into a sitting position and found that she couldn't. She struggled for a moment, blinking rapidly, before realizing there was a pale hand, positioned between her collarbone and left breast, which was applying the pressure that kept her still. It wasn't enough pressure to hold a full-grown adult down though, not usually. That sick bastard at the Elton's must have really worked her over good. The problem was she couldn't feel any pain, like being in a waking dream. Aside from being pressed to the bed, she felt like she was floating, weightless. Boundless.

The hand was reaching out from a black sleeve, loose, like that of a robe. As she looked ever higher, something that was causing her undue strain, her eyes finally alighted on a pale, sickly looking face. One with...*fangs* descending from its mouth...ears that ended in a *point*?

"I told you I'd remember you," it hissed in a silken voice.

Williams screamed to high heaven, blacking out.

II

Williams awoke again briefly, this time finding that her eyes wouldn't come unglued no matter how hard she tried. Her breathing felt as if it was blocked. She choked and found that she couldn't scream. She struggled as hard as she could, and when she found hands on her, pressing her down, she fought ever harder.

All she could think, over and over, was the voice saying, *"I told you I'd remember you."*

Williams struggled like her life depended upon it. It did.

Tears streamed from the creases in her eyes. Pure terror flooded her as blood pounded sickening waves through her ears. She felt tingling numbness start from the top of her head down to the bottom of her toes. The feeling of panic as it fully infects your blood. It felt like at any second her heart would burst; it beat such a sickening rhythm.

A machine off in some corner started bleeping a warning.

She felt a prick at the base of her neck, her brain screaming "*needle!*" and urging her to fight harder. Her last thought as she drifted off was that she would soon be joining the most recent victims of Cemetery.

III

Williams found herself waking gradually. First conscious thought, then awareness of the outside world. She heard the beep of the machines beside her; she heard people walking past and speaking quietly among themselves.

Hospital. She at least had gotten that part correct.

This time, when her eyes fluttered open, they stayed that way. With some tear-filled rapid blinking, the blurriness slowly began to fade.

Just as she was about to see clearly, she heard someone, or something, breathing. She tugged at her restraints, fearing it was the pale figure back again. Her heartrate was about to rocket to all new heights when she heard a soothing voice say, "Abigail, ma'am, everything is okay."

It sounded nothing like the weird voice in the dark. The stark contrast shook her out of her panic.

Williams looked around, trying to see who was in the room with her. It was a nurse. Just a nurse. A middle-aged woman in purple scrubs, her brown hair graying at the roots and pulled into a tight bun. Her face was stern, but not without warmth. A name badge attached to her shirt read "Trudy." Williams let go of the breath she had been holding in, so ready to scream again. She took another deep one, trying to steady herself.

As she tried to sit up, the nurse stepped forward and held a hand on her shoulder. "Abigail, ma'am, you've got to calm down and sit still, please," the woman pleaded.

"Abby...*just* Abby, please," Williams replied, looking down at herself. "Wait, why am I literally strapped down to this hospital bed?"

Trudy looked uncomfortable, but this probably wasn't anything new for her. "You kept waking up, screaming and thrashing, trying to strike anyone near you. You had to be sedated several times and when you kept straining to the point of popping your stitches...the doctors decided to keep you in a sedated state." Her voice trailed off. Williams had a sneaking suspicion she wasn't supposed to be the one to tell her that.

"You guys knocked me out? Jesus, there's a murder investigation going on. How long?" Williams looked distraught. "How long?"

"Eight days, ma'am."

"Eight days?" Williams was furious. "Do you even know what happened to me, where I came from that day? Oh my God, is my partner even alive?"

Williams let out a frustrated groan that drew the attention of the doctor passing in the hall. As she entered, Williams was a sight to see. Her hair was tangled, sticking up at odd angles, and was a sweaty mess. Her eyes were bloodshot; black bags underneath them looked puffy enough to pop. The left corner of her mouth, the side she was leaning forward toward, was losing a battle against a stream of drool and spit, her secured arms keeping her from wiping herself dry.

"Hello, Ms. Williams, I'm Dr. Chen. I've been overseeing you for the last nine days. What seems to be the matter?" Dr. Chen was a lean woman of probably forty-five years. She was on the taller side and wore glasses. She had a black blouse beneath the standard white coat.

"That is exactly my problem, Doctor," Williams replied. "The fact that you've had me sedated for over eight days. Yes, that's a little alarming to me."

"Frankly Ms. Williams, it was all we could do to get you to stop struggling. You opened your stitches three times. They were rather hard to get in there the original time, too, unfortunately. You are incredibly lucky to be alive."

I almost died? Williams thought, *what about Reyes?*

Williams straightened, losing steam. If she had really been such a nuisance, her anger should be pointed inward, not at these people. "What about my partner? Senior Detective Reyes? Did Reyes make it? Did you see an Ed Reyes?" Williams was almost pleading.

"No, Ms. Williams, I'm sorry, I can't help you there. To my knowledge, no one entered the hospital with that name. I can double check for you, but I'm the current trauma surgeon on, so I would know about it if they did." Dr. Chen stepped closer, the clipboard in her hand finally coming into perfect focus for Williams. "You really need to rest, okay? Your body has taken a real beating. It's withstood an unbelievable amount of damage. To your left is a morphine drip. If your pain gets unbearable, press the button. It'll release a dose and help you sleep. I can release the restraints, but your right arm is in a cast and needs to remain immobilized."

Williams was stunned. Absolutely silenced. As the doctor released the restraints and told the nurse to have the chief of police notified of Williams' waking, she just stared blankly at the ceiling above where she lay.

Reyes never came in through the ER, but *dead bodies* never do.

IV

Williams woke up more than a little groggy. If she was honest, she'd hit the morphine button more times than she'd care to admit. She'd needed it and she still had trouble sleeping, suffering from what would be referred to as "tossing and turning" if her arm hadn't been immobilized the entire night. It was terribly uncomfortable, and the pain had remained extreme.

Now she sat propped up, a nurse helping to secure a pillow or two behind her back. Her stomach throbbed, but she wanted to be cognizant for the chief's visit.

She shoveled the horrid lime Jell-O into her mouth. She wanted nothing more than to throw it out, but she needed to prove she could eat and keep food down before getting discharged. She was still hooked up to various machines, a bag of liquid hung above her. She wasn't going to be at a disadvantage by not doing what she was told.

Williams found herself laughing, the slight jiggling of her body hurting her immensely. The anxious pit, then knot—then gaping hole—in her stomach over the last three weeks had become literal. A knot of stitches and rippled skin.

Despite the laugh, Williams was uneasy again. She still didn't know what to feel and think about Chief Carter. He had been acting weird, becoming increasingly rash. More aggravated, more aggressive. There was that weirdness with Evan Rictor, the added evidence sheet to the missing person's file. He had also tried to tell them they couldn't do a wellness check on the Eltons, right after whatever weird performance Brennan and Shotz had put on. It was like he was purposefully halting their progress.

Williams spooned the last of the Jell-O into her mouth as someone knocked at her hospital door. A different nurse from the one last night opened the door. She led in Chief Carter, stopping to ask if Williams needed anything before retrieving her tray and leaving.

Carter appeared pale, like he hadn't slept in weeks. His hair was still meticulously parted, but his eyes were dark and circled, almost purple. He looked like he had five o'clock shadow at eleven in the morning.

"Damn, Chief, who got stabbed, me or you?" Williams broke the ice. "You look terrible."

"Yes, thank you for that," Carter replied, already annoyed. He moved closer to the hospital bed. "How are you doing?"

"I've been better, honestly. They knocked me out for eight days and I still feel like death." Williams chuckled despite herself. "They told me I almost died, so I guess that tracks."

"About that, Williams. I never wanted this to happen. If I had thought trying to call you back would have pushed you on harder, well I would have sent a squad car after you two instead. I just...had a bad feeling about it, I guess. Sounds stupid I know," Carter finished.

"A bad feeling about it?"

"Yes, just out of nowhere, like I couldn't shake it," Carter replied.

Williams repositioned herself on the bed, or at least attempted to. She did it so that the Chief couldn't see her face. Her entire career she had worked under Carter as the chief of police. He had never once uttered something remotely superstitious. A feeling? She'd bet anything he was lying.

What the hell is going on?

"Chief, I almost died in the Elton's house, because I couldn't see with the power out. I let my past slow me down, and I let myself become distracted. This is my fault and I know it. I should have been sharper; better. I get that. But where is Reyes, and why will nobody talk to me about him?"

Carter sighed, running a hand down his face. "A lot is going on at the department right now, Williams. I'm sorry for the lack of communication, but you were sedated, and I swear I came as soon as they let me know you weren't. The FBI have officially moved in, and both of my detectives being out of commission isn't helping my case. It's—"

Williams cut him off. "So Reyes *is* hurt? What happened?"

"Senior Detective Reyes was fine after the Elton's. Some minor bruising and scrapes. But fine," Carter paused. "Physically that is, I suppose. As the paramedics rushed you out, they refused to let him come with you. He was so certain you didn't make it that he took it hard. So hard. We didn't have any information to tell him anything to the contrary either yet..."

Carter stared off, stricken.

"But what about after? I was sedated for eight days, no one told him?" Williams asked. Then it finally hit her. "You said *both* were out of commission, where is he? What the fuck happened to Reyes, Carter?"

Oh god, Williams thought, *if this is my fault, I'll lose it. How is it not my fault?*

The Chief turned back towards her. "Reyes was amped up, drinking as he does, but throw grief into the mix, and he went off the rails. We got a call that became a lead. I told him I would meet him there, that he shouldn't proceed alone under any circumstances. He didn't listen. He drove himself from his house, but he never stopped at the precinct. There was nothing I could do. I got there too late." He shook his head, looking genuinely upset about what happened. "By the time we got to the scene, his car was there, but he wasn't. Simply...gone. I still don't know what happened. We forced entry to the house, but it was empty...not even a single clue. It was like he was never there at all."

"When?"

"Excuse me?" Carter asked.

"When did it happen, Chief?"

"Eight days ago, now, the morning after the Elton's house. We've been searching for him ever since. His car was still in the driveway, a carton of cigarettes on the passenger seat, the thermal mug of coffee he had taken from his house was still hot...it just feels—"

"*Off*," Williams offered. "Like something isn't right."

Chief Carter glared at Williams like he was ready to reprimand her instead of agreeing, but his phone buzzed in his pocket, and he pulled it out instead.

"Chief, the same person, the same thing, that was inside my house came for me here. I woke up...I-I saw them with my own eyes. He was touching me, or *it* was touching me. Holding me down. It looked like a monster; a pale, sickly thing. It said, *"I told you I'd remember you"* in this hissing, silky voice, unlike anything I've ever heard. It came for me, Carter, because I got away."

Carter put his phone back in his pocket, turning his attention back to Williams. His stare was daggers. "You almost bled to death, Williams. The amount of morphine and other drugs in your system could have taken out an elephant. The doctor told me that a little to the left, or right for that matter, and you would have been dead. You lucked out because your assailant used brutality and strength instead of aim and brains. It was a one-off chance..." He paused, breathing, "not that we aren't happy about that part...obviously. But what I'm saying is, there's absolutely no way that anything you saw was real. The nurses and doctors had to hold you down, literally restraining you. Every time you woke you screamed and clawed at them. Your imagined monster couldn't have come that many times—couldn't have gotten in at all for that matter. Do you know where you are?'

"Uh, a hospital, clearly?"

"Yes, obviously, but think of where you are from—Cemetery. One of the closest, and best hospitals in the area, is St. Luke's in Newburgh. There is a literal Newburgh PD detail on the building. Now, I find it hard to believe that they would let a monster come traipsing through, coming after near-death patients, right?" Carter said, smiling at her as you would a small child. "Would *you* let a random '*pale, sickly thing*' come through the doors?"

Williams took a breath and thought. Her first desire was to swing at the Chief, even though she was right-handed, and her arm was casted and immobilized. Her second thought was to spit at him in rage, but that was unhinged. She was just so sick of people telling her to calm down, that she didn't see what she saw, that she couldn't be right, she was seeing things. So tired of feeling like the door mat that everyone walked across whenever they needed a pick me up. It needed to end. She knew what she saw, as clear as day—she would bet on it. Not that it was a bet she wanted to win...but if you couldn't trust your own eyes, what could you trust?

"I know what I saw, Chief. Don't give me the same spiel you gave me in my house. I won't have anyone telling me I'm seeing ghosts, I'm pointing at nothing in the dark, okay? Just leave it," Williams said, a slight edge to her voice that could be a threat as much as a plea. It was a start.

Carter looked like he could scream. His eyes were blazing fires. He took a few angry steps toward the room's window, looking out. "I just got notice that the perp from the Elton's has been identified. He was some nobody that used to work for Elton, a warehouse worker type. It ended badly, and apparently, he couldn't let it go. It was a motivated, premeditated event. Our case is completely unrelated. This all could have been avoided if you both had just *listened* to me. Now I'll have to clean up by myself." He turned, walking toward the door.

"Chief, what day is it? When can I get the hell out of here," Williams asked.

"It's October the twenty-fourth, and the doctors aren't sure. They said that because of the number of times you tore the stitching open your body might reject the healing more than usual. It's not like you're ready for active duty anyway, Detective Williams."

With that, Carter left without another word.

"October 24th?" Williams groaned, throwing her head back against the pillows. She felt like she had missed the entire month. "I need to get the hell out of this bed."

As Williams finally succumbed to the pain, she pressed the morphine button a couple of times, immediately beginning to drift off. As she slipped into a fitful sleep, she found herself wondering if the hospital window could open wide enough to fit a fully grown person.

"*I told you I'd remember you,*" replayed in her mind.

Ch 14

Escaping

I

WILLIAMS SAT UP IN her hospital bed. Three days had passed, but she was still on lime Jell-O. Truth be told, she didn't even like lime. She shoveled it down anyway—no use complaining at this point. She'd spent the first two days in a morphine dream, but the third day she spent weaning herself off it, requesting Advil and Tylenol instead if she could stand it. She wanted to appear strong, ready to go.

The third day—spent in more pain than she cared to admit—had left her with plenty of time to think. She knew what she had seen, what she had felt. Yet when she let her mind wander, she had to wonder if maybe she was just losing it. The strain had been piling on; that much she could admit.

Today, Williams' mother was coming. She had said the only way she would bring work clothes was if Williams also accepted sweatpants and a t-shirt. She'd reluctantly agreed, knowing full well there was no way she wouldn't go straight to work regardless.

In a way, she lived for it. The hunt. The ability to connect the dots. The ability to enable real change. To save people. A chance to prove herself.

Now she might be the only one who could save her partner. Save Reyes. Come hell or high water, she would do whatever it took.

An hour later her mother arrived. She had a bag, presumably filled with loungewear, and a set of hangers covered in the plastic the laundromat used. Williams had a standard for work: dark blue, grey or black slacks, a button-down or blouse on top, usually white, but always a solid color. Sometimes a blazer too, but she usually didn't go full pantsuit. Williams smiled, mostly for her mother…but also for the work clothes.

Their relationship was tenuous at best. The proverbial nail in the coffin, the driving force between them, had always been her father. While the outcome of the stakeout—which had been a colossal screw up—had always somehow fell on Williams' shoulders, at least within her own mind, a part of her had never truly been able to detach her mother from the incident. Why hadn't she stopped him; why hadn't she protected her daughter?

The fact they had a relationship at all was because her father pleaded with her, taking all the blame and assuring little Abby that her mother wasn't involved at all. While she had never fully been able to break away from her adoration for her father, it had been a long and winding road back with her mother.

Williams knew it was unfair, but it also was what it was.

"Hi, my love, you look well today," Elinor Williams said, approaching the bed and trying to kiss Williams on the cheek. She was a short woman, possibly an inch or two taller than Williams. She was thin, lacking the muscular build of her daughter.

As Williams looked at her mother, she realized that time was catching up to her. The crows feet around her eyes had deepened, and her hair was a decided grey now. She knew it had been a while since they had seen each other last, but Williams was embarrassed at how long.

"Hi, Mom. Thanks for stopping at my house before coming," Williams said, surprised to find she meant it.

"It was nothing dear, I was just glad to get your call. I'm so sorry this happened to you. Don't wait for near-death situations to call your mother!" she chided. "I know we've struggled, but you're all I've got. I want to be around more, now more than ever."

"You're right, Mom, I won't," Williams replied. She bit absentmindedly at her left thumb while her cheeks slightly burned. Truth be told she had missed the woman; she was her mother after all. It was just the poor nature of her parents' split. Even though he was definitely in the wrong, her father had stepped up, her mother...hadn't. Even now that Williams could see her immaturity, her mother had backed off, backed away, rather than fight for her place. It had left a wound all its own.

As an adult, it was important to remember her mother was a person as well. She was also going through it. Almost losing her daughter, and on top of that, never being able to look at her husband the same way again. It had to be a lot.

They sat awkwardly for a few minutes. Williams still picking at her thumb, her mother fussing over the state of the room. Elinor straightened the visitor chair in the corner, swatting nonexistent dust from the window shades, all while Williams watched and thought. Neither one of them could ever sit still. The thought warmed Williams a bit. Even through time and space, Williams was still so similar to her mother. Those similarities were not lost on her, as they were so unlike her father. Perhaps a part of her knew that moving forward, that being stronger, more persistent, started here with her mother. Moving on.

She had to laugh—even bedridden from a gut wound, her mother could still be embarrassed over the state of the room. A hospital room no less. The mess was mostly Jell-O cups and gauze packaging anyway, nothing to be ashamed of.

Her mother got caught up in her laughter, giggling and then guffawing herself. Williams laughed until she couldn't breathe, entirely sure she was going to split a stitch again. She held her stomach and laughed. It felt good to let go.

The laughing shakes turned into a breathless sob. Her mother grasped her as tightly as she could while being gentle, and Williams let the dam shatter into a million pieces. There's something so rare, so intangible, about the presence of a mother. Emotionally freeing, healing, even after a lengthy distance.

"I thought I was dead," Williams whispered, her voice barely escaping over the sounds from down the hall. "And still, my partner may be dead because of me."

Elinor Williams caressed her daughter's hair and shushed her. "It's okay, honey. It's all okay."

Williams sobbed into her mother for several minutes before breaking away. "I just have this feeling about the case. Nothing is connecting, and everything feels *off*. Yet no one believes me. The Chief thinks I'm going crazy. My partner even doubts me. And *god*, now he's gone. Maybe I am going crazy…I'm losing it and if I wasn't—if I wasn't, Reyes wouldn't have been alone the day he was taken. He might still be alive."

"Now you listen to me right now. We may not have seen much of each other lately, but if there's one thing I know, it's that you are too steady on your feet, too hardheaded, to go crazy over a single case. Your gut's never been wrong. What's it telling you?"

"Fuck…I don't know anymore, Mom," Williams said, sniffling.

"Well, get your head in the game, baby, you've got this," her mother said, cheering her on. "And watch your language."

II

The last thing Williams' mother brought for her was a new iPhone. The Chief said that hers was evidenced and blood-soaked, so she hadn't argued. She would have been without one for days otherwise. Even in and out of pain and sleep, that's a lot of time to have nothing to do.

Her calls and texts were long gone though, so she had no idea what had stolen her attention the day she was stabbed. Part of her wanted to know just so she could punch them in the face for it.

But deep down she knew the fault laid with her.

With so much time on her hands, Williams had spent a lot of it speaking to Katherine. They texted back and forth for days, their tone growing ever more flirtatious. Part of Williams felt guilty about it, but she just needed *something*.

Tangible, something she could feel. Katherine was just so easy to talk to, keeping the conversation going even when there wasn't much left to say. And Williams was surprised that she wanted it to keep going.

After her mother left, she finally replied to another text. Katherine sent several long, fully capitalized texts filled with punctuation and emojis when Williams told her what had happened. She wanted to visit, but Williams was more interested in getting out.

Be right there, Katherine wrote. Williams smiled, figuring she was just trying to kid around and be cute, but deep down she hoped she was serious.

I better clean up then, Williams texted back. **No one knows I'm leaving. I'm still glued to this damn bed.**

Katherine sent back a screen cap of her Google Maps pulled up for the hospital, making the joke a reality.

Williams sprang up, or attempted to, as her arm was still immobilized in a sort-of tray contraption. The nurses had wheeled it in after she had woken up, enabling her to sit up and lie back on her own by adjusting the level of the tray. Williams had paid very close attention to how they hooked her into it.

In a matter of minutes, she released herself, her elbow bending in ways she hadn't felt in too long. Her arm was in a hard cast, but somehow it still felt swollen—the entire thing hanging at odds with her body, feeling four times the weight it usually did. The doctor said the attack had sliced through something vital, a tendon or muscle, she couldn't quite remember which. She was still doped up at that point. Regardless, the doctor said the cast was necessary for the time being. As long as she could move around and get out, she didn't really care about wearing a cast.

Williams shuffled to the edge of the bed, each move making her gut feel hot and tight, like stretching too much with not enough skin. *Literally*, she thought. She tentatively pushed her feet against the floor. Even with her short period at the hospital, the floor against her feet felt almost foreign. She slowly leaned off the corner of the bed, allowing her feet to take on more and more of her weight.

Eventually, what felt like an eternity later, Williams stood up fully. She edged her way toward the door. There was a nurse's desk a little down the hall to the right, but no one was behind it. They were probably making their evening rounds.

The main desire in Williams' head was to fully clean herself. The first day into her convalescence, a male nurse had come in with a tray of warm water to clean her as if she were a small child, impudent and hiding from their mother at bath time. She had tried to punch him, but her left-handed swing and morphined mind were sloppy. The following day, a female nurse had come in, aiming to do the same, but hoping for a different outcome. Williams tried again and failed, but the second attempt at assault ended the debacle.

Williams shuffled into the bathroom and turned the shower on. She dropped her hospital gown and stared down at herself. She looked gaunter than ever. The same way she had felt before showering the morning after her home was invaded. She wanted nothing more than to stand and soak inside the hot shower, washing away everything that had happened to her. Looking down, she saw the jagged knot of stitches along her abdomen, several inches long. The skin was still an angry red, but at the very least, no longer puffy. She wondered how many stitches there were; how many from the assailant, how many from her tearing them multiple times over.

How many more could be inside?

A whipgraft delusion shook her entire being. The person in the hospital mirror surely couldn't be her. In just nine days, she had become someone she didn't even recognize. She had to slow her heartrate with deep breaths, taking in the bloodshot eyes and hollowed cheeks. She wouldn't look away.

She knew that a shower was off the table for now. Instead, she grabbed a washcloth and soaked it under the showerhead with her left hand. She didn't even have soap, she realized, so she rubbed the steaming washcloth rigorously over the parts of her body she could reach. It felt silly, embarrassing, and more than a little aggravating to be so helpless, but there was nothing else for it. Finally, she leaned to the left and soaked her hair in the hot water. It felt amazing, but she would have signed a contract with Satan for some shampoo.

She stood there, awkwardly hobbled to her left side and soaking her hair until a knock startled her. It couldn't be Katherine so soon...unless her head had been in the shower for far longer than she thought. She grabbed the two towels the hospital bathroom had to offer. Wrapped her hair in one, and her body in the other. The bathroom floor was absolutely drenched, but she didn't really have a choice. She stuck her towel-wrapped head out of the bathroom door to see Dr. Chen waiting by the bed.

"Oh, hi, Doctor," Williams said.

"Ms. Williams, I hope you weren't attempting to shower your stitches too?"

"No. I didn't get them wet," Williams replied.

"I'm glad to hear it. Come over to the bed, I'll clean and bandage them," Dr. Chen said, motioning toward the hospital bed.

"Um, can I not be naked first?" Williams asked.

"Of course," Dr. Chen nodded, "I'll go grab some things and come back in a few minutes."

Williams shut the door completely. She took her time, as her one intact arm necessitated, and gave the rest of her body a thorough drying. She hated slipping into clean clothes while still wet, but she knew there were places right now she simply couldn't reach. She took the bag her mother left for her from the small closet, unzipping it on top of the bed.

Williams sighed. It was already well into the evening. She had work clothes and sweatpants, and she unfortunately wouldn't be getting into work, as much as she wanted to. She found that one handing her way into a pair of underwear was one of the more uncomfortable things she had ever done. Until, of course, it came time to slide on a sports bra. She pulled on the sweats, giving in to fate, and struggled her way into a pair of socks. She pulled out the tee shirt but figured the bra would suffice until the doctor's work was done.

When the knock came at the door, she was ready.

The doctor worked meticulously, taking the time to show Williams what to do and how to do it. "Clean around the stitches lightly with the soap I'm going to give you. It's scent free so it shouldn't irritate. If the stitches themselves are scabby or gunky, you can wash them gently with the soap as well, but don't scrub them at all. Do not use topical cleaners as it can affect the healing of the skin. Don't scratch them, and do not open them again, do you understand?"

"Yes," Williams answered breathlessly, the bruised skin around the stitches pulling and screaming with every touch. "You sound like a school principal or something."

"This is very serious, Detective," Dr. Chen said, her voice stern. "I usually let the stitches breath for a bit and air dry, or you can lightly pat it with a clean paper towel before replacing the bandaging. With your line of work, I figure you might as well keep covering them for now. Here, this bag is some soap and bandages for you to take."

"Wait, you're just going to let me leave?"

"You've been talking about getting out of here since the second you woke up. As soon as I saw you out of the bed, I knew you'd be going. I'd rather you be prepared than end up back in here. You should be fine. Keep that cast dry and do not use the arm as much as possible," Dr. Chen said. She was an astute woman. "Are you getting picked up or do you have a car?"

"Someone is on their way."

"Good, I'll go let the desk know so they get sent up immediately. Be careful Ms. Williams."

"Thank you, Doctor," Williams replied. "And I'm sorry for being such a hassle."

She thought back over the last couple of days. She knew she was lucky to be alive. If luck was involved, that was. She had made it through quite the ordeal and the worst part was that it wasn't over yet. Her mission was twofold now. She had to stop this serial killer and bring them to justice, and she had to bring Reyes back—*alive*, no matter the cost.

In a matter of minutes, Katherine turned up, stepping into her hospital room. She was so caught up in her thoughts, she hadn't thought to put the tee shirt on, and was sitting there in her sports bra still. Her cheeks turned cherry red, and in her haste to cover up, she reached for the shirt with the wrong arm.

Wincing aloud did nothing to remove the color from her cheeks.

Katherine's eyes roved her body for a second longer than they should of. She blushed too, looking away. "Hi, Abby. Your ride is here, but it seems like they ruined our great escape."

III

Williams had insisted on going to the precinct for her gun. She hadn't given it much thought beforehand, or she would have put on the work clothes. She wasn't being irrational or illogical. First the murders, then the home invasion, the attempted murder at the Elton's, and the visit in the night at the hospital.

No, she wasn't overthinking.

Katherine had entered like a knight in shining armor—carrying everything of Williams'—except the shine was from the two of them blushing like mad.

Williams asked her to wait outside while she ran inside the precinct. She had hobbled through the front door, hoping to avoid detection. The second she entered the door, one of the desk attendants called out her name, surprised at seeing her, or surprised at how messed up she looked. The bags under her eyes hadn't lightened up any.

Her desires at stealth were over in seconds. She had missed the arrival of the FBI. Practically seizing control of the precinct, they had made it their home base. The entrance was packed. She wasn't used to seeing so many people up front at once. There appeared to be nine agents in total, or at the least, there were nine still working tonight. They set up shop right in the entryway, shoving desks off to the left and right so they had somewhere to work.

Williams was surprised to see them so active even so late into the night. She tried her best to hustle, grabbing her gun from lock up, as well as an additional box of hollow points.

She couldn't bring herself to go to their office, to see the leftovers, to feel the absence of Reyes. She couldn't. But as she headed back to the entrance of the precinct, a stern-looking woman motioned her over.

She was standing next to a police officer that Williams recognized. Officer Prescott was an average-sized man with a nose that looked like it had seen its fair share of playground fights. He made the introduction. "This is FBI Special Agent Gianna Colfax. I've been appointed as a kind of liaison, at least for the time being, as I actually went to the academy with her before moving back home. Chief figures it'll smooth the process."

She was a brusque and formidable-looking woman; her shoulder length hair was black and straight as a blade. She had high cheekbones with a small mole under her left eye. She took Williams in in a sweeping glance. "I surmise from the getup and cast that your Carter's detective that was attacked?"

Williams wasn't entirely sure how to address her. She seemed like the pantsuit and brooding stare every day type of gal. "Uh- yes, ma'am. Detective Williams."

"The Chief said you and your partner decided to go a little rogue, to not listen to his summons. And nearly got yourselves killed for it, too."

Of course, Carter would start her off on the wrong foot with the person she'd be most likely working closely with in the coming days. "Well, no—that's not exactly how I remember it, ma'am."

"Look, I'm combing through every possible aspect of this thing, and mostly doing so on our own for now. I don't want the interference of any preconceived notions to get in the way of fresh eyes on this thing." Colfax, although speaking in a manner that matched her demeanor, was not coming off as a cold person. "But don't get too relaxed, as at some point I will be expecting a play by play of what you've got so far…looks like you could really use some sleep though. You've been through hell."

IV

As they pulled up in front of Williams' house, she quickly directed Katherine to keep driving, right on by. It didn't feel right. There was a squad car parked out front, which Carter had mentioned would be there, but was now making her uncomfortable. The police detail was nothing more than an additional layer of protection for her after the attack, standard issue, however she was so uncertain of who she could truly trust. That and the fact that the last time Katherine had dropped her off, some sicko had crept inside while she slept. She was almost afraid of entering.

Katherine must have seen the struggle on her face because she told her she was staying the night at her place in a tone that brooked no argument.

Katherine assured her the entire way that it was more than fine. Williams still felt on the fence about it, but not knowing where else she'd go, she accepted the offer. Katherine smiled, changing the radio station more than once, and grabbing Williams' hand to calm her. Williams first impulse was to pull away, but the soft skin of Katherine's right hand felt reassuring, so she let it lie, their palms eventually relaxing together.

Inside Katherine's apartment, Williams looked around and was interested to find a large number of frames around the walls: old family pictures, artwork, posters. She saw a few that were book-related as well. Which, from what she knew of Katherine, made a lot of sense.

The apartment itself was small, a living room that ate up half the kitchenette, a hallway to the right with just enough room for a bathroom door before bleeding into the bedroom. The exact layout Williams had come to know from the apartments inside and around Cemetery. Probably costs a shiny penny or two, too. When rent had gotten over fifteen hundred a month, Williams had said "screw it" and started the mortgage application.

Katherine stepped into the kitchenette and turned towards her, holding her arms out in mock entrance. "So, this is it," she said, blushing. "The lavish lifestyle of a librarian."

"It's awesome," Williams assured her.

"I've actually just changed the sheets, so the bedroom's all set for you," Katherine said, motioning toward the hall. "I'll be right here on the couch if you need anything. The bathroom is right there, and if you're hungry we can order something...I've only got popcorn."

"I actually love popcorn."

"Want to make a couple bags and watch something?"

"That sounds good."

While the popcorn was popping, Williams made herself comfortable on the left of the couch, flipping the TV on.

"I'm not a cable person, just FYI. Netflix or Prime." Katherine came back with a large bowl in her hand filled to spilling with buttery popcorn. "Pick something," she said, sitting directly next to Williams. She plopped her feet onto the coffee table and started picking at the popcorn.

Far be it from Williams to harsh her mellow, especially in her own living space, so she grabbed a handful of popcorn and clicked through the "New Releases" on Netflix. She hovered over a new horror and Katherine stiffened.

"I do not do horror. It scares the shit out of me," Katherine said.

"Well thank god I'm here then," Williams replied, pushing another handful of popcorn into her mouth. "Horror is the best."

They made it through half of the movie before Katherine practically threw what was left of the popcorn into the air, clinging to Williams for dear life. The best part, Williams thought, was that it wasn't a very good or even scary movie—and yes, a horror movie can be scary and good, or scary and bad, or a mixture of either. Scary didn't define its watchability. Williams winced slightly from the grab but didn't pull away.

After the movie ended, Williams excused herself to the bathroom. Taking her bag with her, she brushed her teeth and got ready for bed.

As Williams stepped into the bedroom, she didn't realize that Katherine was getting changed for bed. Katherine jumped, covering her chest with an old tee shirt. Williams couldn't help it; she laughed hysterically.

"I guess I got you back for earlier," she said, turning away so Katherine could get decent.

"I guess so," Katherine said, smiling sheepishly, still blushing. She grabbed a pillow off the bed and edged toward the door. "Well...goodnight, Abby. Let me know if you need anything."

As Katherine stepped out into the hall, Williams pulled the cover forward and awkwardly climbed into the bed. She opened the nightstand drawer and tucked away her Glock 17. Just in case of another midnight visit. The thought of it made her feel weak, queasy even. She knew she wouldn't sleep a wink.

"Hey, Katherine?" she called back down the hall. Was she...biting her lip? She chided herself. This wasn't middle school.

"Yes, Abby?" Katherine called, stepping towards the bedroom.

Williams slid over to one side of the bed, fully deciding. "I've been having trouble sleeping. Actually, without the morphine, I haven't really been sleeping at all. Stay. I-I mean, please stay." She buried herself in the covers, partially to keep out the late October chill, but also to give Katherine the option to back out if she wanted.

Williams felt Katherine slide into the bed next to her, placing her arm around her and laying it ever so slightly on her casted forearm. Williams was nervous, yes; she was messed up from the hell storm of a month she was living in. She was traumatized by attempted murder, she was shattered by the kidnapping of her partner Reyes; and of James, Ebony Bowman, and her teacher. But for the first time in a long time, even through all the other feelings, she felt at peace.

She slept.

Ch 15

RONIN

I

AFTER GETTING DRESSED, AGAIN thankful for her mother bringing work clothes, Katherine had asked Williams if she wanted to stop for breakfast before dropping her at work. As Cemetery natives, the first place that always came to mind was the Cemetery Diner. The thought was a gut punch to Williams. Without Reyes, she wouldn't be going there ever again.

They settled for bacon, egg, and cheeses from one of the town's more popular bagel spots. The bagels were great, the coffee terrible. The wait took longer than expected, a large group of men in *Cemetery Town & Lumber* hoodies walking in just before them.

They hadn't discussed the night before, having woken fully entwined together. Nothing more than sleep had happened, but Williams felt as if they had skipped several hurdles toward a real relationship.

After they finished, Williams threw caution to the wind and kissed Katherine goodbye in full view of the precinct's front door. She figured if everything else was going to absolutely shit, she might as well enjoy the one good thing coming her way. She felt glad that the only bit of embarrassment she felt was from how hard it was to bend over at the driver's side window.

Cemetery had been hit with a seasonally early snow, the roads hardly touched, but the lawns and spots of grass showing several inches. The trees hadn't fully relinquished all their leaves, the added weight of snow leading to several downed trees and powerlines. Williams pulled her coat around her tightly, thankful that the Cemetery PD jackets had buttoned sleeves, allowing her cast to fit.

Inside the precinct, she walked into a round of applause: cheering, jeering, and whooping noises. No matter where you went, even a serious police precinct in a crime-ridden town, men were still dogs. The only outlier was Officer Owens. Brittany Owens was a heavyset blonde woman. Williams remembered her being a bully throughout high school, and she had also taken quite well to precinct hazing. They had never liked each other, and Williams felt certain that only her behavior bordered on homophobic out of the group. Internal Affairs had had more than one field day combing through accusations from Owens taking things too far.

Williams smiled though, enjoying the act of not caring for once.

The rowdiness was ended at the appearance of Colfax, the men quickly dispersing.

Williams gave the FBI a wide berth. She stopped at the precinct kitchen, knowing that the burnt crap that remained in the pot here more often than not would still be better than the bagel place's. At least she was used to this form of bad.

She headed for Chief Carter's office and knocked outside the door. When no answer came, she gave it a minute before knocking again. The longer she waited, the more uneasy she felt. She tried to push it to the back of her mind, but his behavior had been off. Even so, she really wanted to avoid going about alone, not with what happened to Reyes so fresh.

On the third knock there was a small mumble from the other side of the door. Williams entered, and saw that Carter was sipping a coffee from behind his desk. He looked sweaty, pale; tired yet wired. He looked up from his coffee, and, if possible, paled further. "Jeez, Detective Williams, what the heck are you doing here? What are you even doing out of bed?"

"Sir, I'm here to get Reyes back, no matter the cost. To catch the bastard responsible."

"I have to admit, I love the enthusiasm, but not at the cost of my second...my only detective. Not to mention you can't just ignore the enforced leave, Williams. Even if I wanted to allow it—which I don't and won't—my hands are tied."

"With all due respect, he's out there, sir, and he'd do the same damn thing for me." Williams gritted her teeth and forced herself to make direct eye contact with the chief. "I'll get to the bottom of this."

"Williams, I'm with you, truly." Carter sipped his coffee, applying pressure to the bridge of his nose. "Time is not, though. Look at this paper from today, just pummeling us. Nothing we do will keep any of this under wraps now." Carter spun the paper around on his desk and slid it forward. The headline and subhead read:

BODYCOUNT IN CEMETERY ON THE RISE:
POLICE DEPARTMENT'S OWN MISSING

The Chief's jaw was clenched like he intended to break his teeth. He slammed a hand down on the paper. "That information was not released to the public. When I find out who is bleeding information to the press, they're done for!"

"Shit, Chief," Williams paused, not wanting to admit it, but then pressed on. "I asked after Reyes like a hundred times while all drugged up in the hospital. It honestly could have been my fault."

Carter pressed himself fully back into his tall desk chair, breathing heavily. He grabbed his coffee in a swift movement, attempting to sip from it, and hissing as some of it spilled over his hand. "Okay, Williams. I'll let it lie for now. But I don't see you asking after your partner in the hospital being at fault."

"I'd like to get back to the basics today. Nothing crazy. Something I can handle right now. I want to see if the middle school will give me a room for interviews."

"No. I understand the gravity here, but you're clearly not listening, Williams. Even if I could fast-track your meeting with the department psychologist, you're benched. I told you that," Carter said, scratching his chin.

"I feel like it's important."

"I'll see what Special Agent Colfax thinks. If they have the time to spare, she'll get them there," Carter replied. "The FBI is here now; we have to trust them." He reached for his phone to make the arrangements, but seeing Williams' face, said, "Look, I actually have a few things left to go over with the principal at the school. I'll head over there regardless at some point—today even—okay? What I need from you right now is for you to go home."

II

As it turned out, Williams didn't much care for whether or not Colfax found it important. And as much as she did trust the FBI, at least compared to some of her colleagues at the moment, and especially Chief Carter, she wasn't willing to rely on them from the sidelines. Carter had misunderstood her when she'd said, "no matter the cost." It wasn't some platitude—she'd act first, ask for forgiveness second. All in the name of Ed Reyes.

She kicked up a fuss on her way out of the precinct, ensuring she was overheard telling anyone in earshot that she was being sent home for rest. As long as that was what they thought, no one need be the wiser.

At the school, Williams had entered with high hopes. She sat in front of a small table with a pen and pad, a couple of student chairs on the other side for parents, students, or staff. Without recovering the teacher or Ebony, it was hard to tell, but she felt sure this was linked with the other crimes somehow. However, after the first few interviews, her hope began to wane.

Police work often dealt in overly tedious, bordering-on-mind-numbing questioning, but it was a whole new low to be dealing with sixth, seventh, and eighth graders. They either didn't remember, couldn't be bothered, or wove tales so extreme that she had to write off every word out of their mouths.

She had two more interviews, and if nothing came out of these, at least she could be free of the school. The next up was Principal Hayden, to give a character check of sorts on the missing teacher. After that, the final interview was a Susanne Curtis, a seventh grader, who rode the same bus as Ebony. They were apparently friendly. Williams found that she couldn't hold much hope for either. The principal entered now, looking forlorn. He was a tall man, perhaps middle-aged; a paunch looming over his belt, greying, and thinning hair on his head that Williams could only see because he nodded hello to her.

"Hello, Detective, how are you doing?" He didn't wait for a response, plunging on. "An awful lot of strings had to be pulled to set these little interviews up, so I hope it's been fruitful?"

"Fanciful, maybe." Williams said, already at a disconnect with the principal. "As I'm sure you can relate, with such young and imaginative minds, the answers have been all over the place. From alien abduction and police conspiracy to the illuminati. I'll have to work through the notes for any shred of truth later."

"Just so." Principal Hayden sat forward in his chair, awkwardly at odds with the low student seating. "They can be rather difficult."

"So my main line of questioning for you pertains to the missing teacher. What can you tell me about her?"

"Well, she is one of our younger staff members, still passionate for the role, as well as the ups and downs it brings with it. Andrea Nowack has always been on time, dressed neatly, and prepared, with all her work finished." Principal Hayden smiled, "Exemplary, even."

"So in your professional opinion, it seems that you would not believe her to be the kidnapper?"

The principal leaned back into the chair and laughed. He let himself enjoy the thought for a few moments longer, even wiping a tear away from the corner of his eye. "There is literally no one I would suspect less than her. She loves her job, she loves her children, the class. She would never. I simply wouldn't believe it."

Williams jotted a few things down on the pad. This was one of the most useful pieces of information of the day. Was this finally a lagniappe for her due diligence?

"Thank you, Principal Hayden, and with that line of thinking, could you possibly think of anyone who would have wanted to cause her harm?"

"Andrea Nowack having an enemy you mean? The idea itself is preposterous. She's universally liked. Looked up to, even at her young age, for all she does for us. For the staff and student body alike."

"Of course, sir. I understand how you must feel, but in an investigation like this, we have to ask all the dirty questions. We have to look beyond these walls. Perhaps any rumor of her having some kind of aggressive ex in her life? Someone following her, or someone targeting teachers in general?

The principal sat back in the seat again, his spine cracking slightly. He raised a hand and rubbed absentmindedly at his five o'clock shadowed chin. He looked pensive, like he was genuinely trying to give her question adequate thought from every angle.

"Well...there have been a few claims of someone watching the school from the woods. I've taken to having the security guards posted outside more often, especially while the kids and teachers leave the building for the day. But they've yet to report seeing anything."

"Unfortunately, Principal Hayden, sometimes when someone like that sees a change in activity—like added security and an uptick in searching—they bow out. Meaning the target, whomever they were after, is no longer viable. So, in that line of thinking, it's not definitive proof that there was *never* someone stalking out there. I do believe you did the right thing though." Williams penned a few more lines onto her pad.

"Anything else for me then, Officer?"

"Well, yes," Williams leaned forward, wanting a clear look at the man's face. "What are your thoughts on Ebony Bowman?"

His eyebrows arched slightly, and there was a tinge of color rising to his cheeks. "She's trouble...or well on her way to being trouble. Her visits to me have become more frequent. She no longer listens when I talk to her; she's completely disconnected from the teachers. When she entered my school, she was such a sweet little girl, never a problem. I'd never mean to speak ill of the dead, what happened to Lizzy was truly an absolute travesty, but she was the bad influence in Ebony's life. She allowed her to hang around the older kids. Allowed her to take on their traits."

Williams studied him intently during his entire rant. He was clearly more invested in the situation than he was letting on. She thanked him for his time, dismissing him.

"Absolutely and thank you...for trying to stop whoever's done this. I'll send in Ms. Curtis now."

"Back to the Chief now, Principal Hayden?"

"Beg pardon?"

"Chief Carter, sir? Said he had to finish up with you today? I was just wondering if he had arrived?" Williams asked, a little taken aback by his surprised look. She hadn't thought far enough ahead to see the possible ramifications of Carter arriving while she was still at the school.

"Oh yes, quite," Principal Hayden nodded, "He's already gone though, Detective Williams, there wasn't much left."

With relief, Williams welcomed the final interviewee, Susanne Curtis, into the room alone. Her mother had given permission for them to speak as she was stuck at work.

"Hi, it's Susanne, right?" Williams began small. Baselines and all that.

"Yes, ma'am. But Suzy please," she replied, rocking in her chair. She was a small, innocent-looking girl, with brown skin, tightly curled hair, and a pleasant smile. She was small for a girl just on the edge of teen-hood.

"Sure, Suzy, that's not a problem. I'm a detective here in town. My name is Abigail, but if you like, you can call me Abby. All my friends do." Williams smiled at her, hoping to make her feel more at ease with their similarly shortened nicknames.

"Okay," Suzy smiled back at her, a tad less nervous. "Hi, Abby."

"Suzy, I really need help, and I'm sure you can be a big help to me. I was told that you were a best friend of Ebony Bowman's, is that right?"

"Well...we were friends, kind of. I'm not so sure she would have called me a best friend though," Suzy replied.

"Oh. Why not?" Williams asked.

"Ebony always had plans with her older sister and her friends. She even...she even claimed she had an older boyfriend," Suzy said, looking mischievous, as if sharing Ebony's secret was too much for her.

"An older boyfriend? Is that true, Suzy? Do you know who he is?" Williams pressed.

"Well, she would always call him Benny. I thought it was kind of a funny name, but she swore she wasn't lying." Suzy looked thoughtful, "You don't think she was, do you? Lying?"

"I don't have an answer for you, Suzy, but I certainly aim to find out." This development could be interesting. Could that be a name on their list of friends? She found herself hoping that it was someone on the younger side of the friend group, as that was just...gross. "And this Benny, did her sister know him?"

She squished her lips up in that way only children can when thinking hard. "I'm sorry, I don't know. I think she did though. I was so sad to hear what happened to Lizzy...she used to be my babysitter; you know."

"I'm sorry for your loss, Suzy," Williams said.

Suzy smiled, feeling as if she were being treated as an adult. "She got not so nice at the end though."

"Not nice how, Suzy?"

"She would be really mean. She would show up late and have friends over, breaking my momma's only rule. She would eat and drink whatever she wanted, and I think she might have stolen. Just...not nice," Suzy replied in a rush. Like she was still at odds with speaking ill of someone else. She rocked back and forth harder.

Trying to get back on track, Williams smiled again, giving Suzy her best friendly voice again. "I'm sorry that she wasn't nice, Suzy. I hate when older kids and babysitters get mean. It's the worst. I still have to ask one final, not-so-nice question, okay?"

Suzy sniffled, rubbing her shirt sleeve on her nose, and nodded.

Williams continued, "Why do you think Ebony would run away? Why do you think she would go with her teacher without letting anyone know?"

"Oh, no, she didn't, Abby."

"What do you mean?"

"That's not what happened. Ebony walked into the woods that day. Ms. Nowack followed."

"Ms. Nowack, is that her teacher that went missing with her?" Williams peeled the story from her.

"Yes, Ms. Nowack was her homeroom teacher. Ebony walked into the woods first, Ms. Nowack followed. I saw it," Suzy said, still sniffling.

"So you're saying Ebony ran off into the woods and Ms. Nowack ran in to get her? Or that they ran off into the woods together?" Williams waited with bated breath for the girl's response.

"No! It wasn't like that at all," Suzy said. "They just kind of...walked. Kind of like they were possessed or dazed or being controlled."

"Like they were being...controlled?" After all that, now Williams was wondering if this was just another kid's testimony destined for the trash.

Suzy bit her lip. "Yeah...like mentally gone or something. Like-like, have you ever seen *Trublood*?" Suzy didn't wait for an answer before barreling on. "I'm not allowed to watch stuff like that, but Lizzy had gotten pretty bad at the watching part of babysitting. Anyway, it was kind of like they were glamoured by one of the vampires on the show. Like they were being drawn away toward someone...except—except I didn't see anyone. Just them walking towards the woods."

Williams felt like the chair below her was shaking, quaking. She gripped the table as if it really was. It was as if things were aligning for her finally...but because a twelve-year-old mentioned a sex-filled HBO show? She remembered the pale skin in the dead of night. The pressure on her chest in the hospital room. The pointed, irregular ears. *Fangs*.

"That kind of stuff isn't real, Suzy. I'm investigating a string of disappearances. Like your friend and babysitter. Why are you telling me this stuff?"

Williams shook herself and leaned forward, the motion pulling her stitches and hurting her stomach, unsure if she was setting boundaries for Suzy, or for herself.

"You asked, Abby...that's...that's what I saw. At least, that's what it felt like. They were just walking, Ms. Nowack wasn't chasing her. She wasn't running or talking or motioning for Ebony to stop, they just walked...kind of near each other and kind of not."

III

Back outside the school, the heavy October wind whipped, knife-like, through Williams. As she awkwardly plopped herself onto the driver's seat, it was a great relief from the wind, but only a small one from the overall cold. Having gotten to the school before it let out, she was still startled by how dark it was outside. *Daylight savings is a fucking sham.*

Williams' car was parked to the right of the school. She had backed into the spot, figuring it would be easier to leave. Although she had taken longer than expected, she was surprised by how few cars remained. Behind her, the woods loomed larger than life. Now that she had gotten an account claiming the two had gone missing after walking through the woods, she certainly had enough to go on to get another search going. She just wasn't going to do it alone. She'd find a way to get the Chief on board.

She started the car and leaned back into the seat as she waited for it to warm up. She pressed her back into the car seat hard, the seat warmer being the first thing to get hot every time. Prepping to leave, she fiddled with the rearview mirror. In just a sliver of her peripherals, she caught the glint of something metallic in her backseat.

On reflex alone, Williams pounced forward into the steering wheel, letting out a twisted moan at the pull of her stitches. She thanked every god new and old that she hadn't put her seatbelt on. The glint of metal shot forward, plunging into the top of the driver's seat. A *syringe*. Williams slammed herself back, taking advantage of the stuck syringe. She swung an elbow back, once, twice, thrice. Her connections felt weak, with her cast getting in the way. Then on the third, she was fairly certain she had connected with a nose. The satisfying crunch was only slightly less enjoyable due to the painful stinging coming from her injured arm.

At the metallic unsheathing of what Williams was certain would end up being a knife, she threw herself forward again. The swing of the knife caught the collar of her shirt, slicing it open and connecting with the back of her shoulder. She howled and gritted her teeth. She reached for her gun, but it was more of a struggle while scrunched forward. Harder to grab with her clumsier left hand. She grabbed the door handle instead, slamming her body through the door and falling hard onto her back on the pebbly asphalt.

Now prone, she unholstered her Glock 17 and raised it before her. The passenger side door opposite her banged open and she heard heavy feet beating a hasty retreat. Williams cursed and slammed her hand into asphalt. The shock reverberated through her cast, and she felt the corners of her sight begin to darken.

Shit, shit, shit, Abby. Too many goddamn mistakes.

She released her Glock and rolled over to a kneeling position. She looked all around the car, not wanted to risk being surprised by the assailant returning.

Nothing.

Standing and retrieving her gun, she thought she could just make out the slight outline of someone in black trailing into the woods beyond.

Williams leaned back into the car and grabbed the radio. "This is Detective Williams calling in from Cemetery Middle School, requesting back up. Assailant just retreated into the woods, I repeat assailant running on foot, over. All available backup, please respond." *Act first, ask for forgiveness second.* That had come into play much sooner than she was hoping.

"Officers en route, do not engage alone if you can help it. Help is coming, over."

Williams slammed the radio back down. She raised a hand above her head, feeling for the wound the knife had left. Her hand came back bloody, but not nearly as bloody as it would have been if it were too bad to press on. She looked down, seeing blood speckling the front of her white blouse as well.

She breathed deeply and took off at a run. There was no way she was letting this bastard get back to wherever Reyes was being held.

Ch 16

CHASE

I

A HEAVY BOUGH SMASHED Williams in the shoulder as she barreled through the trees. She felt her stitches pulling and stretching, screaming for relief. She couldn't stop.

Williams couldn't believe how short the distance was from the start of the woods to it becoming increasingly dense. It felt impenetrable.

She had gained on her assailant, her years of soccer and keeping in shape clearly doing her some favors now. She was faster than them, and she bet they knew it. Her work shoes beat a steady path through the snow. It had begun melting, but the temperature had dropped with the setting of the sun, each step producing what would have been a satisfying frozen crunch in differing circumstances. Now all Williams could think about was how each step beat a klaxon warning of her imminent approach. She could just make out the shape of them as they ran ahead, zig zagging their way through trees, bushes, and brush.

She tried to focus on her breathing and urged herself onward. The snow's refreezing led to unfortunate but inevitable slipping and sliding. The motion was murder on her stitches—each slide producing an oxygen-stealing grunt from her lips.

As she ran, she found that each turn of a tree, each hop over a branch, each tear through brush, made the outline of the assailant a little less foggy. A little more defined. She chased the outline until each limb became separate from the overall shape, until she saw the outline of the hooded robe they were wearing, heard the crunch of another pair of feet.

Her mind raced, and while this was not at all like her experienced trauma as a child, her brain was never far from it. She remembered the police officer blocking his appearance with the newspaper, hoping to uphold the misdirection that he was her father. Her playing on the jungle gym, running back and forth until she noticed the man. The man watching her from the woods. He had been dressed funny and had white gloves on. Gloves that didn't remain white for long. She should never have been there, been endangered as if her life was worth toying with. But now, her vision was coated in the memory of waving hands and smiles. How he had used the trees to stay hidden from everyone else. Not this side of town, but these same trees that she raced through now.

Almost tripping in her distraction, Williams took a chance and veered to the left. She wound around a particularly large tree trunk, pushing faster under the clearer ground, the tree not yet devoid of all of its leaves. As she cleared its vast circumference, she entered a clearing. The night's stars were beginning to appear above the almost perfectly round area of treeless sky; however, the ground inside was practically snowless. The center of the clearing dipped down into a ditch.

Except it wasn't a ditch at all. As Williams edged towards the hole, she saw that it had been dug out. A manmade hole a mile into the woods? Williams was incredibly curious as to what it could be.

She checked for the assailant before edging further down the slope. The darkness in the spaces around branches and limbs danced, undulating like swaying bodies. The problem with darkness is the possibilities. The feeling of unknown had spooked Williams her entire life. She could handle something definite, that she was sure, but the gnawing factor of what *could* be there, now that had always been too much.

Fairly certain she had heard the assailant continue on, Williams edged ever closer to the pit. She couldn't put a finger on it, but something was inexplicably drawing her toward it. She figured that it couldn't be anything good. She *needed* to know what was in there.

As she leaned over to get a better look, it appeared all the clearing's snow had been shoveled into the center. The pit, for it was in fact a pit, was five or six feet deep, stretching around in an almost-perfect square. Williams imagined the snow had been piled high at some point, but the heat of the day had diminished its height, now reforming into an almost solid block. Jagged peaks and juts stuck out at odd angles, stalagmites forming from the dripping pile.

In the depths of the pile, Williams thought she could just make out the outline of something. A shape in the dark, sticking out against the white of the snow in the moonlight. She stepped as close to the edge as she could get. She leaned as far forward as she could, ignoring the pinch of her stitches, and removed her cellphone. She swiped on the flashlight and gasped...the shape sticking out of the snow was a blued, curled, human hand.

A twig snapped and Williams dropped her phone, spinning just in time to see the figure sprinting into the clearing.

Williams didn't have a chance to think. She had holstered her Glock to grab her phone. She raised her right arm just in time for the assailant's knife to swipe down and dig into the folds of her cast instead of the meat of her shoulder. She used the attacker's momentum against them and swung their arm around, kicking them in the small of their back and knocking them away.

Williams, however, hadn't thought to compensate for how close she was to the hole. She fell full-tilt into the pit at her back, yelping as gravity took hold.

Hitting hard onto her back and shoulders, the wind rocketed out of her. She gasped for breath, trying to fill her lungs, but it was as if cinderblocks had been stacked on top of her chest. She reeled, grabbing for the holster of her gun as she heard movement at the edge of the pit. She thought she saw a sliver of motion from the right corner above her, feeling more than seeing the figure coming toward her. She fired her pistol twice into the night, knowing full well that even a miss could be enough of a deterrent. Exposed and stuck on her back inside the hole, it was now or never if she intended to survive.

Detective Williams intended to.

Certain she saw movement again; she heard a gun fire from above. For a moment, she looked at her own, as if it had gone off without her permission. Someone else was here, shooting at her attacker.

Get the bastard.

As another shot rang out, leaves, twigs, and dirt showered down around Williams, getting into her eyes, nose, and mouth. Someone above her must be scrambling.

Williams sank her head back into the snow as a third and final shot rang out. Being momentarily blinded kept her from being of any use. She had to rely on the unsung hero above to keep her from harm.

She rolled to the side, spitting and rubbing viciously at her gritty eyes. As her eyes teared, working overtime to clear themselves, she could just make out the fuzzy outline she had seen earlier. It was a blue and blackened hand, curled at an odd angle, and clearly frozen solid. Williams scooted away and groaned.

II

An ambulance had been called in, despite Williams' protestations. They looked over her battle wounds, bandaging her neck after cutting away the collar of her blouse. The knife cut was long, but superficial. They inspected, cleaned, and rebandaged her stitches—which had continued to seep—but at least for now, didn't need any redoing. The paramedics had poured some liquid bandaging into the cut in her cast and rewrapped it. Williams would have just as easily settled for duct tape and calling it a night. The top of her shoulders and back were scrapped and bruised from the fall on the hardening snow, but other than some growing aches and pains in the coming days, she was cleared.

Another fucking harrowing escape for Abigail Williams, she thought, leaning back as she sat on the edge of the ambulance. Even though the margin of survival had been paper-thin, she still felt guilty about it. Why her when Reyes had been taken? Or rather, why not her, instead of him? She was the one that felt like she was losing it, questioning herself at every turn. Why had the steadfast, cigarette smoking, brusque professional of the two been nabbed and not her. Especially when she was out cold in a hospital bed.

When Williams had rolled herself over, finally seeing clearly, she saw Chief Carter staring down at her. He had knelt at the edge of the pit, offering her a hand up, and doing his best to pull her out without hurting her one good arm that was left to her. In the moment she felt nothing but gratitude for his timely arrival, even knowing the shit storm she was due for lying to him.

Now, however, stewing with it, her mind pulled at the threads. She knew she had called it in, she knew that Cemetery wasn't all that big, and she also knew that the call in would be treated as incredibly serious, but had the Chief's arrival been *too* timely? Not only making it back to the school in time, but also finding her and the attacker over a mile into the woods in the near-black night. No, she didn't think the threads connected cleanly. She was either missing something, or something was entirely wrong.

The Chief approached her. He looked disheveled, which was so unlike him. Even his hair was a mess.

"Hey, Williams," Carter said, stepping up to the ambulance. "Heard the paramedics got you all squared away?"

"Yeah, I'm all set," Williams replied. "More anti-inflammatory and bed rest."

"You should have just told me, you know," Carter said. He didn't look angry, but rather bewildered. "If you were just honest and told me you were going to do it no matter what I said, I'd like to think I would have figured something out, Williams. And with the FBI breathing down my neck, there's just too much at stake."

Williams sat with that in momentary silence. Would he have? She liked to believe that she had a clear read on the situation, but it was never too late to second guess. However, she was trying so hard to be more direct, to not drop the ball. To be like Reyes. She wouldn't relinquish the fact that lying had been warranted.

Williams decided to change the subject before he tried the benched spiel again. "How's it going in there?"

"We're still combing the woods, but who knows where they lead? I'm not too hopeful in that arena. The team assigned to assist Special Agent Colfax worked fast though. The body is already dug out. They should be bringing it out here soon, I'd imagine. Matter of minutes probably."

The Chief tapped the side of the ambulance and turned to step away. Williams took a breath and called after him, "Chief, how did you find me so fast?"

"Luck, probably? You left one hell of a trail of boot prints through the snow too though."

Williams hadn't considered that.

"But the timing, how did you get to the school so fast, Chief?"

"I told you I was crossing some t's and dotting some 'i's with the principal. Nothing major, but I was still here; my car's right over there. Distress call over the radio almost gave me a heart attack." Carter smiled, looking at her as if she were a silly, forgetful child.

Williams had checked for his car in the parking lot, hadn't she? She laughed and shook her head, then smiled up at the Chief, hoping the October cold would cloak the rose color climbing her cheeks. She thought she recalled a car in the lot, but she had assumed it was the principal's. Maybe she was wrong. "Oh, duh. Sorry. I'm probably just a little shaken right now."

"Understandable, Williams." Carter placed a hand on her shoulder, completely forgetting about her injuries. "You should get some sleep; we can finish up here."

"I'm good, Carter, thanks. As it's related to my case, I'd like to stay."

"Suit yourself," Carter said. He had the air of someone who couldn't care less. Not the type of response you'd expect from someone who had once again almost lost a member of staff.

His story didn't add up, and now Williams had him. The principal had said they were already finished, that the Chief had left. She knew she remembered that, recalling it clearly. So, what then? The Chief was involved...knew the killer...was the killer? That didn't smell right either. Why pretend to shoot at a nonexistent attacker if it was him the entire time? Why not simply finish the job?

What if the principal had been mistaken? Was the Chief simply waiting for him a little down the hall? A little slip-up like that didn't make someone a murderer.

It didn't mean they were clear of it, either.

Two paramedics and an officer broke from the tree line, severing Williams from her ever-darkening ponderings. The three of them supported a black body bag between them, the gurney having no chance of making the mile trek through the snowy woods. Williams stood, stretching herself for the first time since the paramedic had cleared her, and got out of the way of the approaching trio. They stepped past her and gingerly placed the bag in the back of the open ambulance. The two paramedics pulled the body bag further into the ambulance. The officer nodded to them, heading back toward the woods.

Williams stepped up onto the ambulance as the first paramedic moved to the driver's seat. "May I?" she asked, motioning at the bag in front of them.

"Uhh, knock yourself out?" the paramedic still in the back, a woman, said.

Williams nodded her thanks, kneeling and unzipping the bag. The remains of someone far too young to die by the size of them, filled her field of view. The body was still frozen solid, rigid and with limbs at unnatural angles. The victim's fingers curled at disturbing odds with the rest of the body, as if the fingers were trying to claw their way to safety. She was young, that much was obvious. Her skin was a deep brown, but had paled in death, then blued from the ice. Had the snow been shoveled onto her for this exact reason, to preserve her until she could be found?

There was a chance the perpetrator had done it hoping to hide the crime, but if that were the case, where was the dirt from the hole being dug? Why had it been removed? Why hadn't they just refilled the hole, using the snow to cover for the freshness of it? It was an enticing theory that Williams would love to have the answers to.

The body of the young girl was desiccated and shriveled in an all-too-familiar way. The right side of her chest was ripped and torn into, pieces of skin, fat, muscle, and something else Williams couldn't quite identify hung off in bits and pieces. It was clean otherwise, not a drop of blood. Above the hole in her little chest, there were two pricks just below the collarbone...again, could be some kind of teeth marks, or hastily stabbed needles.

Williams shivered.

It was shockingly similar to Lizzy Bowman body's when they found her, but on the opposite side of the chest. The young girl's shirt was missing, but she was not entirely nude like the last victim. She hadn't been left as a spectacle.

Williams would have bet anything this was Ebony Bowman, Lizzy's younger sister. As much as she wished it weren't so, she felt certain.

Where was the teacher then?

As Williams zippered the bag back up, she was stricken with the view of dirt and ice in the young girl's mouth, her jaw opened eternally at a sideways angle. A bone-chilling sight that would follow her to the grave. She said a silent prayer to any god that would listen, and a promise to catch the son of a bitch that was doing this. No one deserved *this*, no one.

Williams stepped out of the ambulance. She figured the paramedics would leave to transport the body now there was nothing left for them to do. The body would go directly to Dr. Kenmore for another autopsy. She could do without further pictures, or another sit down.

She headed for her car, intending to sit inside with the heat blasting for a good long while. As she neared it, the long-forgotten attack in the car came back to her. With everything she had been thinking through, she had forgotten that her car was now part of a major crime scene. An assembly of CSI and forensic workers were combing every square inch of the vehicle for evidence. One of the FBI agents was standing with a clipboard, directing them.

Not that she kept anything inside the car, but she found it eerily invasive.

The syringe! She had forgotten that the attacker's first swing had been with a syringe. It was still stuck deep into the driver's side headrest, waiting to be removed, clear liquid still tucked safely away in the barrel of it.

She stepped toward the woman and held out her casted hand. "I'm Detective Williams."

"Yes, detective?" The FBI agent said, quickly shaking the proffered hand. "Field Agent Sofia Mendes."

She was a slim woman of medium height, who seemed almost tall compared to Williams. She had an aquiline nose, toffee-colored skin, and short brown hair. Her slacks were slim, almost tactical, and she had an FBI coat over a navy button down.

"The person that attacked me in my car, they tried to stick me with that," Williams said, pointing at the syringe that forensics had just gingerly removed. "When it stuck into the headrest, instead of me, they switched to a more lethal approach. Any idea what could be in it?"

"Without testing it?" Field Agent Mendes asked. "Not really...but if your attacker isn't also moonlighting as some kind of medical professional, it's most likely GHB, Rohypnol, or ketamine. Those are most often used by criminals, but if they have no idea what they're doing, or no care, it could also be fentanyl."

"Wait, GHB? Like the date-rape drug they teach you about in health class?" Williams asked, eyebrows raised.

"Well, yes. Why do you think they teach you about it?" she said, shaking her head. "My guess is they aren't some kind of professional, though. That just looks like an awful lot for a single person to get injected with. Could have been just as lethal as whatever else they used against you honestly. At least that's my guess."

"Thanks," Williams said. "I'd like to be notified when it's officially tested, please." She rapped the side of her car and stepped away from it.

Walking back towards the ambulance, the Chief caught Williams' left arm and stopped her in her tracks. "Jesus, Carter, you trying to kill me too?"

"Sorry, I called out to you, but you were distracted with forensics." He smiled at her. "It's my fault. I see they retrieved the syringe from your car. Seems a spot of luck the attacker missed you with that thing, huh? Could you imagine if you'd had your seatbelt done?"

"Yeah...yeah I suppose." Williams tried to smile but gulped instead.

She needed to get away from the Chief, and she needed to do it now. She couldn't let on that she was suspecting anything.

She hadn't told Chief Carter the specifics of the attack yet.

She hadn't told anyone.

Ch 17

Chief Done It

I

Nodding at the Chief, Williams took several deliberate steps backward. "Thanks for the save today, Chief. I guess I'm still just a little shaken. I'll be on the lookout as soon as it's tested. I want to know what's in there. I have a good feeling about it being a lead."

"Don't mention it, just right place, right time—nothing more. You'd have done the same for me." Carter's smile seemed too bright; crooked. "Good call though, could definitely lead us somewhere if we know what it is. Why don't you go get some rest though, if you want me to get the results?"

"No!" Williams practically yelled. "I mean, it's no problem at all. You have to stay here to wrap up the search anyway, right?"

"Okay. Sounds good, Williams," Carter said, eyeing her. "But you head right home after, okay? You've been through enough tonight. Wouldn't want to lose you too now, would we?"

Williams bobbed her agreement and stepped away from the Chief. Why did he want the results first? What the hell was going on, and why the hell was he so disheveled?

What the fuck is he playing at?

As Williams was turning, Brennan and Shotz strode out of the woods, something in both of their hands. *What else could possibly happen in one single night*, she wondered?

Williams slowed down to wait for their arrival before heading near the Chief again. Getting closer, Brennan looked like he was holding some kind of tarp.

As they reached the Chief, she gave herself space to listen to the conversation.

"Chief, we found these tucked away," Brennan said.

"Inside a bush," Shotz added.

"They were hidden pretty damn well," Brennan offered.

"But we're damn good ourselves," Shotz boasted.

"Okay, okay. I get it with the twin act, you two. What did you find?" Carter said, nostrils flaring. He grabbed what turned out to be cloth from Brennan and felt it between his hands. "Some wet cloth? Black...feels cheap...and is that a hood?"

"Yes, sir," Brennan replied. "It looks like some kind of hooded robe, or a cloth poncho of some kind. It's pretty long...feels kind of Halloween costume quality, no?"

"And I got a kind of mask here. It looks like some great quality—movie-set quality even," Shotz held it out for the Chief.

Williams froze, windswept, aching, and chilled to the bone. The right hand on her casted arm, too big to fit into the pocket of her jacket, was turning numb in the October wind. At the sight of the mask in the Chief's hands, a chill unrelated to the cold crept its way up her spine. Williams stumbled backward. Remembering her drug-fueled nightmares in the hospital, she nearly cried out.

A pale, sickly-looking face...one with...fangs descending from its mouth...ears that ended in a point.

Had she really been duped by a Halloween mask this entire time? Addled brain or not, she thought she was sharper than that. *Better* than that. Looking at the mask in the Chief's hands turned her stomach in roiling waves. No matter how good the quality was, in Carter's hands it just looked like...rubber, nothing more.

Their conversation brought Williams back. None of them seemed to notice her nightmarish reverie.

"Yeah, look at it, Chief, it's one of those Nosferatu guy masks," Shotz said.

"His name was Count Orlok, you idiot, the movie was *Nosferatu*!" Brennan yelled.

"Yeah," Shotz fired back. "The guy from *Nosferatu*, isn't that exactly what I said? It's kind of the same thing as the monster becoming known as Frankenstein over time instead of the doctor, no?"

"Well, gentlemen, that is certainly more than enough of that." Carter pinched the bridge of his nose and let the mask go slack in his other hand. "Where would someone even get something like this? The quality is almost...real."

Williams couldn't be certain in the wind and dark, but she was pretty sure Carter had looked directly into her eyes when he said the word "real." Williams wasn't sure where someone would find something like that, but she knew for sure they'd look awfully disheveled after tearing it off their head and hiding it in some brush.

II

Reyes woke with a jolt. Startled and lost, maybe a little dejected, that was how he had woken up for...how many days now?

He was fortunate, but sad to say that the worst thing to befall him thus far was the incredible brain-aching withdrawals from nicotine. If only his kidnapper had taken the carton of smokes from his passenger seat.

He had woken the first day in a damp and dark room. It was almost pitch black, except for a small window in the metal door blocking his escape. The door stood out as a clue...maybe a warehouse or something industrial. The room smelled of mildew, of disuse. Did Cemetery even have anything abandoned like that?

His brain was fuzzy, and he had a temple-pounding headache. He remembered being pulled through the front door into the dark mansion. Chloroform maybe? He couldn't recall seeing a single person inside.

For days, Reyes had been trying to gather information. Anything he heard, any time the door opened to give him food or water—something that was happening less and less as time went on—the off chance that he saw another person. He wasn't sure why he was here, why he was still alive, why he hadn't been drained of blood yet, but he wasn't going to waste it.

No matter how little time he had left.

The previous night he was startled from his sleep by the sounds of blood-curdling screams. The kind of screams that horror movies try to emulate but never succeed at; the kind of screams that can only be experienced, not explained. The screams that accompany incredible, mind-tearing pain. Reyes had screamed for them to stop, but of course they hadn't. He doubted anyone could even hear him. He tore his throat bloody regardless. He couldn't just do nothing, but he couldn't offer more than his voice.

He had to assume the screaming came from either the missing teacher or Ebony Bowman. Reyes was pained to admit that the cries sounded like they were coming from a younger person...a *kid*. Tears stung his eyes as he thought of his own daughter. His Isabell. He imagined finding out a child is terminal had to feel an awful lot like the life-altering knowledge your child was missing. Like a bandage coming off, there is only who you were before, and what was left after.

As the screams petered out to a small whimpering peal, Reyes heard a shuffling outside of his room. He screamed again, struggling against his restraints. "Let me out of here. I'll tear you apart. Limb from limb you bastard!"

The shuffling outside of his room came to an abrupt halt. A scrapping sound replaced it, like someone lifting something heavy.

They stopped outside his door, whoever it was blocking out the light to the small window entirely, plunging him into black darkness. However, a millisecond before the light was blocked from the room, Reyes thought he could just make out a face, recognition hitting him full well.

"I saw your face," Reyes screamed, raw. "You think I didn't recognize you, that I wouldn't see? Williams will catch you; she'll stop you! *I. Know. You.*"

The figure receded from the window, and the light returned and briefly blinded Reyes. He didn't care; he knew who held him.

Too late Reyes realized if they didn't care about being seen it didn't bode well for his future freedom. But he knew in his heart that Williams would figure it out. The hope that flooded him the only fuel he needed to hold on.

III

Williams felt awful, like she was involving Katherine in something she shouldn't. Endangering her in something that wasn't her problem. Then she remembered that they had found a body together, linking her to the investigation in more than just a small way. And she didn't feel comfortable being in the precinct alone anymore. Without Reyes, she needed someone she could trust. Someone who wasn't a cop would do just fine.

Katherine had jumped at the opportunity to help. In the time they'd gotten to know each other, it was one of Williams' favorite things about her; her willingness to jump right in no matter what. Katherine always seemed to be awake and ready.

Although they couldn't exactly count the eight days that Williams was MIA, they had spent next to every moment together since. Katherine texted her encouraging things throughout the day to keep her going. Normally Williams would be turned off, but with the nerves about Reyes, it was like a warm embrace rather than an overstep. When Williams told her the details about what had happened at her house, as well as at the hospital, Katherine accepted the information as fact, not shying away. Nor did she make Williams feel bad about it.

It was after midnight, and the results were back for the liquid in the syringe: propofol. It wasn't even one of the guesses made by Agent Mendes, but as Williams researched it, it looked like the syringe had enough stopping power to put someone under in a minute or two. Fully. That was almost more frightening than a lethal dose of fentanyl. No recollection, no will to fight, and then uncontrollable unconsciousness.

The only good news was that Cemetery PD was practically a skeleton crew. Those who weren't still at the school combing the woods or were covering detail on the list of friends, were out on patrol, or working the desk. There simply weren't enough hands. She had beaten everyone but the forensic lead back to the precinct.

Williams headed out of her office to meet Katherine at the door. She stopped at the desk to sign her in before the officer even saw them.

He was a good guy, Officer Corrin, but he wasn't exactly paying attention.

But as it happened, Williams was staring down Special Agent Colfax, and tonight, that was exactly who she wanted. Colfax would finally get her play by play. Williams filled her in on everything. Not just what she had experienced and uncovered, but what she felt sure of. All the way up to the chief of police finding her way too easily tonight. Way too quickly. It didn't matter whether Colfax wanted to ignore her instincts to rely on the facts; she just needed to get it out in the open.

"There's just something not right here," Williams said, motioning around the entryway of the precinct as she said it. She looked over at the desk to ensure Officer Corrin was still in his late-night haze. "I don't know who to trust, but it's no longer Chief Carter. Everything seems to point to him. I need your help."

Colfax stopped writing on the pad before her, black hair hanging into her face like a solid sheet. "Look, I'm not just going to barge into the guy's office on a hunch. Believe me, as ill-advised as it was, you earned my respect by not giving up on your partner. Office politics aside, I'm not going to tell you when or how to do your job. From my experience though, this Occam's razor approach you're after—the simplest explanation is never it. You trust your instincts, great—bring me something at least suspicious enough to chase."

Williams' phone pinged, notifying her of Katherine's arrival. She couldn't put a finger on why, but she felt a bit of hope as she walked away from Colfax. "Tonight. That's just what I'm going to find you."

She pushed the precinct door open for Katherine, kissing her hello. Of course, this was the part of the night Officer Corrin was wide awake for. Katherine smiled and waved at him as Williams led her down the hall.

Katherine took Williams in. Her wet, dirty, and torn blouse. The blood on her shoulder and stomach. Just because it wasn't a lot didn't mean she still wasn't a sight to see. "People are going to think I'm the horror movie freak the way you keep meeting up with me looking like a final girl."

Williams leaned into Katherine, accepting the silly flirt. "I really need to start leaving clothes in the precinct apparently. Can I borrow your hoodie when we get settled?"

"If I get to help you change into it, maybe," Katherine teased, leaning back.

Williams had considered pulling out the information they'd need and lugging it to her office to give them more privacy, but she decided against it, as the added bonus was that Chief Carter was less likely to know where they were.

She led Katherine to the Records Room. It was in the bowels of the precinct, which in actuality was only two floors deep. Added security and all that. Even with digitized records, Carter had always been adamant on storing them physically. She thought it was weird back then, but it might actually be useful to them now.

For the most part, they used the digital organization system to locate the physical stuff when they needed it, unless they were researching something outside the building. There was just something to be said about having all the information in front of you, being able to flip back and forth, have it all separated in front of your eyes. She guessed you could do that digitally as well, but she wasn't about to try.

She buzzed into the room, leading Katherine to a table in the center. She had already grabbed everything she thought they would need and arranged it on or around the table.

Katherine helped her out of the ripped blouse, gently sliding it from her and crumpling it atop one of the many boxes. The touch of her skin along Williams' back was electric, making the tiny hairs on her body stand on end.

Katherine carefully guided her into the hoodie, taking her time to get it over the cast without causing Williams pain. As she was about to zipper it shut for Williams, she realized just how close that made them, and leaned in, pressing their lips together firmly.

After a prolonged moment of peace, they broke apart, and Williams zippered the hoodie up herself.

"I pulled out past reports of incidents with attempted kidnappings, lurker calls, and stuff like that. The main thing we're looking for is the use of a syringe, or a drug called propofol. A secondary thing to look out for is the description of a person in costume, something that may have seemed silly at the time and gone unnoticed."

Sticking out like a set of fangs.

"Okay, got it," Katherine said. "So you're thinking that the killer could have been doing this for some time? Maybe even starting at an earlier date...like the car accident was the beginning of their escalation, not the start of their killings?"

"Um, yeah, that is pretty much exactly what my line of thinking was. Recidivism in this town in awfully high, *Olivia Benson*."

"Hey, don't knock the crime shows, *SVU* is the greatest. Sickening, but great. And don't forget that I'm a thriller reader too, this stuff is right up my alley," Katherine joked.

"Don't change professions just yet, Ms. *'I don't do horror.'* Someone's tried to kill me for like the entirety of October, remember?" Williams said with a slight curl to her lips.

Katherine took a deep breath in, then released it. She nodded like she had been forgetting the very serious nature of the work they were doing. "Okay, right. Sorry. Where should we start?"

"Some of the boxes are organized by events, some are just date ranges; it all depends. It's sad to say, but in a place like Cemetery, we might have to dedicate an entire section to one thing." Williams shook her head. "Anyway, I didn't really break anything up by date. As I grabbed stuff it got more and more disorganized, so I guess we can just dive in? The boxes are labeled at least."

Williams chided herself for the lack of organization. She had just been so wrapped up in getting it done. She hadn't really given it much thought. But as she looked across at her... date? Girlfriend? Lover? Regardless of whatever Katherine was to her, she was a *librarian*, Williams probably set her mind on fire by throwing everything together.

"Sorry, I should have kept everything together more," she said, heat rising to her face. Much to her chagrin, Williams realized she was leaning toward girlfriend in personal preference. "You've been so helpful and you're always making sure I'm alright. I guess I'm just afraid I haven't earned it."

"Someone attacked you tonight. It's okay to be a little all over the place. It's just files," Katherine soothed. She walked around the table and kissed her softly, more sweetly this time and pulling her into a tight hug. "I'm right here, okay? Now, let's get to work."

They sat in silence for a time. pouring over stacks of police reports and files, descriptions, and witness statements. Every once and a while they would chime in with some small standout, something possibly related, but it was often debunked and put aside. Twice, Williams had excused herself to head to the kitchen for more coffee, each time brewing a full pot. After the fifth, or maybe the twentieth report, her eyes had blurred, permanently bleeding the lines together. She applied pressure to her eyes, rubbing them in tight circles.

No time for being tired, Abby. Reyes is out there somewhere. James Rictor and Andrea Nowack are out there somewhere.

She needed to keep her head in the game. Katherine continued to pour over the reports, with a level of ease that surprised Williams. Maybe she was being strong for her, or maybe it really didn't faze her. Were the thrillers she read allowing her to detach from the reality of the reports? Williams couldn't be sure, but she needed to get it together and act more like Katherine. If anything, reading through these simply reminded her of how much crime there really was in Cemetery. How often criminals got charged, and how often they got away with it.

People want to live here?

It was after the first hour or two that Williams started to think maybe she had been wrong. That her gut feeling was more off than ever before. If nothing was of use here, then it had all been a waste of time. Time she could have used getting an actual lead from somewhere else. Time spent saving Reyes, James, and the missing teacher, Ms. Nowack.

"Shit," Williams said, eyes straining. "This one here says a masked and robed assailant entered the Sanderson residence under the cover of darkness. Startling the victim and—" she quickly turned the page and read. "'Although the victim sustained several injuries, she eventually overpowered and killed the attacker.' Well, that doesn't exactly work."

"When did that happen? I don't remember that," Katherine replied.

"Uh, it says it happened in 1998. So, we don't remember because we were just kids."

Going back to the files, they gave it another half an hour, hoping it would be fruitful, rather than a total mistake. They had made it to the last couple of years, closing in on the end of the boxes Williams had grabbed for them.

"Something here," Katherine called. Going back to the report in her hand. Williams tried waiting patiently but found herself straining as the moments passed.

"And?" Williams blurted out.

"Sorry," Katherine replied quickly. "This report says that a man in a mask tried grabbing a woman as she went from her car in the driveway to the front door. When she drew her pepper spray, the would-be grabber ran. Oh wait." She shook her head in disregard. "It says she thought it was a *Halloween* Michael Myers mask though. So, that doesn't fit."

"Does it give any of the details? Maybe she didn't see them clearly." Williams bit her lip and thought it over. "Just because we found one mask doesn't mean they've never used another. Especially when they tossed it aside in the woods—it's not like they could have returned later to a crime scene. I think that's a good one to set aside. At least it's something."

Katherine put the sheet back into the filing folder and set it in between them. As a librarian, this was her strong suit, and nothing could possibly come close to how exciting this was. Helping with a police investigation? She could pinch herself, but she kept reminding herself of how serious the situation was.

Williams flipped open another folder, tossing the latest rejected file back into its rightful box. She could tell from the first line of the report that it was another dud. She was getting progressively angrier with each useless report. She needed a lead. She felt adrift again, lost in a sea of bloodless bodies and kidnapped children.

Lives were at stake here.

"Another here," Katherine called out suddenly. She leaned forward and read aloud: "'Female teen of approximately sixteen alleges seeing a tall, hooded figure outside her window, lurking and breathing heavily while trying to peer through.'" She scratched her nose and shook slightly. "Jesus, that's so creepy. What the hell."

"Shit like that happens more than you think, sadly. Creeps are going to creep. It's not often that one of them is successful though. What else does it say?"

"She claims to have seen them more than once, alerting her parents, but when her father got outside the house, the entire block was deserted. On this night in particular, the victim claims she awoke to the sound of someone outside her window jostling the screen. She screamed, alerting her parents. By the time the mother and father reached their daughter's room, the victim was on the floor and the window was open. The screen was later noted as having been tossed aside. The victim had struggled, receiving only two small marks above her collarbone. She was observed as wobbly and only semi-conscious. Parents declined an ambulance when shock was ruled out, their daughter having returned to steadiness."

Williams' stomach dropped, but she felt certain this was a thread she could pull. "Can I see that?"

Replacing the report back into the filing folder, Katherine slid it over to Williams. Grabbing the folder, she flipped through the information within. When she got down to the names on the report, she stopped dead in her tracks. The report was written up by Brennan but included additional notes by none other than Chief Carter himself.

When does he ever get personally involved in a lurker call? What the fuck is going on?

Williams flipped the page, seeing the names and address for the invasion. She grabbed her keys, jumping up immediately. She started at a run for the door, calling, "Come with me right now!"

Ch 18

INVESTIGATION

I

SENIOR DETECTIVE ED REYES considered himself a strong man. A strong person. He had spent an unimaginable number of years on the Cemetery Police Force, fighting the good fight. Or at least, fighting the fight to the best of his ability. He genuinely lived to serve and protect, or at least he aimed to. He never took more than he needed, but he gave it all freely. Yes, he may have faltered and let go of himself in recent years, but he didn't think that made him a bad person. He had survived incredible trauma, and while he may have faded away in the process, he never let his work falter. Regardless, if he didn't get to smoke a cigarette soon, he was going to absolutely lose it.

The sweats, the unbelievable headache, the irritability.

After he screamed himself bloody, the noise outside of the room picked up again. The lifting of something heavy, as well as something sliding across what sounded like concrete. Reyes assumed it was the same cold and damp floor as the one he had spent the last week or so on. He'd spent what felt like an entire day wracking his brain for a possible location they could be. Industrial buildings and warehouses weren't high up on his visited real estate, but he felt sure it must be privately owned, or something abandoned. Where else would you stash kidnapped people and turn them into bloodless husks?

Reyes readjusted himself on the floor. The rope that bound him dug at the cracked and reddened skin of his wrists. His skin was the type that reacted to a regular wristwatch, so the intense and over-tight binding was driving him almost as insane as the nicotine deficit.

He stretched his arms out and gripped the stale end of bread he'd been saving, depositing it into his mouth. He had the odd, almost funny realization that he was being held like a medieval prisoner, locked within a dungeon and pilfering the meager rations. Part of him wanted to laugh, part of him wanted to cry. He knew he needed to keep up his strength; if he couldn't, it'd all be over, mentally and physically. Especially with the deterioration from the lack of cigarettes—if he degraded in any other fashion, he'd come unscrewed.

"Come on, Reyes, keep it together. You're better than this. *Survive*."

His pep talk was interrupted at that exact moment by his door swinging open. Someone all too familiar came fully into view. "Back for more?"

II

Williams and Katherine exited into the hall and ran almost headlong into Chief Carter. He was standing in the middle of the hallway with a smile on his face. Williams' stomach churned. She was still clutching the case file in her hand. If he asked for it, she'd have to do some fast thinking to cover for them.

"Woah, ladies," Carter held up a hand to stop them, recognition taking over his face. "What's a lovely civilian like yourself doing in the precinct's basement? It's Katherine, right?"

"Yes, my name's Katherine. I helped with the search in the wood. We're—"

"Katherine here was just doing me a favor. Can't exactly go around doing my job in a cut up, bloody shirt, right?" Williams pulled at the collar of the hoodie she had borrowed. "I was so caught up that Colfax must have sent her straight to me down here."

"How nice of the special agent." Carter stared like he wasn't buying. "Where are we running off to?"

"Uhh, I'm-I'm finally ready to take another crack at that murderer Rictor," Williams blurted.

Carter's eyebrows raised into his hairline. "Evan Rictor? We had to release him. Detective Williams, you were gone for over a week, remember?"

"Shit, I must have forgotten," Williams said. "I was sedated the entire time, remember? Feels like a day or two at most for me, I was ready to continue with the interrogation. How'd he get off?"

"His lawyer finally showed, eviscerated what little 'evidence' we had, and we had to drop him. Don't worry though, guy like that, he'll get his," Chief Carter said, lips turning up. "What have you got there?"

"This? Oh, it's just the file for the missing person we linked to Rictor."

"I thought that was on my desk," Carter said. "I just came from there."

He let the statement hang in the air. A threat. A warning.

"Oh, that? This? No, it's not the report from your office. I meant I was going to get the file for the missing person...didn't know it was in your office though. I guess I don't need it if he's already gone. This folder here is the report on Reyes' disappearance. You know, staying up all wild hours of the night trying to gleam every ounce of information I can about how to save my partner." Williams made direct eye contact with Carter, stone straight. "I need him back. Alive."

"Don't we all, Williams, don't we all." Chief Carter stepped to the side of the hall to let them pass, the smile never leaving his face. "Well, you let me know what I can do to help. Anything at all, I'll make it happen. Ed is an old friend, after all."

"Yeah, alright. Thanks. Of course, I remember."

"Oh, and Detective Williams," Carter called. "Do you remember the name Henry Stiles?"

"Another name from the list?"

"Sadly. I have officers all over his neighborhood. We'll leave no stone unturned; I promise you," Carter replied.

"I was under the impression we had soft detail on pretty much everyone remaining on the list. Didn't Reyes put in for that."

"*Soft* detail is correct. Sadly, it must have happened during a shift change. Nothing was reported, nor seen. It's as if a ghost slipped in and nabbed him." Carter had an answer for everything.

You can overturn every stone out there twice, Williams thought. *You already know he's not there, don't you?*

Williams ushered Katherine down the hall and away from the Chief. As they turned the corner toward the staircase, Williams caught him reaching for his cellphone out of the corner of her eye. She hung back just long enough to see him raise it to his ear and mouth a hello that she couldn't hear.

Who are you calling, you two-timing bastard?

At this point, only two police departments, as well as Jon Elton, knew about the list of friends. And the author of the list was deceased; murdered in the midst of all of this. Williams was ready to bet which side of the Hudson Valley was perpetrating this whirlwind of horror, but just how far did it reach? Williams would bet her life—which she had so recently almost lost—that it was Chief Carter. If it went all the way to the top though, who was to say that it hadn't bled down into the ranks? She could trust no one. Not without Reyes around.

If there was anything Williams was sure of as she walked Katherine back through the station, it was that Reyes would never have been involved in this. He was a good man. He had let go of his appearance in recent years, sure, but he had never shirked on his duty. His job. He would not have stood for this. He still wouldn't. He was alive. Williams felt sure that wherever he was, he was fighting it right now.

III

Williams hoped for a minute alone with Colfax, but like everything else this month, it wasn't working out. She believed that the information in that case file alone was suspicious enough to lead somewhere; however Colfax was nowhere to be seen. Knowing that more information was better in this situation, and having next to no patience, Williams hoped she could get over to the Bowmans' and verify some of her wilder theories before Colfax returned. The less chance there was for Colfax to deny her again the better.

She was a stern woman, but Williams didn't think she was just keeping her head buried in the sand.

Williams led Katherine into the garage, signing out her favorite Dodge Challenger. She was surprised, and pleased, every time it was still in its spot. Her reason for taking it today was because she wanted the Mossberg 590 shotgun locked in the trunk. Something big was happening, and someone was targeting the troubled youth of Cemetery. That, and her car was still evidence.

The onus was on her to stop it if nothing more than for the simple fact that no one else would.

"Where is the Bowmans' residence?" Katherine asked.

"The address says they live on Orchard Street—it's the long winding road right next to the QuickChek. I used to have a couple of friends that lived off that road. Also troubled kids if I'm being honest, but from a different generation, I guess."

"I meant to tell you," Katherine began, cutting into wherever Williams' thoughts were taking her. "I saw on the news that the teacher that Ebony was with still hasn't been found. I work for the school system, and I'd heard that Ms. Nowack was actually going steady with the chief of police..."

"Wait, you're kidding?"

"No," Katherine replied. "I'm just telling you what I've heard. Rumors mostly, but schools are rumor mills even for adults honestly. I guess they had been seen together a couple of times, enough to create talk. Not sure how it ended though, or if it ended."

"What cause would they have to keep a relationship secret?"

Katherine seemed to think it over before saying, "I'm not sure, but I do know that her family ancestors are apparently Cemetery settlers. The kind of family that is engrained into the foundation of the place. Old money type of people. I'm not sure if that has anything to do with it though."

"Wait, Nowack..." Williams said, the thought lingering like a speech bubble. "Like *the* Nowack family? The whole town parade and everything?"

"Yes, that Nowack family."

"Shit, I know it's not that common of a name. I guess I just never gave it any thought," Williams said, lips turned down. She placed pressure on her forehead with a free hand.

For the remainder of the drive, they rode in silence. Their destination today was straight across town from the precinct, so Main Street was all they'd need. The one road let her mind wander. How could the chief of police, someone she had always known as being steadfast, so neat and trimmed, so authoritative, be wrapped up in something so terrible as this? This was the opposite of what she viewed him as standing for. The complete and utter opposite. Not only was he facilitating all of this, but she had to wonder if he was the mastermind of it, too. If he was the one capable of doing such heinous things to teenagers. To anyone.

To kidnap his own girlfriend, really?

Or was she in on it? Maybe she even convinced Ebony to go into those woods? That conflicted with the witness testimonies though.

As she pulled the cruiser into the Bowmans' long driveway, she pulled herself from her thoughts. She put the car in park and keyed it off. She assumed this would be far from pleasant. The department had lost them not one, but two children within a week. They had a right to be angry.

She turned to Katherine, taking in her beautiful face amid the chaos around them. She smiled to herself. "You should probably stay here for this. Sorry."

"It's alright, Abby. I'll be right here."

Williams pushed the car door shut and approached the porch that lined the front of the house, climbing the few steps. It was a long ranch-style house, with cream siding and blue shutters. She thought it was cute, despite the reason for the visit. She raised her hand to knock, but the door was yanked open before she had the chance to connect.

"Uh, I-hi, I'm Detective Williams." She cursed herself under her breath for fumbling, course correcting, "Are you Mr. Bowman?"

"No, I'm Terry Bowman, the girls' uncle. My sister isn't doing too well, as you can imagine. What can I do for you?" Terry Bowman was tall, dark skinned, and had a head full of shoulder-length braids. He was in a pair of sweats and a white tank top.

It was early. Williams was surprised that anyone was up.

"I was just looking to ask them a few questions about a report they filed about someone lurking outside Lizzy's bedroom?"

"Yeah, I remember that. Lit into her when I found out they didn't have Lizzy go to a hospital," Terry said. "Come inside. I'll grab my sister."

The house opened into an open concept dining room and living room combo. Williams saw the kitchen just beyond. She thought it was a pretty standard ranch, the insides a bit outdated, but pretty and homey, nonetheless.

The back of a tall black woman was visible in the kitchen, wearing an orange shift and leaning against the counter over a cup of steaming coffee. She seemed to be taking in the aroma more than drinking it. She stared aimlessly out the window above the sink. Williams could only imagine how she was feeling. What the loss of not one but two daughters in only a handful of days could do. It was truly amazing that she was up and standing.

A testament to her strength.

"Sis, this is Detective Williams. She has some questions and I think you should try to answer them if you can," Terry said, making the introduction. "Where's David?"

"In his room...our room, probably. He's...he's not coping. You know how he's been," Mrs. Bowman said.

Terry headed through the dining room towards the back of the house. Williams wasn't sure if she should start, or let the silence remain until Terry returned. On the one hand, she didn't want to repeat herself. She was sure the questions would hurt enough the first time. However, the silence was kind of killing her.

"Mrs. Bowman, I'm so sorry this happened. I promise I'm doing everything I can to stop it from happening to anyone ever again," Williams said.

"Thank you, ma'am, but right now I want action. I'm tired. So tired. I love both my girls and now they're gone. I have to bury them. No parent should have to go through that once, but twice? Before my oldest baby is even in the ground, and now my baby girl? I don't need well wishes. I need action."

"I have an active theory, Mrs. Bowman," Williams replied. She understood she couldn't relate, but she could empathize. "That's why I'm here, actually. My questions pertain to a suspect I'm after. I'm hoping you can help me."

Mr. Bowman, David, came up the stairs. His eyes were puffy and red rimmed, he wore glasses and a plain outfit. Terry came up from the basement right behind him. It was clear that he was holding the family up. It made Williams smile, but she turned away to hide it. She didn't want to be seen as disrespectful during their time of tragedy. Terry placed his hand on Mr. Bowman's back and guided him to the dining room table. "I'll get some coffee going," he said.

Mrs. Bowman sat with her husband on one side of the dining room table, motioning for Williams to join them at the other. She brought her coffee cup with her, but Williams noticed she still hadn't drunk from it. "So, how can we help you?"

Williams drew in a deep breath before beginning. "So, I have been working the case involving your daughters and—"

"And failing?" Mr. Bowman said before devolving into a wrecking sob. Williams didn't take the bait; she didn't have to. Nor was he wrong, not entirely. She also noticed there wasn't any venom behind his statement, either.

"You're not wrong, and I'll own that, but I am sorry. I am trying. That's why I'm here. I have a lead, and you can help me catch this motherfucker before it's too late." Williams grit her teeth, beyond apologizing.

"Ask away, then," Mrs. Bowman said.

Williams placed the case file on the table in front of her and opened it up. She wanted to have the report right in front of her for this. "So, you called the police for a lurker outside of your daughter's window. Probable forced entry, and your daughter may have been hurt. Is that correct?"

"Someone ripped the window screen off, but our daughter was cleared," Mrs. Bowman said, staring into her mug. "What does that have to do with this?"

"I'm of the opinion that the two are linked. I'm looking to make the connection," Williams replied.

Mrs. Bowman raised her eyes from her coffee for the first time, making direct eye contact. "You think that night was linked to my daughters' murders? Like, they were targeting my daughters the entire time?"

"Well, no, not necessarily, but that is a possibility," Williams said. "It's more that this type of thing could have been going on for a longer period of time than anyone thought. I no longer believe this is isolated to just this month."

"Meaning you could have stopped them then?" Mr. Bowman shouted.

"If your daughter had gotten a blood test that had come back with something on it, that could have led to an arrest. Or at least a wider investigation. We can't know for sure."

"So, this is our fault?" Mr. Bowman said, fire in his eyes. "You going to put it all on us?"

"David," was all Terry said, but it had the desired effect. Mr. Bowman sat back, returning to his random outbursts of sobs.

"No, absolutely not," said Williams. "None of this is your fault. But clues link things for an investigation. More is always more when trying to open a case." Williams attempted a soothing tone. "So, what can you tell me about that night? Is there anything that stands out that maybe didn't then?"

"Well, that main guy told us there was nothing to worry about. He said that it wasn't shock and with her recovering, it must have been nothing. We were all so frazzled, so we just went along with it. He made it seem like the best option. He said it would stop the stress for Lizzy, so we listened."

"Sis, you never listen to police telling you not to get a full report! You know better. What the hell were you thinking?" Terry cut in.

"We weren't thinking! Everything happened so fast. You can't even begin—"

"Ma'am, I'm sorry to interrupt," Williams said, doing it anyway, "but what man are you talking about? The police report I have said you declined an ambulance."

"Now that's bullshit," Mrs. Bowman said. "It was that fella that was just on the news the other day, the chief of police. I used to like him beforehand too, always so clean cut and calm. But not that night. He was all a mess with his hair all over the place. That bastard convinced us that everything was fine."

Ch 19

Hunting

I

The masked figure watched from the tree line above the Bowman's driveway. They had seen the detective step out of the police Challenger; had seen her slip inside the opened door. No one had come out yet. Still, there was another person in the cruiser. She looked around for a time but was now just staring at her phone in a daze as the minutes passed.

Alone and distracted. *Ripe* for the taking. Just how they were taught.

How easy it would be to slip from the tree line and grab her. The possibilities. The chance to take another. A chance to throw a wrench in the investigation. The questioning inside wouldn't last forever. Police were only tolerated for so long.

This one wouldn't fit the MO at all, but they were already too far gone.

The masked figure slid out from behind the trees, choosing their moment to make a move. Instead, they slipped on a rock still slick from the melting snow, rolling down the high-angled decline toward the driveway. The masked figure let out a cry of surprise.

The woman in the car turned to look out the window. The masked figure breathed in deeply, sucking in the plastic taste of the mask; this could be it. If they were seen, it would all be for nothing. A waste.

She popped the car door open to look around, trying to see where the shout came from. She looked up at the thick wall of trees, completely missing the prone figure halfway down the slope.

She couldn't see the danger from the forest for the trees.

The masked figure launched themselves to their feet and barreled toward the woman. As they found their footing, they removed a gleaming syringe from inside their sleeve.

The woman screamed.

II

Detective Williams was finishing up her questioning when she heard Katherine scream. She jumped to her feet and launched herself at the Bowman's front door.

Outside on the porch, Williams couldn't believe her eyes. A masked figure was locked in a fight with Katherine. Katherine was fighting like her life depended on it.

It did.

Williams unholstered her Glock 17, running from the porch. As she rounded the cruiser, she screamed for the masked figure to freeze, an icy edge to her voice.

Katherine pushed with all her might to free herself from the attacker. The second-long reprieve enabled the attacker to readjust the syringe held high. They stretched their hand above their head to plunge down with the syringe. Right into Katherine.

The hit never came.

Williams sprinted forward and crashed into the attacker's left side, taking them to the ground. If she had the time, she might have been proud of the tackle.

The attacker swung a heavy fist, connecting with Williams' jaw. They rolled on top of her and slammed a fist into her midsection, sending an earth-shattering ripple of pain up from her stitches. She couldn't breathe, but the attacker had no intentions of stopping. They rained heavy fists down on her ribs.

After what felt like an endless assault, they reached for the syringe again, raising it to incapacitate Williams for good.

She struggled against them, but the lack of oxygen was sapping her strength. Katherine was leaning against the cruiser, crying, and frozen in panic. Terry was being held back by Mr. and Mrs. Bowman. Williams strained to breathe and dodge the plunging syringe.

As the figure raised their hand for another swing, Williams clumsily struck with her left hand, and ended up striking the attacker across the throat with the butt of her Glock 17. At the same time, Katherine found her courage and raced forward, kicking the attacker across the back, the combination of which sent them flying forward.

The attacker bucked, practically flipping over Williams' head. The syringe sank up to the barrel in Williams' shoulder, the plunger expelling halfway before their finger slipped off. As the attacker's body slammed down on top of Williams, her gun jumped in her hand, letting off an incredible crack as the gun fired.

At such close range, the bullet tore through the attacker's abdomen. A spray of blood and tissue tore from the attacker's back, the bullet smashing the Challenger's passenger side window.

Mr. and Mrs. Bowman, too shocked to move, finally let go of Terry, who ran off the porch and around the Challenger. He ripped the masked figure off of Williams.

Sitting up, Williams' stitches pulled in a strange way. She was wobbly, which may have been from another beating, or the half-syringe of drugs in her bloodstream. Her shirt was bloody, but she didn't know if it was her own or the attacker's.

Rising to her feet, she looked Katherine over to ensure she was okay. She approached the bleeding figure. Terry stood a few feet off to the side. Williams wobbled toward the attacker, kicking the syringe from their hand, and almost tripping herself in the process. She sank to her knee in front of them, the knee of her pants soaking into the spongy grass.

She reached forward and, in a shaky move, tore the mask from the attacker's head.

Shotz. It was *Officer Shotz*.

Williams couldn't say she was surprised. However, seeing someone she had known for years bleeding out in the grass? There was no preparing for something like that.

Fuck!

Officer Shotz coughed, and blood dribbled over his chin. He was dying, and although Williams felt he deserved it for betraying the precinct, she still felt an odd sense of grief. If not necessarily for him, then for the Cemetery Police as a whole.

"They're gonna—" Shotz said weakly, dribbling more blood, "They're gonna fucking get you for this."

Williams leaned forward, grabbing Shotz by the collar. "Who? Who's going to get me for this?" Williams screamed in his face.

"You know damn well, who," Shotz replied, before releasing a breath and sinking back against the grass.

Williams mentally screamed. She was so mad she could spit. Instead, she released her ex-coworker, using his torn-up torso to stand herself up.

"Good fucking riddance," she yelled. As she reached her full height, she almost collapsed, the drugs fully circulated through her body. She was tired. Tired of being attacked. Tired of fighting. Tired of finding out that police officers were turning coat. If nothing else, this cemented in Williams' mind that she was right about them all.

She would stop them.

Katherine stepped forward, placing her arms around Williams and supporting her shaky weight. She sidestepped Williams over to the cruiser and helped her into the back seat. Williams took shaky breaths before leaning forward and vomiting all over the ground. The drugs, mixed with the trauma to her body, was simply too much. It was rejecting any more.

"We have to call this in, Katherine. We can't just leave a dead body here, but I don't know who to fucking trust anymore. I have to speak with Special Agent Colfax." Williams leaned forward again and spit, wishing she had something to remove the taste of vomit from her mouth and throat. "I think my stitches are bleeding down the front of my pants, that or I peed myself."

Katherine laughed, smiling beside herself, but with tears in her eyes. "Yeah, you're bleeding...we'll have to clean that up."

Williams gave a gargantuan effort and raised herself from the car, stepping wide to get past the vomit. She wobbled past Terry, grabbing his arm as she passed, and pulling him toward the family's porch. "I'm so sorry. You all should never have had to see that. To live through that."

Mr. Bowman and Mrs. Bowman's eyes were wide and wild, shocked. Terry still looked angry, ready for action. Williams wished she had a reason to unleash him.

She drew herself up, taking the time to make eye contact with each of them. "I need your help. I can't rely on my colleagues clearly, so I'll have to rely on you. Tell the precinct what happened and get a recovery team out here. Don't let them silence you this time. Stop saying no to interviews. I can give you contact info for a journalist named Meadows from *Cemetery Times*. I trust him to do what's right." Again, Williams looked from each set of eyes, "Can you do that for me—will you?"

Mrs. Bowman and Terry nodded.

Williams applied pressure to her abdomen. A heavy tinge of pain racked her body. It was indeed time to tackle the problem head on. Once she could think and stand straight, she would.

Part III:

Bitter Cold

Ch 20

ACTION

I

REYES WAS PULLED OUT of his room. The metal door scraped open like the yawning maw of death. A masked figure pulled him along by his tied arms, finally reattaching his restraints to what looked like a mobile surgical table.

Strapped in and raised to an almost standing position, Reyes saw that there were a couple of others lurking around the space. More masked figures. His thought process had been correct; he was trussed up in the center of a warehouse's docking area. The entire room, floor to ceiling, being gray, concrete, and rather dank. Points for abandoned too, most likely.

A tall figure stepped forward and tried to place a cigarette between Reyes' lips, but he resisted aggressively. "Oh, come on, it's just a cigarette. If we wanted you dead, we wouldn't poison you."

Reyes relented, leaning his head forward to accept the cigarette. Reyes took a heavy drag. The nicotine immediately set his weary soul on fire after so long away from it. With his exhale came a heady cough, phlegm coming up. "Jesus, what is this, an unfiltered *Lucky Strike*? You really do want me dead."

"You know, for all the cigarettes I've had to see you smoke, I never really cared enough to pay attention to which you smoked. But what do they say, 'Beggars can't be choosers?' It'll have to suffice."

In response, Reyes took a second drag, much smaller, and said nothing. *They've seen me smoke before? Why the mask, then? Where is Shotz? I'm sure that was him through the door earlier.*

"Part of you must see what we're doing here; part of you must know. We're not the crazy, evil people you and Williams think you're hunting. We care for Cemetery, all of us. I work day in and day out for this town. I work night in and night out too, when necessary. I don't want to hurt you; I want to help you."

"What could you possibly help *me* with? You going to make me your next bloodless victim? What exactly can you offer?" Reyes took another drag and shook his head, a motion cut short due to the restraints. It dawned on him, "Wait, you trying to turn me?"

"Turn you?" they asked, the mask tilting slightly to one side. "Oh, you have simply no idea how easy it would be to *turn* you," they said in something similar to a purr. "What I am attempting is to show you the light. With a past like yours, you should be on board already. You could be an asset to us. Possibly even piercing that incredibly thick skull of that partner of yours. The two of you would make us unstoppable. Just...think on it, and enjoy your cigarette, okay?"

Another masked figure was approaching. Although they wore a gorilla Halloween mask, there was something aggressive about the way they looked; their stance. Perhaps it was just unfriendly to conceal one's identity under a damn Halloween mask. Reyes wondered how far this thing stretched. With such a small police force and the high crime rate, he had to wonder how they were pulling it off, unless there was outside help. That line of thinking pointed to the fact that there was.

But who?

The gorilla figure whispered to the other quickly. Reyes tried his best to overhear, but the Halloween masks made it damn near impossible. The first figure responded, clearly giving some kind of instructions to the gorilla. They left, and the first reapproached Reyes, shaking their masked head.

"It seems that your esteemed partner has cooked up her latest plot to halt our progress. A good one at that. So, think on it, and I'll be back. But know this: a good police officer died today. Please don't join them."

What exactly did they mean about his past? And what did that mean that a good police officer died today? For now, Reyes had to believe they were just trying to break him.

If there was anything he had learned about himself in the days he'd been held captive, it was that he had been broken for a long time. Idle threats weren't going to be enough to shake him.

II

On the morning of October the thirtieth, Williams dropped Katherine at the Cemetery Library and headed around the corner to the precinct. The entrance was packed. She still wasn't used to seeing so many people in the building at once. Field Agent Mendes told her that Colfax had been tracking down another lead, and that she was on her way. She wasn't exactly supposed to share, but she said she felt like Colfax trusted Williams—Colfax had made another connection and was busy running it down out of state with one of her contacts.

Mendes told Williams that some of Cemetery's disappearances had already been on the FBI's radar, so that was probably the link that was made. The number of missing persons attached to cold cases was astounding. Reyes had been fighting a very steep uphill battle for years, often losing.

The thought of Reyes hurt to her core. She'd been out of the hospital for days now, had almost been killed more than once, and was still no closer to saving Reyes. The ache at the possible loss of her partner cut her to the quick. She'd trade places in a heartbeat if she could.

Several hours later, Colfax strode into the detective's office. She looked almost as worn out as Williams, each bag under her eyes taking on a personality. They had both been running nonstop.

"I found it. The information you were pressing me for. I told you I would."

"As it turns out, I did some snooping of my own, too, and you're not going to believe it," Colfax said. "You first."

"Combing the files, we found one that seemed a little too suspicious. A masked figure trying to gain entry through a window. That and they possibly drugged the homeowner's daughter. And that daughter was Lizzy Bowman."

Williams watched in triumph as Colfax's eyes shone in recognition.

"Not only that, but it was signed off with odd notes and add-ons, similar to the case file Chief Carter handed me before I interrogated Evan Rictor. So, when you weren't here, I took the chance and went to the Bowman residence, and they confirmed that not only was Carter involved, but he even urged them not to seek medical attention for Lizzy."

"Possibly trying to dissuade them from bringing further sets of eyes onto the scene?" Colfax speculated. Both women assumed that was the case.

Williams had made it to the less favorable part of the conversation. She had been dreading it, but there was nothing left she could do without it coming out. "While I was inside the Bowmans' house, I was attacked again. Well, they were trying to hurt my girlfriend and I intervened—"

Colfax raised a hand, pulling Williams from her deprecation. She prized herself from the desk chair—a process that was getting exponentially harder to do with her stitches and almost daily beatings.

"Williams, it's okay. As long as you're okay. I was already given the details of the shooting during my drive. Standard self-defense...well, if anything in this case can be labeled as standard. I'd tell you to take some time, but you wouldn't, would you?"

"Not a chance."

"It's against my better judgement already, but this does feel earned for you. I'm just worried you'll keep pushing until you're dead."

"If that's what it takes," Williams replied, noticing right away that it was the wrong thing to say.

Colfax exhaled fiercely, flyaway hairs dancing in the created breeze. "I'm going to trust you, okay? I need you to trust me too. You can't do this alone."

Colfax began relaying the information she had discovered with her team. As it turned out, there seemed to be missing files from the records room; items of interest that the FBI had been finding throughout the digitized records. The shame Williams felt at the miss grated against her skin like sandpaper. She should have known better. She'd bet that was why the Chief had brushed off the digital system, so he could hide whatever he liked.

How many times can I fuck this up? she thought, finding it hard to drop the matter. If anything, she blamed herself more because it could have led to an arrest before Reyes was grabbed. Before the others had been killed. *Poor Reyes. Those poor kids. James and Ms. Nowack.*

After Williams had calmed herself, retrieving them both piping hot coffees, Colfax explained that the type of clearance needed to block the information from being transferred was something only Carter could do. Once her contact, an IT type, confirmed it with her, she left almost as certain as Williams. Something was at least *wrong*, but that doesn't make someone a murderer.

In the hours since then, they had been combing through the files, mapping out an area, and trying to triangulate the attackers' location. Colfax was working at Reyes' desk. Williams disliked it, but mostly she was just glad she was no longer alone in the fight. Whoever Colfax's IT person was worked in the background with them from a secure laptop, doing things that Williams would never have been able to do alone.

With the amount of space and relative solitude needed, Williams still had her money on warehouses. She felt certain they were dealing with some kind of gang or cult following. Her attacker behind the school had run further into the woods. Meanwhile, she knew for a fact she'd seen Shotz show up in a squad car, in full uniform—it couldn't have been him.

Williams rounded the desk and stopped right behind Colfax. "What do you have?"

"A projected triangulation, not perfect, but a possible search area at the least." Colfax said. "Could be good. I've forwarded it to the team."

"We need to keep this hidden," Williams said, worried about the hands it would fall into.

"As liaison, Officer Prescott will be waiting for something to go over with the chief. So I disagree. If it appears that we're keeping him in the dark, the chief will suspect us anyway, detective. And you know I've already vouched for him." At Williams' skeptical face, Colfax replied, "look, if it does turn out to be your chief of police, showing this to him could make him unstable. Especially if it's accurate. I'm not saying I don't believe you at the point—because you know I do—but it's not illegal to look disheveled...even if I wish it were for some."

Williams had to smile at the joke. It was uncommon from what she knew of the woman so far, but it was a relief. "Okay, so send it to them, say we're getting close, and that we're going to have the agents patrolling and posting signage, looking for volunteers, that kind of thing. Flush them out."

"Also, I wanted you to hear this from me, but the location that Reyes was kidnapped?" Colfax gestured at the computer screen. "Practically smack right in the middle of the search area."

"Sounds like we better search that property again."

"You think they could be holding and killing the victims somewhere on the property itself?" Colfax inquired.

"A big house on a private road like that? A house owned by a guy that's seldom in Cemetery? Yeah, I think it could be a place to start," Williams paused, realization dawning. "The Chief told me that it was searched top to bottom! At the time I was only getting weary of him, I had suspected, but not felt like I knew for sure. I bet there was never even a search done on the place. He probably never even called the owner like he claimed."

Colfax saw her struggling with the epiphany. "No one can know everything and process it all at once. That's why we work as a team. If you didn't know your team was playing for the other side, that's not on you...it's on them. You can't be everywhere at once."

"It's just," Williams paused, swallowing what could have become a sob, "It seems so obvious now."

"Let's go get these bastards then."

In her haste, Colfax had forgotten that she'd already forwarded the search area to the Chief.

III

Katherine Jackson sat behind the desk at The Cemetery Library. She had already labeled the new arrivals, added them to the system, and shelved all of them save for one. One she wanted to read while she sat behind the counter for lunch. It was a sandwich again, this time tuna with a big leaf of lettuce and tomato. A small can of soda sat next to it that she'd forgotten, having been so engrossed in the book she'd grabbed. One of the parts she liked best about being a librarian was the availability to read through an ever-growing catalogue of some of the world's finest art. Some bad art too, but everyone had a taste for something they'd rather not share. Except with their librarian—perhaps indirectly—as they rented *50 Shades of Grey* for the fourth or fifth time.

Hey, no hate; she read it when it arrived.

She paused, looking up from the book to ensure she hadn't missed someone entering. The library itself had a bell, so she was certain she wouldn't miss anyone, but she often checked anyway. She bit her tuna sandwich and washed it down with a small sip of soda. The tuna was kind of dry, lacking enough mayo. She hated mayo, but somehow also hated when tuna didn't have enough of it. A vicious cycle, especially because she wouldn't make it for herself. She took another bite, anyway, knowing she needed to eat.

She was still having trouble eating and sleeping. Getting nearly abducted, followed up by being nearly shot with a passthrough bullet, hadn't helped her continuous nausea from seeing a murdered body. Now she had seen more than one technically.

She tried to push down the bad thoughts with better ones. Her's and Abby's, most often. She felt like things were going well, possibly getting serious, as they spent more and more time together. It was hard with the investigation, but she was willing to wait.

The bell above the door chimed. She called her hello without even looking toward the door.

A police officer, in full Cemetery blues, came through the chiming door. Katherine was sure she had never seen them before. She had blonde hair pulled back tight, and was kind of heavyset.

She assisted the door as it slowly swung to a close, pushing hard against the weighted hinge, and switching the lock the second it was. Katherine's guts turned to liquid as the fear set in. What was going on? The female officer sauntered toward her. Katherine grabbed for her phone as she neared.

"I wouldn't do that if I were you..." the officer said, letting some unknown threat linger in the air.

"You locked the door at a place you don't work, and you're threatening me?" Katherine wasn't just scared, she was angry. "What do you want?"

"Have you seen Detective Williams lately?"

"She dropped me off at work hours ago," Katherine replied. "What is this about?"

"She's been a little too meddlesome, unfortunately," the officer said.

"Meddlesome? Isn't that basically her job?" Katherine questioned. "And what exactly does that have to do with me seeing her recently?"

"Well, you have unfortunately been getting closer to her...and she's been getting too close to us." The officer let the statement hang in the air again. Then she removed the handcuffs from the back of her belt.

Katherine hurled her sandwich at the woman's face and ran from behind the counter. She just had to make it to the back door, and she would be out of here. She could get away.

As she reached the first bookshelf, the officer's foot jutted out and caught hers, sending her flying into the shelf. Books rained down on Katherine's head as she crumpled to the floor. Struggling for freedom, she blinked the stars from her eyes, the hardcovers from the top shelf giving her brain a shake.

She lifted herself from the floor and ran down the aisle. At the end she cut to the left, away from the back door, but also away from the attacking officer. She'd circle around. The officer didn't know these shelves like she did.

A misstep to the left put her right in the way of a small, circular stepstool. Her ankle connected with the base of the metal. Katherine went tumbling over it, releasing a scream of panicked pain. She hit the rough carpet and rolled, before coming to a full stop. She could tell the ankle was sprained. She heard the officer gaining on her.

Katherine painfully struggled to her feet. It was now or never.

She limped forward at a meager pace, each step pushing her closer to yelling out in pain. She made it back up to the front of the library. For a moment she thought she would be free to simply unlock the front door and go. As she neared it though, she could see a squad car with another officer leaning against the passenger side door.

Katherine let out a small sob but swallowed the rest of the cry down. She still had a shot.

The officer rounded the corner of the left most shelf. It was the furthest she could be from the back door.

Katherine launched herself to the right, wrestling with the pain as she fought for her life.

"Get back here, bitch," the officer yelled after her, starting to run. "There's nowhere to go!"

Katherine ignored them and ran as fast as she could, her ankle a stiff, swollen mass, each step jarring pain through her all the way up to her teeth.

Making it down the middle shelf, Katherine hopped over the spilt books. She took a right this time toward the stockroom door. To freedom. Salvation.

She reached the door and grabbed for the handle. Just as she was about to connect, the door was thrown open in an explosive thrust—the weight of which smashed into Katherine's hand, crunching skin and knuckles.

Katherine screamed, falling backward.

Through the door stepped a tall, imposing figure in a Halloween mask. Not seeing a real face scared her even more.

The officer turned the corner. "I told you there was nowhere to go, bitch. Why didn't you listen?"

The officer stepped forward and reached for Katherine, who struggled, screaming and kicking. The officer raised her up off the floor by her hair. She pulled Katherine's head back at a sickening angle and bashed her head off the nearest shelf, turning Katherine's career and love in life into her demise. She smashed her face into the shelf again, the hardcover books hitting Katherine's face at odd angles, blackening her already swelling eyes.

The final hit opened up Katherine's nose, blood pouring down her chin and dripping onto the front of her tee shirt. The officer pulled her hair and tilted her head straight back. "No, no, no," she cooed into Katherine's ear, "there's a far better use for all the red stuff."

The masked figure stabbed a syringe into Katherine's collar, deploying the plunger and laughing maniacally.

Katherine's vision blurred to black, and all she could do was worry about Abby's safety.

Ch 21

Come to a Head

I

Williams and Colfax pulled up in front of the mansion. An SUV followed closely behind them filled with five of the other agents. The Metlan house was a spectacle, especially in Cemetery. As Williams took in the place, she found it resembled the Old Mayor's Mansion in a way. It had a huge looping circular driveway that pulled right up to the front of the house.

Williams hung back, keying the Challenger off at an angle, a decent distance from the house. It would be best to avoid alerting whoever was inside. Not to mention pulling right up front was its own kind of stupid. She smiled as she thought that it was the exact kind of thing Reyes would have done. However, that thought brought with it the fact that he'd been stupid. Coming here alone could very well have cost him his life.

I'm coming buddy. Hang on.

Williams stepped from the car and popped the trunk. She unholstered her Glock 17, pulling the slide back an inch, ensuring the gun was loaded correctly. Good to go, she replaced it in its holster. She leaned into the trunk, retrieving the shotgun. She chambered it open and reached for the box of shells.

II

Senior Detective Ed Reyes was still trussed up on the surgical table. It had been hours, and something felt different. The air seemed energized. Electrified. Something was happening and Reyes didn't like it.

"Want to spew more of that murderous rhetoric at me, give me the old spiel again? It ain't gonna work."

Reyes felt sure he would have recognized the Chief's voice, mask or not, and he didn't think he was dealing with Shotz any longer either, but there had been something familiar about it.

The masked figure that strode forward was too tall to be either of them anyway. They stuck a cigarette into the corner of Reyes' mouth. Reyes took a deep drag as the figure held a lighter to the end. Putting the lighter away, the figure pulled back and struck Reyes in the face.

Reyes' head did a double take, smacking against the attacker's fist, then smacking into the back of the metal table and bouncing back. He shook his head, shaking the blur from the corner of his eyes. He'd been punched enough times in his life to know when a good one got him. And was that a ring?

Okay, so something is different. Kept my cigarette though.

"You've had long enough to think on it. What'll it be?"

Reyes tilted his head to the side, taking a deep drag. He exhaled in the masked figure's face. "You can tell Carter, or whoever the fuck is leading you idiots, I said they can eat the dirty boxer shorts they've had me wearing all this time. Fuck off!"

The figure struck again, connecting with Reyes' jaw. The fist crunched the lit cigarette up into his face. Reyes struggled against his restraints, groaning as he moved his jaw from left to right, feeling to see if it had broken. He opened his mouth in a snarl, exposing reddened, bloody teeth. "So tough, cracking a tied-up guy," he screamed at the masked figure, blood dribbling off his chin. "And wearing a ring, too, why not just trade it for a pair of brass knuckles?"

The masked figure wiped a string of blood off their hand from the second punch. The corner of a class ring stuck out crookedly as if it was loose enough to spin around.

Another masked figure rounded the corner. Her mask made her look like a real-life werewolf, with frilled sideburns and red, bulging eyes. Reyes could tell it was a woman; the scrubs she wore were a snug fit.

Are nurses in on this too? Reyes wondered. He spat blood onto the floor.

The female werewolf opened what sounded like a drawer out of his line of sight. She stepped back into view, opening a package of surgical equipment. A needle, looking like the kind they use for drawing blood but much larger, came out of the package as well as a long tube. The tube made him shiver. It was long and as thick as a hose. What were they going to do with that?

Reyes worked his brain to do the quick math. So, this group, whatever they were, were removing the blood from bodies, but doing so surgically? Clean and reusable, maybe? Where was the "why" of it though? He couldn't find it no matter how hard he tried. Why the targeted list then?

The nurse stepped forward, rubbing an alcohol swab over his collarbone, his torn shirt giving her the perfect area.

"Get your hands off me!" Reyes struggled against the restraints, hurting himself, but caring little. "What the fuck are you doing to me?"

The tall, masked figure stepped back in front of him, pulling the strap and ratcheting Reyes' head all the way back to the tabletop. "We've got a use for all that red in you. A thirst you could say."

The werewolf nurse sank the needle into Reyes' skin. The size of the needle hurt more than any blood drawing he'd ever received. She snapped the tube onto the back of the contraption, flicking it to get the blood flowing, before applying a piece of medical tape to his chest.

"What...what are you doing?" Reyes' eyes were large, whaled, the only parts of his body he could move. The fear showed plain in them. Escape was now a far-off plea, no longer a possibility.

"Well, this here is a needle, this here is just a tube, but when I connect them to this machine over here it'll start to remove your blood. Fast. We haven't exactly figured out the speed of it, unfortunately. Luckily, we are only concerned with the blood removal, not survival."

It could have been Reyes' fear playing a trick, but he felt like the werewolf mask smiled up at him. Sinister and foreboding, taunting him.

She stepped back out of view. Reyes was left with the tall, masked figure and his fear. He felt an odd tugging sensation on the needle. A strange noise he had never heard before started up behind him. The tugging became more consistent, like the creation of suction, but from inside him. The tube filled with red, his blood pouring from him, betraying him.

No, he thought. *Oh, Jesus, no.*

An echoing bang rang out from down the hall. The tall masked figure spun around, calling out to someone Reyes couldn't see.

"They're too late, whoever it is. It's all going down tomorrow, Reyes. We'll see how it all lands. Happy Halloween." The figure ripped the mask from his head. Brennan. It was *Officer Brennan*. A man Reyes had known for so many years. Standing before him, betraying everything they were supposed to stand for.

Reyes spit as hard as he could, a mixture of blood and phlegm landing on Brennan's face.

Brennan laughed, sliding the Halloween mask back over his face without even wiping it clean. He spun the class ring around his finger; this time it felt more like a taunt.

"Let's go everyone, someone's found us. Move, now!"

III

Williams and the FBI agents approached the porch strategically. Three from the left, three from the right, and one hanging back outside to cover a hasty retreat. Williams wished they had brought an eighth; she didn't like leaving anyone alone. Even the man outside. As she looked at them all, she realized they were about to risk their lives together, and she only knew two of them. If they survived, she'd rectify that.

They filed up the porch steps at an angle, aiming to keep clear of any view holes on the front door. Colfax had finally ditched the blazer, an FBI vest covering a button up, rolled up at the elbows.

As they lined up on either side, one of the agents held up a steel pry bar. Colfax nodded at her, making sure she was ready. She chirped an affirmative "breach" and the agent stepped forward, bashing the steel pole into the door frame. He aimed for just under the door handle. The reverberating sound was deafening in the overhang of the porch. The first bang cracked the door, but the lock held. "Again," Colfax called. The agent planted his feet in a wide stance, drawing the pole back before driving it forward. The door split in two; the side attached to the hinges flew inward, bashing the inner wall. The second half smashed into the floor beyond. Williams led the charge into the mansion, shotgun raised to her shoulder.

She stepped to the left, entering a large atrium-style room. The others filtered in behind her, flashlights and guns raised. They split again into threes. Williams, Colfax, and one agent going left. Field Agent Mendes and the other agents going right.

As they moved from room to room, panning their flashlights and guns into every corner, shouts of "clear!" rang throughout the entry floor. Williams pushed herself harder, faster than everyone else, always the first to enter. Always the closest to possible danger.

With every cleared room William felt as if someone was twisting a knife in her guts. No Reyes, no victims, no blood or struggle, nothing. It was eerily quiet and empty. Had they gone to the wrong place?

They couldn't have. A wrong call now would be the death of Reyes. Of Ms. Nowack, James Rictor, and Henry Stiles.

They weren't wrong. She could feel it.

"Floor's clear!" one of the agents called.

"Team two, upstairs now. Go!" Colfax ordered.

The other three agents disappeared into the darkness.

Williams heard them on the stairs, "There must be something here. We couldn't have been wrong, right?" she said.

"We'll find out soon enough, but no, I still have a feeling we aren't wrong." Colfax echoed Williams' feeling.

Williams started tearing the place up. She tore through closets, dressers, and desks. She found various notes and letters, mostly concerning Mr. Metlan's business. While she assumed he wasn't necessarily on the straight and narrow, the information in the letters had nothing about the current affairs in Cemetery.

Williams moved to the kitchen. It was dark and dusty, the counters showing obvious disuse. She pulled out draws and opened cabinets, revealing old cereal boxes and a knickknack draw filled with old chargers, lighters, and batteries. More nonsense.

She popped the fridge and looked inside. Removing a carton of milk, she inspected its expiration date. "Colfax, come here," she called over, holding the carton of milk out.

The Special Agent nodded, raising her gun back into her line of sight. "Abandoned houses don't typically have fridges full of unspoiled groceries, now do they?"

Team two made it back down the stairs. They hadn't found anything of note on the upper floors. Williams thought that Mendes looked crestfallen. Had she been hoping for a heroic day?

A banging rang out beneath their feet. The kind of thud that's felt rather than heard.

Maybe she can still have her heroic day after all.

"A place this big has to have a basement, right?" Williams asked.

"Find me an entrance to the basement—go!" Colfax ordered.

Williams pulled the fridge forward a foot or two, but there was nothing behind it.

Worth a shot, she thought. *Rich place like this is bound to have hiding spots.*

It was the kind of modernized mansion that would have all of *Tik Tok* going wild for some kind of hidden kid's playroom. Half the house was covered in large, tinted windows, like looking through sunglasses the size of an airplane windshield. Williams couldn't imagine having grown up there, the size and style being so far from anything she'd ever known.

One of the FBI agents whistled from somewhere across the open kitchen. Williams hadn't realized she was so tense until the call pulled her from her musings. She had been holding her breath and clenching her fists, her nails making half-crescent indentations into her palms. She shook herself and retrieved her shotgun from the kitchen counter.

Across the room, the agents crowded around what Williams had written off as a darkened bathroom or pantry, but was actually a tinted glass wall.

Colfax strode toward the glass and pressed at various points on the frame, as well as the glass itself. "How the hell do you open it?"

As she stepped up to it again, hoping to find some kind of release, a single lightbulb illuminated the opposite side of the glass. The light outlined a dark figure in a witch's mask. They wore long, billowing robes that ended at the wrist. The wrist led directly to a drawn revolver.

"Look out!" Williams yelled, throwing herself to the ground. The shot rang out, shattering and showering Colfax with glass as she stumbled out of the way. The attacker fired the pistol into the group of scurrying agents. Field Agent Mendes cried out, falling backwards; blood leaked from a graze to her forearm. Colfax shouted her name as she dropped.

Williams lay prone until she heard the telltale click of the empty gun. Luckily for them, it was only a revolver. She heard the attacker scrambling to reload. Pushing herself off the floor, she stopped in a kneeling position. She began pumping shotgun shells through the hole. Buckshot sparked as it leapt from the gun. In the flashes, she saw the others getting up around her. Each pump of the shotgun sent vibrating pains up her casted forearm.

Williams lunged forward and took up a position against the solid wall next to the shattered opening. All the agents followed except for one. Mendes was angry, struggling to her feet. She favored her injured arm, curling it to her chest.

She dashed into the opening, Colfax hissing after her to stop. She didn't listen. She was still trying to play the hero. That or she was now after revenge. Either way Williams thought she was being an idiot.

As she hurried through the piled glass, each crunch beneath her boots was a declaration of her location. They heard a scream; Mendes was in a physical struggle with the masked witch. The masked witch had swiped across the agent's face with a pocketknife, creating a slice from her forehead down. Now Mendes was locked in a struggle for the knife, her gun knocked away and forgotten. She even used her injured arm, although each yank was visibly paling her face.

Williams stepped over the fallen glass, following the struggle with her shotgun raised. She cursed after a few terrorizing seconds. She'd never get a clear shot at this rate. The agent was losing; her arm pained her too much to keep struggling. The slice down her face sapped her strength further, blood pouring over one eye and down the side of her face.

Williams didn't know what to do, how to help. She thought she had pushed past this, but she froze, the pale skin of the witch's mask drawing her back to her trauma. The white paint on the face of a madman, the disguise of a childhood favorite used to draw kids to horrible ends. An end that was almost hers. Sweat poured down her spine as her knees remained locked. She took in the struggle between them in slomo, both seeing it and not. Superimposed over her memory of gloved hands coated in blood. This was her nightmare.

However, if she didn't fight it, fight through it, her nightmare would always become someone else's as she would always be too late to save them. She had to fight.

Fight for Reyes. Fight for your mother. Fight for Sofia Mendes. And fucking fight for yourself.

In an act of desperation, Williams dropped the shotgun, stepped forward and yelled, "back away!"

Williams unholstered her Glock 17. Mendes screamed fiercely, rallying what strength remained to push the attacker back at arm's length.

Williams fired straight through the witch's mask.

Blood shot out of the back of the mask, spraying the wall behind. Dead, the limp body crumbled to the floor. The female agent collapsed next to the body. Williams wasn't sure if she was even conscious. Or alive.

She had done it. She would live with that. For this woman at least.

"Does anybody else smell smoke?"

Ch 22

A Head

I

Reyes struggled against his restraints. He could smell the cloying scent of gasoline. Could see the thickening smoke. Every few breaths he gave a triumphant heave.

He thought they were triumphant at least. Or rather, the fact that he was still able to heave at all was a triumph. Reyes hadn't recognized it yet, but he was fading. He was pale, his heartrate was slow, and sweat had begun to run like wet rivulets down his forehead and face. His entire body was on fire, or tingling, or *cold*. He could just as easily pass out. Pass away.

He struggled against the thought. Thought of Williams. How hard she would take it. What it would do to her. How they hadn't made up yet, not really. Not to mention he wasn't quite ready either. So what if he was a stubborn ass, stuck in his ways and having been around the block a few times too many, that didn't mean he was ready to bow out. He had let himself go, but not entirely. That was why he had stayed in the service for so long. It was a reason to continue, to fight. He wasn't letting go. Not by any means.

His blood fled from him in pulsing waves, rushing down the tube. Reyes always hated giving blood for this exact reason—having to see it happen. He'd always hated the needles too, if he was honest. His childhood fear had come full circle. He was bound too tightly to the table to move. The machine eked his life from him, and all he could do was watch.

As his vision began to dim, he wondered why he couldn't see flames yet. Wondered where Williams was. Hoped she was okay.

II

Colfax screamed orders at two of the agents, sending them and Field Agent Mendes outside to safety. Williams ripped the mask off the person she'd killed. With what was left of the face after being shot pointblank, it appeared to be a middle-aged man. It wasn't someone from Cemetery PD. She was certain there was something interesting there but had no time to ponder it.

Thick smoke had started to wind and twist its way up the basement passage. Williams ran back into the kitchen and grabbed a handful of old dishtowels she'd seen while searching. She passed them to some of the agents, tying one over her mouth like a bandanna.

The passageway was wide and carved from the stone itself. After several minutes, she wondered how long the property could possibly continue. All the while, the smoke thickened.

She coughed as she descended into the smoke.

III

Reyes awoke to flames. He couldn't tell if the heat was what had woken him, but he was surprised he'd opened his eyes at all.

Flames danced and ungulated all around him. Bright red, orange, yellow, and blues. Where there's smoke, there's fire. Still strapped onto the table, he looked from left to right...looking for what? A means of escape, a way to unbind himself, to survive the nightmare.

Reyes laughed, woozy from blood loss but happy for the momentary levity. The laughs turned to racking coughs that made him thankful the restraints were holding him up.

A harsh smell hit. It smelled like burnt copper or iron, a metallic tinge to the smell of smoke in the air. He looked down, forcing his eyes as far into the corners as he could. He could just make out the semi-shriveled tube attached to his body. The heat must have melted it, boiling the blood inside, and blocking further blood from passing. Saved by his own blood—that was a story he'd love to share with someone. With Williams if he ever made it out.

A desk from the left collapsed, sending flaming debris just feet away from him. The smoke hit Reyes first, thick and strong, filling his lungs with such a lack of warning that the stench made him want to black out.

Only a second later, the heat of the fire hit him. His scream brought on an additional coughing fit. He writhed against his restraints as the fiery heat began to bubble against his skin.

IV

Just as Williams felt sure the passageway leading into the earth would never end, she heard screaming. It was pained, mixed with heavy coughing, and was bloodcurdling. Even with the smoke reducing visibility, she picked up her pace. She crouched as low as her stitched abdomen would allow, but it still wasn't enough.

She would bet the screams were from Reyes. The thought made her sick.

The agents continued behind her, doing their best to keep up. They were all having so much trouble breathing that she didn't blame them for falling behind. They were lucky they hadn't ran into any masked figures. The place seemed cleared out, or at least the passage was. Williams assumed they'd set the fire and fled, hoping to catch the agents off guard and make an escape.

Clearly it had worked, but she was after Reyes.

The passageway came to an abrupt end. She tripped as the floor unexpectedly leveled, smashing flat on her stomach. Black and white dots danced before her eyes. The passageway had opened into a wide cavern-like area. It had the appearance of a rustic wine cellar, but if it was, it was the largest Williams had ever seen.

Colfax stumbled out of the passageway, stopping to help Williams to her feet. Williams mouthed her thanks before remembering the dishtowel, making the gesture unreadable. She wasn't sure she had it in her to speak; she might just as likely cry out in pain instead.

She opened her mouth to try but was interrupted by a final scream. This one was short, weak. She sprinted in the direction of the scream. She was lightheaded, having not gotten the correct amount of oxygen for some time. She coughed, but tilted herself forward, refusing to stop.

She took a right at the first corner she found. It was a corridor with metal doors on each side. It looked like an old office space. The ground here felt different, and she was oddly certain it was poured concrete. It felt like the back end of a warehouse, but with it being so far underground, that didn't make any sense. Did it?

At the end of the hall, she saw billowing, rhythmic flames.

It was a wall of fire unlike anything she had ever seen. The heat in the hallway alone was unbelievably intense. As the wall of flames flickered and danced, she thought that she could just see through it.

Reyes! Shit! What was Williams supposed to do? The flame presented her with an almost unimaginable choice. Her or him.

Just as she was about to jump through the flames, regardless of the price she'd pay, Colfax appeared out of nowhere, pulling the pin on a small fire extinguisher.

Had she had that all this time?

Colfax sprayed the extinguisher in horizontal lines, fighting back the flames. The second there was a big enough opening, Williams darted through.

Reyes was restrained on an adjustable morgue table and tilted up at an awkward angle. She saw bay doors past him, though one was now on fire. There was a stack of blackened wood and debris far too close to him. Williams yelped as she realized it was still burning him.

Without thinking, Williams grabbed at the wood with her right hand, tossing it away from him. She stomped at the smoldering remains until they couldn't hurt him anymore. She prayed to whoever would listen that the damage hadn't been done yet.

She took Reyes in. He had a needle taped just below his collarbone, a tube the size of a hose hanging. The tube was blackened and melted about a foot away from his body. A slow, gelatinous drip of blood occasionally splashed to sizzle on the concrete floor. She ripped at the tape and slid the heavy needle from his skin. It was hot to the touch and when she removed it, no blood came to the surface.

She patted down his body, looking him over thoroughly, to ensure that his clothes weren't burning. On one side of his face, he had burns across his jaw and neck. She cursed herself for being so slow, wondering how many more burns lined his body. His skin looked sallow and sickly.

She tried to rouse him.

"Reyes! Reyes, I'm here. I came for you."

He didn't stir. There was no sign that he had heard at all. She tapped his face, trying harder to bring him to wakefulness. Nothing. She slapped him, desperate. Still nothing.

"No no no no, don't you fucking dare, Reyes. I'm right here! Don't you even think about it!"

She choked out a sob, coughing through her dishtowel. She remembered all of their time together, their late night and early morning stops at the Cemetery Diner. Their highs together of solving crimes. She thought about their lows too. Their arguments; both of their incessant need to be right all the time. How he had tried to apologize, but she wasn't ready. She would miss it all. She couldn't lose it. She couldn't lose him. Not yet. Not now.

Never.

He had become the father figure she never knew she needed. She had gotten time with her own father, no matter how estranged things had become, but Reyes had fulfilled something she hadn't known she was looking for after his passing. He was her partner, an accepting person, and a loyal friend. She loved him. She needed him now.

She felt for a pulse but couldn't find one. His skin was hot and dry to the touch. She wanted to lower the table he was on, to remove his restraints and resuscitate him, but she couldn't figure out how. The table controls looked melted. She was panicking again. She always tried to be so levelheaded and strong, but it was always Reyes' demeanor that brought her back from that line, the panic. Without him, she had been losing it. Without him...

Colfax screamed, "move," shoving her out of the way. She too felt for a pulse, finding one, or perhaps not. She removed something from her belt, stabbing it quickly into Reyes' chest. She waited while Williams sobbed.

Tears ran down her face as she took in her partner. She prayed he wasn't gone yet. She had tried so hard, but she was still too late. This was all her fault.

As Williams was about to scream out her pain, Colfax stepped back triumphantly. "He's got a pulse! It isn't strong, but he's alive. We've got to move him, now!"

Williams wanted to collapse on the spot. Instead, she drew in a deep, smoke-filled breath, holding back her cough, and got to work.

Ch 23

SMOKE-INDUCED FUGUE STATE

I

Due to smoke inhalation, they had sent several ambulances for the agents. Williams forced her way into Reyes' one. She took ragged breaths through her oxygen mask, reviving herself in between rib-shaking coughing fits. She held out her arm toward the paramedic as Reyes was pushed in. She tried to speak but coughs racked her body. The paramedic looked at her like she had eight heads before turning back to focus on her partner.

She coughed again, barking out, "He needs blood, you can give him mine." She held out her arm again, before being consumed by wheezing.

"We don't know anything about him yet, you could kill him, ma'am. I can begin a transfusion with our universal supply now, but he'll need more as soon as we get to the hospital."

As the blood began to flow, Williams felt such a wave of relief that she could have collapsed if she weren't already lying across the ambulance bench. She took in more of the oxygen, the mask fogging with her heavy exhales and coughs. Breath. Something she thought she might have taken her last of.

There was a reason the passageway seemed to last forever. The decline in the path led through the side of the mountain the house sat upon, the long private driveway hiding the warehouse. Williams had to wonder if this information implicated Mr. Metlan or not. Otherwise, he was bound to be awfully upset at the loss of such a property.

Colfax and Williams had fought their way out of the flaming warehouse, but the long driveway had hindered the arrival of the fire department. The house had lit up like a matchbox. They were all lucky to be alive. Even Mendes was being patched up. They believed she would be alright.

Watching the steady blood flow, Williams reached out to grip Reyes' limp hand in hers. He would be okay. He would.

II

The hospital put them all in one room at Colfax's insistence. Most of them were only being checked for smoke inhalation. Colfax and a couple other agents were already up and about. Williams was placed in a bed so they could check out the burns on her hand, as well as her other injuries. Luckily the burns were slight, and for once her stitches had held up.

Sofia would be staying a few days.

Reyes would be having a much longer stay. They still couldn't believe he was alive, and with good reason. The level of blood loss he had suffered and come back from was something they had never seen.

Williams wasn't surprised, she knew he was a fighter. He fought. *Hard.*

Across the room, the agents were discussing what came next for the case. Even Sofia was propped up in her bed, animated. Her forearm was wrapped tight with bandages, as well as part of her face. Williams listened but kept to herself, the nurses and doctor still cleaning her stitches and burned right hand.

"...if they ID that person that was shot, that should give us more of a lead."

"But the detective didn't recognize them..."

"...still a chance dental will turn something up on them either way when they clear up the fire."

"Who could do something like this to other humans..."

Other than random questions and speculation, the conversation never solidified toward one cohesive topic. They never touched upon who they thought was responsible, which Williams was grateful for, seeing they were not alone. She was curious what they thought though. She found that hearing other theories often gave a better perspective to her own.

Having shot and killed someone that didn't perfectly fit into her theory, she had to sit and readjust. Had she been too attached to it being the Chief, or was he still involved in all of it somehow? As Colfax pointed out, there was nothing illegal about being disheveled. It just seemed to match up too evenly, the pieces slotting into place. She often trusted her gut. Seldom did it lead her astray, but she never had a problem admitting when she was entirely wrong.

The problem was that she still felt certain. She wasn't shaken off the scent. She had wondered if he was the leader of the pack or simply a piece at play. Perhaps this pointed to him not being the top dog? Still involved though, that was something she couldn't shake. There were two things she was certainly missing: if there was someone else running the show, who could it be, someone inside or outside of Cemetery? Most importantly, she was missing the why. Why would someone do this, and why were they doing things with peoples' blood?

Could the blood simply be a red herring? How about the mutilated body parts? A missing head, a foot, a heart, a lung. If she removed those variables from the equation, they had next to nothing to go on. Still, it could be just a killer's sick machinations, right?

The thing that stuck out the most was the Chief's disintegrating facade at every timely appearance he made. His appearance at her house? He had practically beaten Reyes, and now that she thought about it, she had called her partner, not dispatch. Reyes was already on the move when he called for backup. Again, at the school, she was certain the principal had told her Carter had finished his business and left. She wracked her brain but couldn't be certain that his car had been gone from the parking lot. She thought it had been, but she wouldn't take a bet. Not to mention the attacker hiding in her car had somehow known that it was *her* car.

Surely a lurker could have picked up on that too, but she was certain she would have noticed something.

Reyes' body convulsed, drawing her from her rumination. His body bucked and his hands gripped at the sheets. He shook for a moment more before going limp.

She rushed to Reyes' side, grabbing his now limp hand, and placing her other hand on his face. His eyes were open.

His eyes were open.

"Reyes?" she asked in a whisper.

"You have to get out there," Reyes said, his voice little more than a groan through his teeth.

"We will, Reyes," Williams promised, her eyes tearing. "God, I'm so happy you're okay. I thought we had lost—"

"Listen to me," Reyes began before turning his head away and coughing hard. "Listen, kid, the people who did this to me, the one I saw without a mask, was Brennan. They're other freaking cops. You need to be prepared."

"I know," Williams said. "Shotz attacked Katherine and I...I shot him Reyes. He's dead."

"Good," he choked out.

"Was there anyone else there, anyone else you saw?"

"Way more people, kid. A troop. Even a nurse. All masked though."

Reyes coughed again, turning his head to the side. Williams saw the mesh bandaging they had used to cover the burns on his face.

When he turned back his face was pale, grim. He was in pain, that much was clear, and he was fading fast. Williams scooped up the morphine button, placing it into his hand.

"Press it, Reyes, it's okay to rest. You've earned it."

"Listen to me." Reyes let go of the button and gripped Williams' forearm hard. "Brennan said something stupid about something big going down tomorrow. He said, 'Happy Halloween' before he left me, thinking I was as good as dead. I think he gave something away."

Something clicked, or more like smashed, into Williams' mind. "Fuck, Ed. They're going to use the cover of the Halloween costumes on kids. They're going to blend in so they can't be found."

Ch 24

Halloween

I

Detective Williams wrung her hands as she leaned against the edge of her desk. She faced the cork board she had been pinning things to for the better part of an hour, her right hand still puffy and bandaged from bare-handing the burning wood, but she needed the outlet for her anxiety—the pain of which was a welcomed distraction.

Katherine hadn't answered her phone all day. She wanted to stop at the library to make sure she was okay, but there was too much going on. Each minute without something to drive her mind was murder.

Sofia was recovering at the hospital. She was still armed, but Williams had insisted on another FBI agent being left behind to guard the door. Williams had loaded and snuck Reyes his gun as well. She was past taking chances.

That only left her and Colfax with six additional agents. They had come back to the precinct with all intentions of arresting Chief Carter and Officer Brennan, but they were nowhere to be found. Colfax had ordered an APB to be put out on them, then she had taken over control as the acting-chief.

Colfax was conducting interviews—more like interrogations—on the remaining Cemetery Police Department staff. She had already cleared some of Williams' coworkers, but she felt more comfortable with the FBI agents.

Until this chapter was entirely closed, she'd always be looking over her shoulder when it came to her coworkers. First her suspicion of the Chief, then the near-death experience with Shotz in a mask. Then Reyes said it was Officer Brennan doing everything to him. Both partners turning against the force? She had trouble imagining that they were all bad.

Misguided or manipulated maybe?

Does that mean there's hope for them?

Williams set her attention back to the cork board. She had pinned up a large selection of pictures from the case files. An array of victims, suspects, and possible leads covered the board. It was true the idea came from TV shows, but it actually helped her to see the case visually. This case came at her so fast in those beginning days that she didn't have a moment to collect herself.

Fighting to stay alive at every turn will do that.

The particular threads didn't want to come together. Chief Carter, Shotz, Brennan. Those three connected, they made sense. The victims—Robbie Elton, Brandon Doty, Lizzy and Ebony Bowman, possibly James Rictor and Henry Stiles—those connected too. They were all from the same friend group, but why were they targeted? Other than Brandon Doty, the oldest and arguably the leader, they were petty thefts at best. Hardly criminals on the police radar. Stoners. Potheads. What did that mean for the case?

Was Carter the new judge, jury, and executioner of pot-smoking residents in Cemetery?

As Williams took in the board, her left hand came to settle on her chin in thought. Brandon Doty had been picked up a few times. So had Robbie Elton, but his parents were certain he had been cleaning up. The lack of anything recent seemed to agree with that. So, what was the common denominator? Why were they victims instead of at home with the munchies? Brandon might have been on a bad path, but she wasn't so certain all the others would follow. Some needed genuine help, others just needed parental attention. Maybe some were destined for prison, but who was to say?

Certainly not Raymond Carter.

Carter, Carter, Carter...where the fuck are you?

Thinking of Carter led her back to the victims. Those still missing too. Then she remembered Katherine had said the school had gossiped about Nowack and Carter being a secret item. And that Nowack was from old Cemetery money. A family like that was bound to have some properties, right? Maybe she could work with that.

Why would Carter kidnap his ex? Had it ended so poorly that he had a vendetta against her? If that was the case, then why had Ebony Bowman been killed first? Maybe her death was more intimate to Carter—maybe it wasn't to be displayed?

She rounded her desk, squished into her seat, and keyed up a search on the Nowack family.

They were definitely engrained in Cemetery history. Various news articles pegged them as philanthropic millionaires. She found digitized news clippings from as early as the 1910s showing the opening of new buildings and storefronts, lending credence to her idea about properties. It seemed as if the Nowack family owned over half the town.

The recent articles online spoke of how worthy and wonderful Andrea Nowack was as an heir to the family estate. Even with the family's wealth, she insisted on pursuing a career as a teacher, wanting to give back more than money alone. She had hosted more events for the school than anyone else, personally funding anything the school could not. She'd been very outspoken about the need for action and counseling for kids in need.

She seemed like the exact opposite of Raymond Carter. Maybe they did break it off, or maybe he had radicalized her. Crazier things had certainly happened before. Was Carter manipulative enough for something like that? If the man could corrupt the police force, the people sworn to protect, he could probably do anything.

Williams tried to narrow her search down further, looking for warehouses or secluded properties. It was slow going as she wasn't exactly accessing a public records forum.

Williams eventually selected a set of five places she thought might fit the bill, overlapping the map with the triangulated area.

Blood thumped in her ears even though she was sitting still.

Could this be it?

She jumped up from the desk chair and ran for Colfax.

II

"You can't do this," an officer shouted. "I want to speak to my union rep!"

Special Agent Colfax motioned to the officers on the door, Officer Prescott and someone she didn't recognize, who stepped forward and began handcuffing Officer Pinsley. The arresting officers' faces were strained, but they read their coworker his rights and led him from the office.

Colfax turned. "Williams, come in. I'm just interviewing officers. Some have proved rather loyal to Chief Carter. Whether or not that implicates them, remains unknown for the time being. My hope is that someone cracks."

"I'm not so sure they will, Colfax," Williams replied.

"Why, what's going on?"

"I've been working through what we have so far, and I think I've got something. Carter was apparently seeing the missing teacher, Ms. Nowack, in secret." Williams leaned forward, absentmindedly picking at her chin. "Originally, I had just pocketed the information. Not to mention I almost got butchered—again—that day. But I've been trying to rearrange the pieces of the puzzle, and I think that could be a big one."

Colfax sipped a coffee and took a seat, rolling the desk chair closer. "Alright. I'll bite. What do you have?"

Williams walked Colfax through the Nowack family history. She told her the theories she'd been brewing surrounding Ms. Nowack and her disappearance.

Colfax's face lit up at the mention of potential locations of interest.

"I've got three locations owned by the Nowack family that are within our triangulated area," Williams said. "Reyes said something big is coming tomorrow. We're running out of time. I think the safest way to do this is if we make calculated raids on each one simultaneously."

"In a perfect world, maybe," Colfax countered, "but how are we going to do that? One of my agents is probably blinded in one eye, your partner is more than half-dead, another of my agents is guarding them. Half the precinct is in an uproar about the Chief being wanted for questioning and the other half is most likely in on it. So, at best we're a team of eight trusted people, us included. Maybe ten. Any more than that and we'll be watching our backs as much as the front."

Williams leaned back in the chair, thinking hard. "You're not wrong. It isn't enough when we don't know what we're getting into. Too much of a risk. Can you request more agents?"

"No," Colfax said. She exhaled and continued, "Probably not in time with such short notice. Not by tonight. What time is it now?" She looked at her wristwatch. "It's already the middle of the morning. I'll try making some calls, but I have my doubts."

"It's a risk I think we have to take."

"It's a bad one though," Colfax pondered it. "It could be the death of us all, or worse, innocent people."

"We don't have a choice, do we?" Williams asked. *Shit.*

"No." Colfax let it hang in the air before finally continuing. "So, what's your plan? We want to end this, but we need to ensure we aren't about to turn Cemetery into a freaking blood bath either. Especially not on Halloween night while the entire town is out."

"What about a curfew?" Williams asked.

"There's not enough time. We don't have the resources to ensure it happens. So what's the plan?"

III

Colfax had vetted Officer Dans, the other cop that Williams had seen arresting their coworker Pinsley. Together, Prescott and Dans had vouched for an additional seven officers, bringing their groups total to seventeen. Still not enough to safely split up, but enough to bolster their chances. Colfax trusted a few others enough to send them on regular Halloween details.

Williams dialed Katherine's cell one final time. She also tried the library, but it rang and rang, without voicemail.

She hopped in the Dodge Challenger and pulled out of the parking lot, the car's window still missing, letting in the cold October air. She bolted the heat on high and whipped the cruiser around the corner to the library. A tight knot of worry grew in her belly as she worked the car around the road. The feelings of anxiety were solely reserved for Katherine's wellbeing.

It was practically a ghost town. She pulled right up front, slamming the car into park and jumping out. The front of the library looked normal, nothing out of place. Williams took a deep breath of the piercing air. The mist and fog had continued rolling in, giving the street an eerie appearance in the overcast morning. Williams looked down either side of the street, the fog distorting in places, clouding in others. The trees lining the street reached overhead, practically touching the trees on the other side. The bare branches of late October made a skeletal dome above her. The opposite side, which wrapped around the town's twin lakes, was hidden entirely. The view was ethereal, a preternatural twitching raising the hairs on the back of her neck.

Williams shook herself from staring, the very nature of which was creeping her out.

She approached the front door and knocked. The sticker on the right side of the door said they should be open right now, but the inside appeared dark.

When no answer came, she knocked again, harder, and the door shook open.

If there was one thing Williams knew about Katherine, it was that she was a stickler for details. She wouldn't have forgotten to lock up, even if she'd rushed out sick or something. A sinking feeling overcame her as she pushed the door wide open. "Hello?"

Nothing looked out of place, at least not in the entryway. She called out again in case someone hadn't heard her.

Could Katherine still be here in the back working on something? She thought it unlikely, as the lights were still dimmed, but she wouldn't put it past Katherine to be so involved in something that she'd have no idea what time it was, working right past opening. The corners of her mouth twitched up at the thought; it was a thing she loved about her.

The levity was short lived as Williams stepped further into the library. There was a heaping pile of books knocked off the front shelf. Leaving them there was something Katherine never would have allowed in a million years.

Williams unholstered and raised her pistol. The bandages over her burnt right hand made it difficult to wrap her fist around her left hand.

A creak from the back drew her attention.

Ch 25

The Librarian

I

Rounding another shelf, Williams had to circumvent another stack of fallen books. These ones, however, were intermixed with drops and flecks of blood, now dried. The edges of two of the shelves had dried blood on them as well. Williams crouched and saw what looked like a tooth shard. She tightened her grip on her pistol, the tension in her muscles growing.

The door to the back office was locked—or blocked by something. Williams leaned her shoulder into it, taking deep breaths before each individual slam. Each one moved it a millimeter, hardly making it worth it. Each try sent a jarring rhythm of pain through her stitches, cast, burns, bruised ribs, and ego.

Enraged, Williams leaned back, and repeatedly Spartan-kicked the door. The results were much more satisfying. The door began to give, splintering, and cracking a third of the way from the door handle. The opening was just wide enough for Williams to reach through and push the blockage back with her left hand.

In the relative darkness of the library's back room, Williams could make out that someone had pushed a small desk behind the door, the top of which stood just below the door's handle. It was lightweight, but perfectly placed.

The space smelled like one giant book. The musk of old, yellowed pages, moisture, and history. Williams didn't have to wonder why Katherine loved working here. She'd bottle that smell if she could.

Underneath it, there was a faint hint of something else. A tinge, a sting to the nostrils from something far more sinister. The smell was of blood. It smelled exactly how the Elton's house had smelled, just in smaller supply. The Elton's...that felt like a lifetime ago. Williams could hardly account for the days anymore. She'd stopped trying, though she stubbornly remembered she was supposed to have three days off in a row...over a month ago.

Raising her pistol again, she sidled further into the office space. There was a long hallway to her right. Where it led to, she had no clue, as the hall itself was pitch black. To the left, she saw more office space. Another desk, filing cabinets, a safe, a shelf in the corner filled with supplies. Otherwise, the space was clean of anything resembling a struggle. She thought she could make out some blood spots on the carpeting, but if they were, they were old.

Williams looked for a light switch while keeping her eyes peeled for anything that might pop out at her. She found the switch, flipped it, then blinked rapidly to stave off the brightening overhead lighting.

The hallway to the right was another long one. With the light on, she saw a staircase at the end of it.

"This place has an upstairs?" she wondered aloud. Then she recalled that the library front had a small, but beautiful, stained-glass window above the shelves of books. She had assumed it was a small attic or storage-style area. She expected one of those rickety out-of-the-ceiling wooden ladders, not stairs.

She crept down the hallway. She thought she heard a soft whimpering or mewling from above.

Slowly she snuck down the hall, keeping her side pressed tightly to the wall. It gave her the best angle toward the stairs. She didn't want any more surprises.

As she climbed the stairs, she was reminded of Reyes' side-stepping waddle up the stairs at the Eltons'. She tried to emulate him now, not making a sound. She kept her Glock 17 raised, and as she crested the top step, could just make out the heap of someone in the corner.

Katherine.

It was *Katherine*.

II

Senior Detective Reyes lay prone on his hospital bed. He was heavily drugged, sleepy, weak. Currently though, he was simply pretending to be asleep.

Field Agent Sofia was still abed herself. She was in a hushed conversation with the agent guarding the door.

"I just don't understand...you're telling me I'm now guarding myself, as well as the detective? Where the hell are you going?"

"I told you already. Colfax needs everyone she can get. You have your gun, your phone, a radio. You've got this."

"I do *not* 'got this'! I'm practically as drugged as that guy," Sofia whisper-shouted, pointing across the room at Reyes.

"It's done, Sofia. The replacement officer is already on the door. Lock the door from the inside if you want the extra safety between you and the police officer. He's to guard the door, nothing else."

"I don't like this," Sofia murmured. Her recent tribulations had sapped her of courage.

So, this is it, Reyes thought. Williams had understood how serious he was and called everyone to action. Just like he knew she would.

She's coming for you, you bastards, and there ain't nothing you can do to stop her.

III

Katherine was pale; sallow. Her skin was wrapped tightly on her beautiful face, as if there were no longer enough to cover it. Her eyes looked hollow and empty. Her lip and nose were busted, and there was dried blood all down her chin and neck. She was unconscious.

Williams saw needle marks on her shoulder where Katherine's shirt had been torn. From where Williams stood, she didn't even look alive.

Williams lowered her gun as she approached her lover. Just as she was about to kneel beside her, a sharp kick came from behind, sending Williams sprawling. Her gun clattered across the floor and was lost in the meager lighting. She quickly raised herself from the floor, looking from Katherine to her attacker.

Officer Owens. Britney Owens. Williams had gone to school with her, been bullied by her, been hazed by her at work, and now she was murdering her girlfriend?

God I'm sick of this shit.

Officer Owens raised her fists before her in a confident stance. Inviting Williams forward.

"You did this? Why? What the fuck could Carter possibly offer you?"

"Carter?" Owens wondered aloud. Then she laughed, a hearty and sickening sound. "Carter didn't offer me a thing."

Williams knew she was stronger than the other woman. Owens was at the bottom of every training or competition the precinct had, but she did have Williams in weight.

Williams lunged over Katherine at the woman. Punching her right in the jaw. Owens' head snapped back like she was in a movie. She really was the weaker opponent. Williams stepped in, taking advantage of her opportune start to the fight. She landed several more punches to Owens' stomach, ribs, and face. A trickle of blood dripped from Owens' nose as she tried to reengage.

Williams stepped in even closer, working to break down Owens' defenses. She swatted away the other woman's weak strikes, dodging those she couldn't block. She planned on punching her until she couldn't raise her arms anymore.

She was going to tear Owens limb from limb for what she'd done.

"You're. Fucking. Dead," Williams growled.

Williams leapt, jabbing Owens in the throat before bashing her fist into the woman's left eye. She was beginning to look like blonde-haired pulp.

Owens landed a glancing strike to the side of Williams' head, making her laugh. The sound was maniacal and wicked, even to her own ears.

As Owens tried to spin away, Williams stepped closer, grabbing the other woman by the shoulders. Instead of cowering, Owens twisted to the right and slammed an elbow directly into Williams' stitches.

Williams dropped to the floor like a sack of cinderblocks, the air crushed from her lungs. Spittle dripped from her mouth as she faced the floor, trying to find oxygen through the crippling pain. The agony was so hot that her ragged breaths did little to draw anything in.

Before Williams could recover, Owens started raining down kicks to her ribs and hips. The pain tore through her with each consecutive strike; she couldn't even cry out in pain. It was like the lack of air while fighting to the surface underwater. The glimpse of drowning is enough to cause panic, the added emotion sapping what little is left. The only thing present is the need to survive. To fight it.

Williams gave one final effort to raise herself, catching a kick from Owens on her elbow, instead of her ribs. The force of the blow sent her sprawling onto her back across the floor. She propelled herself backward with her feet, trying to give herself a moment to breathe.

"You think you can stop all this from happening?" Owens said. "We're the good guys here. I'm not going to let you stop me—"

"You're fucking deluded, is what you are!"

"Deluded? I will say, I did enjoy chasing your little girlfriend through the place. You know...I'm the one that smashed her face up. Over and again. She deserved it for meddling. And it was kind of fun." Owens shrugged, admitting it to herself as much as to Williams. "You know, actually...if it wasn't for you, none of this would have happened to her."

The anger, grief, and shame fired through Williams' body like fuel. Still struggling to breath, she reached with her hands, still sliding backward. Away from Owens. She just needed to give herself a big enough opening so that she could stand.

As she skidded back further, her bandaged hand bumped into something cold and hard.

My pistol! She had found her gun in the dark. She struggled to get her hand around it.

Officer Owens closed the space between them. She removed a stiletto blade from her uniform pocket, flicking the blade open. The steel reflected the slight light from the stairwell, gleaming menacingly.

"You know, I was kind of hoping you would show up tonight," Owens said, smiling.

"I forgot to tell you…"

"Tell me what?" Owens asked.

"I've always hated you, bitch." Williams finally won the battle with her grip.

"Oh, I'm gonna love killing you, just like I loved killing your librarian trash." Owens smile turned into a look of abject rage; she lunged intent to kill.

Williams pulled her Glock 17 up and pulled the trigger, releasing a bullet in a deafening bang that reverberated throughout the top floor. The shot pierced its way through Owens' midsection, the hollow point skewering and destroying her diaphragm.

Williams gingerly climbed to her feet, catching Owens in the middle of her fall, gripping her by her collar and gun belt. With a final thrust she sent the women flying through the stained-glass window, plummeting down to the first floor below.

I can add defenestration to the list of things I never thought I'd do, Williams thought, wheezing. Each breath forced her to feel every single ache and groan of her beaten body, the feeling unlike anything she had ever felt. Existing hurt.

A small whimper from behind drew her back to the moment. She collapsed before Katherine, who was awake. Though barely.

"Katherine, it's me, it's Abby," Williams muttered. "I've got you. It's okay."

She was praying it was.

Katherine's eyes were glazed over until they finally aligned with Williams' and a small smile tugged at the corner of her lips. The tug was enough to pull the split in her lip, causing her to groan. "Abby, you came," she whispered, before coughs wracked her body like breathless sobs.

"Of course. Why wouldn't I?"

"I did-didn't want to burden the case…I know how stressed you are without Reyes."

Williams stroked Katherine's hair, gently, as tears rolled down her face. "Never a burden. You could never be a burden. This isn't your fault."

"They…they must have taken my blood when I was unconscious. I'm so tired, Abby. My hands and feet are so cold I can't feel them. Am I going to die?"

Katherine asked it like a child would. There was no fear, she just wanted to be reassured.

Williams scooped her up as best she could, leaning Katherine's head on her thigh and wrapping her left arm around her in a gentle hug. She used as little pressure as possible, hoping to spare Katherine more pain.

"No, you're not going to die. You'll be just fine in no time. I'm going to help you get better. Then I'm going to take you back to that Italian restaurant we had our first date at," Williams tried to sound reassuring, but the tears kept falling.

"Do-do you think," Katherine began, before succumbing to another coughing fit. "Do you think we could have been happy together?"

The question tore Williams down to something that barely resembled a person. A sob escaped her lips. "I already am happy with you—I am. We already are. The first night that you stayed in bed with me, that was the safest I've ever felt. Now stop talking like that."

Katherine's head became slack against Williams' thigh and her eyes misted over. Williams grabbed her walkie and screamed for help. An ambulance, a helicopter, officers, swat. Whatever she could get, so long as they hurried to the Cemetery Library.

Katherine's voice was little more than a whisper, impossibly far away. "I-I think I lost a lot of blood...I don't know what they did to me, Abby." She fought to raise her arm to Williams' face, wiping a tear away with the end of her thumb. Her touch was cold, too cold.

"It's okay. I'm going to get help. You'll be fine, okay?" *Please!* Williams begged. "Hang on for me, okay...you have to stay with me."

"For what it's worth...I was already happy with you too, Abby. Even with everything it's brought...I-I wouldn't change a thing."

Williams leaned forward, ignoring the stitches searing in her abdomen, and kissed Katherine on the lips. She was gentle, but conveyed everything she felt, everything she could have felt, into that kiss. She wasn't sure what this was—the hellstorm of a month that had followed their initial meeting—but it certainly felt like love, or the loss of it. Holding Katherine like this, this frail, shrunken version of herself, felt like the rending of her soul. Something she'd never get back. She remembered the nerves that had turned to excitement over their first dinner date. Williams had been so angry with Reyes, but the truth was she was excited, she had needed it. She looked down at her bloodied, ruined shirt, and imagined her stomach was filled with those same butterflies, now dead.

"Put them in jail, Abby. That's what you do," Katherine whispered so softly Williams had to lean closer to hear her. "You won't let anyone do this to our town. Don't forget what you stand for."

Katherine's grip slackened, her hand falling from Williams' face. She smiled at Abby, before lurching forward, her face becoming pained. Her breathing slowed until it stopped, her final exhale leaking out of her in a rush.

Williams screamed out in anguish, pulling Katherine closer to her. Katherine's pain finally ended, and Williams had absorbed it into herself. She sobbed, allowing herself to completely break apart in grief. Grief that laid its hand on her so heavily she felt as if a single second longer would destroy her fully. For her loss, for what could have been, for being too late. Always too late.

If only she had come earlier. What then? Could she have stopped Katherine from dying? Did this happen while she'd saved Reyes? While she was stuck in the hospital? Had she unwittingly chosen her partner over Katherine? The unknown was far too much to take. The blame all her own. The blame hurt the most.

Katherine Jackson was dead, her death the price she'd paid for something so simple as giving Williams the time of day. A chance. Now all of her future chances had been taken.

As sirens blared outside the library, Williams prepared herself for the shitstorm.

She didn't know who, but she was going to get the motherfuckers that had ordered this. She would get all of them.

Fuck every one of them. She'd make them all pay.

Ch 26

Halloween-Masked Heads Will Roll

I

SLAMMING HER HANDS DOWN on the metal table of the interrogation room, Williams leaned forward, staring down the crooked nose of the officer before her. Her knuckles were swelling, bloodied, and cracking from the fight at the library, but she didn't care.

She had rushed back to the precinct, grabbed the first arrested officer she set eyes on, and dragged their treasonous ass to the investigation room. If the scumbag wouldn't give up the Chief willingly, she'd pry the information from them *unwillingly*.

To be fair, she had given him a choice. The second time he tried to spit on her had been the straw that had broken the dead camel's back.

"Tell. Me. Where. He. Is," she shouted through gritted teeth. "Now!"

Instead of being intimidated, a laugh eked from his lips. "Don't know what you're talking about."

His head was tilted backward, away from her. She took the opportunity to reach over the table and grab him up by his shirt collar. She pulled on him so hard he began rising from the metal folding chair. Her face was a rictus of fury, deep red and animalistic. She would not relent.

"Alright," he wheezed, "alright!"

"Where is he? I won't stop until you tell me." She paused, tears stinging her eyes. "You can't imagine what he's taken from me. He has to pay."

He laughed again, smirking through chapped lips. "I don't know where he is, nor why you're so set on it. What could he possibly have taken from you?" He coughed, leaning forward and spitting mucus on the floor. His eyes looked unengaged, careless, but she still saw the understanding dawning in them. "Someone of yours got in their way, ehh? It certainly is their way or the highway!"

He laughed weakly, still coughing, breath whistling through his teeth.

Williams saw red. She wanted nothing more than to make an example of this piece of shit. She pointed her anger, her grief, her hope for the future with Katherine, her fear of it too, all at this officer who wouldn't tell her what she wanted.

She feigned a lack of care, turning her face away from him and laughing. As she turned back toward him, she cracked him across the jaw as hard as she could. His head snapped back, and a string of blood shot out from his nose.

Leaning forward, Williams grabbed the officer by his now-bloodied collar. "Tell me where he is. Tell me where!"

The officer's head lolled from the unexpected punch. He shook it violently as he tried to right himself. As he centered on Williams, she struck him again.

"You tell me now!" Williams screamed, shaking him by the collar. "Tell me now or you'll pay for his transgression!"

If he didn't tell her where Carter was, she really didn't know what she would do. She was out of time, out of patience, out of sanity. If Carter could so easily take from her, why shouldn't she be taking from him?

Rough hands grabbed at Williams. She tried to fight them off, tried to keep the officer in her line of sight. The hands dragged her from the room while she still screamed after the officer. They yanked her all the way to the Chief's office before pushing her into a chair.

Special Agent Colfax sat behind the desk facing her, looking disgruntled and at her wits' end. "What the hell were you thinking?"

"He would have talked; I would have cracked him. Let me back in there and I'll get the answers we need."

"At what cost, Detective?" Colfax yelled. "Right before or after the point you forfeit your morals? After you've drained his blood and disposed of his body, maybe?"

The likening of her to the criminals she was after was like a slap to the face—it might as well have been. She felt burning anger at the comment. Confusion, and deep-rooted shame, as well. Later, it would haunt her to look back and admit just how far she'd been willing to go.

She focused her attention on her boots like a chagrined schoolgirl. The scuffs held dried blood that could have belonged to anyone at that point, even Katherine.

"That officer was being held on *suspicion* of working with the Chief, who is wanted under *suspicion* of being involved in all of this. We still need the proof. Now the union will have a field day with him. He's useless to us! Completely out of our reach. What were you thinking?"

Williams took a deep breath. The tears that stung her eyes were from more than just shame. "I guess I wasn't, Colfax. Can you fucking blame me?"

"No," Colfax replied, which surprised Williams enough to raise her gaze to the other woman's. "No, I don't blame you, but I will say I did expect better."

"We have hours left, Colfax, hours. You know we can't hit the three locations separately. Something will go wrong; someone will get away or alert the others. A lack of officers or not, it won't work. It has to be all or nothing." Williams paused, blinking rapidly and fighting back tears. "I-I just thought that if I could get the answer from him, that we'd be able to finally put an end to all of this. All this death...but then he goaded me, and I-I couldn't stop."

A singular tear escaped her blinking, sliding down her cheek. The tear rolled off her chin and splashed onto her ruined pants. The tear felt hot, matching the anger and burning shame she felt. She thought of Katherine in her final moments, thought of her saying that she had to catch them, to put them in jail. Her faith in Williams never wavered. The thought almost broke her again.

She had immediately tilted the other way, blinded by rage and loss.

She thought of Reyes, his insistence on finding the facts. Williams had been more concerned with forcing facts than finding them. About taking the truth, rather than discovering it. She had been ready to beat a man, a colleague, and more—albeit, possibly a criminal one—she had done the opposite of what the two most important people to her would have wanted. What they would have done themselves.

She returned her gaze to the floor, tears burning. "I know she died because of me. I'll have to carry that with me for the rest of my life." Williams sniffled. "If I had stayed away from her, she never would have been caught in their crosshairs."

"There's simply no way you could know that," Colfax said, feeling for the other woman. "The thought alone will kill you. There are too many maybes. Too many variables."

Williams kept her head down, emotions roiling.

"But you can get this son of a bitch," Colfax said. "You can help us get Carter, and every other demented bastard involved in this web of horror. They said Halloween was the night something was going to happen. So help us put an end to it. Help me."

"I don't know how," Williams croaked. "I don't know what the fuck they're after. They've been ahead of us this entire time. One step, one kidnapping, one kill."

"That doesn't mean you can't figure it out. What's stopping you all of a sudden?"

"All of a sudden?" Williams asked with a hiccup. "I feel as if I've been messing up my entire life. When I was a child, my father—for some unbelievable reason—allowed me to be used as bait in a police sting. It all went to shit. A man named Carl Stratton, masquerading as a children's party clown, killed the officer who was supposed to protect me. It's something that I've always struggle with, feeling as if I was at fault. If not in the sting, then in my parent's divorce. It follows me around like a nightmare, but now it's affecting even my waking hours. I froze with Reyes at the Eltons, I almost froze again when Sofia was hurt. And this—this just feels like a continued string in a lifetime of fuck ups. I can't catch up, Colfax, I'm always chasing right behind."

"So, think! You've caught worse before," Colfax replied.

"How would you know that?"

"The staff here talk…I honestly think that the officers still working here weren't corrupted, in part, because of you. They look up to you," Colfax leaned over the desk as she said it.

"That's bullshit," Williams said, but she wasn't so sure. Had she always been too self-conscious to notice?

"It's not. They talk about what you've been able to achieve, the things you've seen. How no matter what you've been through, you still haven't lost that desire to do good. They believe in you, so you should too."

Williams bent forward, intent on putting her head in her hands until she saw how red they still were. She was such a bloody mess.

What haunted her further was the metaphorical blood on her hands. Katherine. Kind, accepting Katherine. That wouldn't simply wash away.

Williams swallowed hard, steeling herself. She tried to take a deep breath, but her nose was too stuffed. She stayed hunched over, breathing through her mouth, and giving herself a moment to regain a sense of calm, her sense of self. If her coworkers could still believe in her, after everything they'd lost, maybe she could too. "I don't believe we can hit the places separately. That wasn't just panic. What do you think we should do?"

"Well, we upped the number of help to seventeen. Do you think we can handle two teams of six and one of five?" Colfax offered.

"I mean, it's certainly better than before, but I still don't like it. We hit all three at the same time, tonight?"

"Tonight," Colfax said, looking at her watch. She looked at the sheet Williams had brought to her hours before with the pinned down locations. "An apartment building, a church, and a warehouse. What do you think the chances of each are?"

"For space, I'd want to say the apartment building or warehouse, but..." Williams petered out. The chief had always been a fan of the spotlight. He enjoyed his power, even when he was using it for good. He had a desire to control. She thought of the portable pavilion he was so fond of, the sight of which drew the townsfolk to him in droves. "The church. I'll take the church. I'd bet it's where he's operating."

"Okay..." Colfax said, "Why do you say that?"

"He's obsessed with power. He'll probably be leading from the pulpit or some shit. Like a murderous pope...well that describes all of them, but you get my point. I think it's the showiest place of the three, so I want to go there. They could be using all three, but I have to be the one to stop him. I will."

II

Reyes woke with a start. His sleep had been fitful at best since he was taken. Not even the morphine could help dull his senses enough to give him a reprieve. He was hyperaware, his brain still not relenting from fight or flight.

A heavy thudding against the hospital door drew him from sleep. His oxygen mask hung loose around his neck, the side of which chaffed his bandaged neck and face. He found that if he replaced it every so often, it kept the lung-popping coughs mostly at bay. He took a sip of the pure oxygen, breathing deeply. A belly roll of minor coughs wracked his body, the quick, breathy exhales making him see stars.

This wouldn't be an easy recovery.

Reyes looked across the room at Field Agent Sofia Mendes. The woman's head was nearly as bandaged as his.

She was staring at the door, her gun in hand. So, Reyes hadn't been hearing things. He couldn't be sure with the meds. He breathed in another gulp of oxygen before signaling for Sofia's attention.

He pointed toward the door and then back at her, signing that it would have to be her to go to the door, but he would still cover her. He raised his snubnose.

Sofia didn't look happy as she slid herself from her hospital bed. Reyes waited with bated breath until he realized that the heightened need to breathe was causing him to choke. He adjusted the oxygen mask over his face and picked up his pistol again.

Sofia edged toward the door, at such a slow pace that Reyes wondered if she'd ever reach it. *Do I even want her to*, he wondered, knowing they were locked inside safely.

Near death experiences, attempts on their lives, bloodless bodies piling up. *I guess there's more than a few things to be on edge about.*

As Sofia arrived at the door, Reyes felt like his heart was readying to burst. The blood pounded in his ears, the speed of it pulsing in his neck, hurting his burnt skin. He wished for a cigarette, but the subsequent cough shook him of that fast enough.

Turning the key in the lock, Sofia yanked the door open rather than easing it. In a great heap, the crumpled mass of the officer guarding them crashed to the floor.

His throat was slit, and his head was bloody at the right temple.

The thudding they had heard must have been his head against the door.

Ch 27

THE PLAN, HICCUPS, A HEAD ROLL

I

Having forgotten the precinct did early trick or treating for littler kids, Williams was unprepared to see the entrance filled with people in Halloween costumes and masks. If Colfax hadn't been standing right in front of her, she might have drawn on them.

The problem with Cemetery is that Halloween is big. Every year it got bigger. That includes the adults. Williams wasn't so far gone that she wouldn't have understood the smaller stature meant children; it was the parents that tempted her. She had to admit the genius of the plan. Carter certainly wasn't a stupid man; he was just sick. On a day like Halloween though, his sycophants would be impossible to find in crowds. The perfect camouflage.

Let's keep civilian deaths at a zero today, please.

Taking a deep breath was still not an easy thing for her to do with the smoke inhalation, but she steadied herself the best she could and stepped away from the entryway.

"So, what first?" Colfax asked.

"I say we gather the teams and cover the plan, then head out on patrols of the town. We have to present a typical Halloween day in Cemetery. Heightened patrols are our normal. Halloween is a good time for crime regardless—let alone when your boss decides to become a serial killer instead of stopping them."

"Alright, I'll gather the team. Meet in my office in twenty?"

Williams nodded her agreement and headed towards the detective office.

Williams stopped in the precinct kitchen, mixing two cups of coffee, before heading to her office. At the door she stared for what felt like hours at the sign that said, "Detective Reyes." Finally, she shut the door behind her, placed one of the cups of coffee on her partner's desk, and took the other to her seat with her. It was still hot, but she needed the caffeine more than ever. She had been living on the stuff since the beginning of October.

"God, I wish you were here, Ed. You'd know what to do, and if you didn't, you'd fake it for my sake. Got to focus on the facts, right?" She sighed. "I really thought you were gone. Fuck, I wish you could be here now."

"I lost Katherine. Forever. Chief Carter had her killed because I got in his way, got too close to the truth...how do you come back from that kind of thing? It's all my fault and no matter how this ends, she'll still be gone afterwards. I feel like I hardly got to know her, Ed, but I wanted to. I really wanted to. And that's your fault, you made me go on that damn date. I don't regret it...but it's a heavy burden now."

She looked up from her desk to find his seat still empty. The tears flowed freely, lining her cheeks.

She stood and headed for the door. "I'm going to figure it out, Ed. For you and Katherine. The other victims."

II

Colfax stood over her desk, which was covered in detailed maps of Cemetery. The three largest were aerial imaging of the locations they planned on raiding. The apartment building and warehouse would be the worst and possibly most dangerous to infiltrate, the number of entrances and exits leaving a lot up to chance.

"Stay together, keep your eyes up, and move slowly. We have some requisitioned SWAT equipment that I had sent over. Earbuds, built-in camera helmets, and a few other things. We won't need it all, but I'm glad I was able to get it in time."

Williams' interest was piqued at the mention of SWAT equipment. As Cemetery didn't have one, she wondered where the items were coming from.

"Remember," Williams began, "we have to get out there soon on patrol or they'll know something is going on. Even the citizens of Cemetery will be on alert. A heightened police presence on Halloween, that's their norm. We have to ensure we give them it, okay? Mix with the trick-or-treaters, talk to people, stop criminal activity as you normally would. We'll be regrouping later. Colfax will meet up with us with the equipment at the agreed upon location, and then we'll all move together. Got it?"

Various nods around the room answered her before they were ushered out of the office.

Williams pulled a bullet proof vest on. It was tight enough that she'd have to alter the way she stepped and turned, but she figured it would hold her stitches better than she had been doing herself. She pulled on a deep navy Cemetery PD jacket over it, zippering it closed. "This is it, I guess."

"We've got this," Colfax answered.

III

Williams pulled the Dodge Challenger cruiser out of the parking lot, heading around the corner with a pit the size and weight of a bowling ball in her stomach. There was no way around it, she knew she'd have to pass the library today. More than once.

It wasn't that she didn't want to remember Katherine, it was that the memory was much too fresh. Too raw. She hadn't had a second to stop, to process, and she feared that the sight of the library would force her to break.

Williams gave a fleeting thought to Owens. She hadn't even crossed her mind since. She was most likely misguided, manipulated, or something in between.

And how had the blood been removed? She hadn't seen a machine like the one beneath the Metlan's. The fire had destroyed any hopes of them studying that one unfortunately.

She brushed the thought aside. As easy as it was to throw her from the window, she cast out the thoughts she was having over Owens.

She couldn't fathom the idea of doing this without Katherine. She had become an anchor for her, something good amid all the shit that was Cemetery. She could have been the thing to fight to come home too. Now all of that was gone.

At the very least, Williams would do this *for* her. She wouldn't give up. Not just yet.

She sped off past the library. She had patrolling to do.

IV

Officer McDonald sidled out of the Cemetery Diner, waiting for a string of cars to pass on the busy Main Street, before crossing the road and heading toward the town's Airplane Park.

The park was named that because of the presence of a real plane restored from the Korean War. There had been a rumor that it would be removed due to its maltreatment, but that never happened.

McDonald walked down the sidewalk at a brisk pace. He shielded his eyes from the rays of evening sun that broke through the cloud coverage. It warmed him through his fingers. Further up the street was a stretch of road with an incredible number of overhanging trees. Officers backed up into the shaded area to remain unseen.

Today, McDonald was on the move, far more of a troublemaker than his badge and uniform would imply.

As he made it to the trees, he skirted around them, pressing his body tight against the brush, ensuring he stayed out of the line of sight. As he rounded the police car, he kept his hip tight to the side, keeping to the mirrors' blind spots.

The driver's side window was rolled down, giving McDonald the opportunity he was hoping for. He raised up a silent prayer before taking a step away from the car and turning to its occupant.

"Hey, I didn't even see you there! Where's the squad car?" the officer said, assuming the uniform meant McDonald was a friendly.

McDonald stepped forward, grabbing the officer's waving arm and pulling hard, smacking his head against the driver's door. McDonald slipped the needle into the officer's neck and pressed the plunger. The officer struggled against his grip for a moment longer before passing out.

McDonald lowered the officer back into his cruiser and straightened him out. He looked like he had simply fallen asleep on the job. Dialing his phone, he alerted someone on the other end to the officer's location. They'd be handling all of the pickups.

Four more times, if he was lucky. Another four unwitting officers and he'd be done for the day. The idea made him sick to his stomach, but he had agreed all the same.

V

Officer Brennan stepped from the side of the shop he was leaning against. The heightened patrols for the day made him blend in seamlessly with the other officers in town. On a day like today, no one paid any mind to another police officer on the street. Their blue-uniform-blindness making them miss the most important part—that Brennan was wanted in connection with serial killing.

He laughed at the thought of it, but he knew better. They were building something, not mindlessly killing. At least that's what he was always told, and why would they lie to him?

Now he walked down the sidewalk, whistling and nodding his head at passing shoppers.

It was too early, he knew that, but if the opportunity presented itself, why shouldn't he pounce on it? He'd be awarded for his cunning. His forethought.

He thought for a second of Shotz. His partner had become like a brother to him. He still couldn't believe he was gone. Then again, he had always been the stupid, young one.

Brennan walked through a parking lot, giving everyone he saw the same attention. No, still not the right ones.

His ire grew with each failure passing him. His squad car was parked around the corner; any further and he wouldn't have a clean break of it. Any further and he would be the failure.

He refused.

Finally, a large family climbed out of an old gold minivan, rust eating up the bumper, the different generations of family pouring out like it was an oversized clown car.

As the family ambled toward the storefront, one of the children lagged behind. The others, arguing loudly about being tired of running errands, didn't pay any mind to the small child nowhere near them.

Brennan removed the syringe from his jacket pocket, waiting for the right moment to pounce. This was exactly what he had been waiting for. What he needed.

With two bounding steps he lunged up behind the child. Pressing the needle into their small shoulder, he covered their mouth with his other hand as he pressed the plunger. The small body went immediately limp. Brennan unceremoniously tossed the limp body over his shoulder, heading behind the store to wrap around back towards his hidden cruiser.

Success. Brennan was filled with pride. He'd done clean work and he was sure no one had seen him do it.

He popped the trunk, harshly tossing the limp body into the back of the car. Slamming it closed, he smiled. Today would be a good one.

"Happy Halloween," Brennan called to a passing couple.

VI

A lean woman with black hair stepped out onto the street. She wore a white cashmere sweater, black skin-tight jeans, and matching white boots. An outfit that would be more fitting for a holiday get together, not late October porch hopping. What stood out the most was not what she was wearing, but what she was covered in.

Blood.

Swatches of red were sprayed and splattered across her outfit, face, and hair. She meandered down the street like there was nothing wrong. Humming and walking with purpose. Heads turned, a few calling out to ensure she was okay, but no one hindered her progress. She smiled at them and continued on her way.

Breaking through the crowds, she turned the corner and walked off the sidewalk, crossing the street and hopping the curb. She stopped in front of a dark, gated parking lot. She slipped the gate open just enough to squeeze inside.

She clicked the gate closed behind her, waiting a few moments to make sure no one followed. People in Cemetery could forget anything, completely ignoring what was before their very eyes. Unless, of course, they caught you in the act. She aimed to keep that possibility to a minimum.

When no one came, she walked through the gated lot, resuming her steady pace and leisurely attitude. As there weren't lights throughout the lot, a blur of white from her sweater would be all a passerby would catch.

At the end of the lot, she turned around the backside of the connecting building, a local jewelers called Nolan's that had been closed for years. She exhaled a breathy plume of white air, the evening air already chilling her to the bone. The sweater would have been warm, if not for the crusting, slightly chilled blood soaking it.

The side of the building was backed by an overgrowth of dead trees and brush, the property surrounding it as much in disuse as the building itself. She edged her way through, avoiding snagging her sweater, as well as keeping her backside from sliding along the old building. Breaking through the opening, she made sure to step into the blind spot of the police cruiser. She was sure they'd probably be sleeping or on their phone. Anything but the job they were paid to do.

She crept closer to the car, removing a switchblade from her jean pocket and flipping it open. Her movements were sure, practiced. Like she had done this before.

The blood soaking her nice outfit proved it.

Part of her was angry at how easy they made this. She held the switch blade behind her back and hopped away from the cruiser. She let out a scream, putting on an anguished, petrified face.

"Officer, Officer," she called, playing up her neediness. "You've got to help me!"

The officer had indeed been dozing behind the wheel of the police cruiser. At the scream he jumped up in his seat, hitting his head off the top of the car and spilling a now-cold cup of coffee all over his police jacket. He sputtered, throwing open the car door and stepping out. His face was as pale as hers with shock.

"My god, ma'am, what's happened? Let me call for an ambulance."

"A man—a man jumped out and grabbed me," she said, laying it on thick. "There was nothing I could do, he simply overpowered me!"

The officer stepped forward; an arm extended in what was sure to be a reassuring gesture. "Oh God, aren't you—"

She stepped forward into his embrace, sliding the entire length of the switch blade into the officer's neck. "There's no need for that, Officer."

Blood squirted onto her face and sweater, hot and steaming as she supported the weight of the dying police officer. He tried to speak, reaching for his destroyed throat, but his movements became slow and shaky.

She let his body slump to the ground. She wiped the switch blade clean on the officer's jacket before pocketing it. She eased herself into the cruiser, gasping at the cold liquid soaking into her pant legs, and gunning the heat on high. "Really wish he hadn't spilt that coffee," she moaned.

Flipping down the visor mirror, she gave herself a once over. "Well, that's one less problem."

VII

Williams whipped the Challenger around for another loop of the town. So far, she had seen nothing indicative of foul play or mischief, but it was only a matter of time.

Several minutes passed in a similar fashion. She finally made it to the point where she'd have to toughen up and pass the Cemetery Library again when her walkie chirped on the seat beside her.

"Williams, you there, over?" the staticky voice asked.

"Go ahead, Colfax," Williams called back, releasing the button.

"We've got a big problem."

Ch 28

Trick or Treat

I

Williams dropped the empty ammo box on top of her desk. Facing the wall, away from Reyes' desk, she took in the set of loaded pistol magazines before her. This was the cusp, whether prepared for it or not. She wished for a state of apathy, to be able to detach, but that just wasn't in her. As she took in the sheer number of bullets before her, their devastating power something she knew all too well, she couldn't help but hope for an outcome where they wouldn't be used. It so rarely happened, but that didn't mean never.

Her phone, on speaker, sat beside them on the desk. After a few extra *rings*, Elinor Williams answered the phone. "Hi, honey. Is everything okay?"

"Well, no. No Mom, it isn't. But—"

"Oh honey, are you hurt again, do you need me?"

Releasing a long sigh, Williams placed a hand over her mouth, blocking a laugh that could just as easily have become a sob. This was happening too often of late.

"I just wanted to tell you that I love you, Mom. I've been trying to work through my own shit, and I know that I placed a lot of what I was dealing with on you, even when it should have been blame I placed on Dad. You know he told me that you didn't even know? In my anger, as misplaced as it was, I couldn't separate it still. It stayed buried for years. It was baggage you didn't deserve. I see that now, and I just wanted you to know...in case."

A minute of silence past as Williams imagined her mother's silent shaking as she sobbed. "I love you too, honey. I love you."

II

Six cars pulled up to the rendezvous point. Williams parked alongside Colfax's unmarked car first, followed by the rest. The officers and agents looked at each other, wondering what had happened to the rest. Their shaky odds had been taken down another notch. Perhaps a notch too many.

"We received calls all day of empty police cars and disappearances. As of right now, I've been made aware of two officers that were found dead. Both stabbed to death while on detail." Colfax shook her head. "The patrols and heightened presence were supposed to help. I didn't expect officers and agents to disappear, too." She shook her head again, defeated. "Gone. Out of thin air..."

"Where does that leave us?"

"You're looking at it," Colfax answered.

"Ten of us? Then we can't hit all three at once, it would be a goddamn death wish." Williams said.

"Yes. Clearly the attacks were targeting those we trusted working with. Sadly, that clears their names for us completely, but is of no use to us now," Colfax said, voice tinged with sadness. "It also means that I was wrong about the others too. Damn it. What do you want to do now?"

"I say we adapt. We'll have to cut out a third destination and go to the others instead. Clear those out before converging on the third?" Williams posed it as a question, but they all could tell it wasn't. There was nothing else they could do.

"The element of surprise will be gone more than likely, but it sounds like our safest route forward," Colfax conceded.

"I'll lead a team a five, you take the other?" Williams stepped forward and popped Colfax's trunk, revealing an array of supplies.

"Sounds good. Or as good as it'll get. Gear up, and let's get it done as safely as possible. Let's put an end to this crap."

Williams took another box of 9mm just in case. She already had her extra magazines with her in the cruiser. With her burnt hand she knew she couldn't handle a shotgun again, as much as she wanted the safety of it. After a moment of thought she bent back in and took out a foot long baton, figuring if anyone surprised them at least she'd have something harder than scabby, tender knuckles.

The officers and field agents gathered around her, eager to grab their own equipment. She hadn't meant to call an end to Colfax's huddle, but she was ready for movement. To put an end to the fiery chasm that had opened below Cemetery, eager to eat them all up.

"I think one from each group should wear the cameras, documenting some kind of evidence," Colfax said.

"Let's hope there's evidence to be found."

III

Reyes reached with all his strength toward the left side of his body. If he could just remove the damn IV, he could claw his way out of the hospital bed.

The burns to the side of his body and neck made his right side swollen and tight, his skin wanting nothing more than to pop open as he stretched out his hand for the other side of his body. Such a simple motion, rarely given a second thought, now so far beyond his abilities.

After Sofia had thrown the door open, revealing the murdered officer, she had dragged the body into the hospital room, and relocked the door.

The hallway beyond had been completely deserted in both directions. However, the hallway was filled with open doors. The murderer could be hiding in any one of them. Just moments away from striking.

Sofia had been a mess ever since.

Reyes gave one final lunge, triumphantly yanking the IV and accompanying tubes from his arm. He was relying on the oxygen mask the more he exerted, his breaths ragged and quick. As delicately as he could, he worked himself to the edge of his bed, his side still stiff, refusing to bend. As his feet finally touched down on hospital tile, a wave of nausea rocketed through his body.

"Check to see if the officer had anything useful on him. We need to get out of here."

"I-I don't want to touch him," Sofia admitted.

Reyes gave as much of a sideways glance as he could manage. "You're an FBI field agent, you've never done this kind of thing before?"

Sofia knelt hard, patting the pockets of the dead officer, and doing her best to avoid getting any of his blood on her. She pulled out a pair of car keys and an extra 9MM magazine. "No Senior Detective Reyes, I haven't. Can't say I've ever been in one single town where seemingly everyone and everything wants to kill you. I-I really thought all through the academy I was ready for action. But this, this all is too much. When I ran at that masked figure in the passageway, it was nothing but adrenaline. Pure rage egging me on. But then they cut my face, and as I struggled under the weight of their arms, waiting to die, it just shook me, okay?"

Reyes ambled toward her, seeing more than a little of the self-conscious Williams in her. "Yeah, okay. But I plan on getting out of here one way or the other and seeing as I'm like a freaking human s'more right now, I need you, Sofia. Okay?"

IV

Williams had elected to hit the warehouse. She didn't really have a reason why, seeing as her end destination was the church either way.

She pulled the Dodge Challenger off the main street, racing down Elm Road, then keying it off behind a copse of trees. Field Agents Doakes, Russell, and Sampson, and Officer Riggs, stepped out of the cars with her, loading magazines, and cocking and stocking pistols and pump action shotguns.

"Listen up," Williams called, the others stepping towards her. "I want this to be clean, quick, and easy. Keep your fucking eyes peeled, and don't let a single one of these bastards get the jump on you. We'll stick together, we'll go room by room, and we'll clean up shop. Got it?"

After a slew of affirmatives, Williams radioed Colfax that they were in position. The thought hit her, that not too long ago she would never have seen herself leading these people—at least not with any confidence. But that time had passed. After a response came through, she switched off the walkie, drawing her own pistol.

It was go time.

The officer taking up the rear, Riggs, drew the short stick picked to don the camera helmet. It was bulky, making maneuvering hard. Williams advised him to stay back and stay low, so long as he didn't get outpaced.

They had surveilled the warehouse and unlike many of the others in town, there were only bay doors and a single front and back exit. Of course, someone could always escape out of the bays, but Williams was willing to bet that less access would siphon off the chances for surprises.

Feet pounded the asphalt as they crouch-ran their way to the front door of the building. It was an old, two-story building that looked more like a shack than a warehouse. It had both the shape of a house and the siding of a storage container. The windows—both those on the ground floor and the second floor—were barred shut and completely dark.

Williams motioned them into action. They all knew the plan. Now it was time to enact it.

Here goes nothing.

She motioned for Agent Doakes on her right to breach the door. He leaned to the side, butting the stock of his shotgun through the glass of the door. Officer Riggs snapped glow sticks, passing them forward. Doakes threw a handful inside, illuminating a small area filled with shelving units.

No lights or alarms blared at their forced entry.

Williams led the charge, stepping into the warehouse space, her Glock 17 and a flashlight raised. She panned the flashlight's beam around the space. It appeared the shelving units could be passed on either side; she chose to go right.

The room was a large rectangle. The shelving units ran horizontally off-center up the room. Williams stuck her body to the right wall, flicking her flashlight and gun up each shelving unit.

There was nothing but dust and disused space.

At the end of the rectangular room, a door led out into the docking area. A row of bay doors visibly ran the length of the building. The place was *huge*. A mezzanine ran straight across the building, recessed halfway back, giving room for the garage doors and pallet loading. A conveyer belt was positioned up the right most wall.

They fanned out, always ensuring to stay close. They cracked and tossed glow sticks in all directions, skittering them along the concrete floor. As the illumination rose, they saw that the place hadn't been cleared out. Several gigantic rows of shelving housed what looked like dusted over clothing, those beyond still filled with shelves of old boxes. Williams could just make out the faint red glow from the "exit" sign still working at the end of the building.

Williams knelt onto the floor. It was dust covered, and aside from the faint impressions from the glow sticks, there didn't appear to be any other disturbances. She waited, hovering her flashlight above the dusted floor, and listened. The warehouse was even devoid of the typical creaks, pops, and bangs found in most buildings. There was nothing. An absolute silence bordering on the preternatural. She waited until the silence sounded more like ringing in her ears, then she stood and crept forward again.

Doesn't mean someone couldn't have come through the back.

She signed to the team to stay vigilant, motioning forward as she took off at a faster pace.

At the end of the row of shelves, they had neither seen nor heard a peep. *Not even mice. In an unattended building of this size, this is just weird.* Williams turned back toward her team, whispered, "all that's left is to check the mezzanine.

I think we got the dud location. We'll check it, check in with Colfax, and move on to the church."

She stepped around the corner of the shelves, just underneath the glowing "exit" sign. She walked a few shelves back, still checking to make sure they were empty. As she stepped into the last one, she realized her feet were making a louder scrapping noise along the floor. She crouched again and released a curse. This side of the warehouse was clean of dust...someone could be inside with them.

Shit!

She stood and spun on her heels, determined to notify her team of their continued endangerment. The front two tightened up when they saw how tense she was, but Riggs, in the back, and so encumbered by the ridiculous camera helmet, was left unaware. It was clear that as he rounded the corner there was someone else behind him.

Williams opened her mouth to shout a warning, but she wasn't fast enough.

The assailant pulled the trigger, shooting Officer Riggs through his helmeted head. Gray matter and blood sprayed onto the two in front of him. His body slumped to the ground, giving Williams enough clearance to fire into the attacker's chest.

The assailant crumpled to the concrete floor, blood already spewing from their mouth. Williams kicked the gun away from their slackening grip. She grabbed the woman by the collar, drawing her closer to her, but she was already gone.

Williams released the now limp gunman to the floor. Even without hesitation, she was too slow. Again.

Clicking on the radio, Williams called out for an update from Colfax. Several minutes later, a series of clicks followed by a staticky bleat from the walkie. Asking for a repeat, Williams waited, anxiety blooming.

"They were waiting for us!" Colfax shouted into the radio, gunfire and yelling in the background.

Too slow again.

V

Colfax and her team moved slowly toward the apartment complex. She had purposefully given an additional field agent to Williams, electing to take the chance with another officer herself. Field Agents Cobble and Holliday took up the rear, following closely behind Officers Prescott and Baxter, in a move that was both strategic and agreeable.

As they hit the doors, Colfax motioned for Agent Cobble to breach…and that was when it started going downhill. Not only did the apartment complex have a slew of entrances, both public and private, but many of the doors were wide open.

She had led her team into the hornets' nest, and the hornets were already buzzing.

They had planned for it; the team entered just far enough that a stealthy retreat was impossible. As they passed their third and fourth apartment doors, they rounded the first corner, almost head on into a group of Halloween-masked villains. Colfax couldn't see their faces, but she felt sure none of them showed any surprise. They knew, and as her team spun looking for any chance to escape, several more had exited behind them, creeping out of what appeared to be deserted apartments.

She had made a shit call; she never should have trusted any of the officers. Maybe not even Williams, although her gut still told her she could.

The shooting started when the masked gang stepped forward with bats, machetes, knives, and shovels. One of them even wielded a chain wrapped around a fist. A few held guns aloft, reconfirming for Colfax that some officers were likely involved. The proof didn't ease her mind.

Colfax was no Batwoman; she wasn't going toe to toe with anyone. Let alone a group of attackers with deadly weapons. She fired at the first of the group, her team following suit. They fought their way into the first open apartment they could reach, buying themselves enough time to barricade the entrance with potshots and an overturned table.

After the first few masked figures went down, their comrades didn't seem too keen on taking a bullet.

As they finally secured the door enough to take a breath, Colfax took stock of the situation. After flicking on the overhead bulb, Colfax saw they were short a man. "Damn it, where the hell is Baxter?"

Before any of the others could answer her, they were forced to throw themselves to the ground, several harsh blasts ripping through the door. The gang was now firing Baxter's shotgun and sidearm.

Think. Think. Think! Colfax wracked her brain for a way out. Bits of door and Sheetrock rained down around her. They all lay prone on the floor, hands covering their ears or faces. How did they end up here? She was so sure they had found the moles within the precinct, but this made it abundantly clear they hadn't.

She hadn't.

This had all been done on her call, her say so. As much as she gave Williams free reign, she was the one with the final say. She did this.

They hadn't let anyone else know about the raids...other than those involved. Colfax raised her hands from her eyes, blinking through the grit, and eyeing each of her team members. Which one? Which one of them would do this? Someone from the precinct would make the most sense, but maybe even one of her own? An FBI agent?

Slowly, each team member met her eyes. She felt as if she could see guilt, see betrayal, in all of them.

A loud crack from the radio startled Colfax back to herself.

As the gunfire from beyond the door halted, Colfax motioned to her team, readying for return fire. They took up crouched positions around the ruined door, trying their best to find a small spot to peer out of. As they began firing the walkie chirped again, asking if anyone was there.

"They were waiting for us!" Colfax shouted into the radio. As she took in the scene, she realized that one of them wasn't fighting. Wasn't firing back.

Officer Prescott was aiming his pistol at Colfax, not at the door.

She opened her mouth to give him more than a piece of her mind but never got the chance.

Prescott fired instead, hitting her hip, just below the end of her bullet proof vest. A searing pain drove down through her pelvis.

VI

Reyes leaned heavily against the IV stand he had requisitioned as a walking stick. The fact that it had a base with wheels was a great help too.

His body ached. Every fiber of his being burned and shook when he tried to walk. His lungs felt like they would shrivel up and die if he didn't take the oxygen with him. However, he couldn't handle the weight of the tank, and they had to get out of the hospital quickly. There was no time left to think about it.

Sofia paced back and forth, her eye still bandaged, giving her the look of an anxious pirate. "We have to get the hell out of here. I can't just sit here and wait anymore."

"Slow your roll. Think I climbed my medium-rare ass out of this bed just so you could leave me alone?" Reyes replied, raising his revolver up as he slid his IV-cane closer to Sofia. "Let's go."

Sofia stalked to the door, unlocking it without so much as putting an ear to it first. Her panic was going to get them both killed.

She stepped out into the hall. "Let's go then, I want to check the nurse's desk."

Ch 29

STORM THE GATES

I

WILLIAMS WHIPPED THE CRUISER as close to the apartment complex as she dared. It was a multistoried building, but it somehow still felt small. Maybe it was because of how deserted it looked, or maybe it was due to the size of the complexes in other towns that dwarfed it, but either way, it still had a small town feel to it. Very Cemetery.

Filled with criminals too, apparently. *So, very Cemetery.*

The outside of the complex was dark, no one in sight. As she stepped out of the cruiser with what remained of her team, she heard the yelling and gunfire from inside. She rushed toward the nearest entrance.

Williams' team followed close behind her. "Keep it quiet as long as possible," she said. "Surprise is our best shot here. They're still distracted. We have to get in there and clear them out, save Colfax and the others. Got it?"

She was met with nods from her remaining teammates. She pulled the baton off her belt, her pistol in the other hand. "Let's stop these assholes."

Field Agent Russell pulled the door open, and Williams bolted inside. She kept her body tensed, ready for action, but there was no one in sight. At least not yet. She came to the first corner, taking up position against the wall, and waited for her team.

As soon as they arrived, she turned the corner, which was also deserted. *What the hell is going on here?* Williams thought as she continued down the empty hallway.

Just as they were about to enter the final third of the hall, a Halloween masked figure backed up from the adjacent space. Their back remained toward Williams' group, and they raised a pistol before them, but it clicked as they pulled the trigger, empty. Williams holstered her own gun, rushing forward before the perp could see them. If there was one thing good about this whole mask business, it was the sheer lack of peripherals they had while wearing them.

Williams took the baton to the back of their knee in a swift jab. Crumpling them backward, she covered the mask's mouth before they could call out. Agent Doakes moved forward to zip tie them.

When the agent returned from discarding the masked figure in an empty apartment, Williams was slowly sticking her head around the corner. The hall opened up into a common area—which was filled with Halloween-mask-wearing cronies. Most had bats, machetes, or knives, though she could see someone closer to the front with a shotgun. She checked each person for additional firepower. She counted five guns in total, but as none of them were being fired, either the fight was over, or they were out of ammo.

Williams' radio chirped on her hip. Before she could reach to turn it off, the noise filled the quietness of the space.

"Williams, I've been hit! It was..." Colfax grunted and hissed through her teeth but didn't let go of the button. "It was a setup!"

Williams unholstered her Glock 17 as every head in the common area pointed their way.

II

Papers, computer speakers, and phones were tossed around the nurses' desk. Either someone had been looking for something, or there had been a struggle. Reyes took the scene in through gritted teeth and squinted eyes; walking was even harder than he thought. His side eked out blood, or blood and pus more likely. He was shaky, his eyes blurred over more than he cared to admit, and his head felt as if an eighteen-wheeler had run it over.

"Were they looking for us, or were they fighting with the staff?" Sofia questioned.

Reyes tried his hardest to pull in a deep breath without coughing before he answered. "Either or. Ain't gonna change anything at this point. The officer posted on the door was probably a shining beacon shouting 'here!' anyway."

"What the hell is going on in this place?"

"Welcome to Cemetery—you'll never forget us now," Reyes quipped.

As Sofia opened her mouth to retort, a figure turned into the hall and started towards them. Every fiber of Reyes' being screamed in pain as he pulled Sofia back behind the desk. He placed his good hand over her mouth while shuffling her back into the dark corner. He forced himself to hold the oxygen in his lungs, straining against the cough he wouldn't let come.

That's all it would take, a single cough, and they'd be dead.

Unless we storm the guy, Reyes thought. *Two guns against a single surprised guy? Pretty favorable odds. But...what's to say he's alone?*

Reyes made his decision. He continued to hold his breath; Sofia pressed against him in the darkened corner. As they tried to make themselves as small as possible, the figure lumbered past. They wore a robe and a monster mask, standing tall over the nurses' desk as they continued on. They turned left and right, clearly looking for something, or someone, but not finding them. Reyes found himself thanking God for Halloween masks and shitty peripheral vision.

They watched as the masked figure turned into their hospital room. He shuffled around without care for the noise being made, so Reyes allowed himself as deep of a breath as he could manage. The oxygen was both a relief and the deepest agony. The very thing keeping him alive was causing him suffering.

The figure stalked out of a hospital room cursing and ripped the Halloween mask off. "Can't breathe in these fucking things!" He leaned his head back and took deep breaths of the unfettered air. He ran a hand through his sweaty hair, pushing it off his forehead.

Reyes almost cursed aloud as he recognized the man.

It was another officer, one that had been with the force for nearly as long as he had. Officer Minges had been a rigid provider of justice, or so Reyes had thought.

Where does this shit end? Where does it lead to?

Officer Minges took a final breath before fixing the mask back over his face. He stalked off toward the end of the hall, the opposite way from where he came. He was searching high and low to find them. Reyes couldn't let that happen.

They watched the officer turn the corner at the end of the hall and disappear. They separated, allowing themselves a second to recover.

"What are we supposed to do now?" Sofia whispered.

In response, the ragged, painful cough that Reyes had been fighting so hard against, ripped its way from his chest. He heaved and sputtered, trying to breathe around the ragged shaking of his body. It hurt so badly; part of Reyes wanted nothing more than to succumb to it.

As the coughing fit passed, Reyes straightened, using the IV stand to give himself strength. It took only a moment to realize the heavy footfalls in the next hall had stopped too.

III

Williams tried her hardest to project control and strength in the face of so many armed assailants. When they ignored her commands to stop, her team had raised their guns to defend themselves. Williams fired a single bullet into the first person charging at them, who menacingly raised a machete.

As the body hit the ground, the machete skittering off under the feet of the other assailants, her team fired. Stepping around people as they ran straight at them, Williams did her best to dodge and disarm with the baton rather than shooting point blank. The FBI field agents didn't seem to have the same compulsion. As assailants continued dropping to the ground, their comrades slipping in the blood of the fallen, the others slowed down to part around them, allowing Williams to try again.

"Freeze! You are all under arrest. We have the complex surrounded. If you resist, if you attack, or if you run, you will meet the same fate as them," Williams finished, pointing at the bodies. Blood soaked from the holes in their chests across the tiled flooring.

The common room of masked figures turned and looked into each other's eyes, each one of them weighing the options. If they all attacked, they had the likelihood of overwhelming the officers, though many of them would die. If they ran, some of them might be caught or killed, but most of them would likely get away. That's if they called her bluff about the place being surrounded, too.

Williams tightened her grip on her Glock until her knuckles hurt. She didn't love the idea of shooting people who had handheld weapons, but she also would make the call to save herself ten times out of ten. Ill intent was simply that; the choice was being made for her by someone else. They never gave her time to weigh her options.

Come on motherfuckers, give up. "You're all under arrest, let's go!"

Some of them lowered their weapons, stepping away and dropping themselves to the floor. They raised their hands into the air in surrender. Others did the same with their weapons but bolted down halls toward the building's many exits. If she intended to arrest those kneeling, she'd have to abandon the idea of catching the runners.

The decision was already made for her. Those kneeling would become runners if she gave chase. It was a lose-lose situation. Her only hope was to crack those she arrested into turning on their comrades. She had never expected the situation to go this easily, but then again, she'd always had hope. If she was right, and most of these people were simple lackies, cronies pushed into service, then it made sense. Their lives weren't worth this.

The masked figures had divided themselves into an almost perfect fifty-fifty, runners to surrenderers. Which was actually good, as there was no way her team could handle arresting, chasing, or fighting them all. Now they wouldn't have to.

Colfax crackled over the walkie again. Whatever she said was drowned out, but it pulled Williams back into action. "Team, I want these people rounded up and zip tied. Folks, if you resist or fight now, my team will not be forgiving. An FBI agent is hurt in this building, shot by one of you. I'm not sure you understand the severity of the situation you're in."

Those that surrendered offered their hands and wrists meekly. They knew the game was up, and they were beyond fighting it. Williams was glad, as whatever came next would not be as simple.

Williams cautiously crossed the common room. As she came to the nearly destroyed door, she heard shuffling on the other side. There was still plenty of debris in the way. "This is Detective Williams of the Cemetery Police. The masked assailants have either fled or surrendered. You can come out." Williams also held the radio's button while speaking. She heard Colfax grunt pained orders from the other side of the door, and the debris started to be cleared away.

They worked hard, and in a matter of minutes, Williams could see within the room.

Colfax was off to the side, half out of view. She looked pale, and each breath seemed to bring her new pain. She gritted her teeth and made eye contact with Williams. "We never even got to search the place. This bastard over here sold us out." She motioned towards a body against the back wall. They wore a Cemetery PD uniform, but a portion of their face had been blown off, chunks of blood and brain littered the wall.

Good riddance then, Williams thought.

Kneeling before Colfax, Williams applied pressure to the woman's hip. Colfax winced, paling further, if that was even possible. "You vetted the precinct, what the hell happened?"

"That shithead set us up and shot me. After we vouched for him—after *I* vouched for him—he turned cloak and tattled." Colfax's head slumped back, immediately dosing.

"I see someone handled the situation already," Williams replied. "You have to stay awake for me though." She shook the woman, bringing her head back up. "Hey, come here, please."

One of the FBI agents stepped toward Williams. She knew his face at this point, but not his name. "We don't have time to wait on an ambulance. I need you to get her to a hospital ASAP. We'll finish up here, but you need to go. Right now," she said, pushing the agent toward Colfax.

His face was set, determined. He scooped Colfax up into his arms. He shifted her, ensuring that he could still draw his pistol in the event it was needed. Williams couldn't promise him it wouldn't be.

With that settled, Williams and the remaining member of Colfax's team followed them out into the common room to see what progress her team had made.

The apprehended assailants were in the center of the common room, every one with hands tied behind their backs. The team had also gone around and removed all of the Halloween masks. For how ridiculous and off she had felt since the start of this investigation, she couldn't help but think that these people just looked...normal. No maniacal laughter, no scary scars, nothing. This wasn't some comic book gang; these were everyday people. It really struck her that anyone could be drawn into something they'd never dreamt of doing otherwise. All it took was one bad day sometimes, and who hadn't experienced a string of those occasionally?

Williams shook the thought off. She wasn't about to make excuses for criminals. In her line of work, she had more bad days than good ones, and no one saw her crying—save for maybe Reyes. No one saw her orchestrating heinous killings. No, this was unforgivable. No matter what anyone said, there was no arguing this.

While she still had the attention of Cobble, Colfax's agent, she told him to stay put. "I'll have you and Agent Doakes stand guard. The rest of us will be doing a quick search through the building. We have to be quick. Anything you find can be brought back here, including the guy we tied up earlier. I'll take the rooms to the left; one of you should follow behind and double down, okay? And keep an eye out for stragglers, just because they ran doesn't mean they left. Got it?"

Williams unholstered her Glock and stepped out of the common room. They needed to be thorough, but they needed to be fast. They had to get to the goddamn church, but they couldn't afford to miss anything either.

The first ten rooms Williams searched were completely empty. Derelict and cleared of furniture. The apartments all had the same layout. They opened into a hall with just enough space for a welcome mat, then led directly into a kitchenette; a small hall ran back towards a bedroom and bathroom. The only thing alternating was the bedroom and bathroom swapping sides in consecutive rooms, Williams assumed for the plumbing. It eerily reminded her of Katherine's—a pang of sadness hit her—she wondered how many ways you could even design an apartment.

Shuffling and clanging from across the hall pulled her back to the present. She stuck her head into the bathroom, then backtracked out of the apartment. She intended to be the first one to head up the stairs. There had to be a reason they were here; she didn't believe for a second it was just a trap.

She just had a feeling.

Ch 30

A Plea for Help

I

Reyes steadied himself on the IV stand and cursed at the powers above to keep him moving. He and Sofia had just rounded the corner at the end of the hall when they heard the masked officer return, their margin for being spotted razor thin.

They heard him ransacking the nurses' desk again, though what he hoped to find, Reyes hadn't the slightest. He placed a hand on his side, the burns so intense they were above pain. A brain-altering feeling no one should have to experience.

The masked officer talked rapidly. Whether he was on a phone or walkie talkie, Reyes hadn't a clue. But he was right. They weren't alone. Reyes let his chin rest on his chest for a second, each moment he spent upright surely shaving years off his life. Reopening his eyes, he saw he was leaving a trail of plasma, his side leaking as he rushed.

Reyes grabbed Sofia's shoulder and shouted at a whisper, "I'm freaking leaking like a colander, Sofia. He just called for reinforcements of some kind, and it doesn't really matter if there's two or a hundred of them, I'm leaving a trail of blood-crumbs right freaking to us. Ain't nothing left for it, you gotta leave me."

"Shut it. He'll hear you, you idiot. I'm not leaving you anywhere. You said you needed me, and I'm right here. Let's go."

Reyes let her lead him further down the hall, the IV stand rolling beside him. His weight had started to bend the thin metal, but it was still better than bearing the weight on his own. He'd have to make do after, but for now, he'd use it for as long as it lasted.

Halfway down the hall, a door with a sign above it that read "Stairwell B" burst open. Reyes raised his snubnose, the violence of the door opening almost enough to make him squeeze the trigger prematurely.

Luckily for them, the new arrival looked down the hall in the direction opposite of where they stood in shock. Sofia slid them two feet backward into an open room. She swung the door shut just enough for them to hide behind it.

Reyes was getting really tired of this. The pain, the lack of oxygen in his lungs, and the fear was becoming too much.

As footsteps approached them, it became clear no reprieve was incoming. They sucked in another breath, each of them raising a hand to cover their nose and mouth, holding it.

The footsteps stopped right outside. A gloved hand gripped the side of the door, pushing it open. Reyes did his best to turn his foot sideways, making his body as small as he could in the hopes the door wouldn't stop on him and alert the attacker. A masked head leaned into the doorway, tilting left and right, before retreating back down the hall.

Reyes let his held breath out, sagging.

Sofia gathered herself, her breath caught up. "We should head straight down the stairwell they barged out of. What do you think?"

"They probably have someone on the doors," Reyes gasped. "But with the both of them here? Ain't no way I'm staying on this floor. Let's go."

Sofia stuck her head out to make sure the coast was clear. Then she stepped back to help Reyes.

As they made it to the stairwell's door, Sofia tensed, alerted to something that Reyes couldn't hear over his ragged breathing.

She stood staring back the way they came, the masked figure they hadn't identified yet was running towards them. Reyes stood as firm as he could. He looked to his right and saw the masked officer running at them from the other end of the hall. They were trapped, and every shoe squeak on the hospital tiles brought their doom one step closer.

Sofia called, "We have to go!"

She started pulling on Reyes' good arm, pulling him backward toward the staircase. Just before he rounded the doorframe, he raised his snubnose and fired in the direction of the sprinting officer.

With a final yank, Sofia pulled Reyes. Twisting into each other, they tripped and fell, plummeting down the stairs.

II

The stairs leveled out to the top floor with a resounding lack of flourish. The floor was dusted over. It smelled of mold and rot and something else. There were tracks in the dust, but it still felt abandoned, as if even the tracks were left behind long ago, past travelers long forgotten.

Williams cut through the dust, making new tracks, and using it to her advantage, muffling her approach just in case. She took her steps at an angle to keep herself quiet. She had a feeling something was coming. Adrenaline aside, every hair on her body stood on end. The downstairs had turned up nothing, but she knew she would find something. She had to.

The smell lingering under the rest was one she knew all too well. In her line of work, it was one she smelt far too often.

The smell of death.

If that smell was anything to go by, they were using this floor for something, and it wasn't good.

The first few rooms she worked through were dustier than downstairs, but no less empty. The air in them smelled of fust, like a tomb being cracked open.

Russell and Sampson had made it upstairs and were working their way through the right side of the hall to catch up.

Sampson broke off to follow behind both of them and started working her way left to right—a second set of eyes to ensure nothing was overlooked in haste.

Williams approached the next door. It stood out as different from the rest, but she couldn't quite put a finger on why. As she gripped the handle, it turned, but didn't budge when she pushed on it.

If the knob isn't locked, what the hell is blocking it? she thought.

Williams gave the door another push. It didn't feel like there was anything locked in—some hidden bolt or some other obstruction—yet it wouldn't give in the slightest.

Then it hit her. It was less wide, but taller; probably something like a maintenance closet or plumbing access for the top floor. The door was a goddamn *pull*, not a push.

So wrapped up in feeling stupid, Williams pulled the door without a second thought.

A string of bodies tumbled out from the newly parted doorway. As distracted as she was, the bodies hit her at the thighs and buckled her knees, dropping her to the floor. Burying her in deceased victims. Her bulletproof vest was the only thing keeping her abdomen from splitting.

The putrid stench of death filled her nostrils and mouth. Holding in her scream was the only way to avoid breathing it in further. The mixture of rot, moldering skin, and liquifying organs was enough to make her eyes water, tears streaming down her face in waves. She tried to scramble back in horror. She clenched her jaw so tightly she thought her teeth might break. It was the only way to keep from gagging.

Field Agent Sampson gripped Williams under the armpits and heaved her up, the bodies rolling off her, arms and legs sticking out at horrifyingly unnatural angles. As soon as she ensured Williams was steady, she replaced her hand over her mouth to keep the smell out.

Williams couldn't help but gape at the nightmarish scene before her. A pile of what used to be five humans was now stacked up, limbs and necks wrapped around each other like a tangle of weeds. She couldn't wrap her head around it. They had been stacked inside the closet, like whoever had dumped them there couldn't be bothered. Unceremoniously tossed to whatever end would greet them.

As she knelt before them, they had the same shriveled, gray, and desiccated look as the others. But these had been left to the elements for some reason. She found herself wondering why. Not to mention who they were.

She took a shallow inhale before leaning forward, fussing about the back pocket of the victim closest to her. She stood, a wallet in her hand, and gingerly thumbed through it.

"Got it," she called. "A Jeremy Martin." She stared down at the ID, shaking her head. "Why is that familiar?"

Russell leaned over her shoulder. "Holy smokes, Jeremy Martin was the guy that disappeared the night before his trial, remember? It was all over the news."

"Jesus fuck, these people were probably double dipping this entire time. Finding criminals then snatching them right out from under the court's nose. No one looks too hard for a criminal, right?"

Williams placed the wallet back on the pile of victims. She was lost in thought, but not so deeply that she had forgotten about her desire to vomit profusely. The stench had grown to swallow them whole, the air on the top floor nearly noxious.

Having tossed around the idea that their plot ran deeper than just a list of criminally inclined sub-adults, Williams wondered just how far the river ran? How long, and how many times had they gotten away with this?

A piercing scream cut off whatever Williams had opened her mouth to say.

She signed for the team to take up positions, leading them down the hall. The scream sounded like it came from the end of the hall to the right, but she couldn't be sure. They would continue their sweep, clearing each set of rooms at the same time, Sampson still covering the other two.

The next four rooms were empty. Each door swing caused Williams to breathe more heavily, the strain of agonized waiting getting to her.

Where the fuck are they?

Another scream.

Williams ran from the last apartment. She strained her muscles to give her more, propelling herself faster down the hall. Russell called out behind her, surprised by her choice to throw caution to the wind. She couldn't stop.

Not another life. Not again. Williams was four or five straws passed the "last" straw; she was done letting these people destroy her town. If there was a shot at saving whoever was up ahead, she had to do it.

Be better. Move faster.

She burst through the final door at the end of the hall, gun raised. A single masked figure was holding a knife against a young woman's neck. The woman was tied to a barstool, her white-heeled boots holding her feet into the chair supports.

The woman wore what looked like it might have once been a white sweater. It was so covered in dirt and filth that it looked dyed grey. There were giant streaks of blood down the front.

Jesus, what the fuck were they doing to this woman?

The masked figure struggled against the woman, trying to force duct tape over her mouth. In their struggle, the knife's tip had slanted downward, creating an opportunity.

"Freeze! Stop what you're doing. Now!"

The shout startled the figure, launching a series of reactions.

The trapped woman bit down on her attacker's hand, causing them to yelp in pain. The attacker, catching sight of them, had given up on the tape and started raising the knife, a stand-off their only chance in the dead-end apartment.

The same thought dawned on Williams. As the masked figure leaned forward, the menace in their movement apparent, she didn't hesitate. Williams' Glock 17 jumped in her hands. The bullet struck the figure in the chest, sending them tumbling to the ground.

Williams darted forward to help the woman at the same time Russell and Sampson moved to disarm the masked figure. As the attacker fell, the blade's edge nicked the woman across the eyebrow, the blood running down disguising how shallow the cut really was. The woman blinked, tilting her head to avoid more blood in her eye. She looked familiar, something prickling at the back of Williams' mind, but the woman was so filthy it was hard to know for sure.

Williams held the sleeve of her police jacket to the side of the woman's head. Not exactly clean, but it was probably safer than anything in the building. "I'm Detective Williams. You're safe now. Can you tell me your name?"

"Andrea Nowack. I'm a teacher. That's where I was grabbed. Is-is Ebony Bowman safe? She was taken with me that day...she was such a sweet girl."

A tear trailed down her cheek, cutting a crisp line through the dirt and grime.

Ch 31

Describe it to Me

I

Reyes groaned as Sofia untangled herself from him. He knew they had to spring right into action, but his mangled body refused his beck and call. "If this is it, so be it" it said. He pushed his damaged body far beyond its limits and now it had nothing left.

He wondered if he even had it in him to fire his snubnose. He doubted it. His breathing was beyond ragged, his lungs sounded more like crinkling cellophane than the air sacs they were. His existence screamed in terrible agony. He knew he wanted to live, to fight, but giving in would be its own kind of bliss. Maybe he should give in. Maybe he deserved it even.

Sofia gripped his arm, yanking him sideways as she fired her gun at the top of the stairs. Each yank sent shuddering pain through his body, a periodic reminder that she was taking the choice from him.

"Come on Reyes, we don't have time. Get up!" she yelled, scooting him further toward the second set of stairs.

The masked thugs upstairs hadn't dared cross the threshold yet, Sofia's firing too close for comfort. Two on two were never good odds, especially if both parties were armed.

Through sheer strength of will, belief in God and all things holy, or unbearable stupidity, Reyes urged his body forward. The pain was so unbearable that every inch his movements bought him sent a vibration cascading through him from head to toe.

He didn't know how long he had, but he would spend it moving.

He shuffled to the edge of the top stair, the descent sending shivers down his spine. His IV-stand cane had been lost to the fall. He sent a foot over the edge, the bend on his burnt side almost sending him tumbling again.

Sofia fired a final time into the stairwell door. She placed herself under Reyes' good shoulder, taking on as much of his weight as she could manage. She dragged him forward, mouthing, "We need to move."

As they hit the bottom step, they could hear the door above. Their escape timely yet again.

The floor they entered looked like some kind of basement. The lights weren't as bright, and it had the appearance of laxity. Stacks of storage bins were scattered around, and the floor could have used a good mopping.

The only door sign in the entire hall said "Morgue." Without conferring, the two of them sent silent prayers to the heavens that it wasn't a tasteless hint.

As they made it inside, it became apparent they were short on places to hide. The medical table in the center of the room had a body on it, only half covered in a thin white sheet. The man was old, probably mid-eighties, and had hopefully died of natural causes in one of the rooms upstairs. However, the milky look in his cataract-ridden eyes somehow still looked present, as if he was trying to communicate with a look alone from the great beyond. What had he seen, and what did his eyes foresee? Sofia made far too much noise leaping in startled shock. Reyes imagined the dead man raising his atrophied arm to point at the door, notifying them of their incoming troubles.

The back corner of the room had a metal filing area with a closable door below the sink. Sofia had just helped Reyes squeeze into its limited space when they heard footsteps.

Her eyes trailed up Reyes, finally finding his eyes. As she slid the door closed to hide him, cloaking him in darkness, Reyes called out "don't!" but it was too late.

"I'll find somewhere else," Sofia whispered.

She finished closing the cubby and crept back toward the morgue door. As she was about to step into the hall, strong gloved hands gripped her by the hair, yanking her head back.

II

"Tell me everything you remember about that day at the school," Williams said.

"Ebony and I were headed toward the playground...she—" Andrea Nowack stopped midsentence, a sob ripping its way through her. "She—she said she wanted to walk in the woods a little. And be-because she was so upset about Lizzy, I just said 'okay.' I didn't know how else to handle her."

Her body shook as she cried. It was evident she felt as if she had caused Ebony's kidnapping. Williams felt shame for having suspected her.

"We have to get to the church; I'll pull over and let you out or something. This'll be dangerous," Williams said, turning the cruiser down another road.

Andrea Nowack turned steely. She stopped crying, gathering herself and putting on a determined face. "No. I'm coming with you."

"Absolutely not. It's too dangerous."

"If you drop me off somewhere, I'll just follow on my own. I know where my family's properties are. At least if I come with you, you can protect me."

A fire burned in Williams that this woman would even threaten something as stupid as that, so soon after being saved. However, she had no choice but to swallow it down, Ms. Nowack was right. She could easily follow behind if she wanted to, and it would undoubtedly be more dangerous.

"Fine," Williams said with gritted teeth.

Williams thought she saw a self-satisfied look come over the teacher. However, when making the next left-hand turn, the face was gone—if it were ever really there. The sniffly, distraught woman was before her again. She tried desperately to wipe the blood from her face with the sleeve of her sweater.

Williams checked the rearview mirror to see if either of the agents were paying attention. Sampson was running a hand through her short black hair. Russell was uncontrollably tapping his leg while reloading a magazine. Williams understood.

An agent had run out with Colfax, trying to save her life. Cobble and Doakes stayed behind to wait for help with the arrested Halloweeners. A team of three was exactly what Williams had tried to avoid all along, yet there they were. She hoped that those fleeing hadn't run straight to Carter. If they had, this might be over much sooner than she wanted it to be. The outcome in question a lot darker, too.

The next fifteen minutes passed without incident. Night was well and truly upon them. Williams hoped the cloak of darkness would lend them a helping hand.

Was she ready to die for this? She had been much more certain when she knew that Reyes was on the other side of the door. There was a new feeling burrowing its way into her stomach; this time it belonged to doubt. She wanted to succeed, to prove herself, but she also desperately, irrevocably wanted to live.

Turning off the road, rough gravel gave way to muddied tracks. Williams rolled the cruiser behind a dense copse of trees. Keying the vehicle off she turned to Ms. Nowack, a nugget of an idea forming.

"This is the original place we intended to rendezvous with the other team. There would have been twice as many of us, and even then, it wasn't enough. What can you tell me about this place?"

Andrea Nowack's face turned up in thought. "It's old, but the shape of a church is pretty standard, I'd think. The front door opens into a large nave. The pews line both left and right and lead right up the pulpit. It's an old Catholic Church. Incredibly ornate with decorations lining every wall and surface."

"Hiding spots, additional entrances, anything like that?"

"Um, yes, actually. The back of the church has an office space and also an upstairs loft apartment meant for a priest. I believe the priest quarters have a separate exit," Andrea Nowack replied.

"Anything else you think I should know?" Williams pressed.

"Well, unlike the apartment complex, the church isn't derelict. It's maintained due to some irreplaceable original wood in the arched ceiling. It could reopen tomorrow even—if Cemetery had use for it, that is. So please, be careful in there. Both for yourself, and the property."

"Thank you for the information," Williams said. "And I'm really sorry about this."

"I know it's not your fault, thank you for saving me—"

Williams pulled Nowack's left hand forward, swinging a pair of handcuffs from her belt. Snapping the first cuff around her wrist, Williams clipped the other onto the passenger side door handle.

"I am sorry about *that*," she said as she jumped out of the cruiser.

Ms. Nowack tried to yell something, but Williams was already gone.

III

The attacker pulled Sofia by the hair and flung her down the hall. Their grip ripped the bandages from the back of her head. She could no longer see out of her good eye, her hair and loose bandages covering her face. Her injured eye felt moist; the knock to the floor had reopened it.

Before she had a moment to think, the gloved hands were upon her again. They gripped her collar and dragged her from the floor. As she blinked through layers of hair, the rubber face of William Shatner met her. She wanted to scream but attempted to punch the mask instead. She missed, her body still struggling to recoup oxygen.

The masked figure slammed her back into the wall, her lungs deflating again with an audible rasp. They pressed her into the wall, sliding her upward with force, her feet leaving the floor.

She desperately fought for oxygen, her double knockout feeling like it was damaging something permanently. Spots danced before her, bright stars and dark wisps swirling before her blinking eye.

In desperation, she slammed her knee up, catching the masked assailant in the groin. They grunted, releasing Sofia, and dropping to their hands and knees with a curse.

Sofia grabbed her pistol off the floor and took off down the hall. She could have ended it, but with the other attacker still about, the last thing she needed was to lead them right to Reyes.

Her feet beat a rhythmic staccato across the tile flooring. She rounded another corner, finally finding her stride. Her eye hurt like hell, but she needed to get them away from Reyes. It was the main reason she was running so loudly. Let them follow, as long as it kept them from the morgue.

She didn't know him well, practically not at all, but she had been left as his protector. He had settled her when she had freaked out, and he had stuck by her side. That was enough for her. She had him now, whatever it took.

The end of the hall let out into a storage area full of medical equipment, sheets, vending machine refills, stacks of tiny apple juices, even extra desks. As she slowed to a stop, she heard the heavy beat of boots. She had just enough time to press her body behind a stack of grey storage crates. She drew in a breath and covered her mouth to muffle the sounds.

Sofia heard them enter the storage area and slow down. Drawing in deep rasping breaths, they started rifling through the stacks. They were careless, loud, throwing and knocking stacks left and right. She held her breath as they walked right past her, continuing their path of destruction.

If she timed this right, she could head back toward the stairwell, the chaser slowed down by their own mess making.

She waited.

The attacker made it to the back of the room, slamming another stack of gray bins. The bins slid sideways down the wall, coming to a precarious halt on a stack of desks. As soon as the bins' weight was distributed against them, the desks came crashing down across the floor, taking other stacks with them. The mess would be hell to get through.

Sofia pounced on the opportunity, sprinting from her hiding spot. She hopped loose bins and juices. Entering the hall, her hunter screamed as he spotted her fleeing.

Sofia ran back down the hall. The noise of crashing desks was probably enough to alert the police a dozen towns over.

At the end of the hall, she turned to head back to the stairs. She rounded the corner and came face to face with the bastard that was trying to kill her. Well, the masked William Shatner face at least...

"Wait, wait, wait—"

Sofia didn't. Her gun let off a resounding blast.

The attacker stared down at the newly made hole in his chest, the blood already blooming across his dark robes. As his one hand gripped his chest over his heart, the other lashed out, racking a hunting knife across Sofia's throat.

Ch 32

Villain Monologue

I

The team knelt in the trees surrounding the church. They were further away than Williams would have liked, but Ms. Nowack hadn't lied—the property was well maintained.

They knelt spread out. It was meant to be strategic, but with them numbering so few, it was just a short fan formation. There were lights on within the church. Every minute or so a shadow would pass before one of the windows.

At least we know there's people inside. No surprises this time, Williams thought. *I wish Reyes were here, or Colfax. A level head would be good right now.*

They had crept around the property looking for anything suspicious. The priest's entrance was completely dark.

Williams made eye contact with Russell and Sampson. If only she could instill what their loyalty and service meant to her with a single look. They had gone out of their way to help. Even if it was their job, she still felt they were taking on Cemetery's problems, and that was a heavy debt to pay. And not just them, but all the others who had already paid with their lives.

The loyal police force meant even more to her. Their ability to withstand the corruption raining down was admirable. She wouldn't forget it. Or their sacrifices they had made. There would be a reckoning.

She took a final look at the church's front. It was beautiful with large, stained windows that ended in beautiful arches. The lights from inside danced in orange, red, and golds across the dark parking lot. The building was stone and wood, the kind of architecture rarely seen in modern times. She wasn't much on religion herself, but if there was a home for it in Cemetery, she found it incredibly odd it wasn't this particular church.

They crept out from behind cover, crouching forward inch by inch. Just as they were about to break away from the tree line, a pair of blinding headlights swung around through the trees.

They dropped prone on the ground; they hadn't even heard a car.

Fuck! They better not have seen us, Williams thought, begged, prayed.

Out of the car stepped a Halloween masked figure. The bane of Cemetery. They stretched, the masked face no longer matching up with their head. Out of the back seat stepped another figure.

Williams hoped this wasn't reinforcements from the apartment complex. Lord only knew what they would do then.

She wondered what had taken them so long. If they were from the complex, they would have left much earlier. Then everything became clear.

The second figure went around and popped the trunk. After a short struggle, they dragged a handcuffed, bloodied person out. One hand was cuffed, and the other was holding the side panel from a car door, a handcuff sticking out the bottom.

It was Andrea Nowack. She still wore the same once-white sweater and boots, but now she was crumbling weakly against the kidnappers as they dragged her toward the church.

II

Reyes bit his tongue in pain, blood tingling along his taste buds. The new pain was at least fresh; something he had done, something he controlled. Finally, with his burned hand, he was able to shimmy the metal door open. Sofia had closed it, hoping to keep him safe, and possibly sacrificing herself in the process.

Once it was opened enough that he could slide his way out, he took several moments to breath after each movement.

Small victories, right...then why do they feel like punishments?

Reyes stood, raising himself with the edge of the morgue table. Various tubes, needles, scalpels, and trocar lined the tray next to the table.

He stumbled over to the wall of cold chambers. The thought of approaching them was enough to gross him out. He rarely found himself all that squeamish, so this was a surprise. Refrigerating human remains just seemed a bit too much. *Leftover neighbor anyone?* The macabre deflection intruding into his thoughts.

Opening the first drawer, Reyes slid the tray along its tracks until the entire body was before him. He wasn't even sure what he was looking for. Something had just drawn him to the coolers.

He was about to push the tray back in when something caught the corner of his eye.

The collarbone of the cadaver had a purple wheal mark, the skin showing the faintest points of dual puncture wounds. Something was just beneath the skin.

Reyes pushed the tray shut, reaching for another. As the body slid further into view, Reyes couldn't fight the tightening of his stomach, the tensing of muscles. He searched the cadaver's shoulders and neck. Nothing. He breathed a sigh of relief. For a second there he thought he was onto something, and the idea sickened him.

He eyed the cadaver a minute longer. Then, as his eyes roved down the legs, he saw the torn ankle. It was just like the other bodies they had found, so where were the needle marks?

His forehead broke out in a cold sweat. It quickly travelled down his body. The juxtaposition of cold, tingling fear against his burned and aching side was its own kind of torture.

Around the torn ankle there were two little marks on the calf. No wheal this time, but clearly they didn't stop at anything to complete their mission.

Reyes felt the burning need to search as many of the cold chambers as he could get his hands on. The bodies, all of them, were the same. Tray by tray, no matter how concealed they were, there they were all the same. Cadaver after cadaver turned out the same result. The shock that these used to be citizens—*people*—was enough to hitch his breath. Did these people all meet the same fate? Were they in the wrong place at the wrong time? Reyes continued down the line, in an almost fugue state, peeling back the layers of depravity.

How was this even possible? So long on the force had prepared him for nearly anything, but this, *this* was something else entirely. How far did this run? This could cripple the entire Hudson Valley. His home. His life and friends. His *people*.

Reyes was just sliding open the final tray when he heard heavy footfalls in the hall. He had few choices, and none of them good. If he left the tray open, they'd be alerted to his presence. Sliding it shut would result in the same. He knew he didn't have it in him to get back in the cubby.

Shuffling against the side of the door, he let out a breath and waited for the inevitable. Reyes hoped the chance of surprising them would buy him what little advantage he could get.

A masked figure stalked into the morgue. Taking in the open tray, they let out a wicked laugh. The figure prodded the body as if it was nothing more than a piece of meat on a cutting board.

The lack of decorum and respect sent Reyes spinning. He growled and threw himself at the masked criminal. His good side slammed into them, the force rocketing them both into the open tray. Reyes' snubnose flew across the tile. The cadaver unceremoniously flopped to the floor.

"That was a freaking human being, you depraved piece of shit," Reyes ground out as he rained fists down on the attacker. The adrenaline and rage fueled him, numbing the pain. His last punch spun the Halloween mask to the side, blinding the figure. Part of Reyes knew he should keep unloading his fear and anger onto the attacker, but he wanted them to see.

Had to know if he knew them.

The mask ripped off easily. The face beneath was one Reyes was sure he had never seen before. For some reason, the anonymity made Reyes even angrier. He jabbed an uppercut into the man's face, knocking him back onto the tray.

Gathering himself, the attacker shoved Reyes back. He wiped a trail of blood from the corner of his mouth and spat on the floor.

Reyes stumbled back, almost dropping to the floor. He caught himself at the last second against the door frame. The pain was beginning to bleed through the adrenaline, tearing its way through his fight or flight response.

Reyes pressed forward, knowing that if he didn't make the conscious effort now, the choice would be taken from him sooner rather than later. The attacker looked as if he was folding in on himself, cowering before Reyes could strike again. However, the man wasn't cowering; he was reaching for something. He swung a blade from left to right.

Reyes leapt back, catching the blow against his good forearm instead. The strike burned through his skin like a million needles piercing through him. He fell right through the door to the morgue, landing hard on his tailbone. He wanted to scramble away from the knife-wielding murderer, but he couldn't get his sliced arm to pull any of the weight, and his burned limb wasn't responding either.

He lay back against the tile floor, breath heavy and strained. A cough wracked through him, shaking his sides and making his eyes blur. If this was it, this was it. There was no beating around the bush. No delaying the inevitable.

The attacker stalked forward; knife held out at an angle, the reflection of the white hospital lights shining with menacing glee. Reyes balked at the realization that his life had been whittled down to a horror movie scene, the worst part being his utter inability to change things. He had known his life was horrific for some time; that was probably why he had let himself deteriorate. He just couldn't help it—the loss of someone so innocent had changed everything he knew of justice—of fairness. Maybe his family would be ashamed somewhere, maybe Maria would be too. Williams certainly would be, but he was letting go. It was decided.

He was ready. He could let it end here. At least he would finally be with his Isabell again. He wished Williams was stronger, wherever she was.

They were eye to eye now. Murderer and victim. One standing above the other in classic form. There really was a level of bliss in letting go, in seeing the end of the road. Reyes could live with that, until he couldn't.

The attacker leaned forward, spittle raining from his mouth, "You assholes just never learn, do you?" Drawing the knife back, he swung.

Reyes closed his eyes and waited for the end. Instead, the attacker's head snapped to the left, blood and viscera splattering the wall behind them as a bullet exited his brain. He slumped, limp to the floor.

Dead.

Sofia dropped her pistol and fell against the hallway wall. Somewhere in Reyes' mind it registered that she had chosen to let go of her slit throat to save him, but it was awfully hard to stay awake.

As their pools of blood spread across the tile, bleeding into each other like eternal lovers, their world faded to black.

III

After the church door slammed shut, Williams waited several agonizing minutes to ensure no one else was coming. She signaled the team, and they crept forward silently. Ghosts in the night—or snakes in the grass, depending on whose view it was. They wrapped back around the building; figuring the recent appearance would be a good distraction.

As they reached the priest quarters, they planted themselves against the base of the building. The space above was still dark, the only perceptible noise the muffled movements from the front of the church.

Williams tried the door; it wasn't even locked. Leave it to a priest to be so trusting. So naive.

The door opened into a tiny mudroom. To the left was a shoe rack lined with patent leather loafers; black peacoats lined the right. The floor was a white-and-red penny tile.

This place really is old.

The mudroom led into a narrow hardwood staircase. The stairwell was dark, but Williams saw the deep red-and-blue runner going up the center of the stairs.

The carpet runner would help them remain silent. Finally, a point in their favor. Williams wondered when the last priest was commissioned here. The thought came and went as she crept up the turn staircase.

As she reached the top of the stairs, the landing was wide and opened into a decent living space. Stumbling, she thought it best to risk a flashlight instead of a broken neck. The flashlight's beam cracked into existence, illuminating the horrors before them.

The missing agents and officers, kidnapped just earlier in the day, were piled before them, greyed, shriveled, and mangled. Several were missing shirts, some with pantlegs rolled up or torn off. Deep, gleaming holes were cut into each body, showing the imprecise movements employed in the butchery of internal organs. The volatile strokes used to remove each almost appeared *ravenous*. Again, Williams was struck with the sheer violence of such an act.

Williams dropped the flashlight in surprised, covering her mouth to hold in the scream that bubbled to life in her throat. She'd been seeing this kind of violence for over a month, and yet, she was still startled by the depravity of it each and every time. It wasn't just inhumane, it was *inhuman*.

Knowing they were alive earlier today, she'd stake everything on the fact that a machine didn't do this. What kind of machine removes blood while accelerating the decomposition of the corpse? None in existence was the only answer. What else could though?

The unbelievable body count, as well as the corrupt officers, was sure to run Cemetery PD dry. They'd have to ship officers in or evacuate the town entirely. Either option was frankly better than this. *This* had to end.

Williams steeled herself, retrieving the flashlight and readjusted her grip on her Glock 17. The last thing she needed was for them to catch her off guard again.

The team made it up the stairs, taking in the scene. Their faces were a mix of horror and steadfast determination.

A door off to the right corner of the living space led into a small office. Williams figured this was where the priests would stay up writing their sermons before bed. The desk was solid mahogany, beautiful, but too large for the space it was in. At the end of the carpeted floor there was another door. This had to be it—the entrance to the church.

Williams crept toward it.

They were in luck.

The door was once again unlocked.

Third time's the charm, she thought. *Or a goddamn trap.*

She recalled for probably the millionth time one of her earliest memories. Her father, ever the pessimist, would take her by the shoulders, look her directly in the eyes and say, "If something ever seems too good to be true, it most likely is. You nod your head along with whatever it is, and then you hightail it out of there immediately. Never trust the easy way out."

The memory only made it harder to recall the stupidity that took place when he allowed her to be used in that damned police sting. Had that not seemed too good to be true, too easy a way out? Or was he so blinded by the idea of helping, or playing the hero that it didn't matter? The indelible memories had been chasing her through her entire life, entire career. The haunting nightmares of Carl Stratton almost getting what he wanted following her through life as if he had. But that was only if she let it—let him win. And she had already decided he hadn't.

Williams swallowed the memories down with all their bad taste. She wasn't a little girl anymore. If he wanted to impart life lessons, he probably should have taken a more direct approach with a child. Should have kept her out of harm's way.

The carpet runner allowed for a much freer range of motion for her team, each of them descending in a way that allowed them to still aim their guns.

At the halfway point Williams stopped abruptly. A moment later, they all knew why.

Just ahead they heard talking. It sounded like a mixture of conversations, one of which stuck out the most. It was Ms. Nowack pleading with someone. Williams' first instinct was to rush in. They had just saved this woman from a near-death experience, just to lead her into another. It was just one more thing to add to the list of Williams' fuck ups, a list that she wore like a brand.

"It's no longer up to you. Sorry, but I'm not sure what you'd like me to say. It's over now. Out of your hands entirely." The voice wafting up the stairs sounded like Carter.

"Please, don't do this!" Ms. Nowack yelled.

A few laughs rang out in answer.

Williams wouldn't let this happen again. Not another life, not another mistake. She raced down the stairs.

She peeked her head out to sneak a look at where the argument was taking place. They were off to the left, Ms. Nowack seated in a pew and Carter standing over her.

To the right, a group of kids and adults were gagged and tied to the pews.

"You can't just do this and expect for everything to go well. It doesn't work like that. Life doesn't work like that."

Life? What the fuck was Carter on about?

While Carter was distracted, Williams worked her way behind the altar. She didn't manage to go completely unnoticed though. Out of the corner of her eye, she picked up on the slightest change in Ms. Nowack's face. A mixture of recognition and maybe hope? Was Williams seeing things or had her lips turned up at the corners the slightest bit?

"Please, Carter, just stop hurting these people. They can be helped. They can be saved! I know it," Nowack cried.

Carter took an angry step toward her, shaking his head, an incredulous look plastered on his face. "What are you even talking about? You're not going to turn this all around on me!"

Russell and Sampson slid across the floor toward Williams' position. They were relying on whatever show Carter was putting on to distract the others.

Nowack closed her mouth and started shaking with intense sobs. She rocked back and forth, tears streaming.

Carter's entire demeaner changed. He knelt, taking Nowack into his arms and wrapping her into a tight embrace. He whispered to her, their voices not carrying back to Williams.

As he was hugging her, he pulled her almost entirely off of the pew. That was the second thing that took Williams as odd. Not just the warm gesture—although Katherine had said the rumor was they were seeing each other—but that she wasn't tied up.

She was just sitting there.

Nowack went from stiff uncertainty to hungry reciprocation. She pulled Carter into her, kissing earnestly. He answered in kind, drawing her even closer to him, hands wound up in her hair.

So much for a private relationship, right? Williams thought. *Strike three, Dad. Something's not right here.*

It was as they separated that Williams saw it. The Chief's gun...but not in his hands.

In Nowack's.

Carter stepped away from her, Nowack's wracking sobs giving way to a disgusting peal of laughter. She raised the pistol between them. "Look at us fighting back and forth like a couple of puppies."

"What the hell are you doing, baby?" Carter cried.

"You were always such a gullible idiot. Power hungry but lacking vision. Your lack thereof is what led us here today. Detective Williams is right over there. And it's because of you"—she gesticulated each word with the barrel of the pistol—"Because of you, and your low-IQ cronies that we're backed into this corner. You absolute imbecile."

Nowack finished her tirade with a flourish of laughter.

Carter turned toward where Nowack had pointed. Now that Williams saw him, Carter looked terrible. The bags under his eyes were a sickly purple, his hair a mess. He looked thinner, sweaty. Like he was drifting away.

"Obfuscation!" Carter said. "That's what you said you needed from me. I set a fake lead, make light of an important clue, forget to set a security detail. That my hands would be *'virtually clean'* so that I could look myself in the mirror. Look at me! It's tearing me apart. You've lied over and over to keep dragging me along. I didn't want to do any of this. Innocent people are dying now, just for getting in your way." Carter's voice broke. His body was tensed, but he was visibly shaking. Breaking apart over his involvement. "You said you loved me...that we would be together. That's why I did it. Placing fake details into that missing person file, trying to keep my detectives away from the Eltons. You told me no one would get hurt!"

Carter's anger flared, getting the best of him. Whether it was a sense of guilt, righteousness, or payback, he stepped toward his maniacal lover, his posture exuding contempt. He reached for her, but Nowack didn't even bat an eye. She raised the gun, firing point blank into Carter's chest.

His own gun putting an end to him. The irony, hatred and pain, clear on his face.

Williams leapt up behind the altar, but there was nothing she could have done. The two of them had been too close to intervene. She would have much rather seen him pay for his mistakes, his crimes than get the easy way out.

Carter coughed, spitting up blood. "I wouldn't have done any of this if it weren't for you."

"I know, I know," Nowack crooned. "That's why I have no use for you, sweety." She fired the gun into Carter's chest again. He shook with the violence of it, a trail of blood dripping down his chin.

Then he lay still.

"You're under arrest," Williams said shakily, her gun raised at Nowack. "The kidnappings, the missing persons, the murders. All of it. And for what?"

Nowack made an apologetic face before busting into laughter again. "I'm sorry, but for what? My family built this town from the ground up and for what? *For what* exactly! For the place to become a cesspool of crime. For rapes, robberies, and murder to run rampant. For the police force to flounder through one crime, then the next? I mean, I always thought things were bad, but wow! You start playing your hand at a few crimes and you truly get to see just how shitty the police are. The amount that gets missed here. You are all pathetic."

"And the officers stupid enough to help you?"

"Stupid? I would argue they were the only ones smart enough to see the folly of the department. They aimed to make a difference at least. What have you done? Nothing but fail left and right. With us right under your nose."

The dig stung, but Nowack wasn't wrong. The truth cut through her more than anything else she could have said. The fact grated on Williams. She tightened her grip on her Glock.

Nowack laughed again. "See! See how fucking easy it is to rile you guys up?" She wiped her mouth and continued. "But enough of that. This isn't an anti-police movement. This was always a fight for our community, for Cemetery. I'm sorry to disappoint you, but this isn't about you."

"Then why the kids? The list of names from Robbie's father. I don't get it."

Williams edged forward, but Nowack sprang up, Carter's gun held out in front of her.

"Why don't you calm yourself and sit down? These fine people behind me are just as armed as you are, and they won't stand for you killing me. You see, all it really takes is to find out which key turns a person. A nurse that sees too much unnecessary death, a police officer that gets shot only to be returned to the line of duty with nothing to show for their sacrifice. Ideology or idealism? Sure. The desire for a better life and riches? Sure. Whatever the buying price, and almost everyone in this awful town has one. Even those that second guessed have no real way out, culpability being what it is and all. Once you're turned, it's over.

"Oh, and the list? Well, that was easy enough. A few late nights spent with that hog of a man, Carter, and it was simplicity itself to get the information out of him. He would never have done anything like that on his own, believe me, he didn't have the imagination, but he was the easiest manipulation I've ever seen. Or done? Whatever."

Nowack shrugged, scratching a thumb along her thigh. "My older sister, Victoria...well she became sick. The kind of sick that haunts the nights of every well-mannered parent, of every younger sister that grew up worshipping their older sister. And you know what, even with my parents' riches, even with everything they had done for this town, they still couldn't get the help they needed. My sister's rare blood type and tween size made it hard for any kind of transplant to stick. And guess what, they didn't find one in time anyway. You wouldn't believe my surprise when Carter told me just how similar Reyes and I were to each other—you'd be astonished the number of similar cases to ours. And you know what? He repelled me time and time again." When Williams opened her mouth to defend her partner, Nowack brandished Carter's pistol at her.

"But where was I, I digress. Those kids were on a dark path. They may have been young, but it's the same old thing. My family's charity has poured millions into changing the circumstances of Cemetery's youth for decades, and for what? Pot-smoking, no-good louts. And that's at best. At worst, they play nice for the handout, running right back to a life of darkness when its gone. My plan, on the other hand, has given them purpose. It's given their measly, pent-up, bullshit lives a meaning. That blood has traveled all over the country to help in life-saving procedures. The stolen organs will be shipped to those in dire need, practically wiping out years on the waiting list, years these people don't have. Years that Victoria didn't have. Do you not understand that? I'm a fucking hero.

"You guys are the criminals for trying to stop me. And all it took was a single set of names matching off a list you'd seen. A missing head and foot to throw you off the scent of what we were really doing. Hook, line, and sinker—you took the bait and didn't see what was right before your eyes."

Williams opened her mouth to retort, but Nowack's face flushed red.

"You see the main problem was believing in change. No one ever does. A leopard can't change its spots, right? Rehabilitation is make-believe. People who land in jail will land there again. And so it goes. These are the facts that the police don't want to see. What is the percentage of recidivism in Cemetery? I bet you don't even know. Because they don't tell you the facts, they want you to feed into and live the lie. Every day you go to work and think you can instill change, that you can save lives. What have you ever done? Put some people away for a few months, years? Pick someone up on shady evidence, on shady circumstances, for the judge to let them walk in forty-eight hours?"

Here Nowack paused, walking to the right-side pews and removing the gag from one of the adults.

With everything going on, Williams hadn't recognized him. It was Evan Rictor. The bastard who had gotten away while she was out cold in a hospital bed.

Trying to play it cool, Williams said nothing, taking the time to look at the pews, hoping to see James and Henry.

"Now wouldn't it just feel *oh so good* to come over here and give him what he deserves? Give it a taste, see how it feels. You just might like it. That's what I offer, that's all I'm doing. He's had his chance. A wife beater, and a child beater. A raging drunk. So much toxic masculinity that he wears it like a cologne. What good is this guy going to do for the world? His blood though, *mmm*," she purred, caressing his face, taunting him. "Now that could do some good. A big muscular shorty like this, he must have a healthy heart, don't you think? A little cut here, a big cut there, we could save someone else's life, don't you think? Maybe even a kid! Someone with a bright future ahead of them, one that the universe is trying to snuff out too soon."

She placed Carter's pistol to the back of Evan's head. "All of this could be yours if you just consent. Should I?" she teased, pushing the barrel against his head, rocking him forward.

"You're wrong you know," Williams offered, no idea where she was going, just knowing she needed to stall for time.

"I'm what now?"

"You're wrong. There's no way of knowing what someone will do with a second chance. I'm a firm believer that it's not up to us, but that everyone deserves one. If we stop believing in others, what's left in the world?"

"Second chances?" Nowack looked stricken. "You really believe that? That even the likes of me could truly change?"

"If given the chance, yes. I believe it's the right of every person to change, to make amends," Williams said.

Nowack sighed. A horrific, tortured look came over her face. For a moment, Williams thought she looked like a real monster.

"Oh well," Nowack said. She pulled the trigger, Rictor's head slamming forward; blood, skull, and brains raining across several rows of pews in front of him. The others tied next to him screamed through their gags, the children crying.

Williams had had enough, pulling the trigger of her Glock 17. A bullet tore through Nowack's shoulder, dropping her to the floor with a shout of pain.

Moving toward the right-side pews, Williams fired at the other masked figures. Russell and Sampson didn't need instructions; they stepped out from where they were hiding and started firing.

In short order, they killed or incapacitated several of the murderers; only one of Williams' team—Sampson from the sound of it—getting clipped. They hid and shot out of cover.

They were outnumbered, but that didn't mean they were outmatched. If they could keep it up, they had a chance.

Every time another one of them was hurt, or ducked out of the way to reload, Williams pressed further. She had to free the kidnapped citizens before the attackers decided to use them as leverage.

Nowack was distracted yelling orders to her men, only firing randomly.

Williams continued to press the advantage, dropping spent magazines and reloading in a practiced motion, her nerves completely lost to the fight.

Williams ducked as a stray bullet whizzed past her head. She had shifted her focus for just a moment as she took in the kidnapped citizens. It almost cost her life.

A scream to the left signaled one of her team was down, perhaps permanently. She didn't know who it was; all she knew was that they were quickly running out of team members. She reloaded again, her jacket pocket getting drastically close to empty. Once that ran out, they'd be fish out of water.

Dead fish.

Williams was filled with rage, fear, and determination to see this through. As she stood again, she made sure to launch herself sideways, so as not to appear from the same spot she disappeared. There was no need to make it easy for them.

She fired off a series of shots, clipping one in the hip who was busy loading a shotgun. She missed the others, but evening the odds was the best she could hope for.

"Shit, shit, I'm out!" someone yelled. Amid the cacophony of sounds, the muzzle flashes, and the screams of the injured or dying, Williams couldn't quite make out if it was theirs or hers calling out.

She caught another attacker exposed, firing three shots, one of which blazed a hole through their monkey mask. They toppled backwards, landing on top of another attacker who had been crouched to reload. Williams fired off several shots before she was out again. She dropped back down, making herself as flat as she could in the bullet proof vest, her head and shoulders bent over the pew.

She dropped out another magazine, this time reaching into her jacket pocket and finding there was only one left.

This really was it. A last stand.

As Williams raised herself from behind a pew, Nowack barreled into her, tackling her to the hardwood floor. The air rushed out of Williams as she tried to raise her hands into defensive positions. She caught Nowack by the wrists, having to release her Glock to do so. Even with a bullet wound to the shoulder, Nowack utilized her body weight as she pressed down upon Williams, finally overpowering the detective's struggling elbows. Batting her arms away, Nowack reached for her throat, pressing down with surprising strength as her fingers found purchase.

Williams kicked her feet out to no avail, Nowack far too high up on the other woman's waist to flip her off. Blinding spots of white and black danced in William's vision as Nowack continued to cut off the oxygen to her brain. Williams fumbled semi-blindly, her arms weak as she tried gripping Nowack's bullet wound and pressing down. The hiss that escaped the teacher's lips was short, but she released one hand from her neck to bat her hand away.

The stream of oxygen into Williams' burning lungs was short lived, but just enough. Her hand scrambled, desperate, trying for anything that could help her escape. Her burned fingers fumbled several times before they finally gripped what felt like a wooden stake. Williams weakly raised her other hand into Nowack's face, pushing against her jaw and trying to distract her. This wasn't what she wanted, but her opponent was overpowering her; was winning. Williams plunged the chipped piece of church pew into Andrea Nowack's chest, sinking it in with a twist as it found her heart. A wave of hot blood rushed past Williams' fingers to drench her face and chest.

Dropping the woman, Williams backpedaled across the floor, feeling for her gun and taking heaving breaths. She had stopped her; she had done it. As much as she wanted to arrest her, to make her pay for the rest of her life, at least her bloody reign was over.

A yell rent through the church, but this one was different. It was authoritative, and one she hadn't heard before. And what were they saying?

The voice called out again; this time Williams heard it loud and clear. She lay back in relief as an FBI agent yelled orders through a megaphone, the remaining masked figures already beginning to stand down. She said a silent thank you to Colfax and wondered if she had made it.

Epilogue

THREE MONTHS LATER

Williams ensured Gianna Colfax was hailed as a hero. Not just in Cemetery; she was determined that people remember. The FBI Special Agent had given her life to a town that wasn't even hers, and even though the chances were small, she'd still secured the reinforcements they needed. Not because she was going to be there, but because she couldn't be. Reinforcements that would later come just in the nick of time to save Williams and her team. That kind of loyalty, that kind of service, was a once in a lifetime thing.

Likewise, Reyes had pushed for the exact same with Field Agent Sofia Mendes. The blood trail they had found leading all the way down the hall to her body, told the story true enough. The exact trail that had led them to a barely breathing Ed Reyes. The hospital had given it their all and had just managed to save him as he clung to life. He couldn't openly share it, but that desire to live had been due to her sacrifice. If not for her duty as a protector, he may have given in.

Now, the two of them stood arm in arm, together again thanks to the sacrifices of others. Reyes was in a new suit, one that Williams had gone with him to buy—vehemently assuring him that he couldn't show up in anything less—and she was happy to admit it fit him well. He was still frustrated with his two new companions, never leaving his side. Since his release from the hospital, he was the not-so-proud user of a cane, at least while his physical therapy lasted. His second friend, literally attached to the hip, was a portable oxygen tank. The mask hung off his lapel so that it looked like it belonged there.

They both spoke at once, smiling when they caught each other. Williams hadn't meant to cut him off, but Reyes simply grinned at this new version of his partner who didn't wait for others to speak first.

He sucked in a breath of the sweet air. "At least you got your wish."

"My wish?" Williams asked.

"I know you always hated my smoking." He laughed, and his recently shrunk belly shook with him.

It was good to hear him laugh. Too much of this experience had caused them nothing but pain, the suffering stacking until the bitter end.

Williams still hoped it was bittersweet when it was all said and done.

"Correction...I hated you smoking in our office, in your car, and pretty much everywhere else. Have you not seen the countless studies on secondhand smoke? That doesn't make it a wish." She smiled at him, and he smiled back. A gleam in his eye.

"The specialist told me that I needed the cane to walk, but that I wouldn't die without it. The cigarettes, on the other hand, may spiral me down a dark, breathless path. So it was time to make a decision...and I finally have." Reyes looked at her sideways, serious. "Abby, I would like you to have my cane to remember me by."

He laughed heartily again as Williams punched his shoulder.

Before she knew it, she was overcome with giggles as well. Such a stupid joke, but she loved it all the same. She had missed him dearly, and him her. Neither had been certain they'd see each other again.

"You did it, kid. And without any help."

"Well, actually, I had an awful lot of help..." Williams trailed off, not knowing how to continue. Katherine, Colfax, and simply too many others had paid the price in this case. The bill had come due, and she was still reeling trying to figure out how to balance the scales.

"You stuck with it. You knew what was in your heart, and you didn't let anyone tell you otherwise. I'm proud of you," Reyes said, his voice catching in his throat. "That's all I wanted to say."

Williams smiled, tears welling in her eyes that she definitely wouldn't let fall. "I can't stop thinking about what happened to Carter. I was so certain he was the one we were after, I ignored all of the signs. That he was suffering. Maybe...like maybe if we had extended a hand instead, he would have reached for us. For me. Instead, I sealed his fate."

Reyes turned stern. "He did that to himself; you can't blame yourself for his crappy choices, kid."

"And there were so many red flags with Nowack." Williams covered her face with a hand, embarrassment and guilt building again. "She told me that Ebony was upset over Lizzy, when I already knew they hadn't told her. She said she 'was *such a sweet girl,*' when she wouldn't have had a clue what had happened if she was being held captive. Ed, those are such major mistakes. And they weren't my only ones."

"Abby, we all made mistakes. But you never gave up. You kept pushing, kept fighting for our town. It ain't always easy, but that's why you're the person you are. My partner. My friend. I'm sorry I kept my personal life from you for so long, I guess it was just easier to hide it away. But god, do you remind me of my Isabell."

"I think we bickered so much because you're like the father figure I never had, but the one I needed." Williams wiped her eyes, centering herself. She placed a kiss on his cheek and adjusted her grip on his arm.

"So, what now for Cemetery's Greatest Detective?" Reyes ribbed.

"Cemetery PD's *only* detective, you mean. Not to mention one of maybe like ten staff members at the moment," Williams replied, the happiness leaving her voice.

"Eleven. Baxter's recovery has been going well. Physical therapy said he should be released to full duty."

"I'm glad you're so hopeful, Ed."

"We'll rebuild," Reyes said. His voice wasn't stern, but certain. "When they had me, I found out that you were on their trail, that you were out there. It gave me hope. Hope's not something we see in Cemetery enough. Maybe it's time we change that."

"Maybe you're right, but how?" Williams looked genuinely curious, not argumentative and ready to butt heads with Reyes like usual. So much had changed. "I still need to find James Rictor. He wasn't among the bodies, and he wasn't at the church."

Reyes took his time answering. "Maybe he didn't like how things were going. At home, or with the case. Maybe after we talked to him, he split town for real."

Williams knew that didn't end the matter, but she let it lie.

"You know," Williams said, "I think the FBI's official report is pure shit. Absolute nonsense to make someone happy. I kept digging before you got out, as you knew I would. I met with someone in the medical field, even double-checking it with our pathologist. The number of kills, the number of disfigured bodies…there wasn't nearly enough blood and organs anonymously donated for it to add up."

"Abby, please," Reyes pleaded. "Not again. You know what they'll say. We can't."

"I know, I know," Williams said, letting out a deep breath. She wasn't satisfied, and she wouldn't stop, even if she had to do it on personal time. While the courts handled Nowack's demonic reign on a public front, she'd investigate in secret.

"Let's get on with it, then," Williams said, smiling again. "Aren't they about to make my partner and closest friend the acting chief of police? I'll play nice. Shake hands and kiss babies. And as soon as they leave, you're giving me full permission. Sound good?"

Reyes opened his mouth to protest, but she was already dragging him through the precinct door and into the spotlight.

The FBI were still deep into the investigation. Therefore, so was Williams. They had found no fewer than thirty dead from those missing and taken, and that wasn't counting the fatalities due to their crusade. So far, no fewer than twenty arrests had been made, with no end in sight. The department was hanging on by a thread, and with the investigation spanning to other towns, there wasn't much help incoming.

One thing was for certain—if a crime was committed in Cemetery, Abigail Williams and Ed Reyes would be there.

Acknowledgements

First, I would like to thank you, the reader. Thank you for giving my writing a chance, and from the bottom of my heart, thank you for reaching the end of the book! As this is an indie release, and my debut, there was always the fear that no one would pick it up, that it would not find an audience. You've proven that fear wrong. If you have enjoyed this story, please remember that reviews and ratings are the thing that keep us going! Whether it's online or dropped on Goodreads or Amazon, it means a lot.

Big shout out to Esther (@ BooksCozy), who has not only championed my work, but read this novel in each and every form. My other alpha-beta readers, who were incredibly helpful: Brenden Rajah, Drew Taibi, Taher Dablan-Azony, Kristen @ Rhode_Reads, Adam R. Bishop, Alex Valdiers, Julie Hiner, Amber Herbert, Shawn Drew. Another huge thanks to anyone that grabbed an ARC, early reviews really mean so much to authors.

A resounding thanks to my family and friends, all of which helped me through a particularly bad year. They also never stopped encouraging me to continue on in the writing process. My niece, Emily and my father's particular pride have kept me pushing on when I wasn't sure I wanted to.

To Ed Crocker, my eternal thanks. Authors always say that without their editor the book wouldn't exist—and wow is it true. The amount of care and talent that Ed brought to *Welcome to Cemetery* cannot be overstated. His developmental work is top tier, and I'd suggest him to any author, writing any genre. Just don't make him so busy that I can no longer book him...

If you've enjoyed this novel, be on the lookout for the accompanying short story collection coming Fall 2025!

Tales From Cemetery

Featuring horror shorts set as background lore & campfire stories from the town of Cemetery

About the Author

C. J. Daley lives in New York. He is the author of *Welcome to Cemetery*, his full-length crime thriller debut, as well as a full accompanying short story collection. *BestGhost* was his first sampler on the road to release and the collection is coming Fall 2025. He enjoys smaller pieces that give hints to his created worlds at large, and he loves blending genres with dark descriptors. He hopes this won't be the last you hear from him, and if you enjoyed, please consider leaving a review on Amazon, BookBub, Goodreads, StoryGraph, Literal Book Club—or share with a friend.

Follow along for more news @ CJDsCurrentRead / @ CJDaleyWrites on social media

For more goodies to come, sign up for my newsletter